Montesereno

Montesereno

The Chaplain's Garden

Benjamin W. Farley

RESOURCE *Publications* • Eugene, Oregon

MONTESERENO
The Chaplain's Garden

Resource Publications
An Imprint of Wipf and Stock Publishers
199 W. 8th Ave., Suite 3
Eugene, OR 97401

www.wipfandstock.com

PAPERBACK ISBN: 978-1-5326-5668-2
HARDCOVER ISBN: 978-1-5326-5669-9
EBOOK ISBN: 978-1-5326-5670-5

Montesereno is a work of fiction. Aside from historical personages and places, the novel's characters, events, and situations are purely fictional. Any resemblance to actual persons, living or dead, is coincidental.

Manufactured in the U.S.A.

To
Alice Anne

When I look at your heavens, the work of your fingers, the moon and the stars that you have established; what are human beings that you are mindful of them, mortals that you care?

—Ps. 8:3–4

Contents

Preface

The idea for *Montesereno* was inspired by two principal events, if we may call them "events." The first owes its inception to the many visits my wife and I have made over the years to the Pisgah Inn and its panoramic view of the mountains, west of Asheville. The drive to the Inn, through the Parkway's many tunnels, past its oaks and firs, wildflowers, cliffs and laurel has always cast a spell of wonder and solace, regardless the season. Walking the Inn's grounds, its narrow trails, and staring far off across range after range of distant mountains, as well as gaping down into its sunlit or shadowed coves has equally provided levels of restful calm. So I set *Montesereno* and its villa grounds in a wistful location similar to the grandeur of the Parkway's scene.

The second "event" is traceable to reading Kay Jamison's *An Unquiet Mind* and the revelation of those unchartered vistas and thwarted delusions so common in our society today. Could the two realities—the unquiet mind and the healing solace of the Parkway's mountains—be woven into a story worth exploring and telling? As one who is not a psychologist but a professor emeritus of philosophy and religion, I began perusing the more current common disorders to create a cadre of characters and situations to match the characters' needs and the disorders' symptoms. Thus did the story evolve. I began it in 2009, and have worked on it each year since. It is far from the dream novel I wanted to write, nor are its characters perfect in any way, let alone its central figure—Darby Peterson, PhD, retired professor of philosophy. But I sensed it was time to conclude the adventure and bring its hero and his hopes to an acceptable denouement. I can only hope readers enjoy it, or find it to be of some value, or at least worth reading, as much as I felt driven to write it. As the old Greek playwrights used to say: "So hath it fallen here."

Columbia, South Carolina, 2018

PART ONE

Autumn

Chapter 1

With each swerve of the Parkway, the mountains bore Darby higher and higher into their manicured wilderness. Bank after bank of scarlet and yellow hues, hemlocks, pines, and wind-sheared firs swept past the windshield. So too its gray cliffs and rills of laurel. But however grand the landscape, its autumnal glory could not mask the misgivings Darby struggled to quell. What was he getting into? What ever made him think he could pull it off? What if he failed and had to go back? What if there were no "back" to return to? Was it too late to say, No?

He slowed the car to enter a tunnel; then switched on the lights. Darkness rushed over him, swallowing the headlights' funneled beams, snuffing out all but the faintest glow of the domed cavern's reflectors. Suddenly, the car swept back into the sunlight. Once again the oaks and maples burst into color.

Ahead, the road opened onto a wide overlook. Darby broke the car's speed, pulled up beside the shoulder's stonewall, and stepped out. Everywhere the sun's rays illumined the panorama with delicate softness, tinting the sky a graceful blue, while daubing the mountaintops umber and gold. Darby cupped his hands about his eyes. To the east in the sunlight's sheen lay Asheville, less than 25 miles away; while to the west, beneath the sun's ochre smudge, stretched Waynesville, a distance of 35 miles or more. He glanced at his watch. Dusk would soon be falling. It was time to look for the intersection that crossed the Parkway.

When twenty minutes later Darby arrived at Montesereno's gates, he placed his car in park and stared down the pebbled driveway at the Villa. Its tall Italian windowpanes shimmered silver in the dusk, bathing the pink façade in a luxuriant light that only evenings create. Its sandstone window ledges and embossed cornices added a mystique of antique elegance. To his left, an edge of the Villa's slate deck peeked out from behind the mansion's rear entrance, and, still visible in the evening's glow, slumbered the Villa's guest cottage, flanked by its garden of azaleas and ornate flora. Darby drove down to the mansion. After parking, he mounted its worn, semi-circular steps and raised his hand to knock on the Florentine door.

His knuckles hesitated. Old memories rushed forward. Her hands drew him down. Her lips smothered his, wet with kisses. It was the night of their honeymoon, their season of boundless passion. How they had raced through the Villa's grounds, scattering the crisp and lustrous leaves, sending them afloat in clouds of raspberry-pink and yellow flame to the blush of morning mists and the purple of sunset haze!

It seemed so long ago, and yet was it? He—the ex-priest with a PhD, first in his class and first to be hired; and Julia Laine, his bride—a Medieval archivist, excellent in every way, his equal. It had all unfolded with such promise—the move to Georgia, the University of Oglesbee, with stipends to travel to Berlin, Paris, and Rome. He stared at the door, a casualty of his Socratic quietude, a facet of his personality he knew he would never be able to slough off. He smiled to himself, knocked quietly, and waited.

"Ah, Peterson!" Garnett Nelson greeted him, as he swung the door open. "Thank God you've come!" stated the tall, pallid-faced figure. An unkempt head of graying hair matched his sallow complexion. A linen napkin dangled from his white shirt above a gray tie. His swollen milky eyes burned in the hall's semi-light that emanated from the dining room's chandelier. "Come in!" he motioned with his hand. "We'll take your things to the cottage, afterwards." He turned toward the dining room. "Linda! He's here! Our own Dr. Peterson!" He struggled to clear his throat, but the guttural rumble remained. Darby knew what it masked. Perhaps they would talk about it later.

Darby peered around the hallway into the lighted room. To his right, a frightened young girl's eyes caught his; then the anxious glances of an older man, seated opposite her, clad in a tweed jacket, sporting a yellow tie. To his left, sat a surprisingly stylish woman, beautiful to say the least, dressed in a bright blue blouse, wearing a pearl necklace with matching earrings, and, opposite her, a young male, slumped forward in a suede jacket, with dark and jealous eyes. The young man had been touching the woman's fingertips, clasping them across the table, but looked up uncomfortably when Darby stepped in.

Just then Linda entered the room through a swinging door between the kitchen and dining room. Anorexic in size but energetic and aglow in a pleated green dress of silk, she squeezed her small frame between the chairs and breakfront to hug him. With her brown eyes and cheerful lips, willowy face and short black hair, she drank in his features with overt excitement. "Darby! How wonderful! Garnett's told us all about it." She kissed his cheek. In turn, he embraced her about the waist. Still on her tiptoes, she straightened his shirt collar, where it poked up under his maroon sweater. "It is such a right thing to do. Even Jon Paul concurs. Oh, Darby!" she kissed him on his mouth, her eyes radiant with a shameless blush.

"And yourself! Lovely as always! And how is our chef?"

"Unchanged. He'll be out in a while. Look, we've set a plate for you, at the head of the table no less."

"I believe that's the opposite end," Garnett muttered, suppressing a cough. "But tonight, who cares?"

Darby scooted the chair back and took a seat. As tall as Garnett, but with a decidedly muscular frame, a head of white-and-pepper hair, tanned face, and bronzed hands, his appearance easily belied his vocation as an academician. "Well!" he greeted each with a polite nod. "I apologize I'm not in jacket. I'm Darby Peterson. Please don't believe a word Nelson says."

"Darby's our Renaissance man. Our Plato in residence," Nelson mumbled in his weak voice. "Dr. Peterson's the retired head of the philosophy department at Oglesbee University, or at least he's been willing to risk an extended leave, just for us. He's a PhD from Princeton and as world-traveled as Job's Satan, if I may add. And, at one point, a Catholic priest," he feigned a smile.

"Please! That was long ago, and only for two years," winced Darby, unfolding his napkin as he looked up at Linda. Linda's lips brushed pleasantly past his left ear. Artfully, she set his pear salad of greens and cottage cheese in front of him.

"Were you a priest?" the young girl asked. "And a professor, too? I've never met a professor before. I applied to Charleston's Ashley-Cooper College, but my writing skills weren't up to par, or so they said."

"Well, I'm sorry to hear that, but, sad to say, I am a professor, or was. As well as a priest. But that was long ago!" He glanced up at Linda, so fair in the table's light.

"What happened?" asked the male opposite her. "I thought once a priest always a priest." The man was just then lifting a glass of white wine to his lips. A shiny drop of condensation slipped down its stem and dripped onto his salad plate. He grasped the stem with his napkin and hunched slightly forward. His tight grey eyes never blinked as he stared at Darby. His narrow and somewhat elongated nose twitched at the tip. He fidgeted with his glass as he awaited Peterson's reply.

Darby could feel his chest tighten. He wished Garnett hadn't introduced him so. He hated labels. They changed you into an object instead of a person. "When I was younger, I tended to be reticent, more of an idealist than a people person—even as a priest. But that was thirty-five years ago.

It ended when I surrendered my celibacy and married, just before my PhD. What about yourself?"

"Oh! An art dealer of sorts, and dabbler in this and that, you might say."

"Nonetheless, the best!" Nelson confirmed.

"If I may ask, what's this reference to Job's Satan?" the man beside the girl interjected. There was an air of casual challenge about his voice, if not a rigidity concealed behind a visage of uncertainty. Darby could sense it in his eyes, coupled with an undisclosed fear of something that needed to be shared, but which he, obviously, couldn't. Slender to gaunt, the man brushed a strand of his black hair past his right ear and focused exclusively on Darby. He couldn't be more than twenty-nine, guessed Darby. He sat with his left leg crossed over his right and rested his chin in his right hand. "I'd like to know," a slight leer played about the edges of his mouth. "The Catholic Church has always intrigued me with its love for secrecy and whatever else it's up to."

"Like what?" Darby reacted. "Pedophilia? Is that what you're hinting?"

The man's face filled with embarrassment.

"Hah!" the woman with earrings smiled. "He got you on that one! Dr. Peterson—my husband," she iterated. "Mr. Martin, no less."

"Sorry, sir! I apologize," the man sought to regain what dignity he could. "You go for the jugular, don't you?"

"Only when I have, too," Peterson smiled. "Forget it! As for Job's Satan, he was part of Yahweh's court in the Bible. Let's say he operated on the margin of God's domain, a sort of spoiler. In the Book of Job, he travels to and fro about the earth, giving Yahweh grief whenever he can."

"Not a bad definition," smiled the coat-and-tie man, still tweaking his wine glass's stem. "Incidentally, I'm Tunstan Hughes. And specifically, I'm an art fraud investigator."

"Now you know why Peterson's here," Garnett coughed. "He was thrice recipient of the Excellence in Teaching Award and has authored many books. He's what we've needed for years."

"I have a question," Martin's wife stated. "I'm Celeste, Celeste Martin," she nodded toward her husband. Still smiling, her short black hair rendered her boyish in appearance, but her eyes sparkled with seductive playfulness as she stared at Darby's lips. "I've always wanted to know the meaning of 'pluperfect.' I know that sounds stupid, if not silly, but the word seems so important," she stared at his brow and face.

"Not much to explain, Mrs. Martin. It's from the Latin. Means 'more than perfect.' It's a combination of the past tense and the perfect, sometimes called the 'past perfect.' Example: 'I *had thought* you might ask a question I *had heard* before.' I know that's lame, but that's it!" Darby could tell that his answer was hardly what Mrs. Martin wanted. No doubt she had hoped for a more intriguing definition.

"I prefer it in expressions," Hughes scowled. "Like, 'that artist is a pluperfect ass.' Or, 'that woman in Manet's *Bar at the Folie-Bergère* represents the pluperfect essence of Parisian life in the 1880s.'"

"Like our pluperfect dreams," Darby stated.

"Dreams! All I have are nightmares!" the young girl announced. "My name's Stephanie, Stephanie Gay," she extended her hand to Darby. "Have you really had pluperfect dreams? Mine are nightmares. I wake up running away from voices, terrifying faces and old houses with ceilings falling in."

"Mine are quite normal, I guess," he released the girl's hand. "But you needn't be afraid of your dreams, or even your nightmares. According to Jung, dreams are our best friends. They never lie. They bring us compensation at a level too deep for words, and in *shapes* that emerge *strange* and *unintelligible*," he feigned with a smile. "Perhaps we can talk about it sometime, if you'd like?"

"I'd love that!"

"Well, let's plan on it. Maybe tomorrow."

"I must say, I am quite interested in all this banter," the art investigator remarked. "What was your dissertation on, anyway? Jung? The subconscious? Some modern theory of the self?"

"No! In fact, it embarrasses me to tell you. My doctoral dissertation was entitled: *Nietzsche's Übermensch as Icon and Archetype*. It was published in the *Journal of Philosophy* over a period of three issues. Later, it was published as a monograph. As for the word *Übermensch*, it's Nietzsche's term for what he hoped would become a futurist figure, a person capable of overcoming whatever obstacles and petty judgments others might harbor. Kind of a tough call, I know," Darby smiled.

"That's just one book of many," Nelson added. He stared around the table as Linda brought in the main course: a pot roast in dark gravy, garnished with peas, onions, and tomatoes, along with parsley-sprinkled russet potatoes, grilled spears of asparagus, and a side dish of relishes and pickles.

"Bon appétit," she pressed Darby's shoulder with her fingertips as she returned toward the kitchen.

He glanced up at her as she slipped away. Where were his thoughts? Then he turned back to savor the dinner, a feast as fitting for its guests as his fleeting ideas served to fete his philosophic palate.

"Someone please pass the red wine," coughed Garnett, struggling for breath. "Please help yourself. There's more in the cellar."

"I'm an MBA," stated Parker. "I really am sorry for my inappropriate jibe," he acknowledged, his face still flushed pale red. "Celeste here's into

marketing. I do have a question, however. Is it true that we all have a philosophy of some sort? If I've got one, I sure as hell," he paused, glancing
toward Stephanie, "don't know it. I try to be ethical, but in the bond market,
that's damn near impossible."

Darby eyed Parker with a thoughtful smile. "Technically, we're not all
philosophers, if you mean that in the critical sense. You know, Socrates was
put to death for chiding his fellow Athenians. He accused them of ignoring
what was best for the self, and for caring nothing about honor and virtue.
His favorite 'jibe' was: 'the unexamined life is unworthy of a person.' Most of
us are content to bump along. But you did say, 'ethical'?"

"I wouldn't jump to conclusions," Parker replied. "I live off commissions. That means I have to hustle and spin bonds and stocks in my favor. It
doesn't needle most consciences."

"That's why I'm into marketing and public relations," Celeste said as
she nudged off a piece of roast with her fork. Her lips hung partially open as
she studied Darby. "Besides, why can't you just enjoy life as it is? Why have
to examine everything, or keep looking for meanings that aren't there? Like
honor and *virtue*? Why not enjoy life as it comes along, day-by-day? I find all
this nonsense about a 'purpose-driven life' obnoxious. Don't you?"

Before Darby could answer, Tunstan stopped eating and placed his
fork along the edge of his plate. He glanced about, clicked his neck from
side to side, and loosened his tie. "If we're into confessions, I might as well
share mine. That's why I'm here! I botched a major project as an art sleuth.
I was confident the piece was a forgery. It didn't look anything like the canvas I had seen in Vienna, though there were telltale brush strokes and light
touches that looked familiar. The Vienna Museum of Fine Arts listed it as
missing. There it was in front of me! But I was cocksure it was a fake. A
masterpiece, yes, but a fake! So I announced my findings, the house holding
it put it up for auction, and it sold for under $2,000. Then the buyer took
it to Sotheby's. Their people pored over every detail. And, you guessed it!
They judged it to be authentic. Worth $13 million! I was shocked. Vienna
demanded it back. To save the auction house embarrassment, I resigned.
I've been in flight ever since. And that was eighteen months ago. So what do
I do now? I couldn't get a job as a curator of the least significant museum
in America." He grasped his wine glass in both hands before taking another
sip. "Oh, well! So much for aesthetics. It's back to the rag shop, for certain."

Darby stared at the man. "History records that during the fall of Rome,
Aristotle's dialogues were consumed in the flames. We don't know the name
of the curator in charge of their safety. Or whether he escaped the sword, or
fled to Africa as so many did. But if he fled, who'd have the right to condemn

him? Why not reintroduce yourself by letter to the houses you represented, or to new ones that possibly aren't so famous?"

"Sure! Just like that!" Hughes arched his eyebrows. "No wonder your types are accused of dwelling up in the clouds; no offense."

Darby dropped his voice. He could see his students before him. How they twisted their pens and counted his steps as he paced back and forth. "I hate to think of how many students I let down until I learned what real teaching requires. It took time to learn that teaching ideas is one thing, but teaching kids, another. I had to stare into their faces and eyes. I had to coax them to ask questions, goad them in the very midst of my lectures. That's the truth, Mr. Hughes!"

Everyone sat silently, even Tunstan. "Perhaps we can talk some. What I do is incredibly technical, as intuitive as it is scientific."

After dessert and coffee, Nelson signaled for Darby to accompany him to the office. "You will excuse us," Nelson said. "The professor and I have a few things to cover before I depart in the morning. I'll be heading first to Atlanta, then to Oklahoma, and hopefully back here by the Holidays. It's been my pleasure to dine with you tonight. Perhaps, we shall see one another again, and soon at that," he surmised. Once more he suppressed a cough, before turning with a slight bow.

Both Hughes and Martin stood. If they knew the reason of Nelson's departure, neither voiced it.

"We shall miss you," Hughes uttered. "I'll be leaving myself after the weekend. It's been very pleasant. I'm glad the professor came at your summons. I'm looking forward to a few days of chat with him," he glanced toward Darby, then back at Nelson.

Nelson nodded and bowed again, this time toward Celeste and Stephanie. "I'm honored that you chose Montesereno. Santé to each of you! I'll be gone before breakfast. Good night, ladies! Enjoy the living room and fireplace. Again, good night!"

"Good night, to you, too," Parker shook his hand. "We love coming here and look forward to returning."

Darby noticed Celeste's eyes as she looked up at him. Her glance was quite transparent. Darby lowered his face and followed Nelson into the hallway, past its winding staircase, and into Garnett's study. Portraits of Garnett's parents and grandfather hung in large gilded frames suspended on wires from the ceiling's high molding. Bookcases, lamps, a leather sofa, and three black-lacquered captain's chairs encircled Garnett's mahogany desk.

"Let's crash here," Nelson said as they approached the sofa. "You'll be staying in your favorite quarters, the petit cottage. The rooms are ready—all two of them. Plus wood by the fireplace. Everything you need."

"I can't thank you enough. Montesereno's just what I need," Darby replied, repressing his uneasiness with a smile.

"By the way, I know this is personal, but whatever happened between
you and Julia Laine? You two seemed so perfect. I know I should stay out."

"No, no! Not at all! I've hidden a lot of it, even from myself." He stared
thoughtfully at Garnett. "She wanted children but couldn't conceive. I was
buried in my work, up to my neck in lectures and writing. She too was busy
but needed more. She needed me home, wanted me home, and wanted to
travel." Darby looked away from his host, then back. "She was needy in a
way I couldn't fulfill. She got the house, then sold it and slipped off with a
millionaire sportsman. I was angry, bitter at first, but it was for the best. No
point in fighting the inevitable. They live in New Mexico, near Taos. I've
been there. It's beautiful. Yes, it took time to get over it," he glanced down,
then back at Nelson. "And I did love her! I truly did! Still, I welcome your
invitation to be here. I was prepared to teach longer and may go back, but
Montesereno is what I need; at least just now."

"Well, enjoy it. I know our clients and guests will enjoy you. Plus, you
don't have to worry about a thing. Linda and Jon Paul manage the Inn.
They're responsible for registering the guests, providing whatever they
need, plus keeping a list of drugs or prescriptions they bring. The law requires that. We rarely take alcoholics anymore, but a few show up. We're not
equipped to be a detoxification center, either, but some come just the same.
Leave them to Jon Paul. We've a cabinet stocked with bourbon and scotch
and plenty of club soda. When my father ran the Villa, he hired a physician
to dispense anti-depressants. But we've dropped that service. Now we focus
on providing rest and a change of venue. For alcoholics, we do offer cold
showers and wet towels," Garnett coughed, paused and wiped his face with
a handkerchief. He placed it back in his jacket's pocket and stared at Darby.

"Most of our clients today," he continued, "are upscale, mainly suffering from depression. Which leads me to warn you about Stephanie." He
retrieved his handkerchief and wiped his lips. "Her grandmother brought
her. She's been here two weeks. The child's suicidal, her grandmother claims,
though I've not seen it. She stays mainly to herself. Her father and mother
used to come here, years ago. But that's another story," he said with a cheerless glance and sadness in his voice. "The girl's on Xanax, which Linda
makes sure she takes. You do know that Linda used to be a Licensed Practi-
cal Nurse. As for the girl, she's scheduled to go home Sunday but wants to
stay longer. I wish I knew how to help her. Maybe you'll figure something
out. She likes you. I saw it in her eyes the moment you walked in. As for
Hughes, he's just in a state of self-pity. He takes long walks and likes to sit in
the Garden. He'll be a pest I fear. As for the couple, they're a mystery. They're

not on anything. They've been here a week. Real distanced from each other when they arrived—moody, impish, wanting sex, but aloof and secretive. God only knows what problems they've brought. Maybe you'll get them to talk. That's about it." Suddenly Garnett leaned forward; sweat beads popped out on his brow, and he struggled to catch his breath. "Damn!" he groaned. "I can hardly breathe."

"What is it? I have a right to know, you know. Throat cancer? Is that what it is? Lung cancer? Emphysema? Or something worse?"

"No. Throat cancer. And there's nothing worse. That's it. My doctor in Atlanta's scheduled tests for me at a Mayo clinic out west. That's where he completed his residency." There were tears in Garnett's eyes as he fought for his breath. "He thinks transoral laser microsurgery is what I need. That's less invasive than the traditional jaw-breaking, disfigurement process. You know, where they slice your neck open and rip out your thorax and voice box, gutting you like a fish. I'm not looking forward to it, I assure you," he swallowed, choking on his own phlegm. "You'd best get on to your cottage. I'll see you in the morning before I leave."

"Sure! In the morning!" Darby repeated as he rose and laid his hand on Garnett's shoulder. "See you then. You'll have to write."

"Oh, that reminds me!" Garnett fought to regain his breath. "We don't receive mail delivery here. Jon Paul picks it up twice a week at the post office in West Asheville. We've a box there. In case you ever need to go down, the key's in the drawer here," he pointed toward the desk. "Top drawer on the right. The box number's on the string. There's a business credit card next to it. You'll need that, too."

"I'll remember, thanks. Till the morning. Good night!"

Chapter 2

Driving around the Villa to the cottage stirred Darby's memories again. They had spent the happiest hours of their honeymoon by its fireside, in its dayroom, so cozy and warm. But the past was past; he hardened his jaw. Hegel had put it best: *every moment is a compilation of the past, as well as a revolt against it.*

He entered the cottage. In the glow of its hearth, he and Julia had melded into their first pluperfect throes. For years they had loved each other intensely, cooking together, studying, writing, traveling, until Julia completed her own degree as an archivist. Still, from the beginning, the feeling that something was missing never dissipated. He bit his lip. That she wanted out destroyed his wholeness, his grasp of himself. No, he couldn't fault her. Nor should he fault himself, a psychologist had assured him. Life is never that simple. Slowly, he made his way into the room. It was a good place to live, to dwell, however long Nelson should need him. Then return to Atlanta, if they'd take him back. The Dean had pretty much promised he would.

He had his clothing to bring in—his laptop, reference books, and personal items. He returned to his car and completed the move. Now as he scanned the cottage's bookshelves, he was surprised to find his own works closest to the room's reading lamp. Garnett must have arranged them to create the effect. There they were: his dissertation, his two volumes of *The History of Western Philosophy*, two novels: *Au'voir Paris* and *Christopher Rex*—a fable set at sea—and *Orion*, his first and only book of poetry. Just as he sat down, someone rapped at the door. "Hey in there!" a voice called. Darby recognized it as Jon Paul's.

He rose and opened the door. With only a thin smile, he stared at the stout, medium-sized chef of hefty chest, his head a stream of godlike blond hair tied in a wiry pony tail dangling down the back of his neck. There was something about him Darby had never been able to trust. It was in his eyes, the silent cant that never smiled. "Come in! What a sight you are!" he belied his feelings. "Thanks for everything."

"Hey, it's not me to thank! It's Linda and Hettie. They spent all yesterday cleaning and dusting this place for you. We get some real crazies, you know. Sometimes it takes two to take them down. Enjoy your night. Who knows what tomorrow may bring! If you need anything, let me know. Otherwise, I'll see you at breakfast."

"Thanks. I'll do that."

Jon Paul's eyes scrutinized Darby's for a moment. A look of distance crept into them. Suddenly, he shook Darby's hand, then, slipped back into the night.

Darby watched him disappear toward the Villa. A thin fog had begun to form. It settled ever so subtly about the mansion's flagstone walkways, its tall ornamental urns and rhododendron bushes that hunched numb in the cold. Darby rubbed his arms, closed the door and lit the logs in the fireplace. He had scarcely begun to relax when another rap sounded at the door. It was softer and hesitant, but nonetheless a knock. "Come on in!" he called. "The door's unlocked."

"Yes!" a young voice answered. It was Stephanie. She eased the door open and stepped in. She quickly closed it behind her. "Please Dr. Peterson, don't be angry! Please, sir! This is totally unlike me. But I'm frightened. May I sit for a while? I, I won't stay long. I promise. I won't tell anybody, either. I'm just . . . lonely, . . . sad."

Darby glanced at her trembling hands. They were white, almost blue from the cold.

"Well, you're already in. Sit down and we'll just be lonely and sad together," he smiled.

The girl's lips parted, creating a warm, expansive grin. "I . . . I can't believe that," she stammered. "I thought you had it all together!"

"Well, your smile eliminated any sadness. Sit there by the fire and tell me about yourself. Why all this sadness? This self-doubt? You know, there's always a reason for the way we feel, and we can choose to feel differently. That's the truth."

"I wish I could," she mumbled as she sat in front of the fireplace to warm her hands. "Do you really want to know about me? To hear the truth? I'm not even sure what it is. I've told my counselor a thousand times, but it doesn't do any good. I feel guilty taking up her time. I just sink deeper it seems."

"Maybe there's nothing wrong with that, sinking and sinking until you feel the ground?"

"Please!" Stephanie winced. "I don't need that." She looked at him with disparagement in every pore of her face; then placed it in her hands and began to cry. Her sides and shoulders shook, as her voice broke into sobs.

Her fingers glistened with tears. She inhaled her sobs and stared at Darby. "My daddy left us when I was just a little girl. It broke my mama's heart. She took her life after that, leaving me to grow up with my grandmother," she paused to wipe back tears.

"Here!" said Darby, as he handed her some tissues from the bookstand beside his chair.

"Thank you!" she mumbled, half snorting and half strangling. "I always felt it was my fault. That maybe I was to blame. My counselor tells me that that's quite normal. I guess it is. I wish I knew."

Darby sat quietly and waited for her to continue.

"The horrible thing is, Daddy ran away when we were *here*. He and Mama had been fighting, picking at each other, always finding fault. I never knew which way to turn. Mama liked coming here. Daddy did too. They called ahead, and we came. But this time it was different. Mama claimed Daddy was seeing someone, some woman from Tennessee. That he didn't love us anymore. Daddy swore that wasn't true. They said terrible things about each other and to each other. We went to bed, but the next morning Daddy was gone. 'I knew he would leave us!' my mother cried. 'I bet that wench was waiting for him on the road.' Mr. Nelson phoned the sheriff's office. The sheriff sent out deputies to search the area, just in case something had happened. Daddy liked to walk, to take long hikes. Maybe he had gotten lost, or slipped on a rock somewhere. Sometimes he'd talk to himself. That's how he handled his sorrows." She took a deep breath. "Maybe I inherited his sadness, like some kind of gene."

Darby sat forward, his fingers intertwined. "Maybe, maybe not."

"At home, when not in school, I just sit in my room and stare out the window. I used to play with a bunch of girls down the street. They all had mamas and daddies. I guess I was eleven or twelve before I realized how sad I was. I would come home and cry. Their moms were sweet to me, but I knew when it was time to go home. I don't mean to sound like a cry-baby, but I've lived with that so long, I just feel numb inside: unwanted and worthless. I tried cutting my wrists once, but was too scared. I did leave a patch of red scratches on my arms, which my homeroom teacher noticed. That's when they sent me to the nurse, and later to see a doctor. To be evaluated. I was so embarrassed. When I returned to the classroom that first time, the kids snickered. I hated them after that, every fucking one! Yes, every *fucking* one," she affirmed. She inhaled again and fought to regain her composure. "I'm sorry," she suddenly said. "I'm sorry." Fresh tears trickled down her cheeks and slid off her nose.

"That's fine," Darby said. "We're all free to say what we need to. Life's sparkle dimmed after that, didn't it? A hurt beyond words?"

"Yes!" she muttered, sniffling back more tears. She shook her head in the affirmative, as she attempted to smile. "Yes, sir! It did!"

Darby looked away while she cried more.

"You never said much about yourself," she sat erect. "We just all fell into blabbering about ourselves in there, didn't we? Aren't you married? Don't you have a wife and children? A son or daughter? I'd love to meet them, if you do."

"I'm afraid not. I'm what you see and nothing more."

"I don't believe that! You're just trying to blow me off. I could die in this room and you wouldn't care," she retorted with a teary huff.

"Now that's what I mean about choosing the way we feel. You could have said: 'Hey! You've had it rough, too, I bet? No ring, no wife, no family, no kids. Just you, alone! There must be a story there.' Or, 'I don't want to talk about myself anymore. Can we talk about something else? Like maybe your life? Huh?'"

Stephanie smiled. "You don't have to rub it in. You're as bad as my counselor. She's into cognitive behavioral therapy, whatever that is, but if you ask me, it's a pile of crap. Or it is with her."

"She might care for you more than you know. It's just that deep down she doesn't connect with what's happening to you. Is that possible?"

"Yes, sir! It's like she's hearing my voice, but not *me*. But I feel better now." She dabbed the corners of her eyes with a handful of wadded up tissues. "I guess I look terrible," she stated with one last sob.

"Tell you what! Why don't we pursue this some more tomorrow, if you want? I'd love to explore those dreams you've had, especially about the strangers and the old houses falling in. I've had dreams like that, too. Is that a deal?"

"Yes, sir!" she clutched her hands together between her knees. She leaned her head sideways. Her mouth, face, her eyes, cheeks, and chin seemed to smile in unison.

Darby rose and walked her to the door. "Better turn up your collar. It'll frost hard tonight. Here! Let me walk you to the Villa." He accompanied her past the urns, to the first steps of the Inn's back entrance. Warm light streamed through the French windows of the rear doors. The guests were seated about the fireplace. Darby could see them through the muslin veils that hung between the enormous gold drapes that framed the windowpanes. An air of long-ago opulence caressed the room.

"Good night!"

She turned to hug him. He caught her hand and pressed it. "You're going to make it, Stephanie. Reach down inside your soul; you'll find more courage than you realize!"

She hurried inside.

For some bizarre reason he thought of *Ivan Ilych,* the magistrate in Tolstoy's story. Seeing the drapes must have aroused the association. Ivan had injured himself while hanging drapes, in nothing more than a simple fall—just a simple fall. But the persistent wound changed his life. Never was he the same again. Darby stared into the room, let his benumbed feelings float up and slip away, then turned and walked back to the cottage.

Chapter 3

Darby awakened cold, his right arm numb. He opened his eyes and stared at his watch: 5:00 a.m. It didn't matter how early he retired or how late he stayed up, his internal alarm functioned with incredible regularity. He hated to get up. He'd rather return to his dream. The road had climbed through a rocky gorge over the crest of a vast ridge to fade into a grassy lane before ending near a field with a path that led into the distant woods. He had gotten out of his car, looked around, only to realize he had no idea where he was. Yet he recognized the path, the woods, the field, the lane, the ridge, and rocky gorge. He had traveled this road so many times, always to awaken in a state of disorientation. He pulled the sheet and blanket up over his shoulders and tried to fall asleep. He wanted to follow the path that led toward the woods. But it was no use. Whatever REM sleep he longed to reenter had expired. He rolled to his right and struggled out of bed.

With his feet still in slippers, he turned on the coffee pot; then wandered toward the fireplace to stir its white ashes with a poker. Not a single spark, not even a faint ember glowed in the gray fluff. After several minutes, he poured himself a cup of coffee, donned a woolen jacket, and stepped out into the morning cold. All was dark in the Villa. Jon Paul and Linda would be waking soon, along with Garnett. He didn't envy the man's drive to Atlanta, or the surgery that awaited him in the west.

Darby peered out into the dark quietness. Ever fresh, new, and different, each morning seemed to possess a mood, a mode, an elusive essence all its own. Instantly, the cold seized him and, shivering momentarily, he stared up into the night's predawn vault. How its radiant stars burned bright! He clenched his cup tightly in both hands. Toward the west, the faint ridges of the Parkway's mountains poked black through layers of morning fog. The cup of The Big Dipper tilted bright in the northeastern sky. Its neighboring stars twinkled in their blurred infinity of trembling light and distant galaxies.

When he turned back toward the house, lights had come on in Garnett's room and the kitchen. Garnett would be leaving soon. Darby expelled a pensive sigh. He knew he needed to shave, shower, and prepare himself for whatever the day might offer.

* * *

"Well, it's off to Atlanta!" Garnett stated, as he clattered his cup in its saucer at the sight of Darby. "What time is it, anyway?" he glanced out toward the hall's clock.

"6:30!" said Darby. "It's awfully foggy out there, especially down the mountain. When do you have to be at the airport?"

"Oh, that won't be till later. First I have to meet with my own doc. I've plenty of time. Plus I need to stop by the post office. I'll make it, I'm sure."

Jon Paul poked his head into the dining room. He hadn't shaved, and his face bristled with blond stubble. "What'll you have?" he asked Darby. "Linda's sleeping in. I'm scrambling eggs for Garnett, with a side of sausage links and wholegrain toast with rhubarb jelly. Same for you?"

"That'll be fine! Thanks."

"No problem!" the husky chef intoned.

"There'll be a new group of guests arriving mid-week," Garnett said. "Linda will fill you in. Relax and enjoy yourself. I'll keep you posted once I'm done with the procedure," he poured himself a fresh cup of coffee. "Here," he filled Darby's cup as well. "Cream?"

"Thanks."

"I never asked you if you're working on anything new? Another novel? Essay? Or scholarly work?"

"The latter. My *History of Philosophy* never accomplished what I wanted it to. It was more a survey. You know, a summary of major timeframes and their philosophers' views. Mainly for students, with selected readings."

"And there's more?" Nelson smiled.

Darby smiled with him. "You know the two volumes never touched on the real nuances that elude us. Like, what are philosophers for in a time such as ours? It wasn't until I read Heidegger's *Poetry, Language, Thought*, that I realized the value of philosophy. Up to that point, I treated the discipline more as a history of theories than a study of ourselves. Rorty's *Philosophy and the Mirror of Nature* changed that, especially his essays on 'the problem of personhood.' That's what I want to investigate now, and I've found a clue to it in a discourse I want to develop: *From Wittenberg to Weimar*. That's all I can divulge at the present."

"I'm certain it'll be over my head, but a work I'll want to read. Can you put it in layman's terms, where it will speak to real people with real needs? Why can't philosophers do that?"

"Many have and do! Nietzsche did. Plato! Rousseau! Hegel! Deep down, philosophy's more of a work of poetry than a science of propositions."

"Could you put that in a novel? In a story that a person could read and think how remarkable it was that the story of their life had finally been written? Why can't you do that?"

Darby stared at Garnett. If Garnett's life were a story, perhaps he could do it. But how would he end it? In a tracheotomy, a curse of silence, or a newfound life? He thought of Hemingway's novels, of *War and Peace*, *The Red and the Black*, even the Zane Gray novels he had read as a boy. "That would be nice, wouldn't it?" he managed to reply.

"Oh! Incidentally," Garnett added, "here!" he said, reaching into his pocket. "It's the key to the study. You'll need to squirrel away in here from time to time. Just lock it behind you. Too many personal files, you know. But you're free to peruse any you need to."

"Thanks!" He slipped the key into his pocket.

After bidding Garnett farewell, Darby wandered back to the cottage to pick up the threads of his thoughts. He paused to gulp in a breath of raw air and watch as the amber eye of the sunrise illumined Montesereno's eastern face. He would take a walk to clear his mind, he resolved, up to the right, past the Inn, through its orchard, and out to an overlook he had come to love. Yes! To let his thoughts bubble up, evaporate, and take him wherever they must.

The path to the orchard led through the Villa's garden. Its slate-paved terraces created a sense of ascent. The garden sported two slender fluted white columns and wide beds of rhododendron, laurel, and azaleas. A lone ginkgo biloba grew encircled among shrubs. He paused to run his fingers across its fan-shaped, yellow-lobed leaves. A broad smile gladdened his heart as he walked on.

Somewhere he was in Paris, near the Menagerie. Yellow ginkgo leaves had fallen, dappling the sidewalk and iron grills with cobbler's patches. Julia Laine leaned against his shoulder as he turned to kiss her.

Midway along the orchard's path, he noted a jogger through the trees. The man was running up the gravel lane that paralleled the estate. Someone—no doubt Jon Paul—had recently repainted the white fence that separated the Villa's grounds from the lane's marl-colored gravel. The lane would end at the property's overlook. The runner appeared to be the investor, Parker Martin. Darby stopped to take a second look. Dressed in a yellow T-shirt, black shorts, white socks and running shoes, the man jogged past Darby, unaware of his presence beyond the fence. The man ran with an easy gait that only youth possess. Darby had to smile. He once too had run cross-country in college.

By the time Darby reached the overlook, Martin was gazing out across the ridges, the latter still shrouded in fog. "It's peaceful here, isn't it?" the young man said. "So beautiful. Do you come here often?"

"Whenever I'm visiting I do. Once the clouds clear, there are nothing but mountains—all the way to the west, south, and north. There's a drop off below, too, and an old mica mine, with a bit of silver in its creek and sand. Its brook becomes a trout stream farther down. Plus, there's a logging road right over there," Darby pointed behind the Villa, "that wends down to the creek. It's in decent enough shape to hike."

"You've been here quite a bit?"

"No. Not really! But enough to know where to wander about."

"You must have come up through the orchard," Parker glanced toward the Villa. "I apologize for being such a smartass last night. May I walk back with you, when you're ready to leave?"

"Sure! I'm ready now. And forget about last night. I could use another cup of coffee or hot tea myself. I doubt if most of the guests are up."

"Certainly, Celeste isn't. I'd love to bend your ear, if you don't mind."

Darby stared closer into the young man's face and deep dark eyes. He tried to smile as empathically as he could. "I'm listening. You'll need to watch out for rotten apples and a few deer pellets along the way. Just follow me."

The two swung onto the path, with Parker slightly behind Darby's left shoulder.

"We're here trying to restart our marriage," stated Parker. "I guess that's no secret. We're coming up on our fifth anniversary. The first two years were great. In fact, fabulous! Then something came over Celeste. She didn't want sex anymore, at least not from me. She asked if we couldn't have an open marriage." Parker stopped, dead in the path, then resumed following Darby. "She 'needed space,' she said. A little 'more action,' as she put it. Something 'wild,' with more than 'one partner.' Would I do a threesome? Would I go online with her and experiment? 'What's wrong with you?' I replied. I was angry. I must have pouted a hell of a lot."

"Here, let's pause for a minute," said Darby, stopping in his tracks. "That's quite an opener."

"It was," stated Parker, resuming his walk. "Anyway, she became cold and distant after that. We began sleeping in separate beds. We stopped having dinner together. Each night she came home later and later. I could smell other men on her. Musk! Perspiration! The odor of cigarettes! Men would call. 'O God, fellow! Sorry wrong number!' Some would even leave a number for her to call back. Sometimes there'd be bruises on her arms and thighs, neck and wrists. She would sit in front of our dresser and stare at her small breasts or wrinkle her mouth in a wry smile. Then, one night she came home crying. She was sweating and scared. She went straight to the shower and stayed and stayed and stayed. 'Are you all right?' I asked. 'I still love you,' I said. 'My God, sweetheart! What's happened? I want to know. I want our marriage back. I want you again. Just you!'" Parker paused, inhaled a long breath; then fell silent.

The two men continued to walk. Parker kicked a fallen apple out of his path. It left a reddish-brown smudge on the toe of his running shoe. He inhaled another deep breath and released it slowly. "She never answered me. She just came out of the shower, still crying. I handed her a towel. 'Please! Just leave me alone,' she said. 'Will you fix me a drink?' 'Gin and tonic?' I replied. 'Yeah. That'll do. I need another towel for my hair.' And so after that, we began having dinner together, and sometimes sleeping together. But no sex. 'Just hold me,' she'd say. 'That's all.' And that's all it's been, even till now. I'm sure you don't need to hear all this. Life's a mess, isn't it? I never thought it would happen to me."

"Whatever, the hurt is still there. I know about it, too," Darby added.

"Yes. Well! Here we are!" he exclaimed, as the two entered the Garden by the ginkgo tree. "I guess I'll shower and have breakfast. Thanks for listening."

"Chao!" Darby smiled. "It promises to be a beautiful day."

Just then, Darby glanced up toward the house. Someone on the second floor had drawn the drape to one side. It appeared to be a woman in a gown. Upon seeing him, the person's hand immediately let go of the curtain. Darby watched the drape settle back, as the hand disappeared. He wondered if it were Stephanie's or Celeste's. He guessed he'd learn soon enough.

Chapter 4

After Darby returned to the cottage, he browsed its library for whatever Garnett might have collected on depression, bipolar conditions, marital counseling, and personality disorders. To his consternation, very little caught his eye. Perhaps, Garnett housed them in his office. To his relief, however, he did find the eighth edition of Lippincott's *Professional Guide to Diseases.* He pulled the volume off its shelf and perused the sections on "Sexual Disorders of Men." He wondered if Parker suffered from a low libido or inadequate testosterone levels. None of those considerations, however, made sense. As for Celeste's disinterest in Parker or compulsive desire for sex with other men, nothing in the book addressed the subject. Perhaps it was there, but he couldn't locate it. He would have to consult more specific studies. Hopefully, Garnett's library possessed a few. His field was philosophy, he reminded himself, or had been; Eastern religious thought, logic, and Western literature of a metaphysical nature. But now it was couples, the estranged and depressed he was being asked to assist, even to act as a consultant on private sexual anomalies. With a wave of angst in the pit of his stomach, he realized how inadequate his background for counseling of any sort. Still, as he mulled the matter, his task didn't require him to "fix" anyone's problem, only to listen. No one can fix another person's problem, he assured himself. They have to do that on their own. Yet, he wanted to help.

Opening his laptop, he leaned back in the couch and stared down at its screen. He clicked on the document *From Wittenberg to Weimar*, but his mind rebelled against anything metaphysical. Stephanie's image cried for his attention, along with Tunstan's dilemma. Moreover, fall's seasonal colors and azure skies begged for priority. Why not pick out a book and sit in the Garden and ruminate? Winds would soon scatter the Villa's red and golden leaves, whirling them into rusty piles for Jon Paul, or Hettie's husband, to mow under or rake away. He closed his computer, picked up a book, and slipped out the door.

As he entered the Garden, he caught sight of Stephanie, gathering apples in the orchard. A quality of enthusiasm emanated about her, an excitement in engaging in so simple an activity. She was dragging a large burlap sack and filling it with the choicest fruit she could find. Occasionally, she'd pick up an apple, turn it in her fingers, laugh and hurl it at a tree trunk. The rotten missile would disintegrate in a loud splatter. He laid his book down and walked in her direction.

"May I join you?" he called, as he slid on a slick core.

"Oh! You scared me!" she laughed with a startle. "Yes!" Suddenly she bent down, scooped up a mushy apple, and lobbed it in a playful arc toward him.

He dodged the slop as it splattered near his feet. He bent down and picked up an apple of his own.

Stephanie shrieked and ran toward the closest tree. Darby hurled it so as to miss her but, nonetheless, create a gushy splash. "Oh, gross!" she groaned as flecks of peeling struck her shoes.

For the next few minutes, the two lobbed a dozen or more overripe apples at each other. "Truce! Truce!" Darby finally called. "You win! Here, what are you doing with all these anyway? They'll rot before you get them home."

The word "home" suddenly brought a cessation to her smile. Her ebullient countenance fell. She stopped, looked down at her sack, and peered inside. "I've bruised them!" she muttered. "They're just a brown mess! Look!" she exclaimed, as she turned the sack upside down and dumped its contents on the ground. Her faced turned sad and eyes glistened in the bright air.

"I'm sorry. Come, look, there are plenty of apples in the trees. They'll last a lot longer. What you say?"

"Ok!" she replied. "Actually, Jon Paul sent me out. He said he'd make us a pie for supper, if I'd pick enough. But these are a pretty sorry lot."

"Well! Don't worry. Let's get the firmest and most luscious we can."

Her faced filled with smiles. Soon, the two filled the sack with a bulging load of firm red apples.

* * *

Lunch at the Villa was never more than a tray of sandwiches, chips, fruit, tea, soda, or water. Garnett had mandated the policy since assuming management of the Inn. Linda arranged the mid-day repast in buffet style in the dining room, and guests were free to serve themselves between noon and one o'clock. Darby carried his sandwich of tuna fish, pickle, and chips to the cottage and ate in the privacy of its nook, alone.

Afterwards, he turned anew to his "Weimar book," but, once again, the pleasant October air and warm sunny skies lured him outside. For a long while, he walked about the grounds and up its exquisite driveway. Pausing, he stared back at the *grand palazzo* before returning to the Garden to meditate and read.

Someone had beaten him, however, to his favorite bench. Tunstan! The man looked up from a large book he held in his lap and motioned for Darby to come over. "I want you to see this!" he stated. "I want you to see what I mean, first hand."

Darby peered down at a painting of the *Mona Lisa*. As he stared at the famous work, Tunstan ran a large magnifying glass slowly across the painting's face. "Note the symmetry and geometrical lines, the way Da Vinci employs proportion and shadows. He's famous for that. You can't see the brush strokes or true pigments in this photo, but Da Vinci's style is recognizable anywhere. Fakes can't quite capture the haunting quality the master packed in his work. What counterfeiters do is create sketches they try to pass off as authentic drafts. Right now they're the bane of the market. And who wouldn't want an original sketch with all its delicate and intricate lines? He was an engineer, remember? A master designer of bridges and war machines. They were in huge demand in his day. But if you've ever seen the originals, then you recognize a fake the moment you see it. What's so aggravating, however, is that today's counterfeiters can create the spidery cracks and multiple coats of varnish so common to masterworks. But what they fail to capture is the authentic dress and hairstyles of an era, or the right length of a nose, or brow, or a smudge that plagued the original. But, damn if they don't come close.

"Now take a look at these Impressionist pieces of Van Gogh and Renoir," he continued as he turned several pages. "They're unique, and you can generally detect a copy in an instant. Nonetheless, they're out there and hanging in a lot of galleries, too. You just don't know about them until they show up at an auction."

"I fear I'd be duped in a second," Darby confessed. "Of all the courses I neglected in college, art appreciation leads the list."

"Don't they, for most!"

"As a young man my wife and I saw our share of great paintings in galleries all across France, Spain, and Italy. I can still see the *Mona Lisa*, Rembrandt's *Bathsheba*, and Goya's *May 3 Firing Squad*. For that matter El Greco's *Annunciation* also, along with Raphael's *The Transfiguration*, and Michelangelo's ceiling in the Sistine Chapel. I especially enjoyed the battle paintings that hang in one of the galleries at Versailles, along with Jean-Louise's *Napoleon's Coronation*. What a colossal scene!"

"And color!" Tunstan added. "Speaking of which, I can never behold autumn leaves without thinking of the Austro-Italo-French War. At the

Battle of Solferino, the multi-sided forces lost a total of 38,000 maimed and dead. Think of it! The battlefield glowed with blood as evening fell across the carnage. Armies of 242,000 troops had fired volley after volley into each other. That was on June 24, 1859. The Minnie ball had just come into vogue. My God, if the South had had an observer present, would there have been a Civil War? The color *solferino* was coined that day. See those trees. Those tall ones with the purplish, blood-red hue?"

"Sweet gums. They're called 'Sweet gums.'"

"That's the hue artists call *solferino*. Imagine! A field scintillating in purplish-dark red! Several painters tried to capture it. You might have seen the more famous of the paintings at Versailles. Aldophe Yvon painted it. You probably wandered right past it without realizing the savagery that Yvon's work masks. Forgive me, but all these sweet gums ooze of that sorrow."

Darby looked up at the rich, purplish red leaves. Soon they would be gone. "*Solferino*," he whispered. "I think I'll take a walk. See you at dinner."

Once past the Garden, Darby sauntered around to the front of the Villa, entered, and sought out Garnett's study. As he jiggled the key in the lock, he glanced quietly over his shoulder. He didn't want to be observed. Surely Garnett's office housed enough books to cast light on Celeste's behavior. He opened the door, entered the room, and locked it silently behind him.

He switched on the light and began browsing through the shelves. Books on schizophrenia, psychotherapy, the borderline patient, and other disorders lined Garnett's many bookcases. Jamison's *An Unquiet Mind* caught his eye, along with a host of pop-therapy books. A brown accordion folder tied with a shiny shoelace lay wedged between several volumes on sexual disorders. He slipped the folder out and unwound the lace. He peered in. It contained sheets of printed studies on "Compulsive Sexual Behavior," all of which lay loosely shuffled together. He glanced inquisitively through several. They covered everything from symptoms to causes, from risks to treatment. It was a comprehensive study by the Mayo Clinic.[1]

Darby clutched the folder in his hands and sought out the leather couch. Within seconds, the research drew him into its well of hypersexual definitions and warnings of how an enjoyable sex drive can become a compulsive obsession, a trail of fantasies pursued beyond the boundaries of accepted behavior. If untreated, its writers claimed, its end would lead to destroyed relationships, the loss of self-esteem, and one's own career, if not physical and mental health. Some of its forms disgusted Darby. Crossdressing! Pedophilia! Scatology! Asphyxiation!

---

1. See Mayoclinic.org. *Compulsive*. Mayo Clinic Staff.

The symptoms varied from mild-to-wild: intense impulses beyond one's control; an inability to refrain even from disgusting activities; the need to escape boredom, anxiety, depression, and stress; an indulgence in spite of recognizing risks, all resulting in the ultimate disparagement of committed relationships. The warning signs equally disillusioned him. As he read them, Darby sensed the unraveling of a cultural heritage he had valued since childhood. Yet, in truth, he had fantasized them all. Why pretend otherwise? Here was the universal dark pit of the soul, Freud's libido in all its erotic allurement—from the desire for multiple partners, to sex with strangers, free of any and all emotional attachment, to the twisted and exacerbated world of lurid pornography. No wonder Celeste had come home silent, ashamed, haunted by her inner darkness, or was he over-reacting, jumping to conclusions never meant to be drawn. Was he staring into the heart of Julia's own soul? Were the lusts symptomatic of her disorder? Or of his? Yes, his? Reading the study had aroused him! He could feel his own groin swelling.

Somewhere in his memory, a youthful girl leaned across his desk. It was winter, cold. She was clad only in a yellow cashmere sweater, white shorts, and red sneakers. He could see the impression that the slight tips of her nipples made under her sweater. Her breasts were full, firm. With a smile, she watched him pore over them. "My parents will die if I don't get a B," she stated. She leaned in a little closer, her lips glistening with just enough lipstick to entice even God. "It's not like you're married," she whispered. "No one will know."

She wasn't the only one. As he sat there he began sweating. His groin tightened more. He was no saint, at least not in his heart.

He read on. That the symptoms were caused by an imbalance of serotonin, dopamine, or other neurotransmitters struck him as absurd. How sterile! Was human desire, including his own, nothing more than frustrated neural circuits? At what point were one's own desires indicative of a self in search of itself, or of a self, crying for its own wholeness? Whatever happened to plain old hedonism, with its revulsion of manipulation by prigs and self-righteous monitors? Damn! He sighed. He wondered what Nietzsche would have thought. He slid the sheets back into their folder, placed it in its niche on the shelf, and returned to the Garden. Any earlier euphoria he had felt had dissipated. As he gazed up into the avenue of the Villa's oaks and hickories, he remembered Woodworth's lines from "The Tables Turned"—

> *One impulse from a vernal wood*
> *May teach you more of man,*
> *Of moral evil and of good,*
> *Than all the sages can.*

He thought of the girl at his desk. Thank God his super-ego, or own wretched heart, had said, "No, Darby. No! Never! Never! No! No!"

Chapter 5

Evening came quickly. In what seemed like only seconds, the sun's warm rays turned into a pale soft pink, before sinking into a blur of iridescent purple. Instantly the air became cold. Darby entered the *palazzo* and made his way to the dining room.

"Well! Well! Here's our host! He did make it!" Tunstan exclaimed as he raised his wine glass to hail Darby's entrance. "We were wondering where you were."

"No place in particular. Just enjoying the fire and the cottage's warmth."

"I can't believe you weren't doing something," Stephanie commented. "All those books! I bet you were reading something."

"I'd be embarrassed to tell you," Darby smiled. He took his seat at the head of the table and unfolded his napkin politely. "How's everyone doing? You know, when I was studying group dynamics as a priest, we were discouraged from asking anything personal. Like: 'How are *you*?' Or 'What are *your* thoughts?' Instead, we were instructed to ask: 'Well, how's *it* going?' leaving the person to define *it*. Frankly, I found that impersonal. You're either fine or not, happy or sad, reflective or garrulous. So, I trust everyone did have a decent day, however miserable it might have been."

Parker smiled. "I took a jog in the afternoon. Even coaxed Celeste to go with me," he turned sheepishly toward her.

She looked up hesitantly toward Darby, smiled; then glanced away. He focused on her mouth, her lips—how tightly she pursed them—before he too glanced at the others.

"I saw that!" Tunstan quipped as he observed their interaction. "I once had a paramour. Paid for her studio. Taught her how to paint, to blend pigments and create shadows. She was young," he said haltingly, glancing toward Stephanie. "She went on to higher and bigger and better things, then dropped it all to marry a Spanish bull breeder. Imagine that? A toreador's consort! I wish I knew where she was. Her husband's ranch was somewhere between El Greco's Toledo and Velazquez's Madrid. Maybe one day she'll resurface and take up the brush again." His lips parted unable to disguise his disappointment. "It makes you wonder, doesn't it? Do I dare ask about you?" he confronted Darby.

"Ask all you wish. But some things aren't divulge-able! I know that isn't a word, but that's the case."

Celeste, who was seated to Darby's right, laid her fork beside her salad plate and stared directly into Darby's eyes. "Come, Professor Peterson! Even philosophers stumble from time to time. Bertrand Russell, anyone? Or Sartre or Abelard? No?" she smiled in a deliberate challenge. "You don't strike me as being a 'mouse of the scrolls.'"

"Mrs. Martin, I've made my mistakes, many of them, I assure you. But life goes on, even for us mortals," he replied with a pleasant smile.

She drew her face back slightly, placed her napkin against the edge of her lips, and touched his forearm with her left hand. "That's what fascinates me—the going-on part. *Us mortals!*" she repeated his words. "Here we are, for whatever reasons we've come, and none of us knows each other's secrets, nor needs to. But I wish I knew what I wanted out of life. That always seems to evade me. You're supposed to have the answer, aren't you? Or at least an idea? Isn't that what philosophy's about?"

"My science teacher says it's dead!" Stephanie piped up. "Philosophers don't have answers, least not important ones. Only science can provide them. Or so he says. No offense, sir!" she smiled at Darby with imploring eyes.

"None taken, my dear! In part he's right, you know. Ideally, philosophy's task is to make us critical of the *unexamined* answers we end up settling for." He lowered his voice momentarily. "In truth, it can't give us the answers we need. It can only encourage us be *honest* with ourselves. To what Heidegger calls, the search for 'an authentic existence.' I don't think the search ever ends. If there were some one purpose, above all purposes, that we're to live by, wouldn't we have discovered it by now? It's just that at various stages some purposes make more sense than others, and later we exchange those for others."

"I don't know what I want," said Stephanie. "I just want my life to be happy! I wish my father would come back, wherever he is. I wouldn't even care where he's been. I just want him home."

"I'd say that's pretty sensible!" remarked Tunstan. "I'm still searching, too."

"Good Heavens!" Linda moaned, as she entered the dining room. In one hand she carried a platter of braised chicken, and in the other a tray of yellow rice and broccoli. "You all look morbid. Darby, you're supposed to enliven our guests, not turn them into zombies."

Everyone laughed.

"I'd say he's doing a good job," Parker announced. "I hope were having apple pie for dessert. I've been smelling it all afternoon."

"That's right. Our own Stephanie picked them," she smiled at the girl, "plus the philosopher here," she nudged Darby's right shoulder with her left hip.

"Well, here's a story for you," Darby smiled with a fey sigh, "if that's what you want. Maybe it'll make all of us *misérables* happy. I forget the source—perhaps Durant—but once upon a time there was a philosopher who lived in the Duchy of Luxembourg, back in the era of Napoleon. He wrote philosophy books, all of which he dedicated to the Prince. One day the Prince called him into his study and demanded to know why the court's critic constantly found fault with the philosopher's works. 'Doesn't that make me look bad?' questioned the Prince, 'since they're dedicated to me?' 'Well, your Excellence, you have to look at it this way,' replied the philosopher. 'A book is like a mirror. If an ass looks in, don't expect to hear an angel sing.'"

"Now that's more like it," chuckled Linda. "The next time Jon Paul's shaving, I'll ask him if he's ever seen an angel."

"Well, wait till we've had our pie," said Parker. "Then we can all look in the mirror."

"Speak for yourself!" sighed Celeste, as she glanced, eyes down, toward Darby.

* * *

Following dinner, the guests migrated to the living room. Stephanie wandered over to a CD player and began sorting through a stack of CDs. She found several she liked and placed them in the player's tray. Soon her selections filled the room with their hip-hop and light-rock sounds. Tunstan appeared a bit annoyed, until "Soul Sister" came on. Its spirited melody and hypnotic lyrics opened something deep of long ago in his being. He rose from the chair, in which he had slumped, and took Stephanie's left hand. "May I have this dance?" he bowed.

"Of course!" the girl replied, as she rolled her eyes toward Darby. "I'd love to."

Quickly Parker turned toward Celeste, where she was standing by the fireplace, and took her hands. "You know we haven't in a long time," he said. He drew her hungrily against his chest and began to move to the beat of the music. Her body submitted to his tug. Her feet stepped gracefully to the CD's rhythm. Darby watched with envy.

About that time, Linda entered the room. He held his hands out to her. "Will Jon Paul mind?"

"Don't think about it," she smiled. "He's a fabulous cook, but two feet in reverse on the dance floor." She glanced up at Darby. "Hold me, Darby. Just hold me, that's all," she whispered.

More discs were placed in the player: shag, rock-n-roll, tunes from the 70s and 80s. Darby continued dancing with Linda, then Stephanie, and finally Celeste. He knew Parker's eyes scrutinized their every gesture, glance, and movement.

"I guess he told you everything," she looked up into Darby's eyes. Her intense gray pupils bore into his manhood. It was as if they were inviting him to, to . . . he dismissed the thought. His chest rose and fell with silent pleasure. "He told me he talked with you earlier," she whispered softly.

"I listened."

"I bet you did!"

Darby didn't answer.

"He didn't tell you why. Did he? Why I came back?"

"Not really."

"I loved it. I couldn't get enough. But I was slipping, slipping into something I couldn't control." She leaned out, pulling away from him slightly, before placing her hot cheek against his shoulder. "He's watching. I can feel it. I'll have to go to him. I was becoming a whore and loving every moment of it with any and every man. I knew I had to stop." Tears formed in her eyes. "Something died in me that night. I just stood there in the shower as it died. I don't know what it was or if it'll ever come back. I just knew I had to stop." She brushed her eyelashes with the back of her fingertips, smiled, and slid away toward her husband.

Parker opened his arms and clasped them about her waist. He looked silently toward Darby. Darby couldn't discern what the man's thoughts were or even imagine his feelings.

As he turned to leave through the French doors he felt a nudge at his elbow. Tunstan was struggling into a leather jacket and adjusting his tan beret. "May I exit with you?" he clasped Darby's arm. "I'll be leaving tomorrow. I want to show you something. I want you to take it." He bowed his head, almost ushering Darby along.

Outside, Darby followed the now dour-faced art investigator toward a Mercedes, parked alongside Parker and Celeste's Lexus. Hughes fumbled in his jacket's pocket, found his keys and unlocked the passenger's side front door. He opened the glove compartment, hesitated momentarily, then handed Darby a small handgun—a 9 mm, semi-automatic Beretta. "Here! Take it!" he glanced up at Darby with remorse in his voice. "I was going to use it. What the hell! You might need it some day. It's registered, but no one will know."

Darby examined the gun carefully before slipping it into his pocket.

"I need to get on back to Philly, visit some relatives there, and return to Boston. I want to get started again on the only thing I love." He hesitated; then clicked his keypad, as his trunk door snapped open and rose upward. He smiled. "A little something for Stephanie before I depart. I plan to give it to her in the morning."

Darby stared into the trunk. There lay a watercolor of Montesereno's villa. Tunstan had captured its Italian beige and golden-pink hues, its ornate door and iron grillwork with a whimsical flair all its own. Nor had he left out the Villa's spacious grounds, pebbled approach, sprawling lawn, and ancient oaks.

"Take it to your cottage," stated Tunstan. "It needs to dry more. We'll both present it to her tomorrow, at breakfast, or whenever she gets up."

Darby lifted the canvas with extreme caution so as not to smear a single brush stroke.

"Maybe it'll inspire her to paint one day. She's a sweet kid. If I could afford to stay longer, I'd teach her how to paint. I need to get back. There's an art show coming up, and I need to be seen again. Art dealers will be there from all over. Wish you could come yourself."

"I, too."

"Maybe I'll paint you one day. I rarely, if ever, forget a face. 'The Professor's Cottage!' Or maybe better 'The Chaplain's Garden.' I can see it now." He waved his right hand in a majestic arc. "The ginkgo tree; the *petit maison*; the garden, and, *voilà*, yourself, seated in contemplation beside the laurel!"

"Sounds rather cruel to mar nature so. Maybe you'd better stick with still life or poring over lacquered layers of brush strokes and fingerprints."

Tunstan shut the trunk door with a loud thump. "In the morning," he said. "Besides, I think someone else wants to see you," he nodded toward the house.

Darby looked back. Celeste stood in the door light, cloaked in a fur coat that covered her slender shoulders down to her ankles. She clutched the collar of the fur, enwrapping herself in its shiny sheen, and stepped down.

"Goodnight!" whispered Tunstan. "Get that painting in the cottage." He tipped his beret to Celeste and returned indoors.

"I'm glad he's gone!" Celeste said. "Has Parker come out?"

"No! Not that I can see." Darby leaned the painting against Tunstan's car. "I've got to get this painting inside. Did you want to talk?" he asked, lamely. He could feel the blood pounding in his temples. He didn't want his stay at Montesereno to begin like this, or end this way, either.

"I need more than talk." She reached for his hands, clasped them, and clenched her fingers about his. "At least, let's walk." She put her forearm under his coat's left sleeve and began walking slowly toward the Garden. "Sometimes, I never talked with them, you know. We just undressed, ran our hands over each other's genitalia and had sex. Often with multiple partners. Sometimes we used cuffs. They'd pull my hair back and choke me." She looked away; then raised her face searchingly toward Darby. "I miss it. God, but I do. As for Parker, he's like a deer in the headlights. He knew what I was doing. He wanted me, too. He wanted to watch. Yes! Watch! He didn't tell you that, did he?" she stopped, before lifting her eyes to stare into Peterson's. "Well, he did! I took him once. He wanted to go back. He made me feel more like a whore than the others. That's right. They just wanted sex, their libidos fulfilled. Parker wanted humiliation." She pulled Darby along, slowly, while all the while clutching his arm. Her hands were trembling. "I don't think our marriage can survive. We're too far-gone. He wants me now only out of carnality, out of anger. Maybe love. I don't know," she choked on her words. "I don't like what I've become. But I crave it! I want you to take me. He'll never know. He won't care, anyway. He just needs me because his job's in jeopardy. Come!" she pulled on his hands, on his arms. She climbed on her tiptoes to kiss him.

Just then car lights loomed into view. A dark limousine entered the Villa's gates and approached the house. The two stood there, looking up past the corner of the Inn, hand in hand, and watched as a second vehicle, a black Crown Victoria, swung in behind the first. The cars pulled up under the lamplights in front of the house. Five men got out, three from the limousine and two from the black Ford. They ascended the front stoop, knocked, and appeared to enter. Darby could hear the door close.

"They're either state police or politicians," said Darby. "They love riding around in Crown Victorias!"

"Maybe they're celebrities!"

Moments later, the French doors opened and Parker stepped out into the cold. The light of the living room cast his silhouette large and bituminous against the velvet dark, illuminating the patio's plants and tall urns. "Celeste! Please come in! We've been asked to remain quietly in the living room. Jon Paul said he'd explain in the morning. We're not to ask questions. Please, Celeste, come in! That goes for you, too, Professor."

Celeste gave Darby a quick glance, released his hand, and hurried toward her husband. Parker glared at Peterson but said nothing. He held the large doors open for his wife. He closed them as she entered.

Darby quickly returned to Tunstan's car to retrieve the painting. Just as he unlocked the cottage's latch, the backdoor to Garnett's office opened and Jon Paul stepped out. "Peterson! We need you in here. Please!"

Chapter 6

Inside the study, Jon Paul stood uneasily beside Garnett's desk. Standing with him were the five mystery guests. Two wore black leather jackets and dark tan trousers, one with a brazen smile, the other younger, slender, with a hint of high cheekbones. He slouched forward slightly in his dark-brown cowboy boots. A third figure of medium build, gray hair, black eyes, and a flattened Roman nose eyed Darby with suspicion. A rumpled, wide-lapelled, olive-green sports coat drooped cape-like about the man's shoulders. Darby estimated him to be in his late-sixties. The remaining two wore dark suits, one with a beige shirt and red tie, the other in a blue shirt and gold tie.

"We're with the Witness Protection Service," the taller of the latter spoke. A full head of wavy black hair obscured his brow. His face seemed unusually pale. A scar ran horizontal along his cheek, just past his right eye. He leaned forward to shake Darby's hand, his shoulder holster clearly visible. "Hal Gunn!" he identified himself. "Jorgan and I," he glanced toward his partner, "are Federal agents. Donaldson," he nodded toward the booted man, "and Jeffries are US marshals. Mr. Dominetti here's in our protective care. You, Mr Wagner, and his wife, Linda, are the sole residents to know this. You'll need to keep silent until he's gone. He'll be here no more than a week, if that long. Is that clear?"

"Yes, sir! Quite!"

"Not even your staff is to know, if others work here," he directed his comment toward Jon Paul.

"Hettie and Curly will not be informed, I assure you," the chef stated.

"Who are they?"

"Housekeeper and grounds-man. They're here only between guests, or as needed."

"Well, try not to need them for a while. Mr. Dominetti's identity is to remain undisclosed. If anybody asks, he's a retired fireman from Albany, on his way to visit relatives in Florida, his *family*—so to speak. Jorgan and I, along with Jeffries, are entrusting the don to your villa. Donaldson will remain behind. They'll share the same room, or at least rooms side by side, eat with guests or alone, and wander the grounds as they please. Help them fit in as naturally as possible. Dominetti's due to testify in federal court next week—in Newark. He likes cigars, wine, and liquor. We've brought him boxes of each."

The Italian shifted his jacket about his shoulders and smiled. "My name's Angelico, named for my grandfather's brother, a priest," he extended his hand, first to Jon Paul, then to Darby. "You need somethin', just ask Angelico!" he croaked in a hoarse, throaty voice. The man all but crushed Darby's fingers as he enfolded them in his massive grip. "I give you my *parola, come il cacio sui maccheroni*! You got nothing to fear!"

"I'll look forward to it," Darby smiled. "Perhaps you can enjoy *la vita di Michelaccio* here. The food's *magnifico* and so is the view."

"You speak Italian! I like that."

Darby blushed, as he knew no Italian. Only phrases, blurted out occasionally by a former colleague in the hallways of the Humanities Department or occasionaly by an older priest. "Perhaps we can discuss Dante or the popes of the Renaissance."

"Ahh!" he grunted with indifference. "Better their wines and *dolce bagascia*! But opera? That's my true *amore*. Caruso! Pavarotti! Puccini! Verdi!"

Darby wondered what *bagascia* meant.

The Italian stuffed his hands in his pockets. Suddenly, he produced a rosary. "Forgive me for saying *bagascia*! My father would not have approved. One of his wife's sisters was a *whore*." He twiddled the rosary's beads in both hands while the agents waited for Jon Paul to sign several papers they had placed before him.

"He's all yours till next Sunday!" said Gunn. "Donaldson will see he's protected. Goodnight, Dr. Peterson! Mr. Wagner! Remember, mum's the word. Dominetti's new name is yet to be assigned. What'll it be, Angelico?"

"Dominetti! I will remain Dominetti till the day I die."

"Don't be silly!" Gunn replied. "We need you alive. Not dead! Dr. Peterson, come up with a good name for him, until then."

"What about Domino, at least around others? That'll preserve the *Dom* in your name."

"*Bischeros*!" he muttered. "But it'll do! Domino Ruffini! Thank you, Dr. Peterson. Dominettis don't forget friends. Somehow, one day I'll repay. I promise with my life."

"Well, keep it through next week!" Gunn added. "Adieu, everyone! Donaldson, he's all yours."

The young marshal nodded, studied his quarry momentarily, and shook Peterson's hand. "I like your style," the marshal stated. "I don't know beans about Dante or Puccini, but I know plenty about the mob, how they function, prostitutes, and whores," he bent his head toward the living room.

He must have noticed Celeste, was all Darby could surmise. That's all they needed. A capo and young marshal! He glanced at Jon Paul. The latter lowered his eyes. So he knew they were coming, but couldn't or wouldn't say anything.

Chapter 7

The purr of the running engine awakened Darby before his eye lids deigned to open. Rolling to one side, he rubbed them sleepily; then glanced at the clock. Six a.m. He sat up, yawned, slipped into his robe, and opened the cottage's door. The taillights of Tunstan's Mercedes glowed red as the car slipped out of sight around the Villa. Moments later, it re-emerged on the opposite side of the house. He watched as it headed up the lane. Once past the gates, the silvery vehicle sank out of view. So began his day.

* * *

"Oh, I love it!" Stephanie exclaimed as she held the canvas in her hands. "He's such a nice man! Isn't it beautiful?"

"That you like it, would please him."

"I do! All night I kept thinking about his girlfriend and how beautiful Spain must be." She set the painting beneath a dining room window before seating herself. She glanced about, then whispered: "Did you see those men last night? Two of them stayed here. They're in a suite at the end of the hall. I heard Mrs. Martin come out of her room in the night. They're two rooms down from me. Someone else came out. I could hear Mr. Martin's voice. He was upset. I fell back to sleep. I like him. I wish I were older and he was single."

"Stephanie, there's enough going on around here without that. OK?"

"You don't have to be so bossy! You have a mean voice sometimes. You know that?"

"Not intentionally mean. If so, I got it from monitoring certain types, especially during exams. They'd crimp cheat-notes inside their belts. They'd cough as they brought up their hands. Bad boys! There are a lot of them out there, Stephanie."

"I know," she said with a flirtatious smile. "Who are those men, anyway? Mr. Wagner's supposed to tell us."

"Firefighters, I believe. On their way to Florida or somewhere."

"I don't believe that. That one in the cowboy boots is cute."

"Stephanie, that's enough! You've got to get back to school before you slip down the drain."

"I know! It's hard to be upbeat when you're sad."

"There are some good argument patterns that can improve writing, you know? They'd make an admissions committee think twice before rejecting a candidate. Might even result in a callback interview. You game?"

"If you promise to be sweet! Why not?" a sparkle of hope gleamed in her eyes. "Yeah! You're on!"

"First thing, once it warms up. We'll sit in the living room or out in the Garden."

* * *

After breakfast, Darby returned to the cottage. Neither the Martins, nor Donaldson and his witness had come down for *prima colazione* or *le petit déjeuner*. He guessed Linda would have to provide room service. She'd probably become accustomed to many mood swings, based on what little he had already observed. Darby looked about for some pads and pens in case Stephanie should follow through. He turned over a multiple slate of ideas for starters. Best to let her choose her own.

He stirred the embers in the fireplace, threw on a new log, and sat in the chair with a sigh. He closed his eyes and fell asleep.

He recognized his classroom. Students were staring at him. He opened his folder, but where was his lecture? Not a single sheet, note, or memo lay in the folder. What class was he in, anyway? Logic? Metaphysics? What day was it? Monday or Tuesday? Had he shown up at the wrong hall? The students looked familiar. O God! He had forgotten their test scores again. Nor had he graded their papers in weeks. What would he do if the Dean found out? He was already in enough hot water.

The bed! Look under your bed? Yes, the bed. Darby got down on his knees, threw up the bed's coverlet, and pulled out a long plastic storage tub. Bundles of dusty ungraded papers lay in rubber-band-wrapped clumps. His heart sank! Someone was at the door. Quickly he slid the tub back under the bed and dropped the coverlet. Just in time, too. They were still knocking.

Darby woke up with a bolt. A subtle waft of perfume tingled the hairs in his nostrils. Its sillage would have awakened anyone. He opened his eyes. There stood Celeste! His neck felt cold and clammy, his face hot. "I must have been dreaming."

"How about snoring!" she bent forward and kissed his cheek. "But just lightly! Wish I had been in the dream with you." A far-off sadness flashed briefly across her eyes, then crept softly into her mouth. "We're leaving now. Just wanted to say good-bye!"

Darby sat up, wiped the corners of his lips, and rose to his feet. She embraced him and kissed his mouth, quickly but hard. "I'll be back! Take care of yourself," she looked away. She stepped back and closed the door quietly behind her. Darby could hear her sharp heels on the pavement stones. The Lexus cranked up and drove off. The delicate scent of her perfume still lingered in the room.

Darby expelled a slow breath, slipped into his woolen jacket, and left the cottage. Halfway through the orchard he heard men's voices along the road. He peered through the apple trees' limbs, past the property's fence and dried vines. Donaldson and Dominetti were strolling along. They appeared to be returning from the overlook. They seemed not to notice Darby. Dominetti was gesturing with his hands, while the marshal was listening.

At the overlook, Darby stared out across the bulky mountains. The foliage would soon be gone. A few hickories and oaks retained a smattering of citrus-brown leaves. So too, scarlet bunches of sumac emblazoned the slopes below. A cold wind stung his ears; a russet colored hawk spread its wings and cried overhead. The lonesome shriek pierced Darby's soul.

Back at the Villa, Darby entered the living room in search of Stephanie. If she wouldn't come to him, perhaps he should go to her.

Hettie, Garnett's housekeeper, called to him as he shut the door. "Well, well, if it ain't Mr. High-n-Mighty hisself! I figured Mr. Wilson would call on you. You ain't still teachin', are you?" She paused with dust cloth in hand to rest beside an end table. The tiny woman had bunched her red hair up in a bun. Her forearms were splotched with bruises and age-spots. The roots of her hair were turning gray. "I ain't broke nothin' yet," she fretted. "I'd rather it'd be you than some shrink. They ain't worth the prescriptions they scribble. Been to one and that's all. He didn't care a hoot for me or Curly. We was just white trash. Poor Curly's losin' it, Doc. He cain't remember half the time who I am. He's got dementia bad. He's out there right now helping Jon Paul rig up that rusty tractor that ought-a been trashed years ago. Well! How are you?"

"Hettie, I'm alive, I suppose. You haven't changed a bit. It's good to be back. You look as fit as a fiddle."

"Well, hell, I ought to be! I don't do nothin' but slave around and cook for that worthless husband of mine," her face lit up with a frown. "Lord, I'd be lost without him. What cha lookin' for? I ain't never seen you when you wasn't lookin' for somethin'."

"Stephanie. The young girl!"

"That one? With the sad eyes? She's out there with Curly and Jon Paul. Like she's gonna help 'em or something. Poor child."

"Hettie, you'd make a good shrink yourself. Thanks for telling me."

Once outside, Darby found Stephanie easily enough. The coughing, chugging, ear-popping sounds of the tractor's exhaust gave their presence away. The sinewy, gnarled man next to her smiled as Darby approached. His brown brogans had long since lost their color, and the cuffs of his jeans had disintegrated into scruffy pale threads. Gray hairs poked from his ears, alongside a mole near his left chin.

"She's doin' right fair," Curly commented as he looked up at Darby. "How's yerself?" he asked. "We ain't seen you in quite a while."

"They're letting me drive," Stephanie exclaimed.

"Be careful!" Curly warned. "Don't let up on that clutch so fast."

Suddenly the tractor jolted as it rocked unwieldy forward. Stephanie gripped the steering wheel firmly and guided the huge tractor slowly toward the orchard, pocketed with its intermittent patches of grass.

So much for delving into critical thinking! Darby mused. If the girl were happy, wasn't that therapy enough?

Following lunch, Darby returned to the cottage. He selected a few books to browse, namely, Plotinus' *Enneads* and Nietzsche's *The Birth of Tragedy*, and searched for the sunniest spot he could find in the Garden. He adjusted one of its metal chairs to face the sun, sank back, and, with closed eyes, raised his visage toward the orb's warm rays. After indulging himself, he turned his attention to the *Enneads*. He hadn't read the Neo-Platonist's chapter "On Beauty" since assigning it last semester. Somehow the autumnal colors and Tunstan's painting had reawakened an aesthetic undercurrent that wished to surface. He turned the pages slowly, noting the Greek text on the even-numbered pages and the English translation on the odd. The world of Neo-Platonism came back to him with nostalgia. The ascent of the soul from the material to the intellectual, and thence to the ideal, the good, and God, struck him as inconceivable anymore—especially in light of the immense intellectual distances that separated the modern era from the classical age.

> What then is our way of escape, and how shall we find it? We shall put out to sea as Odysseus did, from the witch Circe . . . not content to stay though delighted by the eyes and the beauty of sense . . . For one must come to the sight with a seeing power made akin and like to what is seen . . . You must become first [of] all godlike and all beautiful if you intend to see God and beauty. First the soul will come in its ascent to intellect and there will know the Forms—all beautiful—and will affirm that these,

the Ideas, are beauty. [For] that which is beyond we call the nature of the Good, which holds beauty as a screen.[1]

Darby closed the book and stared at the aurora about the sun's outermost
sheen. Its blinding glow forced him to look away. Slowly his eyes readjusted
to the light his retinas allowed him to see.

While still basking in his contemplative shell, the sweet notes of
Pavarotti's voice emanated from the French doors of the Villa. Bemused,
Darby turned to see what was happening. Amid the majestic urns, Signore
Dominetti had seated himself in the sun, to listen, no doubt, to the tenor's
arias. The CD player had been turned up full blast. Just inside the door, sat
Donaldson, vigilant, yet relaxed. Darby listened to the aria being sung. It
was Aquinas' *Panis Angelicus*, written for the Mass in the thirteenth century.
It was all he could do to keep from humming it under his breath.

Panis angelicus

Fit panis hominum.

Should he speak to the old man, or let him imbibe his sacrament of loneliness? After several interludes, the gray-headed don rose and walked out
toward Darby. "May I sit with you?" he asked. "One can only take so much
opera! *Sì?*"

"My honor, sir!" he replied, as he stood up to shake his hand.

The two reseated themselves. Dominetti spoke first. "My father, he
loved music. The arias of the church. Our uncle, the priest, raised us to
cherish them. You know, we are a dying breed. This trial coming up, we're
one of the last families to go. The Russians and Chinese have moved in. The
Ukrainians, they are the thieves. Now it is the Internet and politicians. The
great families are gone.

"You know, with us, it was a way of life. *Sì*, crime; lots of crime. But for
a reason. You are a priest, no? A professor, too? Yes. You were? *Sì?* So Linda
has told me."

"Yes. Both at one time, or other," he smiled.

"Well, the priest I like," he half-crossed himself. "Did you ever study
Sicilian culture? Huh? Yes, or no!"

"Not in the way you're asking. No!"

"Well let me tell you. It was our way of life. Since the fall of the Roman
Empire, someone had to take charge. Someone had to expend a little mus-
cle. Even in its last days, there were grandees, dons even then. They owned
what estates remained. Gathered what armies they could. Yes, imposed

---

1. Plotinus. *Ennead*. I. 6.

themselves, determined what ports were open, who sailed what and where, and what fees collected. Bribes, yes! That's how it worked. From the lowest shops in villages to the highest *signores* in towns, even to the papas, the grandees skimmed off profits. You moved nowhere without their will. As Italians, we inherited all that. No?"

"I'm listening."

"It's always been that way. *Sì*? Our first family to come over brought it with them. New York was hard. Families had to band together, protect themselves; take a little here, a little there, bribe the police, the judges and bailiffs, whatever. You wanna a job? Only the don could get it for you. Your sons needed shoes, then the shoemaker knew he had to provide. Simple, but it worked. I grew up that way.

"My father, he owned the butcher shop in our *vincinanza*, our neighborhood. It was a front. Sure, we had to pay for the slaughtered cows and pigs, but we made the best sausages in town. Mama made pasta! Myself—my brothers and sisters—we cleaned up; we had our chores to do. I was always big, big hands, you see," he clenched them. "It became time for me to collect the rents, you know. I was smart. Once I beat up three men, bigger than me. No one held back after that. But change was coming. Unions, the dockworkers, cabbies, drugs, police, bookies, racketeering big time. I moved into prostitution and strip clubs; kept the cops bribed. They was the easiest to corrupt. They had families, ya know, and mouths to feed. Plus, they had grown up with us in the streets. But you know the rest. We got into politics, bribing senators and majors, paying them off big. My first murder involved using these," he held up his hands. "I was sent out to strangle a capo. Yeah, he had insulted a neighbor's sister-in-law. I was good at it. I left no fingerprints behind. I became my father's *negotiator*," he smiled. "No one ever double-crossed us. My father was proud. Then, another family moved in. Killed a carload of cousins. We struck back, but only through the police. The judge was one of ours. All of them got life! Things settled down." He glanced uneasily toward Darby. "You know what I mean?"

Darby nodded in concurrence.

"We did a lot of good, especially my father. The family honored him. On feast days and saints' masses, people in the Bronx brought gifts to us and laid them in front of my father. At every wedding and funeral, he was seated first, down front, along with my mother, before the service could begin. But an uncle became jealous. He wanted to be the don. He undermined my father's business, set up a rival gang, and murdered some of our family. Then, the worst happened," Dominetti paused. His voice turned hoarse, barely audible. Tears welled in his eyes. "They came to me with a threat. I was to leave the family, or they'd kill my father, along with my mother and sisters. My wife was already dead, my only son, in college—now a lawyer. I refused to budge. We rallied and fought back, tried to regain what we could: brothels, unions, casinos, retirement funds, judges, you name it. I knew too much. They knew it too. They put out a contract on my father. Two months later they killed him, right in front of our shop. My mother got away, but not my sisters. That's when I went to the cops, to the DA. 'Hey! I'll make you a deal.' They knew who I was. They showed me their file. 'OK!' they said. And, so, I'm here. Dead meat," he smiled. "Cowboy there," he motioned over his shoulder. "For all I know, they've bought him off, too. Why not have a glass of wine with me! I'd appreciate it."

"Of course! The Villa's got quite a cellar. But what a story! Here, let me show you the way. Come on."

They went by way of the kitchen to find Jon Paul and Linda. "Good!" said Dominetti. "After this, I'll bring a bottle of my own down for supper." All four of them descended the steps to the cellar.

"Hey, whut's goin' on here?" asked Curly. He'd crept down in the basement to check on the pipes. "Ain't you got no respect for me or Hettie?" he coughed with a smile.

"Tell her to come on down," Jon Paul motioned. "But, remember, one of you has to drive home."

"Huh!" snorted Curly. "Since when's bein' sober got anything to do with drivin'?" He held out a cup from a rack near the wine, grinned, and wiped his lips in anticipation.

Within minutes, Hettie joined them. Darby took a long drought and excused himself to search for Stephanie.

He found her sitting on the front steps of the Villa in its cold shadows. "It's warmer in the back, you know," he nodded. "Kind of cold here, isn't it?"

"I don't feel like basking in the sun," she said, as she glanced up. "I don't want to go home. Grandmother's coming in the morning," she looked out despondently across the drive. "I don't deserve better, I guess. I'll probably end up being a waitress somewhere, if I don't get off my butt. I know it's my fault. That's what everybody tells me. 'Stephie, you have to try harder.' Like I'm not trying all I can. I can't focus like the rest. I'm the butt of everybody's jokes. They think I'm weird, different, some kind of kook. But I'm just me. Just Stephanie Gay, shy, like any other kid from a broken home—not that Grandmother doesn't try. There's just no way she can understand. Motivation's not my thing. The Zoloft I'm on doesn't work. I wish I were dead or had never been born. You ever feel that way?" she forced herself to smile.

Darby reached out and clasped her hands. "Come on," he pulled her up. "Let's walk up the road. I'm a sun person, you know. In another twenty years, I'll be dead, or lying somewhere in a cold grave. Eternity's a long time. Why not enjoy the sun while we can?"

"You're right! I wish my daddy was here! Or someone to be proud of me. Girls laugh about their dads, how silly and clueless they are, but their eyes light up when they talk like that. Come!" she pulled on his hand. "I want to show you where I mowed. You'll like it!"

Darby followed her to the orchard. She had concentrated on the area under the trees and about their grassy perimeter. In the process, she had created an oval design, lending a touch of grace under the gnarled limbs of the knobby trees. "Not bad for a waitress!" he teased. "Maybe you should be a cosmetologist!"

"No! I'm going to be a painter, a writer, or scholar. I'm gonna work my butt off. Charleston's Ashley College's not the only place I can go. You'll see."

"I've never doubted it. Not for an instant! Let's eat an apple, if we can find one, and gather a few to throw off the cliff."

"I like that! I really do."

Soon they had collected an armful each. They ran happily through the orchard toward the overlook. "Here's to you, Admissions Committee!" Darby hollered, as he lobbed one far out and over the face of the cliff. They waited to hear it splat, but the bottom was too far below to accommodate their hope. "Ah! That's life!" Darby laughed, as Stephanie hurled one farther out than his.

"Look at it sail!" she said.

Far better to throw apples off a cliff than oneself, he thought, as he cast a worried but buoyant eye toward the girl!

Chapter 8

Just prior to dinner, Curly came by the Villa to bid "Good Night!" Darby answered the door. He could see Hettie in the couple's pick-up truck. Linda and Stephanie sat in the living room in front of the fireplace. Donaldson and Dominetti had stationed themselves in the kitchen to observe Jon Paul's culinary arts. The shadows of evening lay cold and dark across the grounds.

"Won't you come in?" Darby asked.

"No, Sir! Ain't necessary," Curly addressed him. "There's a strange car parked up at the overlook. Ain't nobody in it, but the license plate's marked 'New Jersey.' I walked up there when I seen it. I think maybe the driver was in the woods, relievin' hisself. But that ain't for certain. Just thought you needed to know, especially with them 'fire fighters' of yourn hangin' about here. Well, you'ens come and see us." He tipped his cap before descending the steps. "Oh!" he turned, "Hettie says to say, 'Till next time.'"

Darby waved to her as the truck drove off. "Linda! Did you hear that?" he asked her quietly.

"Yes!"

"Better call Jon Paul. Let Donaldson know." While she hurried to the kitchen, Darby nodded toward Stephanie. "Stephanie! You're not to know about this. Just sit loose until we know more."

She shook her head in approval, her eyes wide with fear.

"Gentleman!" the marshal called, as he came running from the kitchen with Dominetti and Jon Paul: "If what your Curly said is true, we might be in trouble. Do you have a gun, or weapon?"

"Of course!" replied Jon Paul. "I keep a .38 in my room at all times. Why?"

"You're going to need it, if that car's from New Jersey. What about you, Professor?"

"Yes. I've got one in the cottage. A 9 mm semi-automatic. But I've never used it."

"Mr. Ruffini, are you comfortable staying here with the professor while Mr. Wagner and I look around? We'll come back instantly. Mrs. Wagner, lock all the doors. Do you mind? Is that OK, sir?" he directed his question toward Dominetti. "Do you feel safe?"

"*Holy Mary, Mother of God*! Stop calling me *Ruffini*! Do I have a choice? I could of warned you how this would end! Just protect the girl," he groused bitterly. He held up his hands. "I, Angelico, would love to use these again! To crush their throats!" He snapped his knuckles as he clenched his fists. "Find them. Dead or alive!"

The tall marshal unzipped his leather jacket, checked his revolver, and spun-clicked the chamber of his Colt .45. "Mr. Wagner. Please get your gun. I'll wait for you at the back door. I'm going out the front now to look around."

"Linda! . . . Stephanie! . . . Mr. Dominetti!" Darby quietly enunciated each name, "let's adjourn to the living room and . . . see what happens. . . . *Sì*?"

"Only for the sake of the *Signora* and *la poca raggaza*, yes!" Dominetti smiled reassuringly, giving Stephanie a hug. "Come, little one. I have grand-daughters older than you."

Time passed slowly. Darby sat nervously with restless misgivings, while Stephanie fidgeted with a doily under a lamp. Linda stared restively into the flames. All four listened for sounds of the night, from the faintest stirrings of leaves against the windowpanes to the terrifying possibility of crashing glass. Their prolonged silence was about to reach the breaking point, when suddenly Dominetti pointed his index finger toward the backyard. "Shhhh! Did you hear it, that zippin' noise? That's a silencer! Get down!" Immediately upon his warning, Donaldson's .45 roared—once, twice, a third time! The popping sound of Jon Paul's .38 punctuated the ensuing clamor. Dominetti bolted up and raced toward the French doors. He flung them open to crash abruptly into the chest of a large figure in a woolen overcoat. "You!" Dominetti exclaimed. He seized the man by his throat, lifted him off his feet, and, twisting him sideways, broke his neck with a shocking snap. Darby heard the man's upper vertebrae crack as his body collapsed on the steps. "My own kin!" the exasperated don swallowed. "May God forgive me!" he crossed himself in anger.

Darby stepped out into the cold. Dominetti had bent down. He was stroking the dead man's cheeks. "O Frankie! Why? Why? I wasn't gonna rat on you. O Frankie, we were friends!"

Peterson looked up. Donaldson was on his cell phone. Jon Paul's hands were trembling. "I shot him, but I missed!" he stammered. "The marshal killed the other one. He was hiding in the Garden."

Darby could hear Gunn's voice over Donaldson's cell phone. "We'll be there within two hours!" the agent stated. "Stay indoors and keep calm. Don't let Dominetti out of your sight!'"

"Can you help me?" asked Donaldson, directing his words toward Peterson. "We'll need to drag them out to the parking lot under some lights," he emphasized for Jon Paul to hear. "That large one there's going be heavy."

Within moments, Jon Paul flipped on the outside spotlights. Linda placed her hand on Angelico's shoulder.

"Hey, I'm all right!" he grumbled. "How's the girl?" he turned toward Stephanie. "Are you OK, sweetie?"

The girl looked at him, her large eyes filled with shock. Her shoulders quavered from the excitement. She opened her mouth to reply, swallowed; then, without warning, she threw up.

"Ah!" groaned Dominetti. "We all puke the first time. Jesus Christ! Here!" he bent forward and mopped up the vomit with a handkerchief from his pocket.

*　*　*

Just prior to nine o'clock, the agents arrived in a hearse. Darby was surprised, yet fascinated. He stared down at Frankie's body. It had already begun to bloat and ooze with stench. Gunn stepped out of the long gray vehicle and opened its rear doors. A second agent got out as well. The two men, along with Donaldson, secured the two corpses in body bags and heaved them into the back of the hearse.

"Do you have the keys to their car?" Gunn asked Donaldson.

"Yes, sir! That was the first item I removed. Neither has an iota of identification."

"I'm not surprised. We don't need the car. Remove its tags and obliterate the VIN. Drive it off the Parkway, if you have to. Just ditch it. I'm coming back for Ruffini," he glanced about, using his fake name, "probably around Tuesday. Just stand guard. We still don't know how the mob found out. My God, it was almost instant! Watch him around the clock. I'd take him with us, but we'd only have to find another place first."

"Why can't we just impound the car? It'd make great evidence later."

"That'd involve the locals, the sheriff's department. No. Just get rid of the damn thing. OK!"

"Yes, sir! I savvy."

*　*　*

Not until ten o'clock did the guests finally gather about the dining room table for their evening meal. Angelico had provided the wine from his own larder upstairs.

"I'm still not hungry," said Stephanie, "yet I want something to eat."

"Nervous energy," smiled Donaldson. He had seated himself across from Dominetti who sat beside the girl. The marshal's smile warmed his otherwise grey face, framed within his neck-length cropped blond hair. His eyes could not conceal his attraction to the girl. "How old are you?" he asked.

"Seventeen! I'll be eighteen in April. What about you?"

"Twenty-nine! My first name's Joel. Straight out of Tulsa. With a BS in chemistry from Oral Roberts. Been a marshal since 2002. Mainly in New York."

"That's right!" uttered Dominetti. "That's where *babyface*," he nodded toward Joel, "infiltrated the mob. They had him selling 'coke' in the Bronx schools. I was his contact. He had us fooled." Dominetti set his fork down and raised his wine glass. "Now aren't you glad I brought this vintage!" he said, as he turned the glass of translucent *vino* in his hand. "You couldn't of asked for a sweeter wine to go with this *pollo e pasta*. No? *Sì!*"

Darby raised his glass. He wished Linda had joined them, but she rarely, if ever, compromised her role as the Villa's hostess-server. The creamy white sauce on the pasta, which Linda had ladled over the crumb-encrusted breasts, could not have been richer. "I've never eaten this soon after a death, or *murder*, I should say. Strange, but I feel no guilt."

"Yes! It's like a wake, a *vègila*!" Dominetti smiled. "Too bad for them; perfect for us."

"If you say so," Darby rejoined.

"It was a close one, though," Dominetti admitted, first refilling his own glass before pouring the professor's to the brim. "Tomorrow, we must talk," he stated with raspy seriousness. "There is something I must tell you in secret. No offense, my pretty one, or marshal," he deferred to the girl and Donaldson. "Somethin' just between the Father and me. Mr. Wagner did say you were a priest? *Sì?*"

"Yes, and a professor!" beamed Stephanie. "All in one guy."

"The good don here's just being gracious," Darby smiled. "And I'm honored, sir, with the title, but the priest part was long ago."

"No matter. Tonight we celebrate!" Dominetti raised his glass anew. "Tomorrow is different." He looked down at his plate. His jubilant countenance had waned. He looked up at Darby, with something of an absence of mind. "I must retire. Please excuse me!" he announced, as he slid his chair back and stood up. "Give my compliments to the chef."

Stephanie hopped to her feet to give the Italian a hug. "I'll be going home in the morning, in case I miss you," she kissed his neck. "Thank you for being so sweet."

"My dear!" Angelico croaked in his harsh voice. "You are the sweetest of all." He hugged her tightly with a tear in his eye. "May our Savior's Mother watch over you all your life."

Chapter 9

Darby watched as the black Nissan slowly crept down the pebbled driveway and came to a stop. It was still early morning, and the sunrise had yet to clear the oaks and Fraser firs opposite the Inn's gateway. An elderly driver in a petite gray hat and white gloves peered through the windshield before cutting off the engine. Slowly she opened her door and crept out. She looked about and glanced up timorously at the Villa. Her hat sported a red band. In her hands she clutched a red purse. A long black woolen coat hung loosely about her frame. Darby estimated the cautious lady to be in her late seventies, if not older. Surely, this was Stephanie's grandmother. Darby opened the front door to greet her.

"Mrs. Gay, I assume? I'm Darby Peterson, Mr. Nelson's fill-in until he returns."

"Yes! I heard you were coming. It's a pleasure to meet you." A thin smile formed before disappearing from her lips. "I suppose I'm early," she added, as she climbed the steps, holding to the iron rail with both hands.

"Allow me to assist you," Darby stated, as he stepped down to take her arm.

She looked up and smiled, but her expression was cheerless. "I trust the child is ready. I know I have to write the check first."

"I can't say about either, but please come in. I'll inquire."

Darby escorted her into the hallway and walked with her toward Garnett's office. Linda, having heard the commotion, stepped from the dining room to greet her. "Please, Mrs. Gray, would you care for some tea or coffee while we tell Stephanie. She's been expecting you since dawn. Couldn't sleep, she said. Had breakfast with Dr. Peterson here at seven o'clock."

"How nice!" the woman replied, as she held to Darby's arm. "May I sit down in your office to write the check?"

"Of course, but if you wish to pay only half now, we can bill you for the remainder after November."

"No!" the woman said with a stiffened lip. "I just hope Stephanie's better and ready to come home."

50

"I believe you'll find her in good cheer," Darby offered. "She's a marvelous girl with a sound and inquisitive mind. It's been a joy to know her."

The woman let out a guarded breath. "We'll see," she answered indifferently. "That's what they all say."

Linda led the woman to the office while Darby took a seat in the living
room and waited for Stephanie to come down. He could hear her footsteps
in the stairwell, along with someone else's. He rose and looked up. It was
Donaldson. He was standing with Stephanie, with her suitcase and Tunstan's
painting in hand.

"Stephanie, I wish you all the luck in the world," Donaldson reassured
her, as he kissed her cheek.

The girl smiled as he walked her to the door. Just then her grandmother emerged from the office, somewhat started to see her "child" with
the lean "cowboy." She placed a hand over her mouth, as if to suppress her
thoughts. Her arched eyebrows, however, conveyed her disapproval. She followed them to the door.

Suddenly, Stephanie turned and raced toward Darby. He was standing in the living room. She flung her arms about his neck and kissed his
ear. "Thank you! Thank you a thousand times," she muttered with tears in
her eyes. "I will write you as soon as I can." She stepped back and, looking
admiringly into his face, turned and ran toward the door, down the steps,
and out to the car. Joel was waiting with her items by the trunk.

The elderly woman released the trunk latch. Donaldson lifted the suitcase and painting and placed them inside; then closed the trunk and held the
driver's door, while Mrs. Gay seated herself; then he helped Stephanie. The
grandmother started the car and stared back again at the Villa. Darby stepped
out and walked down to stand beside the marshal. Both waved as Stephanie
craned her neck to wave in return. The sun's yellow morning bands had crept
now into the trees and its bright aura blinded them as they watched the Nissan
pass through the gates and out of view.

"Well, what to do with the car?" Donaldson enquired. "Is there a cliff
along the Parkway that no one would notice?" he queried in jest. "What
does Gunn expect me to do?"

"I still don't understand why the car can't be impounded for evidence?
Why have to destroy it?"

"I wish I knew myself. It could lead to a lot of other leads, but that's
not my decision. Mainly, it's to keep the local sheriff's department out of the
picture. They don't need to know about our business, or how we go about it.
Now, what to do with this car? Any suggestions?"

"Jon Paul likely knows plenty of places you could ditch it. It's a shame
someone can't use it."

"Again, that's not our problem. I'll remove the tags and see what I can do to the VIN. I can't leave our witness unguarded. Any ideas?"

"Actually, yes."

"Oh?"

"There's a logging road behind the Villa that's negotiable most of the way down. The bottom opens into a little valley of creeks and tall oaks. A mica mine flanks it to the left. Lots of abandoned debris and rusted drums molder there. Sometimes trickles of silver leach out of the mine. Lots of kudzu, grapevines, and honeysuckle everywhere. And tangles and tangles of briars! A car driven into all that would scarcely be noticeable. When you're ready, give me the keys and I can do the rest."

"I'd go with you if I could. Maybe the old man and I could walk down and meet you partway back. How long would it take you?"

"A half-hour to an hour down. Two to three hiking out. I'm a little out of shape. It's a long way down and back but beautiful this time of year. It's a great place to fish in the spring."

"Let's plan on early afternoon. OK?"

"Fine! Let's say by one o'clock!"

* * *

Creeping down the logging trail was not as easy as Darby had fancied. Deep ruts, fallen branches, and washed out rainbars created a driver's nightmare. Darby guided the mobsters' vehicle cautiously over the rocks and roots, down the road's gravelly descents, along its narrow ledges and clay curbs. Occasionally, he stopped to admire the forest's red and yellow leaves, browns and stone-white grays. Many had fallen, affording a visibility of hundreds of yards along the mountain's slope and ravines—dark green with thickets of rhododendron. With his heart still pounding, he finally made it to the bottom, eased the car toward a bank of dried honeysuckle and floor-boarded the petal. With a violent lurch, the big Chrysler plunged into the tangle. It was all Darby could do to force the door open and crawl out. Once in the clear, he leaned back and stared up at the gray cliffs, below the overlook. If it weren't for the wall there, he and Donaldson could have pushed the car over, and that would have settled it. He released a sigh, looked up toward the sun, and began his hike up the trail. He paused to listen to the tinkling murmur of the stream, faintly audible over his right shoulder. He could see its banks and moss-covered rocks through the alder bushes and beech trees. He must come back. As he began his ascent he noticed the uprooted ground cover deep in the woods where wild hogs had despoiled the forest floor.

Their menacing presence did not bode well. Hopefully, they'd remain in the wooded glades and not discover the orchard.

At least an hour and a half or more elapsed before he met up with Joel and his Star witness. The aging Italian had paused to rest on a smooth granite ledge to enjoy a cigar. Darby could smell the Havana's aroma while still out of sight. The don scooted sideways for Darby to sit and catch his breath. "After dinner, save me some time to talk, a kind of *confessione,* you know," Dominetti whispered quietly. "You can never be sure. Right now, I want to enjoy the view. We ain't got as much in New York, 'less you go off to the lakes and Adirondacks. Me? I am a stranger here. My life's in the city, in its noisy neighborhoods with trash in the streets and rats in the alleys. And not just rodents. I mean real rats! Wire singers, *sapatos e fannuloes.*" He shook his head in the negative. "What have we here but the fire of the sun and the smile of angels! No? Behold, we look

Nel giallo de la rosa sempiterna.[1]

That's what my father used to call my mother: *la rosa sempiterna,* his 'eternal rose.' Come! Pull me up! *La lucerna del mondo* will soon go down," he waved his cigar toward the sun.

As evening approached, Darby sought out Linda. "I know we'll be having dinner soon, but I need an item, a piece of cloth hopefully you have on hand."

"What kind?" she asked, somewhat amused. "Have you ripped something? Torn a hole in your pants?"

"No! Not that at all!" he blushed with embarrassment. "I need a purple stole, or something as close to that as possible. You know, a priest's stole, a vestment he wears about his neck!"

"Are you serious?" she cocked her head with a smile. "Is this some kind of joke?"

"No! It's partly your fault. Signore Ruffini has asked me to hear his *confessione.* He wants to talk to me in private. He said you told him I was a priest."

"I only hinted at it," Linda blushed. "I like it when you get peeved," she pursed her lips as if to kiss him. "There. Now calm down."

"Well, he's Catholic, you know," Darby picked up the threads of his thoughts. "Priests don a purple stole when they hear confessions. I don't have a choice," Darby stared into Linda's eyes. "I can't let him down."

Her thin face filled with reflection. He could tell her mind was sorting through closets, or searching through drawers for whatever might match his

---

1. Dante, *Paradiso,* Canto 1.

request. "Yes!" she stated. "There's a bolt of lace border upstairs. It's lavender, but it's all I have. I could cut off a section."

"Good, you're a dream," Darby kissed her right cheek. "That'll work. Say, two yards. You don't need to iron it."

Following dinner, Darby remained in the living room for a while, determining what to do. Jon Paul had re-stoked the fire. Now its orange flames provoked a radiant wave of pleasant warmth. Should he return to his cottage or wait longer? He paced the room, stared at Garnett's walls of books and paintings, moved toward the central couch, and flopped in front of the fireplace. He couldn't imagine what being a mobster was like, least of all a don or godfather, however minor or common. He never thought of the *Cosa Nostra* as being American anyway. Or for that matter, New York Italians! They were so entrenched in their culture's past! Provincial? Yes, he was provincial! A Provincial with a PhD! He smiled at himself. Still, he had his dreams. Poor Garnett. Probably still undergoing tests. Darby glanced at his watch. He listened as the hallway's grandfather clock chimed eight-thirty. He drew in a deep breath and rose to leave.

"Hold up!" Donaldson called from the hallway. "Angelico wants to see you. He wants to walk in the Garden. I've told him to wear his overcoat."

"I need one, too," replied Darby. "I'll meet you by the cottage. My jacket here is too thin," he flopped it open. Outside, he walked thoughtfully toward the cottage and clad himself in a warmer coat. He adjusted the lacy lavender border about his neck. It wasn't a stole, but it didn't look bad. Would Angelico be offended or even notice? Darby closed the door behind him and waited.

Soon, the don stepped out into the night. A white scarf glowed visibly about his throat. He had wrapped himself in a handsome black topcoat. Darby recognized the garment as a Hart Schaffner Marx. A folded white handkerchief poked out of its lapel. A cool vapor encircled the man's gray face. He saw Darby and walked immediately to his side. Donaldson appeared in the doorway. The lean marshal stepped out and stood by one of the urns.

"You know I have to talk," Dominetti began. "Yesterday, it could have been my last. My uncle, the priest, would understand. So, you've not said if you're a Catholic, but you're a priest, or were one, right?" He looked up at Darby, just then noticing the stole. "You're okay, you know that? Huh? You know what I'm tryin' to say? Here, I will show you the kind of man I am. Take my arm, and I'll take yours. See! Like this, and we can walk."

Darby glanced down at his stole. "They say it's the color of penance, in memory of the Christ's robe, before they stripped and beat him. What do you think, Mr. Ruffini? Do I offend you?"

"Ah! You are a good one! No, no! I'm not Ruffini! I'm Angelico Dominetti. The last son of my mother's six boys. Yes. She had six. Six boys and four girls! Ten! Ten in all. And all lived. At least for a while! Now, listen, I may not make it till next week, or long after that. The mob, they know everything. You can't really hide from them. This program the boy there represents," he nodded back over his shoulder, "it doesn't work. They find you anyway. So I need to say something, to get this thing off my chest," he coughed in a rasping voice. "I, I killed a lot of people, maybe as many as twenty. I don't remember, nor want to. But," his eyes grew moist and his voice broke, "I strangled a child once, yes, a little girl, 'cause we were afraid she'd talk. We didn't mean to. You see, after we killed this guy, this little girl ran out from behind his counter. We'd gone to his clothing store to collect rents, you know, protection money. We beat the guy senseless. Then here's this little child that runs out. A little girl! 'Daddy, Daddy!' she's screaming. I grabbed her to shut her up. But she struggled. I was young, tough, I told myself. This was business. A guy doesn't pay, so we teach him a lesson. We gave no quarter, nor wanted any. So, I'm Mr. Big, Mr. Tough Guy, you see! Sure! I placed my hands around the little girl's mouth, as tiny as it was, and, yes," tears welled in his eyes, "I crushed her vocal cords until her neck snapped. Mother of God, I did! I didn't mean to, but I did! I don't deserve purgatory. Hell and Death are too good!" He paused and inhaled a long breath. "You know, killings after that was like killing myself. I did it with gusto. I am so sorry to God and all his angels. Before Mary and all the saints, I am sorry, Father. Yes, Peterson, sorry for what I did. And it doesn't matter if I'm forgiven or not. I just want God to know, for you to know, for a human being to know that I'm sorry for that little death. God Almighty! Holy Jesus and all his saints, I'm sorry. Listen, just one more thing. You know that Jew, the one who wrote about bad things happening to good people. He got it wrong. The Jew doesn't know what he's talking about. That's not the problem. Not at all! You know what the problem is? You wanna know? The problem is this: why do good people do bad things? That's the problem, Father. That's the real problem, the real mystery, and there's no answer to it, from what I know." He stared into Darby's face, clutched the makeshift stole, and buried his face in it. "Thank you for coming out here! Look! I am holding the hem of Christ's robe!" he held up his hands as he gripped the cloth. "God forgive me! Holy Mother of God!"

Darby placed his arm about the Italian and let him sob.

When two days later Dominetti and the marshal left, something of Darby left with them. For several hours he wandered the grounds, up through the orchard, out to the overlook, and back behind the *grand maison* and its outside outbuildings. He stared down the old logging road. The imprint of the mobsters' car's tires was still visible. That wasn't good. Hopefully after a rain, they'd fade away.

Chapter 10

Whatever free time Darby thought he had, evaporated the next morning. "You're in for a shock this time," Linda greeted him at breakfast. "A lady's book club has booked the Inn for the evening. They plan to stay overnight. You're going to have to be on your toes as well as on your best behavior," she teased. "Better have something up your sleeve to say! They're a sharp group, and the liberal warden among them will go for your jugular! She's something! Let me tell you. You could opt out, except Garnett told them that you'd be here, and what a wonderful conversationalist you are. How's that for friendship?"

"I can think of several words to say," he smiled. "Tell me more."

"Well, they like politics and social issues. They love to travel. Bore one another with pictures of children and grandchildren. They talk about where their kids are going to school, where they've vacationed last. Where to find great jewelry at bargain prices, antiques. Who's divorcing whom! Other than that, they chat about their favorite menus, authors, and always exchange books," she hummed with good humor. "You'll survive it, I assure you. They're just girls, doing what girls do. And don't get that look in your eye! They're well heeled, but *ladies*! There'll be no Celeste in this crowd. She was a temptress, wasn't she?"

"You know too much!"

"No! You can always spot a woman on the hunt. They're eyes and lips give them away, even when they're only studying you. You'll be safe."

"You had me hopeful there for a minute."

"Just be prepared. I wouldn't come in for dinner until you have to," she gave him a knowing look. She smiled before filling his cup with more coffee. "Seriously, Darby, just be your charming self, that's all."

Being one's charming self was hardly a reassuring thought. Darby wandered back to the cottage to peruse its bookshelves. His two favorite women philosophers were Hannah Arendt and Simone de Beauvoir. He'd often incorporated their concepts into his lectures and had urged his conservative female students to read them. So, also, some of the guys. He began scanning the bookcase. Huh! There was Arendt's *The Human Condition* and *The Life of the Mind* shelved right alongside *Plato's Complete Works* and Heidegger's *Being and Time*. He looked for de Beauvoir's *The Second Sex*, but it wasn't to be found. Maybe Garnett had it in his office, or in the living room. But whether the erstwhile book club's appetite cared for such fare, would remain to be seen.

More to his sorrow was Dominetti's conundrum about good and evil. Why do good people do bad things? Simply writing it off as a facet of inordinate pride or lustful concupiscence missed the point. Nietzsche was closer to the truth with his *doctrine of resentment,* or Dostoevsky with his horror of humankind's *perversity.* Then, of course, there was Arendt herself, who, after the Eichmann trial, stunned the world with her catch phrase: "the banality of evil." He shook his head. Why do good people do bad things? Out of perversity for certain, yet out of mindless indifference, too. Still, the most disgusting explanation was the one scientists labeled: "the absence of serotonin uptake inhibitors in one's brain." But what if closer to the truth people err and make mistakes just because they're human? Just because "we're mammals," he told himself, Homo sapiens with egos and libidos?

Toward five o'clock, a Lincoln Continental, followed by a sleek black sedan, pulled up in front of the Villa and disgorged its cargo of book club members. Darby watched from the Garden as a group of four emerged from the Continental and three from the sedan. Amid laughter and shivers of cold, the women made their way good-naturedly to the entrance. A part of him wanted to assist carrying in their bags, but another voice advised leaving well enough alone. What if the warden resented the offer of a "gallant male" to *assist* them? Of course there'd be others who'd be grateful. The male in him wanted to help. But his Socratic muse urged *caution*! Better to walk back to the cottage and read before dinner.

As the hour arrived, Darby entered through the rear hallway door to reach the dining room. On a stand near the stairwell, he noticed a stack of new, glossy covered, hardbacks. He paused to read the covers of several: *Goddesses in Everywoman*, its tenth anniversary printing; Betty Frieden's *The Feminine Mystique*; a collection of essays entitled: *Women's Ways of Knowing*; and Susan Douglas's best-seller: *The Mommy Myth*. In a separate pile on the floor lay more stacks: bestsellers by Baldacci, Greg Isles, Nora Roberts, Dorothea Benton Frank, Jan Karon, Sandra Brown, and others. A nice mix, he thought. Maybe it would be a pleasant evening after all!

As he entered the dining room, he was surprised to find the table surrounded by the club's members, all standing as he walked in. "Good evening, Professor!" they chimed, as if on cue. They laughed and watched while he slipped between their chairs and the breakfront to take his seat at the head of the table. Darby lifted his hands, palms up, in gratitude of their respect. "I hate to think what might be coming!" he smiled. "But I approve of the start. Please, be seated!"

All took their seats amidst an immediate outbreak of amiable chatter and glances toward him. Then all grew silent.

He noticed that the woman on his right had remained standing. Quickly he acted to rise, but she placed her left hand on his shoulder. "Please don't!" she insisted in a firm voice. She was tall, with neck-length black hair, tiny pearl earrings, and a minimum of face powder on her cheeks. Only the thinnest line of red lipstick glistened on her mouth. A rouge patch of fine crowfeet etched the corners of her eyes. With a casual, yet all-knowing glance, she looked about the table and then down at Darby. "Dr. Peterson, Mr. Nelson has told us *so much* about you. We trust he's well, and we're honored to be with you tonight. If our views seem a bit abrupt, please don't be offended. As you know, times have changed, and, we of the Ernestine Lucie Marie Book Club—as we call ourselves—have dared to change with them. Honestly, we're looking forward to this, as we've only had a few sociologists and psychologists meet with us before, and, of course, one or two writers. We love *intense discussions*," she emphasized. "Incidentally, I'm Beverly Wallace Hutchinson, our club's president." With something of an awkward gesture, she seated herself.

"I love good stories and novels!" a friendlier voice spoke up to his left, near the end of the table. A younger woman, perhaps in her mid-forties, had leaned forward, just past the woman on her right, to bathe Darby in a warm, trusting smile. Her eyes twinkled in the chandelier's light. "My name's Dianne—Dianne Riley. The *warden* there," she nodded toward Hutchinson, "doesn't speak for us all the time. But we do like sincere discussion."

"That's right!" added several voices concomitantly.

A slender woman seated immediately to Darby's left extended her right hand. As he shook it, he noted how long and thin her fingers were. "Anna Pelson," she smiled. Dark pouches sagged beneath her green eyes. Worry lines furrowed her powdered brow. She noticed that he had observed them. "Two daughters will do that to you," she smiled with a mother's wounds in her eyes. "Not even good men can prevent some things," she stated, as Linda entered with a tray of salads to place around.

"My favorite!" the youngest of the seven piped up. She was seated opposite Dianne. An air of innocence defined her entire countenance. "Waldorf! With raisins and apples!" She looked straight down the table at Darby. "My name's Amanda. Beverly tells us you're a retired philosophy professor. I took one course at State and hated it. The professor never got past Plato. 'By knowing all about Plato,' he boasted, 'you'll know the essence of philosophy.'

All I got out of it was headaches. I made a B+ but had no idea what he was talking about half the time. I majored in biology after that. I'm a lab tech now, and love it. And my favorite author is Anita Shreve. That's probably more than you want to know."

"No! Not at all! Plato's a good place to begin."

"Well, I wish I knew why?" the young woman responded.

"He had a hunger for something his world didn't have. Stability, you might call it. Its gods were too fickle."

"Like today's men!" someone laughed mid-table.

"No, really, he wanted to believe in something higher, in something reliable in a world that was violent and changing."

"Keep going!" Hutchinson inserted, with a teasing leer. "You've not convinced us yet."

"Seriously!" Darby replied good-naturedly. "What would life be like without the Good, the True, and the Beautiful? I can see why your professor chose Plato," Darby smiled toward Amanda. "I wish I had had you as a student. I would have welcomed your dismay. That's the whole point of philosophy."

"Well, I never took philosophy or aspired to it," a fourth woman stated. Her smile seemed genuine and so too her swollen eyes. A bit on the corpulent side, she adjusted her weight in the spindle-back chair. She bent over her salad, obviously hungry. Bangs of dyed blonde hair dangled in her face. "Oh, I'm Mildred Devon!" she paused, while still chewing on apples and raisins. "Incidentally, what's your view on 'eugenics'? Does it really go back to Plato?"

"Let me take that!" Hutchinson interrupted. "It has to do with pairing people with compatible partners, based on their genes, especially if their families have had problems with Down-Syndrome offspring, or children with genetic disorders." Then with something of a smug air, she continued. "Plato based his theory on social classifications. You know, the poor being forced to marry the poor, the brightest the bright, the dumbest the dumb, while the wise, the rich, and the aristocratic to whomever they wished. It was meant to keep women in their place," she pronounced with emphatic displeasure. "It's a form of androcracy. Every society has its caste system," she glanced toward Darby. "Ours is no different. I like de Beauvoir, because she reminds us of how the French bourgeois males deliberately exercised their *masculine prerogative* to despoil young girls of the lower classes. Of course, the nonsense lives on, like in the case of the Duke of Windsor, or the Prince of Wales, who must, God-forbid, never marry a Commoner!"

"Perhaps we need more wine!" Darby suggested, as he rose politely to pour a glass for whomever wished it. Only the woman with bangs turned him down. "I don't drink!" she whispered quietly. "But thanks."

"Her husband's an alcoholic!" Hutchinson said. "A curse that affects us as much as men, I regret to admit."

Darby reseated himself, picked up his fork and began reworking his salad. What to say? What not to say? "Whatever brought you together, if I may ask?" he addressed Hutchinson and the fairer pair at the end of the table. "Are you members of the same country club or church?"

"Most *definitely not!*" Hutchinson replied. "That's a typical male judgment that feminists reject," she said with open relish. "To assume that our aspirations are limited to our husband's social clubs or assemblies is really demeaning. I should have thought that by now any astute male would have grasped that," she glanced with triumphant gleam about the table. "Well? Isn't that right?"

You miserable bitch! He bit his tongue. "So there are higher reasons that brought you together? My apologies for being an old-fashioned male."

"Dr. Peterson," Dianne interjected. "Personally, I love old-fashioned males. My father was one, and especially my grandfather. They remained clueless about the National Organization of Women or women's movements in general. But they *were* loving—blusterous at times—but there when I needed them. However, I know the type Beverly means. I'm an attorney and have to face them down every day: arrogant, self-serving, bullying their staffs around, goading clients to file suits, knowing their cases are unwinnable, but glad to collect retainer fees. We don't have to be that way, nor do men. That's part of our mission."

"Well said!" the women about the table attested.

"I don't disagree," muttered Darby. "But as a male," he smiled with a twinkle in his eye, "you realize, I hate to give up my bourgeois sentiments about women, or their role in society as child-bearers and icons of amorous pleasures!"

"Oh, don't get us going there!" Mildred coughed. "If you knew how often husbands abuse women, you'd never make remarks like that, sir, teasing or not. It is so good to be away from all that, as these girls know."

"Mildred speaks for all!" Hutchinson commented. "You probably think the same of political correctness? That it, too, is a joke?"

"Actually I do! And why? Because it's a form of spite, not a principle of fairness or wisdom."

"And how's that? I find your dismissal puzzling, if not, to be frank, *offensive!*"

"I can understand. But at heart, political correctness is a twisted principle, designed to deny freedom of expression as well as freedom of thought. It wants to get inside a person's soul and change it, to censor and crush a person's views before they can even think them through; to eliminate dissent before it's heard. It's a form of tyranny, if you please! And, sadly, it's promulgated by legions of people who insist they're advancing it for the sake of *tolerance*, but who do so in the most *intolerant* and self-righteous fashion. If I have a passion, that's it. I would love to see us move beyond it."

"I love it!" clapped Amanda. "I love what you say. Yes, I want equal rights, equal pay, equal opportunity and treatment. And I want men to stop acting like assholes. Still, I want them to be empathic, strong, and sexy!"

"I see we have our work cut out for us!" Hutchinson quietly retorted, as she fought back her disappointment. "This whole thing is so systemic. So pervasive! It's political and global. There are cultures that still enslave women and mutilate girls. If we, who know better, withdraw from the battle, then the evilest of evils will win, as it has always won when it comes to women. That is my *passion*, Dr. Peterson. Mine! But, enough!" she smiled, as she suddenly leaned sideways and touched his arm. "I do love men too, even my own hunter/gatherer husband, who's out in Iowa shooting pheasants right now. Our burden never ends, sir. Like I say, we love a spirited debate."

"Oh!" Mrs. Pelson suddenly spoke up. "Smell that delicious aroma! What is it?"

"Salmon!" reported Linda, as she entered the room to take up their salad plates. "Our chef has prepared two large filets of salmon, smothered in butter, cream, lemon juice, peppercorns, and white wine sauce, just for you. Potatoes and parsley, too. And dessert? A big surprise. Not even our host knows."

Soon they were feting on Jon Paul's exquisite dishes, when Mrs. Hutchinson turned abruptly toward Darby: "I would be interested in your views on gay rights and abortion. I think we all would," she glanced about the table. "But I think I can guess where you stand."

"Oh please, don't go there!" Mrs. Pelson objected, as her eyes filled with a deeper sadness than already present. "I think you all know that Savannah, my oldest daughter, is lesbian."

"You see! That's just what I mean! What we're all having to fight against!" sighed Hutchinson. "Anna, there's absolutely no shame in your daughter being lesbian, whether it's genetic or by her own choice. We must celebrate her and you. Goodness! When will this ever stop?"

Darby laid his fork aside and leaned toward the two women. "Mrs. Pelson, Mrs. Hutchinson, if I may, I've never considered myself a moralist. May I explain?"

"By all means, do!" Hutchinson perked up.

"There's a qualitative gap between morality and ethics. Morality hinges on how we *feel* and how we *view* certain actions, as well as the people who engage in them. Like: gays are bad, or all gambling is wrong, or prostitution should be outlawed, or liquor stores closed on Sundays. In many cases, we've been habituated to think like that. I am *not* into morality. That's *not* what philosophers do. Ethics, on the other hand, has to do with rules and duties that reasonable people agree are justifiable grounds for laws and legislation. These are always up for debate, since our ideas change. People should be free to hold any *moral* views they wish and act on them as well, but only so long as they aren't harmful to others. They don't have the right to impose them on their neighbors. That's probably not the answer you want, but it's the best one I know to offer."

"So, you're in favor of gay rights and abortion?" Hutchinson smiled.

"And pedophiles and rapists?" Pelson interjected. "O God, I hope not!"

"Come on now, be fair! No! I'm not in favor of coddling the sick and the twisted, or the perverse and evil. No! But, given the complexities of democracy, I support equal rights for all—men and women, gay or straight. Nevertheless, that said, I'm still for profiling and common sense. One can preserve the rights of minorities while protecting the rights of others. Whatever happened to common sense, anyway? There are sound arguments for it, you know."

Dianne applauded, along with Amanda.

"What do you really think of women?" Pelson asked, uncertain of Hutchinson's glances or possible disapproval.

"I thought you'd never ask," he smiled. "I love women and miss my ex-wife. I loved her, but it didn't work out. In truth, I miss a woman's arms, a woman's whispers. Just a woman's presence makes me feel like a man. But I know it's different now. I watched our coeds over the years. Many are engaged in professional careers. I value their grit and right to succeed. I hate it too when they're passed over, or abused, or bullied—even by women—'cause I know that goes on. But I'm just a male, your typical male; and being a trained philosopher hasn't eroded my ragged ontology one iota," he smiled, as he squeezed Pelson's hand. "I won't ask you what you think of men," he deferred to Hutchinson. "Like us or not, we'll still be around, whatever happens, ready to want you and cart you off to our caves. It's in our nature. It's the one tenet of de Beauvoir's I reject. *Essence does precede existence sometimes.* It's in our bones, our DNA. We can't help but choose to be men. What man wants to be less than a man, even if he doesn't know what that means? I think that's true of gay men as well. They just express it differently. Remember, you represent our missing rib, and we are incomplete without you."

"Well, we can drink to that!" Beverly raised her glass. "There's nothing in feminism opposed to good men! And who wants to settle for artificial insemination, if George Clooney's around?"

"Or Johnny Depp!" added Amanda.

Everyone laughed as they sipped on their drinks.

"And what is our secret dessert?" Mrs. Devon asked, as Linda returned to remove the dinner plates.

"*Lady fingers!* Of course!" she replied. "No, no! A delicious, brown, crusty, crème brûlée! One of Montesereno's signature finales!"

* * *

As the evening meal drew toward a close, Beverly reached into her purse and displayed a card for Darby to see. It was a 4 x 6-inch card, with printed material in numbered rows. "Dr. Peterson, here's a statement of what our book club endorses. We've taken a little from here and a little from there. It expresses something of our stance. It's not a requirement for membership, just a guideline. I hesitated to give it to you earlier, lest you'd bolt up and run off," she laughed. Many members laughed with her.

"Read it with care!" Dianne warned, with an affectionate smile.

Darby scooted his water glass to one side and read silently:

We of the Ernestine-Lucie-Marie Book Club pledge ourselves to the following:

1. *to encourage each other with diligence and propriety*

2. *to promote the reading and dissemination of good books*

3. *to challenge harassment and discrimination wherever possible*

4. *to budget funds for regional educational opportunities for women*

5. *to promote healthy lifestyles for ourselves, our families, and friends*

6. *to befriend single and abused mothers and defend the right of abortion*

7. *to be sensitive toward all, yet resolute in our actions.*

Darby looked up at Hutchinson and the other women. "Thank you," he said. "I'm in your debt. It's been a lovely evening." He rose and smiled politely. "Perhaps I shall see you in the morning."

"Please! We shall look forward to it!" several replied.

"Adieu!" he said, as he left the table.

* * *

"Precious God!" he moaned under his breath, as he returned toward the cottage. "I guess it could have been worse," he mumbled to himself. Hopefully he hadn't offended anyone. He guessed he'd know by morning. He knew he had talked too much. After all, his assignment was to listen, to facilitate conversation, not to dominate it. Oh, well! Sweet Linda would apprise him of any complaints.

He settled into the big leather chair by the fireplace and turned to Chapter One of Arendt's *The Human Condition*. It was good to read it again and enjoy her analysis of Greek culture. Here was at least one woman who understood the mystery of human transcendence and a longing to resolve it as best she could.

For the next two hours he read, well past the middle of her book, when he heard a sound by the door. Someone knocked faintly, then a second time. He rose and opened it.

"Hi!" It was Dianne. "May I come in?" She peeked inside the cottage. She looked up at him and into his eyes. "I'm the one who kind of cheered you on at the end of the table. Remember?"

"I do," he said.

"I've been through a divorce, too. I know what you were talking about. The uncertainty and loneliness," she smiled.

"Please come in," Darby volunteered awkwardly.

"Yes, thank you. I was afraid you weren't going to ask," she smiled again.

With something of a visible blush, he ushered her in to the central room; then closed the door.

"It's so warm and cozy," she said.

"May I take your coat?"

"Yes," she half-whispered, as she slipped off her gloves.

"I'm not very good at holding garments," he said, as he slid it off and laid it over the back of a chair. "Forgive me, but it's been a while. Thank you for dropping in."

"I had to," she looked up at him. "I'm the one who needs forgiveness. I wanted to come. I wanted your *presence*, that presence you were talking about. Can we sit by the fire and just relax?"

"Please, by all means!" he offered her his hand. "I left feeling so awkward. I hope my comments weren't inappropriate."

"Not at all! Hutchinson loves to goad males. You grow tired of it after a while. What did you think of our statement?"

"Quite tame, I thought. I was prepared for something far worse."

"Well, I subscribe to it in principle, as I helped write it," she smiled, "but we leaned heavily on the National Organization of Women at the time, when all I really wanted was a statement about books, their helpful ideas, and comfort when alone and depressed." While still standing she ran her eyes across the bookshelf. "What's this one about?" she pointed to his *Nietzsche's Übermensch as Icon and Archetype*? Sounds dreadful!" She placed her right hand on his left shoulder and smiled.

"It is!" he laughed. "Here! Let's sit down," he motioned toward the couch. "I guess at the time, it said what I needed it to say," he stated as they sat together. "We all have our icons we admire and archetypes that struggle within. You know, Nietzsche was as much a psychologist as he was a philosopher." He had planned to say more, but he realized she wasn't listening. She was just staring, thoughtfully and quietly into his eyes, maybe past his face, and back toward the fire's, into somewhere far away.

"Tell me about your ex-wife. Did you really love her, or were you only saying that?" she toyed with the earring on her left ear.

"Maybe some of both. But, in truth, yes, I loved her. What about yourself? What kind of a man was he?"

"Noble born, you might say. Scion of a wealthy pipeline empire. His parents had subsidiaries everywhere. He managed the ones in South Carolina and Georgia."

"What happened? If I may ask?"

"Control, jealousy! He wanted me to stay at home, rear children, look beautiful, and be his mother's social secretary. I wanted to practice law, be my own woman, establish my own agenda. His mother disapproved. She set him up with one of her friend's daughter. Encouraged them to meet together, you know, to dine out just to make me pull the plug. So, I did. And now, look at me! Forty-six! Single! Divorced! A bit worn about the edges!" she turned her eyes to one side. "The bloom of youth gone!" she flicked back her hair. "But, I guess you could say I'm adjusted. Imagine, living in such a world! Adjusted! Adjusted to what? Not being loved. Not being wanted. Just getting up every morning, alone, going to work, alone, and then coming home, alone?"

"I take it you didn't have children."

"No! Once I realized what his mother wanted and what that would cost, I went on the pill; we just sort of lived together, occupied the same house. But his mother saw to it that he got all the quality time he needed with her friends' daughters." She laid her head against his shoulder. "My father was still living. 'There's someone out there for you,' he'd say. 'Chin up, girl!' And all that," she turned her face, eyes, and mouth toward Darby. "You never said as much about your ex!"

Darby wasn't certain what to say. He hadn't expected a guest to open up so suddenly, to come into his . . . privacy . . . so casually . . . so unassumingly, even like Celeste had. He wasn't ready. He looked at her, at the stately loveliness of her face, at her eyes, her mouth, her hair. Whatever he was trying to deny wasn't working; his mind wasn't buying it. "She left for other reasons," he stammered haltingly. "She took a huge hunk of my *whatever* with her." He paused to gather up his thoughts, to calm the unanticipated feeling that was swelling within. "I felt unworthy at first, guilt-ridden, obsessed with remorse for the longest time. It took a while to get over it, but being here," he looked down, "I feel pretty normal."

"I'm not certain how good I am at this," she smiled, as she lifted her mouth closer to his, "but I'm willing to try."

He placed his arms about her shoulders and kissed her. She returned his kiss with one of her own. She stood up and extended him her hands. She clasped his, as she pulled him up and looked into his eyes. "Do you have someplace more comfortable?"

"Yes," he whispered. He could see his reflection in the pools of her deep green eyes. Her slender nose and warm mouth beckoned him closer. He placed his arms hungrily about her body and drew her tightly toward his chest. Her wet mouth opened, his lips slipped nervously along her own, "I'm not certain how good I am, either," he whispered, "it's been a long time."

"I won't run away, if you won't."

"Here," he took her by the hand and led her into his bedroom. She slipped off his jacket and unbuttoned his shirt. In turn, he pulled up her sweater; then, as she put her back to him, unfastened her brassiere. He cupped her soft breasts in his hands and ran his fingers tenderly across her nipples. Together they slipped off their remaining clothing and tumbled in the bed.

She laughed as he pulled the covers back and buried his face against her neck. They kissed each other, fondled one another's flanks and loins, and slipped blissfully into the rhythms of the heart's cry. The long exile he'd endured welled up, burned within; then it sailed away, like an eagle mounting the sky, flapping its great wings in a stiff breeze.

For a long while afterwards, they lay there, staring up at the ceiling.

"I guess I'd better go back," she kissed him once more. "Will I see you at breakfast?"

"Provided I wake up from this dream!"

She nudged him. "Help me get dressed!" she muttered. She ran her hands through his hair and curled it about her fingers. "I've had too many dreams, Darby. I'm tired of dreams. You're a reality! I will miss you! Strange!" she whispered. "Being a woman can be so wantonly hard."

Each helped the other dress. Darby held her coat. Slowly, he walked back with her to the house.

"Good night!" she pressed his hand.

"Good night! If I don't see you at breakfast, it doesn't mean . . ."

"Shhhhh!" she placed the index finger of her right hand to her lips. "I'll understand." Suddenly she reached up, put her arm about the back of his neck and drew his face down to hers. Their lips met and kissed. "Good night!" she whispered a second time.

PART TWO

Remember the Night

Chapter 11

October passed. The Parkway closed; still guests sought the refuge of the Villa. Now the route brought them up the scenic winding state road that ended at the overlook. The first weekend in November, a group of bikers broke the usual spell of sequestered residents. A touring club out of Greenville arrived exhausted, clad in their gaudy colored tight Lyric jerseys of green and black, yellow and red, blue and white. They came cycling in past the gate posts in slanting waves of sparkling spokes to drop their bikes along the pebbled drive to the grinding clack of their hard-soled shoes. Darby watched as they sprawled on the Villa's grounds, or stood motionless beside their bikes before sipping from their plastic or aluminum water bottles.

They filed to the back of the Villa where Jon Paul and Linda feted them with hot-cross buns, hot tea, and coffee. Darby mingled with the group briefly before returning to his cottage. They left in the manner they had arrived—in a colorful array of gleaming handlebars and spokes, silver helmets and black shoes. Up they stood as they peddled past the entrance to disappear down the narrow road. Darby watched them from the cottage's window. What humankind will do for pleasure! They had probably spent the night in Asheville. Perhaps they might make it back as far as Hendersonville before dark.

That evening at dinner, Darby noted that their newest guest sat with unusual resignation midway along the table. According to Linda, the men on either side of her were battling alcoholism—while she, depression, following a month of frantic activity. As Linda put it: "She's about as bipolar as anyone we've ever had."

Darby studied her quietly as they ate in silence. Neither ugly nor pretty, her short red hair created a convex bowl about her neck and ears, masking her pasty composure. Expressionless and emotionless, she hunched forward, staring down at her plate, not having lifted her fork a single time.

"Please, Gloria! You need to eat somethin'," the older of the two men said. He was seated to her right. He had registered as Jeff Horne. His elongated jowls glowed red from years of alcohol abuse. Spidery purple veins crinkled about his nose. Gray hair flowed down the back of his neck in comb-grooved strands. Deep lines in his face belied his age—fifty-five, according to Linda. He looked seventy. He owned an automotive supply store in Raleigh, named for himself: *Horne's Body Parts! Best in Town!*

"Would it matter?" the woman answered. She placed her hands to her face; then slowly dropped them to her sides. "I'm not hungry," she mumbled. "Just thirsty."

"It's that lithium!" the sallow-eyed large man to her left offered. This was his last week. He was scheduled to return home to Myrtle Beach in the morning. He had signed in as: *Andrew Johnson, former architect, unemployed.* "It makes your mouth feel like cotton. God knows my youngest daughter's already a wreck. Last spring she swung into a manic episode that lasted three months. Before she crashed, I started drinking again. We were both hospitalized, in my case a week. I got off the bottle, then got right back on." His hands shook as he spoke. He had not shaved. A horseshoe of curly black stubble bristled from ear to ear. He patted her left hand. "Look! At least we're up here for a while. Plus, we've got our own doc and nurse, all in one place; our own Alchemist!" he smiled toward Darby. "If only you could conjure up a job! That would be nice!"

"Don't I wish? As for alchemy, I might as well be a practitioner. Would that I could change this water into an elixir of happiness—for you, me, and for all of us! Now with wine, I have no trouble changing it into water. With enough ice cubes," Darby feigned a chuckle. "No offense, Mr. Horne."

"You know, it don't bother me if you drink or not," he replied. "I get depressed on my own, all by myself," he smiled. "It begins with self-pity, then moodiness. The next thing I know, I'm on the bottle. I've gone for weeks, not knowing who I was, or where I was, or what I was doin'. More than once, I've waked up in jails, or in some room in a private clinic. After this, it'll be hospital wards. My son's paying for the stint here. He's quite a guy. Not like his sister or me. More like his mom. God help her!" his voice cracked, as he continued eating.

Seated opposite Gloria and her two tablemates, a more refined gentleman and his wife eyed Darby and the others with mixed empathy. It was evident to Darby that the tall man with his graying moustache and his slender wife would have preferred to have dined alone, but Garnett's house rules were specific. "Everyone must eat together, at the same time. It's essential to healing." It was on a placard in the kitchen. As for the couple, all Linda had told Darby was that the "Gibsons" were from Gainesville, Georgia and had lost numerous assets in Helena with the downturn of the economy. "Craig," she added, "has taken it harder than Ada. They own enterprises all around

Atlanta, plus an outlet in Commerce. They're not exactly poor!" Linda had winked. "They've been here before."

Mr. Gibson, for all his reticence, shifted in his chair and addressed Johnson. "Ada and I hope to launch a new development soon, near Athens. We could use an architect in the initial phase, if you've ever designed office or residential communities. If you have a portfolio, I'd like to see it." Gibson sat back and quietly awaited the bearded man's response.

"Yes, sir!" Johnson sat erect in his chair. He dabbed his eyes with his napkin, before wiping water beads off his stubble. He stared at his hands momentarily and flexed his fingers. "I can have one to you in less than a week. I'm free to travel. Myrtle Beach's not that far from Athens. It's been a while since I've been there."

"Most of your work, you could do at home. But I'd show you the site first. Send me what you have; we'll take it from there. I like your honesty. No one's perfect."

"Gloria?" Ada addressed her. "What do you do, if I may ask? You've been so quiet." The slight woman sat erect with a smile. She had drawn her dark brown hair back behind her neck and had fastened it with a blue diamond clasp. The tight pull had stretched her frail skin about her pink brow, creating a web of tiny wrinkles deep into her scalp. Her face reminded Darby of photographs of Wally Simpson.

Gloria did not respond immediately. With weak, brown eyes she stared at her water glass and silverware. Carefully, she smoothed out the tablecloth about her plate as unobtrusively as possible. "I don't have a career," she answered. "I did at one time."

"We'd love to hear it," Ada said gently. "We're strangers, yet Dr. Peterson's made us all feel welcome," she deferred toward Darby. "I've had my share of antidepressants, too, dear. There's no shame in acknowledging that. I assure you."

"I don't need your pity!" Gloria muttered. "If you must know, I was an office manager for a homeless organization. We collected food, staples, bedding, money, along with clothing for a shelter in Charlotte. I had an important position. I lost it. I don't like being bipolar. I don't like taking drugs! I like to drink. Yes, drink! And party! I just want my life back. Not some addict's!" she gasped with a catch of phlegm in her throat. "So, I need help now! What's so demeaning about that? Tell me!" her shoulders shuddered in a series of trembling jerks.

"Nobody's said you aren't important, or aren't valued! Jesus, woman!" Horne interjected. "We all need help from time to time. There's no shame in having disorders. Half the mechanics and clerical staff in my business are as loony as hell. Some of 'em are barely educated! That's right. But they know how to install parts and are damn good at it. You don't have to hold a degree to be smart. I did have to fire one, cause he was abusing his mother. Then I got to thinkin' about it and hired him back. I sent him off to a counselor. He needed someone to talk to; maybe some meds. That was all. They put him on Prozac. It took a year for him to get his shit together, but he did. You can do it. Hell, look at me! I'm not exactly your paragon of virtue. Or some pillar of the community. But I do run one hell of a good business." All this he said while shaking his head and running his hands through his long thick locks. He wiped his fingers on his napkin and picked up his fork again.

"You haven't done what I've done!" Gloria mumbled. "I felt so good at the time. I mean grandiose! I could feel it. I started slacking off my medications. Then quit them altogether. I felt great. I could do anything, I told myself. I drove all over Charlotte telling people how important I was and how much we needed their donations. They needed to increase their pledges, I insisted." She looked about, toying with her fork momentarily. "I spent money the organization didn't have. Thousands of dollars! I even finagled money from CEOs at Wells Fargo and the Bank of America. I stood right there as if I were the most important person in the room. After that, I started buying up box loads of clothing from Big Lots and Wal-Mart. I charged hundreds of dollars of my own money. Of my husband's. Then I took a plane to Richmond. Don't ask me why. I felt so great! So emancipated. I spent four days and three nights in a five-star hotel with marble-top bars. I bought dresses and handbags, the most expensive I could find, and tipped big. I was celebrating my success. I was high! I, I . . . , " she caught her breath amid a horrid expression on her face, "I *fucked* three different men. I don't remember their faces at all. Nor a single name." Her voice became tiny, a whisper, as if drifting up from a deep pit. "Yet, I don't feel sorry. It's just something I did." She stopped and stared at each guest around the table. "My husband had to come for me. He sent me to my gynecologist. He was ashamed of me. Bitter. But he took me back." She looked up, staring hard at them again. "After all we have children: two girls and a boy. He says I'm sterile, without love or passion. I never think about it," her words dropped off into silence, dragging her eyes and lips into her exile.

No one said a word. Darby thought of the myriad things he might say; then cleared his throat. "Life has always been hard, even for the happiest. Anyone here ever heard of Arthur Schopenhauer?" he glanced about the table. "I used to recite paragraphs of his lines from memory, just to nudge students out of their lethargy. He was a pessimist and never really succeeded until late in life. Give or take a few words, here's a sampling of what he said:

> It's incredible how meaningless and void the course of life is for the majority of mankind. It's a weary longing and complaining, a dream-like staggering through the four stages of life to death. . . .

A smirk crept slowly across Gloria's face. She noted others were watching. "Well, go on," she blustered. "I'm listening."

Darby regained his composure:

> The life of every individual is a tragedy . . . the restless irritation of the moment, the desires and fears of the weak, the never satisfied . . . and . . . frustrated efforts, the hopes unmercifully crushed by fate, . . . all of it is always a tragedy.[1]

"I know it's melodramatic. In one form or other we all have to cope with depression, however much or little lithium we may take. We live in a chemical world now. And it's reduced metaphysics to a plethora of disorders. I find that upsetting but the truth."

"Well, it's over my head!" Horne grumbled. "I just need to keep sober. How I'd love a drink right now!"

Gloria's eyes suddenly lit up. She turned and stared into Horne's rocky face. A helpless seam of libido seemed to glow in her irises; she shifted uneasily in her chair. Ada noticed and glanced quietly toward Darby. Darby caught it, too.

After dessert, Darby wandered into the living room to warm his hands by the fireplace. Out of the corner of his eye, he watched as Gloria and Horne ascended the staircase quietly. Johnson sauntered in and collapsed in the room's largest armchair. Its yellow and black, Oriental-print coverings swallowed the rejuvenated man, giving him the appearance of a Chinese lord, enthroned in solemnity. Alchemy! The elixir of eternity! Something of the mystery of the *Tao Te Ching* seemed to cloak the big fellow as he sank back into a dreamy solitude. His countenance reminded Darby of portraits of ancient China's emperors during the third-century BCE. What fortunes they squandered in search of elixirs of immortality and pills of eatable gold!

His mind drifted. The darker side of Paris came to memory. He had passed the man in the street before realizing what was happening. The reek of body odor and the sight of sockless feet caught his attention first. Then he saw the man's eyes: bloodshot and sunken in a pit of bearded red night. Lighter fluid glistened silver on the rag-wrapped man's lips. Paris! Along the Boulevard St. Michel, no less. Suddenly, Darby's mind came back to reality. "What? I'm sorry. Forgive me."

---

1. Beardsley, *European Philosophers*, 710. Altered slightly.

"We've enjoyed our stay here," Mr. Gibson muttered. He had walked in behind Darby and had approached him by the fireside. "This whole thing about depression, you know. I read where between 1987 and 2007 the number of Americans being treated for depression had quadrupled from less than one percent to over twelve percent. Now it's up to eighteen percent. Yet, just when people need it most, few are seeking therapy. Why? Because of serotonin drugs! That's kind of sad, isn't it?

"How can a drug alter your mind in a vacuum of personal contacts? Especially of talk therapy?" Gibson moaned. "I don't know anything about metaphysics, but I know that you don't market ideas without one-on-one contact."

Darby was about to reply when he noted Linda, standing in the hallway, with a worried look on her face. She was nodding in the direction of the dining room. "Excuse me, sir, but I see our own hostess is summoning me. It's still a woman's world."

"Yes! I'm afraid so," the developer smiled.

"What is it?" Darby asked, as he entered the hallway and followed Linda into the dining room.

"Our guest, Dominetti. He's dead! The mob gunned him down on his way to the courthouse. It was on the evening news. Donaldson was shot, too, but's in stable condition. He knew he'd never survive. I loved the man in spite of his macho swagger. He was like the rogue uncle we all wish we had. I thought you needed to know," she hugged him.

Darby stood motionless beside her; then kissed her cheek quickly. He struggled to smile. "If you can find out where Donaldson's recovering, I'd like to write him. Maybe Stephanie would want to know. A few cards would do him good."

"I have her address. I thought she'd write by now. I have Gunn's number, too. I'll give him a call in the morning. Jon Paul thinks you'd better sleep with your pistol nearby, just in case the mob comes back."

"You mean, *negotiators*! I doubt they'll come. They got what they wanted: revenge!" He exhaled a deep breath. "It's been a tough week with Horne and Johnson, hasn't it? I wish I knew more about Gloria."

"Her husband brought her doctor's files with him. I put them in Garnett's office, on his desk. You have the Villa's permission to peruse them. They're mainly notes of past episodes, medications, thyroid levels, and warning signs, but not a reference or summary of any counseling he offered."

"Incidentally, how is Garnett doing? Where is he? Do you know?"

"No! We still haven't heard. I'm beginning to think they've sent him to one of their clinics in California, or is it Arizona? He must be terribly discouraged. I'll get Jon Paul to look into it. You know the hardest thing

I have to do is to keep up with guests' medications. They don't always tell me what they've brought. Trying to manage this place is hard enough," she cocked her head to one side with a smile.

Darby looked down at her petite frame, delicate features, and black irises. How he wished she could have been his wife! It was there in her eyes as well. "I don't know how you do it!" he muttered. He cast his eyes downward, to avoid staring again into Linda's. Then, he glanced up toward the hallway and living room. Gibson was still standing by the fireplace, awaiting his return. To be polite, Darby knew he had to accede, but the news of Dominetti's death and Joel's wounds had swept away such a nicety. He wished only to withdraw, to slip off to the cottage, or examine Gloria's file for what it might be worth. He raised his hand in a respectful gesture of "Good night" for Gibson to see, looked deeply into Linda's face, and stepped out into the cold.

Halfway to the cottage, a loud crash interrupted his retreat. It came from the second floor. Someone was cursing. It was Horne! The tinkling sound of glass accompanied the commotion. Darby wheeled around and ran back inside. Ahead of him, Johnson and Gibson clambered up the hall's stairwell. Together, all three raced toward the uproar. Gloria was standing in the hall, outside her room, clothed only in a pair of torn pink panties, her bosom in full view. At the sight of the three, she wrapped her arms about her breasts. They were large and pendulous. Inside her room, Horne lay wallowing on the floor. "You whore! You bitch!" A broken chair piece flew out the door. Johnson entered first, then Craig, while Darby followed. The architect bent over Horne, tackling him near the bed. Darby rushed to pin the man's arms behind his back. Gibson looked on. Horne rolled over and stared up drunkenly.

"She's to blame," he drooled. "She enticed me. Let me up," he rolled to one side. His breath reeked of sour bourbon. An empty bottle rolled slowly out from under the bed. "I'm sick." With that, he curled into a fetal position and vomited. Darby heard someone enter the room. It was Jon Paul.

"Here! Let me handle this!" he blurted.

Sure, thought Darby. The bully in disguise!

"Darby, pin his arms back. Johnson, Mr. Gibson, secure his feet. Up, now! Up with him! It's down to the tank, ole boy!" Jon Paul stated with a smirk. "This way, gentleman. The shower's in the basement, just past the wine racks. Darby, you've been there. Show 'em how to find it."

Yes, thought Darby. Indeed, he had been down there. And with no one less than Linda. Julia Laine had remained upstairs, with JP in the kitchen. It was their fourth visit to the Villa. He could hear Jon Paul's cleaver, thumping on the heavy cutting board. Then all grew quiet. Incredibly still! "Shhh!"

Linda had whispered. "Here, help me with these bottles." She handed him two. Both were holding their breath. Something wasn't right. The thumping noise was scarcely the sound of a cleaver. First a look of puzzlement, then a wry grin slipped across Linda's face. Her eyes shimmered in the cellar's dim light. She pressed against him, placing her fingers to his lip. "Let's wait a second, before going back up." Suddenly, the thumping quit, amid an awkward silence.

"Well!" Jon Paul stated. "He's not going on his own! Just drag him!"

Darby struggled to control Horne's powerful torso. The man was flailing the air with his elbows, almost striking Darby. "Leave me alone!" he slurred. He jerked with violent kicks, twisting and squirming to free himself.

In the hallway, Linda and Ada were draping a blanket about Gloria. It was obvious that she was equally drunk. As the four men stumbled past, Gloria snuffled back a gleam of tears and scowled contemptuously at Darby. Why me? He wondered. But when he turned to look at her again, she was weeping.

When thirty minutes later, exhausted and drenched, the four had mopped up the remaining water and vomit in the shower's stall, they watched as Linda wound the sullen Horne in a huge white bathrobe, adorned with the Villa's crest. Delirious and half asleep, the scruffy guest leaned heavily against Darby, as if he were his sole friend. With guided difficult steps, they made it out of the basement and back to his room. "I didn't mean no harm," he moaned, as they dropped him in his bed.

"Makes you not want to drink," Johnson mumbled, "makes you see how pitiful you look."

Gibson said nothing.

After calm returned, Linda, Gibson, and Darby sat in the living room to recoup. Jon Paul uncorked a bottle of champagne and poured each a flute full. "Well, I have to thank you," he said. "He was a lot heavier than I thought."

Johnson had retired to bed. Ada had remained upstairs with Gloria, a sacrifice far beyond the latter's worth in Darby's mind. Ada's last words to the disoriented woman had shocked him. "Come now," she had whispered, "it's been a tough go, hasn't it? You can do this, Gloria. Deep down inside, I know you can."

Darby sipped thoughtfully on the bubbly drink. Not once had he considered the woman's feelings, though the well of darkness he had seen in her eyes troubled his conscience and suppressed his self-rectitude. Ah, God, as if I had any, he moaned to himself. He drained a second glass, rose to his feet. "Good night," he muttered. A comment Goethe had once made came to mind. He wanted to quote it, but kept it to himself: *Live as so to hate no one, to despise no one, to mock no one, to be angry with no one, and to envy no one.*[2] He glanced about. Holy Mother of God! Who could live like that except the Christ, or maybe the Buddha, or Mother Teresa? It was time to go to bed.

2. Kaufmann, *Shakespeare*, 54.

Chapter 12

"Well, you just missed them," Linda stated, as Darby walked down the hall for breakfast.

"Who's that?"

"Mr. Johnson and our dear Gloria Gandy! They left about thirty minutes ago. Talked him into returning to Myrtle Beach *by way of Charlotte*. I think she was afraid of facing Horne. He's still asleep. I don't think she recovered at all, or benefited from being here. By the way," she blushed, "what was that glare of hers all about?" she feigned with a roll of her eyes.

"Projection. I'm not sure. Maybe self-loathing. Or a sorrow too deep for words. You can't save them all, Linda. Celeste and Parker weren't exactly the Villa's poster couple, either."

Linda arched her eyebrows and stared into his face. "Darby! I'm glad that woman's gone. She wanted you. You would have been just another knot on her purse string. Supposedly, we're here to provide healing, a time to reflect and recover. Few drive off like she did. Listen, Horne won't demand our services beyond JP's capacity to handle them. Why not take the day off? Drive down to Asheville or Waynesville. You deserve it. I'll not expect you till dinner. Seriously!" she smiled. "Go on! Enjoy yourself. Go on, now! Get out!" she puckered her lips for a kiss.

He complied with a smile. "Why not call Gunn's number for Joel's address? I'd love to write a card."

"Darby, go on! Enjoy yourself. You need the break!"

* * *

The drive down the state road to Waynesville consumed more than an hour. With the Parkway closed, the devilish road that twisted with unbanked curves and steep drop-offs constituted a challenge to negotiate. Yet every turn and narrow straightaway opened to meadows of purple grasses and Fraser firs. As he dropped below the five thousand foot level, red, black, and white oaks, in addition to scarlet maples, Scotch pine, and yellow poplars framed the drive. Cliffs of granite, dazzling with trickling gleams, added to the beauty of each cove as he descended. A white tail deer bounded across the road and down the mountain slope to his right. A buck in hot pursuit followed. Down, down, the road descended, as Darby guided his car, shifting its transmission into the lowest gear to break the speed. He slowed at the forks of the road, glanced to the right in the direction of the Asheville turnoff; then continued left toward Waynesville. Toward the bottom, he let the car cruise.

For two hours he wandered the shops of Waynesville. Many tourists were present, shopping for the coming holidays. While browsing in the Mast General Store, he discovered a display of handsome pocketknives made of horse shinbone and steel blade. He purchased one for himself, one for Curly, and, after a moment's hesitation, a third for JP. What the hell! In a snazzy boutique shop, he spotted and purchased a purple-and-white pullover sweater for Linda. "Yes! Gift wrap it," he smiled. He located a bookstore, stocked with out-of-print books and rare collector's volumes. Amid its dust, he discovered a copy of Whitehead's *The Adventure of Ideas*, Goethe's *Autobiography*, and Etienne Gilson's *History of Christian Philosophy in the Middle Ages*. He bought all three, ate lunch, and considered driving out to Lake Junaluska until he glanced toward the sky. All across the Tennessee Mountains, black clouds threatened the horizon. He couldn't remember if the car carried snow chains in its trunk. Probably not! A crisp breeze blew a Styrofoam cup along the street. He returned to his car and drove anxiously toward the Villa. Already tiny flecks of hail bounced off the windshield. By the time he made it up past the first three thousand feet, the sleet metamorphosed into a blinding snowfall. Beautiful but treacherous, it swirled in falling flakes, filling the road, trees, and ravines with its white, mesmerizing coverlet. When he reached the meadows and graceful firs, he could scarcely see through the windshield. Twice he stopped in mid-road, got out, and whipped handfuls of heavy flakes off the blades.

Within the next few minutes, darkness began to conceal the roadway. This was hardly a place to mire in drifts, or wait for assistance. None would be coming. Slowly, his car slid sideways. Its tires spun. Darby hunkered forward helplessly as the car slid into a ditch. He pushed on his door to climb out, but the ditch was too deep to open it. He glanced at the fuel gauge. Less than a quarter of a tank! If he had to spend the night that might keep the engine running till morning. He closed the door, turned off the headlights, and sat in the snowy darkness. He glanced at his watch. Six o'clock. He had not carried his cell phone. Linda would worry about him soon enough, he hoped. Maybe, he was close enough to walk the rest of the way, but when he tried to wedge the door open again, it wouldn't budge. He leaned to his right to crawl out the passenger's side, but after several efforts elected to remain in the car. Minutes, then an hour passed. No one came down the road! Just then, he detected lamps shimmering ahead in the darkness. Closer and closer the lights grew, one swinging to the cadence of its carrier. It was Jon Paul on the tractor and Horne trudging in the snow beside him.

Darby pressed the switch that rolled down the passenger's window. "Am I ever glad to see you!" he smiled.

"Not half as glad as we to find you," Horne huffed as he knelt down to hook a chain to the vehicle's under carriage. "Keep your car runnin' and just go gentle on the pedal. We'll do the rest," he said. "Steady, now. Here we go!" Horne waved for Jon Paul to put the tractor in reverse.

The machine strained, its tires slipped, the chain rattled and grew tight. Slowly the tractor backed away, taking up the chain's slack with it. Twice, three times the tractor roared as the chain stretched taut, pulling the car closer to the road. Its tires spun, slinging snow everywhere, but on the fourth attempt Darby's car lurched with an audible whine of tires into the roadway. "Careful!" Jon Paul shouted as Horne stepped back. Horne unfastened the chain and looped it about the tractor's grill. He waved for Jon Paul to turn about, as he piled into the passenger seat beside Darby.

Ten minutes later, they were home. Linda was standing on the front steps, bundled in a bright red woolen coat, with a bright red scarf wrapped about her throat. Jon Paul waved as he drove the tractor around the house to its shed. Darby followed in his car. Linda came to the hallway's backdoor and watched as he and Horne emerged. "Thank God you're safe!" she blurted. "Get in here! That's the last time I'll ever order you away!" Snowflakes had caught in her eyelashes. Or were they tears? Darby couldn't tell. He and Horne each gave Linda a hug as they entered the hallway.

That evening, as Linda, Darby, and Horne sat about the fireplace with the Gibsons, Horne cleared his voice and, with embarrassment, began: "I don't remember last night, only wakin' up cold and wet. I'm sorry, you know. Just one taste is all it takes. Then another, and I go out like a light!"

"Yes!" Linda replied. "But you seem fine now."

"I am a little shaky," he held his hands out palms down. "Getting out there in the snow revived me. I hope I didn't hurt Mrs. Gandy. All I recall is goin' into her room." He rubbed his face with his callused hands; then slicked his hair back with a comb he produced from his shirt pocket. His eyes loomed amber, with a touch of jaundice, in the fire's glow.

"Luckily Dr. Peterson was here to assist," Ada offered. "No one is resentful of your actions."

"She means it!" her husband added. "My delusions debase me enough. Which reminds me," he turned toward Darby. "While you were gone, I found a copy of your dissertation in Garnett's office and started reading it. Why in the world did you want to write about Nietzsche and archetypes? That is a fair question, isn't it?"

Darby smiled. "Please, don't make me bore you," he smiled again as he glanced around the room.

"Please do," Gibson smiled in return.

"Well, I chose the subject because deep in our subconscious we carry emotional and metaphysical freight of a universal type. Both Nietzsche and Jung exposed that fact as well as espoused it."

"I never knew the two were linked together."

"Yes," Darby offered. "As you know, Jung maintained that in the same way our physical bodies and brains have evolved over the millennia, so has our *sub-conscious,* or *unconscious.* It's retained eons of emotional reactions and memories of how to cope and survive. I suppose our DNA chain best encodes this physiological development, or what some philosophers call 'the problem of consciousness,' but I think Jung's right. Such subliminal suspicions and fears, repressed fantasies and insights, remain below the level of consciousness. Within each of us, they vie for attention and release. For Jung, this mystical repository of behavioral moods conforms to types that are both universal and *arché,* and thus he dubbed them *archetypes.* They can't help but shape the way we think and act, filling us with subliminal impulses that can make us perverse."

Darby glanced about to see if his audience was still listening. He chuckled and smiled at the group.

"Please go on," Craig sat forward. "This may be repetitious to you, but not to me."

"Nor I," said Ada.

"Might as well," smiled Horne.

"Well, then as for my own use," Darby continued, "I owe that to Nietzsche. His favorite archetypes were Dionysus and Apollo. Dionysus was his symbol for the dark, twisted, and perverse side of our personalities, the god of self-abandonment and inebriation. Apollo, on the other hand, was the symbol of enlightenment, of our hunger to know, even to become like God. Nietzsche wanted to blend the two—exuberance and wisdom—and thereby create a nobler race, his Superior Man, or *Übermensch.*"

"I guess that means I'm as screwed up as you can get," drawled Horne. "My doc tells me alcoholism's a disease. That's comfortin' to know, but useless once you taste whiskey's nectar. I'm just a diseased ambulatory disordered archetype!" he grinned. "I like that! I'm Dionysus at his worst, when I get drunk!" he shook his head with sarcastic modesty. "I envy you," he stared at the four. "I'm not going to wallow in self-pity, though. You people are educated in ways I'm not. You're refined, genteel, and gracious. I'm different, rough, if not downright crude. I broke a lot of furniture and fine china last night, but you folk cleaned me up and put me back to bed. Of that, I'm grateful," he smiled as he swept his hands back through his curly locks. "But don't worry; I'll pay for every penny of it. I'll carry my Dionysus back to Raleigh and make his ass listen to Apollo." He swept his hands once more through his tangled hair and cracked his knuckles.

Darby flashed a faint smile. If philosophy had taught him anything, it's that sometimes you just need to keep silent.

Chapter 13

As morning broke over the Villa, Darby sat at breakfast, clasping a cup of coffee as Horne shuffled in. "Haven't seen this much snow so early since last year's twelve-incher," Horne observed. Bending forward, he squinted past the blinds of the window. "That booger closed everything down in Raleigh, even my shop." He pulled his chair out and sat down. "Any places to hike around here? I love trekking through snow. I've got a pair of boots in my room, just for the purpose. It's my exuberant side," he smiled.

"If you're serious, yes. There's quite a hike right behind the Villa. An old logging road descends toward a creek. It's out back, waiting for you now. It takes about an hour or so to hike down, and two or so to hike back. I'm game, if you are."

The shop owner poured himself a cup and stared across the table at Darby. "Just say when. I'm ready."

"Let's eat first. I'll have to find my boots. We might jump a buck on the way, or a grouse. I used to hunt the area. That was years ago. How about you?"

"Love fowl huntin': ducks, geese, quail. Got a lot of 'em east of Raleigh. Belong to a hunt club there. We harvest our fair share every year. Marvelous time. Wish I'd brought my shotgun or rifle, but, who knew? Besides, my wife drove me up and won't return till tomorrow. What is it today, anyway? Thursday?"

"That's right. I'm glad you're feeling better."

"Me too!" Jeff smiled as Linda brought in a stack of buttermilk pancakes, sausage links, and a silver pitcher of hot syrup. "Lord, woman, it'll take me an hour to recover if I eat all that."

"You won't be alone!" Darby added. "The sun needs a chance to warm up the woods, anyway."

"And me, too," said Linda. "It was *cold* in here last night, even around the kitchen. I mean frigid. Jon Paul has a rifle if you want to carry it."

"Thanks!" said Darby. "A ski pole is more what I'll need."

"We've got those, too; plus skies," Linda added.

"I'll carry the rifle!" Horne spoke up. "We might see a deer. Do y'all care for venison?"

"Jon Paul will cook it, if you'll clean and skin it, but we're scheduled for tenderloin tonight, filets for everybody."

"Just a ski pole!" Horne grinned. "I don't have the energy to clean one. Besides, tenderloin sounds perfect!"

"I'll see you have a jug of coffee when you're ready. We've got personal thermos jugs, just for the purpose. You'll welcome them on your way back."

* * *

The long hike down fulfilled one of Darby's persistent joys. Wading in the deep snow, feeling it crunch under the weight of his boots, smelling the keen, nostril-stinging air, shielding his eyes against the blinding sunlight, listening to the snow's thump as its mushy clumps slid off tree limbs, and hearing its gurgling runoff in a million tiny streams filled him with a love of the forest's primeval call. Here truth and beauty became one, perception and reality inseparable.

The two trudged their way to the bottom before either spoke.

"Did you see those deer tracks back there?" Horne observed.

"Yes! They were probably feeding in the orchard last night. It is cold, isn't it?"

"Yep! Let's indulge some of Linda's coffee."

They found a stump on which to rest beside the creek at the base of the high overlook that rose behind them. Icicles glistened suspended from the crevices on its granite wall. Darby could hear the ice crackling in the morning's light and the quiet patter of its melting drips. Darby brushed the snow off the stump as they sat down to enjoy the coffee, each sipping from his thermos jug's lid. He hoped Horne would not detect the vine-draped car, buried under its silent cape of snow, deep in the dark rhododendron.

"Did you hear that?" Horne stated, as he rose to his feet. "Listen!" He stared down the lane in front of them. Cold shadows hovered over the snow-filled bramble where the lane disappeared into the woods.

"A deer?" Darby ventured.

"Hogs!" replied Horne. "They're heading this way. Damn, I wish I had carried the rifle. We'd best find some place substantial to hide. A hog can do a hell of a lot of damage, you know. Snow or no snow."

"There's a mica mine, just behind us. It's just across the stream," Darby pointed toward the base of the cliff. "We can observe them from there."

Standing by its entrance, the two waited, watched, and listened as the group drew closer. The squeals and grunts of the passel grew louder.

Suddenly, a large black boar stepped out into the open, his coat silver with ice and snow. A sow and smaller pigs scurried behind him. The boar raised his head and grunted. With ugly nostrils he sniffed the air, before sweeping the snow with his tusks. He snorted louder, squinted in their direction, and trotted menacingly toward the creek. Horne stepped forward, picked up a sharp rock, and hurled it across the stream at the boar. The ugly monster stopped, emitted an ear-splitting grunt, and bolted back into the woods. His panic set the drove—sow and all—fleeing behind him. Horne smiled. "That'll give them something to remember! How's that from the pit of my exuberance?" he chortled.

Darby couldn't help but smile. "That was a splendid throw! Where'd you learn to pitch like that?"

"Didn't! It just comes natural," his red jowls swelled as he laughed.

Chapter 14

Saturday morning arrived to the sounds of a snowplow clearing the road near the gates. Back and forth it worked, breaking up the ice and scraping it to one side. Within an hour, it had cleared most of the ice along the road; however, a few patches of slick packed snow remained. Darby had enjoyed watching the activity. If only it had arrived yesterday? That's when Horne's wife was to have picked him up.

"She can't do it now!" the gruff guest had sworn.

"Just call her and have her spend the night in a motel," Gibson suggested, "and we'll take you down in the morning, if they clear the road."

Now that they had, Darby helped the Gibsons set their suitcases in the trunk of their car.

"Marvelous time!" Mr. Gibson shook Jon Paul, Linda, and then Darby's hand. "Come Christmas, we'll be back."

"If not earlier," said Ada. "We'll strive for Thanksgiving, if possible." The white shawl drawn about her hair accentuated her thin face and gaunt appearance. Still, her countenance remained upbeat. "Good-bye!" she waved her gloved hand as Jeff opened the door for her.

After closing it, Horne turned and bid his own farewell. He climbed in the back seat of the Gibson's car, glanced toward Darby; then smiled for Linda and Jon Paul. He was still adjusting his seat belt, as the car drove away.

"Incidentally," Darby began, "I forgot to ask about Donaldson or Stephanie. Were you able to get hold of Gunn, or their addresses?" he asked Linda.

"Yes and No! Gunn's line was dead. No way to contact him or Joel. Stephanie's address is in the book. But I hate to contact her yet."

"You two are getting too 'touchy-feely,'" JP groused. "Why bother? We've enough to do as it is." With that, he turned, mounted the front steps, and reentered the Villa.

"I need to shovel off those steps, don't I," Darby mumbled. "It'll give me something to do," he smiled, as he caught Linda's down-turned eyes, no doubt a smart from JP's comment.

"Who's next, anyway?" Darby asked, as he followed her into the hall-way. "You haven't said."

"Two tomorrow. Their flight was delayed coming into Asheville. They'll arrive by limousine."

"That's a long ride."

"It's an heiress with her nurse, from Ohio. Her name's Virginia Lee Thompson. They've been here before. The old woman suffers from Seasonal Affective Disorder. She should go to Arizona or out west, I've told her, but she prefers the view here. She and her husband used to frequent the Villa back in the 90s. Very elegant lady, aristocratic, but very prone to depression. Her nurse is actually her niece, my age, but talkative, and sole heir of her aunt's estate." With a knowing smile she turned toward Darby. "Don't get any ideas, ole boy. The niece is no fool. She wants it all for herself! Plus, she's ugly as sin. Then, after that, it's our Thanksgiving crowd! Your favorite guest, Hutchinson and her husband will be here, along with rooms full of others. It's the only time, other than New Year's, that we fill every room. That's when we go buffet. You can be the wine steward!"

"My joyful day! I'll have to brush off my tux, except I didn't bring one."

"Garnett's will fit. Black tie and all!"

"Why not assign Curly to that ineluctable task?"

Before cleaning the steps, Darby stepped into the living room to gaze about. Why, he didn't know. Probably one of his archetypes acting up, some subliminal inkling drawing him into the *casa's* luxuriant womb. Whatever, he would humor it. He walked past and among the room's divans, deep-cushioned chairs, Italian tables, and vases. He paused in front of the entertainment center, packed with videos, CDs, cassettes and old records. He picked up one of the latter. "Bing Crosby's Favorites," the label read. "1956."

Somewhere Darby was home in the parlor with his mother. Before her on the piano's music rack rested Bing's latest hit-songs. His mother's bare feet moved nimbly across the foot pedals, while her fingers glided gracefully along the keys. She smiled at Darby and sang that incredible song: "I've got a bimbo down on the bamboo isles." He smiled. Would Hutchinson ever denounce Bing for that!

As for his mother, there was woman to favor! How he had savored those moments beside her, perched on the corduroy ottoman, wondering where his father was—somewhere in Korea. Now both were dead, entombed side by side in Abingdon, Virginia, on the hill overlooking the farm.

Someone had slipped a CD of Beethoven's *Fifth* out of its case. Beside it rested CDs of Chopin and Shostakovich. Not exactly Horne's choices, in all likelihood. Yet, who was to say? Perhaps Craig or Ada had enjoyed them. Ah! Dominetti! There lay his selections of Pavarotti's arias, including *Panis*

Angelicus. He picked it up, held it to his lips, and placed it in the player. As the disc clicked in place, he sought out the oriental armchair that Johnson had favored. He sank back in its soft cushion, closed his eyes, and listened. Soon, he fell asleep.

The large tent flap slapped back and forth in the wind. The orderly standing inside could not secure it. Hands from without kept prying it open. Bombs exploded in the distance. Red flames leapt skyward. "We can't take you," the orderly moaned. Darby waited for the next blast, his time to die!

He was swimming desperately. Wave after black wave washed over him. Two girls in the sea cried for help, their blonde hair bobbing in the water. A man hunched in a small red-and-white boat was observing them from nearby. He stared at them, indifferently, before looking away. Darby realized the man was their father. He fought the oncoming surge, rose above it, and struggled to reach the girls. Only then did he see the shark's fin cutting through the sea. The angular gray *form* slid straight in his direction. He turned about, treading water franticly. Two more fins appeared in the sea's swells. Voices broke overhead. A beach clogged with green and yellow seaweed undulated just beyond reach. Women and children floundered in the weeds' tendrils. Legs and ankles thrashed helplessly in the water. Once ashore, he stared horrified into the hold of a ship, into its freezer locker where bodies were stacked, being thrown in alive among frozen corpses. With bony hands, they reached up to clutch him. Their hideous faces resonated with laughter.

He bolted awake! Where was he? Pavarotti's last aria reverberated with its "ho, ho, ho!" He sat forward, blinked his eyes. Thank God he was the room's only occupant. He gripped the chairs great arms, struggled to his feet, and rushed out into the cold sunlight. He took a deep breath; then exhaled, as he walked toward the Villa's shed in search of its snow shovel. Once he completed his task, he returned by way of the Garden and its leafless ginkgo. Poor Adam, he must have looked as pale and white as the naked ginkgo, once expelled from Paradise.

* * *

When late the next afternoon the airport's limousine deposited Mrs. Thompson and her niece in front of the Villa's iron-railed stairway, Darby watched from the hall, but with little enthusiasm. Into his seventh week, he felt exhausted, mentally drained. Still, he rose to the occasion to carry in their bags. Thank heavens he had cleared the snow off the steps. Ice still clung to the base of its metal rails.

"Please be careful!" he advised the elderly lady.

"You are such a dear!" Mrs. Thompson thanked him. She attempted a smile, but seemed distracted. A tiny gray cap, adorned with a long, brown pheasant's feather, reminded Darby of hats his mother wore in the '50s. It complemented her tall willowy frame, loose gray skirt, beige blouse, and pearl necklace—all visible beneath her long black coat. At some point in her youth, she had plucked her eyebrows. The black ones painted across her brow arched up unevenly. He wondered if she realized it.

"Not at all!" Darby replied.

"It is so good to see you again, Mrs. Thompson. And you too, Martha," smiled Linda, as she hugged the two.

After Linda registered the pair, Darby carried the women's suitcases up to their room.

With an audible sigh, Mrs. Thompson waited impatiently while her niece opened the door. Once open, she threw her right hand to her forehead. "Martha, please close the blinds!" she ordered. "The glare's killing me. I've had this headache long enough."

"But Ginny! You need the light! That's why you're so depressed. And cranky, if I may add?"

Darby studied the niece carefully, guessing her to be somewhere in her early fifties. He couldn't help but recall Linda's description. *Ugly as sin?* Well, not really! If anything, she had been born with a craniofacial disorder. The poor woman's face appeared to be lopsided, her lips too thick, and chin and eyebrows reminiscent of Neanderthal proportions. Maybe such disorders did preserve something of an Ice Age genetic code, filtered down across the centuries to manifest itself in select individuals, but only an anthropologist, or geneticist, or, far better, a craniofacial specialist would know. In any event, he felt an immediate affinity of mixed emotions for her.

Darby carried Mrs. Thompson's two valises to the center of the room, glanced about the spacious suite, and bowed from his shoulders with a nod. "Dinner's at seven," he put on his best smile. "With Mr. Nelson gone, I'm the dinner host now, as Linda probably mentioned. I look forward to your week at the Villa and getting to know you."

"Well, we're not here to fraternize, or impose on your time," Mrs. Thompson replied curtly. "Linda did inform me, and Martha and I shall do our best to enjoy our respite, while not interrupting your time. She said you write and have a life of your own."

"Ginny! The poor man's just being friendly! He doesn't need a lecture."

The old woman stared face-to-face at her niece. "Take my coat now. I want to lie down. Then I'll look out the window."

The light shall have waned by then, thought Darby, but no one had asked for his opinion. "Until later!" he muttered. "Good day, Ms. Thompson," he addressed the niece.

"Oh! Just call me Martha! My last name's actually Reese, my mother was Ginny's older sister. Aunt Ginny'll feel better once she's rested. I assure you."

Seven o'clock came, seven-thirty, then a quarter to eight.

"They're not coming down!" Linda concluded. "Might as well serve you. I'll send Jon Paul up to check on them later. Tea, coffee, water, wine?"

"What's for dinner?"

"Poultry. Roast chicken, yellow rice, green beans, and buttered carrots. Why not polish off one of Dominetti's Toscanas? A little bubbly but superior to our chardonnays. He left a whole case in the basement."

"Why don't the two of you join me? Everything's set for three."

"Don't tempt me! No! I'll take the tray upstairs myself. In all likelihood, Martha will be down in a minute. They don't like to be rushed, or appear as slaves to a clock. Very independent and a bit withdrawn. When you're a member of the privileged class, you set your own boundaries. The old woman's never accepted orders, or apologized for being late. O, good! Listen! That's Martha's footsteps."

"I am so sorry!" Martha stated as she entered the dining room. "Ginny's just not up to company—no offense, Dr. Peterson. Trying to get her to socialize is almost impossible, especially after a flight and all the falderal at the airport. They searched her handbag twice. Imagine? Inspecting an eighty-eight-year old lady's purse twice! As if she were a criminal!"

Martha sat down with her elbows on the table. Realizing how awkward she must look, she quickly sat more erect. "Exhausted. We're just both exhausted." She had applied too much lipstick to her lips, creating an even more distended image of her face. Darby felt so sorry for her, as he knew her physiognomy resulted from conditions far beyond her control.

"Would Mrs. Thompson care for any dinner, or an appetizer now?" asked Linda. "I can run it up while you two are having salad."

"Oh, no! She'll feel better tomorrow. Perhaps a cup of soup would do, or a light broth, maybe. She likes that when moody," the woman smiled. "If the sun shines tomorrow, she'll behave much better."

"Darby, why don't you show Ms. Reese the wine cellar, while I refresh your salads. We need to reheat the carrots, anyway."

"Certainly!" Darby replied, as he rose to assist Martha from her chair. "You would like to go?"

"Goodness, yes! I haven't seen a bona fide wine *cave* since Auntie and I were last in France." She struggled out of her chair and followed him past the kitchen, to the staircase, and down to the basement. "O the wines of France," she began. "The Loire, Le Rhone! *Le Tour D'Argent.*" She intoned the latter, with a hard accent. "O Professor Peterson, the food there was simply divine! And the service! I loved it, but Auntie refused to dignify anyone. Not even the Maitre D. Have you dined there yourself?"

"Actually, twice!" Darby replied. "Once during De Gaulle's era, and then later."

"Well, I would have *never* guessed that!" she placed one hand to her breast. "You must be a connoisseur yourself? And did you visit Marseilles and the French coast? So unique! Ginny loved it, but Uncle Sydney despised the odor of the plough, the muscles, and the hors d'oeuvres. I loved it, though. So different, robust and charming! 'N'est-ce pas?' as they say in French. Isn't that marvelous! Oh, this wine, the one there. Le Cote du Rhone. Let's take it!" she pointed.

Darby slipped the bottle out of its rack and dusted it off with the palm of his hand. "*Mis en boutteille en France.* 1989! Let's hope it's still good!" he placed it under his arm. "I can tell you plenty of stories about French wine cellars if you'd care to know," he smiled, not wanting to offend her.

Suddenly, Martha grew very quiet and swallowed hard.

"Perhaps, another time!" he said.

Dinner passed ever so slowly, with Martha monitoring her selection of topics. "You have been to Ohio, perchance? Dublin? No doubt!"

"Only passing through, on my way to Michigan. I'd love to wander Ohio sometime."

"Dublin's where we live now. A beautiful little town! Uncle Sydney's office was in Cleveland. Shipping, you know. His was the largest cargo container line on the Lakes, thanks to the St. Lawrence Waterway. But Dublin you'd love. It's just that it's so cold in the winter, and damp, with dreary days and deep snows. Ginny's spirit plummets the moment the first flakes fall."

"I can imagine. The Asheville weather station's calling for fair skies tomorrow. Temperatures in the low 50s, though colder here. There are still patches of snow on the ground, but I've cleared the path. Mrs. Thompson should be able to sit on the patio, or in the azalea garden. You'll need to bundle her up, though."

"That I can do! I've been her caretaker since Uncle Sydney died. Died of a massive coronary in his office. They didn't discover his body until the next morning. He's buried in Dublin, with the rest of the family—all forty some, stretching back to the mid-nineteenth century. You know, his own grandfather led a regiment at Petersburg during the Civil War, under Grant," she waited for his response.

Darby smiled. Should he tell her of his own family's heritage, or of their losses during the War, or of his mother's grandfather's house, which was burned to the ground? He smiled again. "This has been very pleasant!" he said, as he excused himself from the table. "Let's keep our fingers crossed for a sunny day tomorrow! And hopefully, a cheerier one!"

Before exiting to the cottage, Darby stopped by Garnett's office. He wanted to peruse any literature his friend might have filed away on narcissism or narcissistic behavior. When teaching his Introductory course in Philosophy, it had never occurred to him to link hedonism with narcissism. The latter he considered a disorder, not a viable goal. Hedonism, or a life pursued for its pleasurable ends, however, he deemed legitimate. Ayn Rand's egoism was another matter.

As he scanned Garnett's files, he discovered a box full of clippings and articles on narcissism. One in particular caught his eye. It too had been written by staff members of the Mayo Clinic. It listed a number of common traits of narcissists, such as an exaggerated sense of self-importance and entitlement, along with a tendency to exaggerate one's achievements, and a need to take advantage of others. The authors suggested that a willingness to reassess one's own relationships with others and talk therapy might open one to a less selfish sense of life.[1] Not bad, Darby thought. He placed the article back in the box.

Outside the night blazed with bright stars. A frigid halo hovered about the moon. All through the orchard, its sheen shone brightly on the snow. Hopefully, tomorrow would be a good day! It was time to retire to the cottage. As he approached its door, he noticed a message attached just above the lock. He recognized Linda's handwriting.

> Didn't want to bother you while in Garnett's office. According to the news, there's been a fire in a clinic in Los Angles. An Asheville man, recuperating there, is reportedly missing. Garnett is listed as one of the residents. Do you suppose it might be he? Also, Mrs. Riley called on our cell and asked to be added to the Thanksgiving list. Where I'll put her, I don't know! Darby, be careful. Sorry to be so jealous. Linda.

Such good and bad news—all at once! Darby's heart sank to think that Garnett might be among the missing. Surely not! But where had he been? And how had he gotten to Los Angeles? The Mayo Clinic had several western units, true. But their main one was in Arizona, or so he thought. They must have transferred him after surgery. Surely, that was the case. But the news about Dianne! How wonderful her coming sounded. How quickly it

---

1. Mayo Staff Members. *Narcissistic*. Mayoclinic.org.

eclipsed his concern for Garnett. He had to flinch. Who was the narcissist now, the hedonist behind the mask of self-respect?

Darby entered the cottage and collapsed in the couch by the fireplace. Unattended all day, its blaze had gone out. A few dark embers glowed red under a veil of gray ash. He struggled to his feet and fanned the coals into bright flames again. Satisfied, he added on a small log. He would read before retiring to bed. But what to read? Gilson's book? Goethe's *Autobiography*? Whiteheads *Adventure*? No! Something lighter, an escape, if possible! Yes, even indulgence in some fantasy? Yutang! Lin Yutang! Why not? The consummate hedonist with a love for the simple joys of life. But did he still have the book? Was it on the cottage's shelves? He had put it there himself, years ago. He ran his hand across the books, up and down the shelves. There it was. *The Importance of Living*! He slipped it off the shelf and opened it.

> Human life almost reads like a poem. It has its own rhythm and beat . . . It begins with innocent childhood, followed by awkward adolescence; then reaches a manhood of intense activities; at middle age, there is a slight easing of tension, a mellowing of character like . . . the mellowing of good wine, and the gradual acquiring of a more tolerant, more cynical and at the same time a kindlier view of life; then in the sunset of our life, the endocrine glands decrease their activity; . . . finally life flickers out and one goes into eternal sleep. . . . There is no good or bad in life, except what is good according to its own season . . . It is curious that Shakespeare was never very religious . . . I think this was his greatness; he took human life largely as it was. Shakespeare was like Nature herself . . . He merely lived, observed life and went away.[2]

2. Yutang, *Importance of Living*, 30–32.

Chapter 15

Long before daybreak, Darby's internal alarm jolted him into the harsh revelry of a new day. A bitter cold gripped the room. He had forgotten to reset the bedroom's thermostat on the baseboard. He rose quickly and moved through the darkness toward the fireplace. Fortunately, a few coals still glowed beneath a soft crust of ash. With minimal stirring from the hearth's poker, the logs reignited, creating a low red flame. Soon, the fire blazed hot, while the heating elements raised the cottage's temperature to a pleasant warmth.

Outside, the pre-dawn darkness twinkled with stars. Eyes glowed in the orchard, amidst the snow. Darby stepped out and closed the door quietly behind him. He listened as the small herd of whitetails dispersed, leaping in different directions behind the garage and several outbuildings. With tails hiked high, down the logging road they bounded. An owl hooted, annoyed at the disturbance. Darby could hear its wing-beats as it flapped away. A good omen, he thought to himself.

Darby entered the hallway and made his way quietly to the kitchen. The automatic coffee maker had already performed its task, and the aroma of fresh brewed coffee filled the kitchen and dining room with mellow richness. It was still early: 5:45 a.m. Linda and Jon Paul wouldn't rise for another half-hour at best. After pouring a cup, Darby stole into Garnett's office and switched on the television set. At 6 o'clock, the morning news should come on. The young female announcer seemed confused as the broadcast opened. Darby listened with curious interest:

> The Associated Press reports that a Mr. Garnett Nelson of Asheville and owner of the Villa Montesereno may have perished in an overnight blaze in California. No additional details are forthcoming at this time. Nor is anything known specifically about the alleged victim, or so-called "missing Asheville person of importance." Now to the weather report and morning news.

Darby shook his head with disbelief. He flipped off the station and returned to the kitchen. Jon Paul had just emerged and was in the process of pouring himself a cup.

"Have you heard the latest?" Darby asked.

"Yes! Just moments ago," he grumbled, half asleep. "It isn't good."

"What if it's true? And how do we find out?"

"The clinic or Garnett's doctor in Atlanta should call us. Who knows? His attorney lives in Asheville. I suppose I ought to clue you in."

Darby took a seat by the kitchen's oven.

Jon Paul pulled up a chair and sat beside him. "Months ago, when all this began—his throat cancer—Garnett called Linda and me aside. His attorney drove up to meet with us." He stared at Darby, somewhat reluctant to continue.

"Well?"

"Garnett made us his heirs as well as 'guardians of the Villa.' His father endowed this place years ago. He did it with lumber money. Lots of it! This place survives in good and bad times. And our salaries, too! We're to ensure that it remains operational *in perpetuity*, if possible. Once it fails to be viable, the will directs us to sell the Inn and donate half its proceeds to the Asheville Mental Health Foundation. Linda and I are determined that that will not happen. Montesereno deserves a better fate than liquidation. But all this is premature until we know what's happened. We'll simply proceed as usual. We've too many bookings to cancel a single one. You don't have to stay if you don't want to, but . . ." He looked squarely into Darby's eyes. "For right now we need you. I can't say about later."

Darby stared at the floor. Some invitation! He looked hard at Jon Paul. "Supposing it's true? That he's dead? If so, I won't stay."

"No! Don't leave yet. We'll know in time. At the moment, our fates are bound together. Thanksgiving's coming, and we've a hell of a lot to do. We need you, at least through the winter and into the spring. You'll just have to forgive my bluntness. Deal?"

Darby released a long slow sigh. He was too fond of Linda to leave her at the mercy of this ass. "Ok!" he uttered with a hard voice and firm handshake.

"Good!" Jon Paul quipped with a firm grip of his own.

Darby rose, walked to the sink and emptied his cup. He zipped his leather jacket tight about his chest and, without glancing back at the chef, walked out through the dining room, down the hall, past Garnett's office, and into the cold. He had not planned on this. Indeed, he had made no plans at all. He felt homeless, like a pawn, a beggar at fate's gates. And Garnett? Where was Garnett? What would Garnett have wanted him to do? If any man had been a saint, it was Garnett. Like his father, he had lived for Montesereno, traveled state and nation wide to establish its name, and now not even the local stations knew or cared for his existence. *He merely lived, observed life, and went away.* Maybe the last two, but not the former! Hopefully, they would hear that he was alive! Until then, like JP said, there were guests to care for, disorders to mend, and wounds to heal. Darby walked toward the Garden along the path he had cleared. Dawn would soon arrive. He glanced about the area. There had to be at least one spot where Mrs. Thompson could sit and enjoy the sun's rays. He moved among its metal chairs and stone seats, brushing off as much snow as he could with his cupped hands.

She did not appear for breakfast, nor did Martha; however, to Darby's relief, Mrs. Thompson asked for his assistance just prior to noon.

"Auntie wonders if you'd sit with her for an hour," Martha implored. "I told her about your tour of France—I assume it was a tour—and that piqued her interest. May I tell her you will?"

"Please do! I've already selected an ideal site and brushed aside any ice or snow. She'll enjoy ample sunlight to brighten her day. But it's very cold! Still in the mid-40s."

"Oh! She's prepared, with warm scarves and mittens! I'll not be with you. She wants to chat alone," Martha's voice dropped at the last two words.

When the old woman descended the stairs, she took Darby's arm and glanced up with a smile. Martha stood on the last step, awaiting further orders.

"I wasn't particularly gracious yesterday, was I?" the heiress began. "Grumpy, to say the least! I'm sure you understand." She turned and looked back toward Martha. "That'll be all, dear!" she waved her away.

Martha's face filled with hurt. She sought to avoid Darby's eyes, nodded and returned upstairs.

"I understand!" Darby replied. "Traveling is always tiring, especially under today's conditions."

"I told Martha you would. She can be slack, you know?" she said, as she glanced over her shoulder. "She's my sister's child. Never married. Of course, her features have been her curse. You've noticed her face, haven't you?"

Darby did not reply. He stared politely at her gnarled hands. He guided the heiress through the hallway and out its backdoor. "I've selected the sunniest seat I know, just over there," he gestured toward the Garden's slate benches and iron chairs. Though somewhat shaded by laurel and azaleas, sufficient sun still bathed the chairs and shrubbery, despite the cold. "Your seat comes with a cushion," he added, "as does mine. A little extra protection from this weather."

"That I don't mind, the cold! It's the gray skies and months of darkness that wear me down. For years I was oblivious to it, until my husband's doctor suggested that my depressions might be the result of seasonal dreariness. Well, here we are! How nice! Even the snow. Please sit with me. I don't want to be alone." She released his arm and sat down.

Without interrupting, Darby quietly took the seat next to hers.

"Sixty-eight years ago, last night," she continued, "Sydney and I were married, in Dublin, no less. That's right: 1942. For the next two years I didn't see him, until he returned from the war. We had two children, but they died. As Sydney's business grew and success continued, we grieved over having no heirs. I wanted to adopt a child. But when Martha came along—and she was adorable at first—we settled on her as our heir. As you might expect, a corporate board runs the shipping line. I know all the men; Sydney hand-picked everyone. But now they're growing old, Dr. Peterson," she turned to study his eyes, "it's not easy growing old, having no real son or daughter to care for you, or about you, and no one to whom to leave your life-long business, save a niece. And if you're half the man I think you are, then you know she's not astute enough to run it. That's mean of me, if not selfish, I know. But how it weighs on my mind! And how can I say that to Martha? I can't. She's all we have. Plus the Board."

The sun's oblique rays filtered through the Garden with soft light. Their warm beams caressed the elderly woman's tired face, in whose wrinkles Darby realized she had applied a smidgen too much of pink powder. Her gray hair needed extra grooming, too. A little longer under the gentle strokes of a caring brush would have highlighted its luster. Tiny granules of powder lay matted in her necklace of yesterday. He wondered if she had slept in it.

"You've been kind to listen to all this," Mrs. Thompson mumbled. "I don't mean to complain, but I've little to look forward to. An old woman's life is a misery unto herself. When I was younger, life filled our days with alternate hours of headaches and joys. Both children died of illnesses: the older boy before he was seven, his brother at age five. We traveled after that to soothe our grief. To France, Austria, Italy, and Greece. Martha says you've traveled, too. Is that so?"

"Yes. I studied in France several years, and later spent a sabbatical there."

"With good memories, I trust?"

"Yes! Many! I fell in love with Paris, as all young men do."

"Youth is fickle, isn't it? My love was Venice! The Square, St. Mark's Cathedral, and those stylish gondolas. I flirted with a gondolier who gave me his hat. Sydney tipped him wildly. Said it was worth the man's smile. Later we rented a car and drove to Perugia, Assisi, and into Rome. But when the little beggar boys showed up outside our hotel, I became sad. All I could think of was our two dead sons." She put her hands to her face to catch a tear. "I'm sorry, Dr. Peterson," she turned with a smile, placing one of her hands on his cheek. He clasped it and held to his lips. "Oh, so *gal-lant!*" she pronounced the word correctly in impeccable French—*gah-lonn*! "Well, we cancelled the rest of our tour and flew home."

Darby noticed that the sun's angle had dipped past Mrs. Thompson's face. Only a sliver of warm light illuminated her cold visage. Deep wrinkles created long shadows down her cheeks and past her lips and mouth. He could count the fine white hairs on her chin. He glanced at his watch. "Perhaps, Mrs. Thompson, we should wander back in. Some hot tea and one of Jon Paul's biscuits might elevate our spirits about now."

She turned with a thin smile. "The tea, yes! His biscuits? The butter disrupts my stomach," her words slipped quietly from her trembling lips. "Yes. If you would be so good as to assist me," she raised her right elbow, while extending him her left hand.

Inside, Linda had prepared sandwiches and hot soup: a hearty chicken broth with peas and dried flakes of onion. Biscuits, honey, cubes of cheese, and celery stalks accompanied the broth and chicken salad sandwiches. "Why not sit at the table?" Linda offered. "Or, if you prefer, I can bring you a tray to your room."

"Have Martha bring it to the room," the old lady stated. Any warmth or affection had entirely vacated her voice.

So now she has come to her *iron age*, thought Darby, as Goethe once put it, with no one to care for her but her niece.

* * *

Toward mid-afternoon, someone knocked on the cottage's door. Darby rose from the couch to open it. "Linda! What is it? Please come in!"

"It's Garnett. He's dead! His doctor from Atlanta called. He wants to know what Garnett's burial wishes were, if any."

"Ah, Linda!" Darby blurted. "Forgive me! Did he have any, I mean wishes?"

"No. But his parents are buried in Hendersonville, near the old Wolfe monument, you know, the angel. Jon Paul called, but there's no plot available near them. We're thinking we might bury him by the orchard. His body will be flown back this weekend. We're thinking of a graveside service next Tuesday, just before Thanksgiving. Kind of bad timing, isn't it? Just thought you should know." She paused. "You will officiate, won't you? Just a few words? Surely an ex-priest can do that?"

"I'll do what I can. But I'm not a priest anymore, just a memory, Linda." He looked away; then back at her. He knew he couldn't say No. "Oh hell, I'm sorry. I'll do what I can."

"I knew you would," she stepped forward to kiss him. "There! Don't leave me. I need you. JP told me what he said to you. I'm the one who's sorry."

"You're fine. I wouldn't ever leave you without your insisting I go."

Large tears welled up and hung heavily in her eyelids. She tried to smile, while struggling to regain her composure. "Where were we? Oh yes, his funeral. We'll get Curly to select a spot. Somewhere near the overlook where you can see forever. Maybe you can help him. He likes you. It'll just be the few of us. We'll keep it upbeat!"

"Indeed, upbeat!"

That evening, Linda whispered the news to Mrs. Thompson. The elderly lady glanced up from her place and stared hard toward Martha. "That's what I want. Graveside only. Remember that, and keep it cheap. In fact, we'll plan it when we get home."

No one said anything. Darby resumed eating quietly. Maybe Yutang was right. Sometimes it's best merely to live, observe, and wait for guests to go away.

Chapter 16

"Doc, I ain't no *es-thuh-tition*," Curly pointed, as he and Darby stood on the edge of the orchard, "but this here spot, lookin' out over the mountains, ain't bad, I figure. Only one problem, sir!" he fidgeted with his cap in his right hand, "even with the snow gone, this here grounds too shallow and hard to dig a grave in. Them rocks under here ain't but one-to-two feet below surface. Ain't no place to sink a grave, or one of them expensive caskets. If'n you want my advice, I'd say, cremate his body and put his ashes in an urn, right around here somewhere. That's what I'd do?"

"Curly, that's the wisest advice I've ever heard. You'd make a good logician. In fact, you are."

"Well, it don't take no education to be smart. Sir, some of the dumbest people I know are professors—beggin' your pardon. Hell, they're educated an' all, but they ain't got a grain of sense. Hettie cleans sometimes for a professor's wife. He teaches economics. His wife says he ain't worth a poot—well, she didn't use that word—but he ain't worth a damn when it comes to fixin' a thing as simple as a leakin' commode, or reparin' a lock, or changin' wiper blades on his car. Plus, he's had to file for bankruptcy twiced! Now ain't that somethin'!"

"Careful!" Darby smiled. "I'm only good on two out of those three qualifiers you mentioned. I like your suggestion—about cremation—and maybe an urn here, or a monument of some kind. I'll pass it on to Linda."

"Thank you, sir!" Curly replied, replacing his cap on his head. "You ain't offended none about what I said, are ya?"

"About professors? Heavens no! I've known too many myself. But a scholar, now, that's a different animal," he smiled.

"I figured as much; you ain't never put on no airs with me."

* * *

"I like the idea," said Linda.

"I too," added JP. "I'll call the home and ask them to hold his body till after Thanksgiving. We'll have it cremated and store Garnett's ashes until later. Well, we'd better get back to work. Hettie's preparing the rooms now for the big event. Thank heavens for Thanksgiving! It's a mother lode that covers a lot of costs."

* * *

Much to Darby's despair, Dianne was neither among the first or second wave of guests to arrive. The Hutchinson's Lincoln pulled in around three p.m. Dinner was scheduled for eight o'clock, with heavy hors d'oeuvres and champagne at seven. A harpist was to play prior to dinner. However, at six, still no Dianne.

The flavorful aroma of baked turkey, ham, dressing, green beans, and gravy saturated all the downstairs rooms. Linda had opened Garnett's office to afford additional space, and tables were set up throughout the downstairs to accommodate spillover guests. The harpist finally arrived and began playing. Jon Paul had dressed Curly in Garnett's tux, but his wiry hair and beard created quite an anomaly amidst the well-dressed crowd of guests. Curly smiled at Darby, as the latter entered the living room. "A glass? Your honor?" he bowed in droll fashion with a mischievous wink. "Ain't never thought I'd do this. But here I am!"

Darby caught sight of Mrs. Hutchinson. He assumed the gentleman beside her was her husband. He returned Curly's wink and drifted toward the couple. "Good evening!" he addressed them.

"Oh, Dr. Peterson, you haven't met Boyd, have you?" she acceded to the ruddy stocky figure at her left. "Boyd, this is the professor I told you about," she rolled her eyes toward Darby. "Dr. Peterson, Boyd Hutchinson, in the flesh!" she chortled.

"My privilege," said Darby, as he clutched his champagne flute in his left hand and shook the man's right.

"Heard you gave her as good as you got!" Boyd said in a husky voice. "Pleased to meet you. My first time here," he added, as he glanced at the ceiling, the room's furnishings, bookcases, and pictures on the walls. "Some digs! I should build one so good!"

"I'm confident you do," Darby replied. He turned to Beverly and was about to speak when she touched his hand.

"She's coming!" Beverly affirmed. "She had a last minute client pop in. She hasn't stopped mentioning you since we were here," her eyes smiled with jealousy.

"That's reassuring," he stated in a low whisper. "I trust the club's reading something good for a change. Like *Going Rogue*!""

"Oh my stars! Nooo thank you! We'll not be sitting at your table, that's for certain!" her eyes teased with ruthless glint.

Darby tipped his glass toward Boyd and turned to mingle with the others. To his joy, he spotted the Gibsons. "I should have known you'd return," he addressed Ada.

"Yes! We've driven over every year since I can't remember. We heard about Garnett. We read it in the *Atlanta Journal*. I was shocked. So sad! So very, very sad! Will there be a service?"

"Yes?" inquired Craig. "The paper didn't mention one, nor was there an obituary."

"Things are on hold until arrangements can be announced. In truth, I don't know. I expected as much, but not his dying in a fire. How horrible a way to go. My flesh crawls at the thought."

"Oh, don't say that!" Ada gasped, as she sipped on champagne.

"Listen!" Craig interrupted. "What's that the harpist is playing? It's a hymn, isn't it? A Mozart melody! No?"

Darby strained to identify the musical notes above the din. Yes! But what was its title? He had hummed it to himself countless times. But so long ago. What was it? His heart thumped to the soothing melody of the harpist's hands as the young woman's fingers plucked nimbly across the instrument's wires. "*It is Good to Sing Thy Praises!*" he suddenly smiled.

"Of course!" Craig replied.

"Please excuse me," Darby answered. "I need to check on Linda and our chef."

"Indeed! But I could stand here another hour, easily, listening to the harpist. Such a pleasure!"

As guests in double lines filed by the buffet, Darby walked to the front door and peered out into the night. It was now past 8:30 and still no sign of Dianne. A light fog had settled about the Villa. Its outside lamplights glowed pale in the darkening gloom. He closed the door behind him and stepped down into the damp fog. Thrusting his hands in his jacket's pockets, he walked slowly toward the gates and stared down the road. The air had turned frigid. Rime ice would soon form on the trees' damp limbs. He listened for the sound of tires or an engine's purr. All was silent, wet, and gray.

He turned to walk back when the faintest hint of car lights peeked through the mist. Instinctively, his feet moved toward the lights and to the side of the road. Slowly the car came into view. The driver's window gaped black. It had been rolled down. Dashboard lights illuminated a woman's frightened face.

"Dianne!" Darby touched her door, then her hand. "It's me, Darby! Thank God you're safe."

"Darby! I all but went off a thousand times." She was trembling, cold.

"Here! Scoot over. Let me in. I'll drive us around back to the cottage. Then we'll go in. Are you all right?" he kissed her, as he slipped in.

"I did this only for you."

"I know." He wrapped his arms about her shoulders and kissed her lips. He sniffed the fresh fragrance of her perfume. "Gardenia!" he whispered.

"Maybe!" She titled her head back and returned his kiss. He sat upright, raised the window, and drove through the gates and around to the back. "Lots of cars!" he mumbled. "Will you stay with me?"

"Yes. We don't even have to go inside. The Villa, I mean."

"Linda will scold me, if we don't. You'll feel better, too. Besides, the champagne and turkey would feel neglected if you snubbed them." He parked the car. "Come. Take my hand. Let's go in."

* * *

"O my gosh! You made it!" Beverly hugged her. "Look, Boyd! She did! Now we can chat and eat, gossip and drink all night. If only poor Mildred were here! She'd love it!"

"You had me worried," Linda hugged her. "Darby, please help Curly with the wine. He's beginning to drink more than he's pouring. Better let him slip downstairs, till Hettie can join him. I've fixed a bed for them under the stairs. You may need to help, if he falls asleep."

Darby kissed Dianne on the neck, then Linda. "I will never be free, will I? So much for my missing rib."

"Get on!" Linda pushed him aside, "before Curly embarrasses himself and us. Go on, now!" she glared with protective eyes toward Dianne's face.

"Till later, Mrs. Riley!" Darby smiled. "Would you prefer white, champagne, or red?"

Linda and Beverly turned instantly toward Dianne. "Whatever you answer, darling, stay away from that man," Beverly smiled. The three women laughed, as Linda and Beverly guided Dianne toward the buffet.

"You know, I ain't one much for talkin'," Curly nudged Darby's elbow as he welcomed Darby's help, "but I've been meanin' to share somethin' with you for a looong time," he looked up at him, then looked away. The smell of wine was strong on his breath. "I should a told ya earlier," he glanced nervously over his shoulder. "Mr. Nelson's father didn't want no one to know, but there's a body stowed away in that mine at the bottom. Yes, siree, there is!" he stated flatly. "It's a man's. His skull's crushed an' bones broken.

Course, he ain't nothin' but a skeleton now. I he'pt him put him there. He'd flung hisself off the overlook, some twelve years ago, or either fell."

"Stephanie's father?"

"Might be! It ain't fer me to say." He glanced away uneasily. "What makes you so sure?"

"Just suspected. I wonder if Stephanie's mother knew?"

"No! Onced we found him, Mr. Garnett's father was a' feared it'd hurt the Villa's reputation an' all. I was sworn to secrecy. Jon Paul don't even know. But it's been on my heart a long time. Yes, sir, Doc. Seein' all these people brung it back. That ain't no lie. Kinda sad, ain't it? But I heard Linda sayin' that the girl's coming back next week. Just for a day or so. That artist man sent some money for her. Well! Just wanted you to know."

Darby slipped aside and made his way slowly toward Linda. She and Hettie were refurbishing the chaffing dishes, busily adding slices of turkey breast and ham. "It would be nice if Stephanie could enjoy this," he mentioned to Linda. "Poor girl! I wonder how she is!"

Linda's face paled. "Strange that you should mention her! She'll be here next week. Mr. Hughes is treating her to a weekend's stay. I meant to tell you. Talk about a coincidence! Listen, Garnett's attorney wants to meet her *and* you. We'll need to talk after this is over. A codicil's been added to the will." A fazed twinge of fluster reddened her face. "I'm so sorry," she stood on her tiptoes as she kissed his ear. There were tears in her eyes. "O God!" she whispered in a small miserable voice. Her hands were trembling. "Don't say anything, please, until tomorrow." She looked him squarely in the eye. "Darby, I . . . I," but she never completed the sentence. She squeezed his hand, with a jealous glance toward Dianne. "Nothing till tomorrow."

Darby nodded in agreement. The ends of her short black hair brushed against his cheek; she pressed her small breasts and slender right arm against his shoulder and chest. He wanted to reveal his own emotions, but how could he? "I'm good at secrets," he whispered. "Even when it hurts."

Darby searched for Curly. "Thank God you're sober!" he feigned. "The guests will soon be relaxing in the parlor or going up to their rooms. Can you and Hettie handle the cleanup and the dishes afterwards? I know that's a sorry thing to ask."

"Man o man! You've said it! But I've ascertained the reason why," he grinned, as he glanced toward Mrs. Riley. "Bet you didn't know I knew such words as *ascertain*?"

"I do now."

"Sure, Doc. Go on! Ain't many pleasures left for most us, no how."

"Thanks! I'll make it up in the morning."

Turning toward the back hall, he walked quietly toward Dianne. She was sipping on a glass of wine and visiting with Ada. "I hate to interrupt," he smiled, "but perhaps I ought to help you with your bags before it gets much later," he offered. "You know she got in late, right in the fog," he explained to Mrs. Gibson, embarrassed at the effrontery of his lame excuse.

"You know, we've never been caught in rime ice before. It's kind of scary," the tall woman replied. "Please, I've taken up enough of this delightful lady's time," she backed away. "Good night, dear. Such a lovely place, isn't it?"

"I'll get your coat," Darby whispered. His heart thumped as if an appendage of his throat. His body all but trembled. Dianne's eyes glistened with a passion equal to his.

Once in the cottage, they all but ran to the bedroom, stripping off clothing as they stepped past the chairs and furnishings along the way. Darby flung back the quilts and top sheet, enfolded her in his arms, and, laughing together amidst hot kisses, the two tumbled into bed.

When Darby awoke the next morning, Dianne was gone. So also her car. Had he said something wrong? Done something wrong? Assumed something he ought never have? Standing half-dressed in the cold, he realized no rime ice had formed. A raw breeze whipped the limbs in the treetops and rattled the cold rhododendron leaves. A forester had once taught him that the tighter the leaves curl, the colder it is, and they were curled, almost closed. His body shivered as he re-entered the cottage.

When by noon the last guests had departed, he walked back to the kitchen to face Linda and Jon Paul. "What's up?" he asked. "What's this codicil, and how does Stephanie or I fit in?"

"Let's sit in the office and talk," Jon Paul said. "You're named in Garnett's will. It's a hard pill for us to swallow, but the truth is the truth."

Slowly, the three made their way through the dining room, down the hallway, and into Garnett's office.

"Please don't be angry with us!" Linda said, as they fumbled for seats. "We're so sorry. It's like all we did wasn't enough."

Darby listened, numbed but not shocked. He thought of Goethe's words about assessing blame. "I understand. I'm not here to contest anything."

"We know that!" Jon Paul replied. "It took us by surprise, that's all. We don't know the details, only what the attorney said, that you were included. It's the Stephanie clause that's got us puzzled. We're to call the attorney once the kid arrives." He shook his head, still in something of disbelief. "Oh, well! I'm sure we can work it out."

"Yes," said Linda, turning her face away from Darby.

Chapter 17

That Saturday, as Darby returned from a morning walk, he noticed a checkered cab idling in front of the Villa. In the back seat sat Stephanie, about to exit the taxi. He hurried through the remainder of the orchard and strode eagerly across the estate's yard. As she stepped from the cab, her youthful eyes radiated excitement. Her mouth opened wide with a smile. "Dr. D! O goodness, forgive me for not writing, but do *I* ever have good news! The College has accepted me! I resubmitted my essay and was re-interviewed. I wrote about Mr. Dominetti. And they liked it."

"Here! Let me help you," he hugged her, as the driver opened the taxi's trunk and set out her lone valise. The man waited for Stephanie to pay him, counted back her change, and moped about momentarily.

"Here," said Darby. He pulled out his billfold and handed the man a five-dollar tip.

"Thanks, Capt'in!" the man smiled with a mouth full of black-stained teeth.

"How'd you know to do that?" Stephanie asked, as the taxi drove away. "He wasn't all that friendly."

"Maybe not. But some things you just have to do," he smiled, as he picked up her bag and followed her into the house.

"Stephanie!" Linda greeted her with upraised arms. "O my!" she hugged her. "It is so good to have you back. You're our only guest this weekend! How about that?"

"I know! Isn't Mr. Hughes wonderful? But what's this notice I got from Mr. Nelson's attorney? It came yesterday, by Federal Express. Have I done something wrong? Is that why I'm here?"

"No, no! Absolutely not! We don't know ourselves, but Mr. Sheratt's to drive up as soon as we call him. Take the first room, Honey, upstairs on your right. We'll call the attorney now." She paused; then looked at her watch. "My goodness! You must be hungry. Come back down for some soup and salad. I'll call his office now. Oh!" she added abruptly, *"that beautiful ring*! It's a ruby, yes?"

"Yes! Joel sent it to me. He told me about Mr. Dominetti's death. He wants to see me as soon as he's well. I am so happy!"

* * *

Two hours later Linda, Jon Paul, Darby, and Stephanie were still waiting in the living room for Sheratt's arrival when Stephanie exclaimed: "Would you look at that!" she nodded as she stared out the room's front window. She pointed to a red BMW convertible that had just pulled in front of the entrance. "Imagine! Owning a car like that!"

Darby readied himself to meet Garnett's attorney—Winthrop Sheratt—with an equal share of misgivings. As he stared at Linda and Jon Paul, he could tell that Jon Paul had all but lost his patience.

"Dammit, I'll be glad when this is over," the chef blurted. "Codicil? What in the hell has he added?" he stared at Darby. "My understanding all along is that this property belongs to us—Linda and me—if anything happened to Garnett." He eyed Darby with anger in his eyes. "Sorry, Darby! Stephanie! I'm just unnerved," he released a heavy stream of breath.

Linda opened the door, as Sheratt came up the steps. She quickly led him into the living room.

Sheratt, a surprisingly shy man, took a seat, and, adjusting his pair of black slender reading glasses, looked up at all four of them. A petulant leer formed about his eyes and lips. Small in stature, with a rooster's comb of thick reddish-pink hair, he shifted the legal papers in his lap, removed his glasses, and began: "The bottom line is this. And it's twofold. One, before Garnett left Atlanta for California, he wired me the following codicil, which, as you know, is something you add to a will, sort of like a proviso. Here it is—in summary. '*I, Garnett Nelson, do this 12*th *day of October, make Dr. Darby Peterson my third partner to inherit the Montesereno Estate, along with Jon Paul and Linda Wagner, and do name him a co-equal inheritor with them and guardian of said estate, should anything happen to me.*' That's in his own words. That's the first item."

"I knew it. The moment you said there'd be a codicil, I knew we were going to be screwed," Jon Paul retorted. He looked at Linda, then Darby again. He shook his head, still in disbelief.

"That's just the first item," Sheratt ventured, dropping his voice slightly. "The second," he picked up another sheet, quite yellowed in appearance, "was written by Garnett's father, the late Fulmer Daniel Nelson, some twelve years ago, and," as he peered over his glasses toward Stephanie, "it has to do with you, young lady." He smoothed out the sheet and read: '*On the morning of June 3*rd, *1998, Mr. Curly Bell and I discovered the body of Arnold Gay at* *the bottom of Montesereno's overlook, where he had apparently fallen, been pushed, or leaped to his death.'"*

"Ahhhhh!" Stephanie gasped with disbelief. "That's a *lie*! That' a stinking lie!" She shrieked. "Mama said he ran off with a woman, that my daddy's still alive! You have to be mistaken! Daddy's alive! He'll come back someday. You'll see!"

The attorney's hands grew white as he clenched the paper and stared worriedly toward Linda. She too appeared shocked. Whatever Jon Paul was feeling he kept hidden within his eyes. Nonetheless, the earlier hurt was there. Darby could see it clearly.

"Please!" Sheratt said. "Now settle down, Ms. Gay. Control yourself! Dr. Peterson, watch her! Hold her if you have to. Now, please, there's a reason for all this. If I may continue!" He addressed his words to Linda and Jon Paul. "*We carried his body into one of the shafts of the old mica mine and covered it with timbers and dirt. I made a terrible decision that day, as I bound Mr. Bell to secrecy, for I feared knowledge of this event would hurt the Villa's image. Now as I near death, I disclose that I deposited $20,000 in shares and stocks of my investments, to be set aside for Mr. Gay's young child and to be placed in her hands upon the her acceptance or decision to attend college or upon the age of 18. This I do to assuage my conscience as well as provide for the child when she comes of age. The shares are deposited with the First United National Bank of Asheville, and the key to the deposit box is entrusted to my attorney, Winthrop Sheratt, and shall be found in his office safe.'* Which it is," said Sheratt. The lawyer looked up, removed his glasses, and slipped the papers back into Garnett's folder. "Ms. Gay, the shares are yours whenever you wish them. I had their value assessed last Wednesday, just before Thanksgiving. Their net worth is $38,000. Not the best, but not the worst, and in no way expunges the trials your mother or you suffered. I'm as sorry as you are," the little man's voice broke, as he glanced miserably at the girl.

Stephanie buried her face in her hands. "O Daddy! O Mama!" she sobbed. Her chest and arms shook with convulsions. She reached for Darby's hand and wept against his shoulder.

Linda's eyes filled with tears. Jon Paul stood up and stared out the room's front window. "We are sorry. We didn't expect any of this!" he turned and glared at the others. Linda wiped back her tears, her only thoughts on the girl.

"Daddy! Daddy!" Stephanie's voice rang throughout the house.

Struggling to remain calm, Darby stared up at Jon Paul, while holding the young woman's hand.

Mr. Sheratt cleared his voice: "I will need you to sign this affidavit, declaring your cognizance of Mr. Nelson's last will and testament. Then, I shall leave. But," he looked toward Linda, "will there be a service for Garnett of some kind? And if so, where and when? I shall want to come, along with my staff."

"Yes. But we don't know when. Garnett's body's at the undertaker's now. We're going to have it cremated. Maybe in the spring we'll have a service."

"I wanna see my daddy's body," Stephanie spoke up. She wiped her hands across her eyes. "I want to see his *tomb*. I want to touch his shoes, his boots, his hands or skull, even if he's nothing but rags and bone. I have a right to. Don't I have a right to that, even if he's dead?" She placed her face in her hands and ran them across her brow and down the back of her hair. "I wanna see my daddy."

"Stephanie!" Jon Paul suddenly turned, and, in a surprisingly tender voice, said, "it's dangerous down there. We've got enough trouble up here. Besides, I've never been in the mine itself, but by now the timbers have probably collapsed inside. Rats and snakes, bats and lice cover its ceilings and floor. Plus there's a creek trickling through it."

"I don't care! If that's my Daddy's grave, I wanna crawl inside and cry. I want to take his bones home, or bury them here," she turned toward Darby. "Isn't that possible? Dr. Peterson, you'll go with me, won't you? There's still plenty of daylight outside. Please! Just this once! I promise, I'll never ask again. Please! Please say you'll go?"

Darby stared down at his hands, his feet. "Stephanie! It can't be that safe, or easy. Like Jon Paul said, it's dangerous," but when he observed her again, he knew what he had to do. "If you have to, really have to, I'll go. Linda, you'd better find some boots for her, if you can. And a flashlight."

When an hour and a half later they approached the mine, the sun's orange rays were barely visible to bathe the mine's entrance in a sheen of eerier late afternoon light.

"You sure you still want to do this?" Darby asked. He held out his hand for Stephanie to grasp and helped her cross the stream. "It's wet, cold, and dank. Take a whiff!" He sniffed the air. "That raw, rank odor? That's hog feces. They've been here, too."

Stephanie stepped quickly across the creek, hopping from rock to rock. She could see the pigs' hoof-prints herself. "Phew! It's strong, isn't it?"

"Quite! Once the pigs move, it'll get better."

"To think, my father's been here all this time, in all this stench!" she placed her hands over her mouth. "You first."

Darby puffed out his cheeks; then inhaled a deep breath. He bent down, peered inside, and swept his flashlight's beam in circular motions about the mine. The entrance tunnel was more like a cave. Seeping water dripped from the ceiling into quivering pools. Slug slime glistened in the flashlight's path. "Come on, then," he said. "You'll have to stoop pretty low."

Fallen rafters blocked the way. Bat guano glowed iridescent, green, and pale yellow as Darby swept the light about. "Careful," he muttered as he held her right hand in his left and crawled over a timber. Wet mire slid off the mine's wall as the timber shifted. "This isn't good!" he said. "We'll go a little farther." More mud and slick particles glittered in the light. Silver sparkles scintillated in the dark. Crumpled shards squished under their feet.

"How far back would they have taken him?" Stephanie asked. A shudder ran all the way through her hand and up Darby's wrist.

"Probably enough to be out of sight. We'll try another few yards. Then we've got to turn back." Increasing amounts of wet grit sloughed off the tunnel's walls and landed at their feet. Bending low, they slogged carefully yard-by-yard through the crumbling gloom. Supporting beams had long since rotted. Brushing against one inadvertently set off a wave of vibrations as particles of ceiling dropped about them. Darby reached out to steady the timber he had brushed against, but it gave way at the touch of his hand. "We've got to turn back," he said.

"No, no! Not yet!" Stephanie pleaded. "What's that?" she suddenly pointed over his shoulder. "There, in that niche? See?"

Darby shined the light to his left; then to his right. A shoe poked out from under a rotten timber. Then the bones of a foot, still clothed in its sock.

Stephanie let go of Darby's hand. She all but collapsed in the mine's mud. Her hands glimmered with mica and quartz flecks. "It's Daddy! Daddy! Isn't it?"

Just then a hunk of ceiling splashed in the shaft behind them, showering both with muddy glitter. A vibration, at first distant, but now rumbling shook additional debris onto their heads. Louder and louder it grew until a timber cracked behind them; then another.

"Come!" Darby seized her hand. "Quick! The mine's caving in. Hurry!" he pulled her. "We've got to get out of here." Behind them, beyond the tunnel's darkness, the sun's dying rays flooded the black hole with eerie light.

Stephanie fell, emitted a cry, and huddled in the glistening sparkles. "Daddy! Daddy!" she called. "I don't want to leave my daddy." Suddenly, a loosened section of the ceiling overhead dropped in another shower of mud.

Darby stuffed his flashlight into his shirt, placed his arms under Stephanie's chest, and dragged her toward the light.

"No, no!" she cried. "No! No!"

Darby fell down, struggled back up, and dragged her out the entrance and into the cold air. He rolled over and sat up. Stephanie's face was covered with glowing mud and tears. She hugged him; then slumped quietly beside him. Finally, after a long while, both struggled to their feet. Tears marred Stephanie's cheeks. Salty speckles glistened on her lips.

"I just had to see Daddy! He was my daddy, Dr. D. My daddy. In that grave!"

Chapter 18

It wasn't until mid-December that the Hopkins Funeral Home notified the Villa. "The ashes are ready," the home called.

"Why don't you drive down and retrieve them," Jon Paul suggested. "Two new guests are arriving tonight, and I'm still debating what to serve them. Linda's preparing their rooms. That would be a huge help." He studied Darby's demeanor carefully, if not testing him. "Sorry about what I said about the will. No point in denying the truth."

"I understand. I'd probably feel the same way. I'll be glad to," said Darby.

The drive to Asheville took about an hour, but locating the funeral parlor another. He found it past the Biltmore Estate in a cluster of older shopping centers. Just ahead in the street, a police officer had stopped a car and was questioning its female driver. Darby recognized the woman as Dianne. She seemed distracted. He waved and pulled into a side street to wait. He parked his sedan and stood behind his car. Moments later, Dianne pulled in behind him and rolled her window down.

"What's up?" he asked. "I miss you. What's the trouble?"

"I know! The officer was warning me. One of my client's uncles has threatened to kill my client's landlord if the woman doesn't drop charges against him. But, that's how things go among my clients. Molehills become mountains, and mountains the reverse."

"I think of you a lot, you know. I'd love to date you, if that's possible. If there's someone else, that's all right."

Dianne glanced down at her lap before lifting her eyes to reply. "No! It's not that. But there is someone," she looked up helplessly. "I met him in Charlotte, just before I met you," she fought to minimize the effect of her words. "I do hope to come up one more time. My law firm's buying out partners. It's been horribly contentious; no peace at all. They want to transfer me to Durham. That's a long way from here," her eyes sparkled faintly. "I hate to take a case I can't win," she stared into his eyes and then down across his mouth and lips. "A good lawyer hates to lose."

"Who says you'd lose?" he leaned inside her open window and kissed her.

She placed her left hand on his cheek and kissed his lips in return. "I've gotta run. Darby. There's so much I'd love to say. Need to say!"

She glanced into her rearview mirror, backed slowly up, and pulled away. She turned left at the next block. She blew him a kiss from her window.

A car's horn blared behind him. He was still standing in the space where Dianne had parked. Darby acknowledged the driver with a wave of his hand and returned to his car.

When he arrived at the funeral home, the management conducted Darby to its elaborate office, just off their "show room." Photographs of distinguished families gazed from the walls. Darby had to smile. One of his older colleagues had often joked that when waiting in line at visitations, "Keep moving!"

"Here they are, Dr. Peterson. I'm Henry Hopkins. Mr. Wagner called to say you'd be picking them up." The tall, trim, well-groomed owner handed Darby a small chest of cherry wood. A silver nameplate graced its top. It displayed Garnett's name, date of birth and death. A tiny latch fastened the box's lid tight. "Go ahead! Open it!" Hopkins smiled.

Darby unfastened the latch and raised the lid. Inside, a pound or more of white ashes glistened through the sides of a heavy cellophane bag. Beneath it lay a handsome blue felt pouch, embroidered with Garnett's name in gold letters.

"The sparkles are bones!" Hopkins stated. "I wanted you to see those before we placed them in the pouch. If you will sign here," he indicated toward a sheath of papers on his desk. "Our services are now complete until further request. And we do look forward to providing as many as might be desired." With that, he lifted the bag of cremated ashes from the chest and placed it in the pouch.

"Thank you, sir!" Darby penned in his signature. He saw where the bill was to be sent to Sheratt. "$11,000!" Darby whistled under his breath.

"Yes, Dr. Peterson. Only the best for our families. There were numerous costs: original preparations, airfare from California to Atlanta, a hearse from there to here, flowers, Sir! We did place flowers about his casket until the Villa notified instructions. I could go on," he reiterated in a sanctimonious voice.

"I'm certain you could, Mr. Hopkins. Montesereno is very grateful."

Darby picked up the box and cradled it tightly under his left arm. In his right hand he clutched the Villa's copies of the itemized mortuary's expenses. "Good day, Sir!"

* * *

Upon returning to the Villa, Darby placed Garnett's chest of ashes on a decorative mantle in the office, then filed the funeral home's invoice in a special folder. He was about to sit at Garnett's desk—his desk now—when Linda walked in.

"The two guests coming could not be more diverse," she began. "One's apparently an abusive type, on furlough to cool off for a while; the second a rather pitiful mother, accused of child neglect but still loved by her children. The man's served at least three nights in jail and one in a hospital for observation. The mother's children have been put in foster care. The man's company is paying for his visit; the woman's father-in-law for the mother. How to provide them space and rest will be quite a challenge. If you can keep them calm at dinner, Jon Paul and I will do the rest. There's ample reading, lounging, and walks they can take in the meantime."

"You know I'll do my best. It's strange standing here, knowing this is my office now. And, of course, yours too!" he added. "It serves both purposes, I guess."

"Yes. Those cabinets there," she pointed, "hold the Villa's guest records. These by the window: ledgers, invoices, and day-to-day business expenses. You're welcome to Garnett's room," she nodded her head toward the door between the office and the north wing of the mansion. "Shower, bed, sitting room, everything you need."

"I like the cottage, if it's all right. I'm already spread out. Plus, I love the fireplace, the privacy, and nearness to the Garden."

Linda smarted slightly at the word *privacy*. "Darby, I worry about you out there." Her eyes conveyed more than she meant to disclose. Darby could see it in her face.

"You know I'm discreet," he said.

"And our guests, too?" She stepped in closer and placed her hand on his shoulder. "We're all in this together, Darby. We can't afford to let Montesereno fold." She stood on her tiptoes and kissed his cheek, smiled, looked back, and left the room. Her perfume's essence lingered on his skin; then dissipated slowly. Darby had not planned on this. Montesereno was one-third his. If he had to leave it, where would he go? No doubt back to the University. He wandered out to the cottage to rest before the new guests arrived.

As evening fell across the grounds, Darby walked thoughtfully along the path through the orchard and out to the overlook. The sun had set, leaving a dark ruby smudge spread out along the western horizon. Above it, the night sky reflected the pale sheen of the sun's sinking orb. Below, the forest and its cold ravines lay locked in an indistinguishable landscape of darkness and shadow.

* * *

At the table, a bearded man with a massive chest and girth stood up. Long slick, uncombed black hair hung about his neck and shoulders. He had rolled up his shirtsleeves. His forearms were quilted with red, black, and yellow tattoos of snakes. "Good evening!" the man hailed in a commanding voice. "So you're our host!" he grumbled, reseating himself.

"In the flesh!" Darby replied. "And you, Madame?" he smiled at the worried person on his right.

"I'm Edna Miller," she extended her hand. "Mrs. Wagner said you're a wonderful gentleman. I am so pleased."

"And what did she say about me?" grunted the bearded man.

"And your name, . . . sir? I forgot to ask Linda," Darby said with no small embarrassment. He glanced down at his place and took his seat.

"You mean, *you* don't know! Huh! What a start? And who are you, other than our host?"

"Darby Peterson, co-owner of Montesereno, along with the Wagners," he smiled. "Your name again?"

"Jonas Sumter! From Augusta. Is this the usual pleasantry you subject guests to?" he retorted. "I'm hungry. Where's the food?"

"Right here!" Linda said, as she entered the dining room and slipped past Darby. She winked as she served Edna first, Darby second, and Sumter last.

The large man looked up at her, annoyed at being served last. "Urrrmmph!" he cleared his throat. "Beef medallions, tomatoes, peppers and potatoes, on metal skewers. These could be dangerous, you know. Do you serve coke or beer? I despise wine."

"Both," said Linda. "But your Haldol prescription shouldn't be taken with alcohol."

"Water, then!" he grumbled.

"That's on the table, sir!"

"I'll pour it myself," he said with a captious jerk of his shoulders.

Linda glared at him, suppressed her emotions, and returned to the kitchen.

"Mrs. Miller, how was your ride up today? I forgot to ask Linda where you're from, if I may?" smiled Darby.

"Greenwood. Just south of Greenville, SC. It's an old mill town. All our mills are gone but one."

"I know the area. I've several friends there, students I taught. Two are attorneys and one's a physician at Self Memorial."

"I've been there, you know. Before my husband left, he attacked me. I had to be admitted for facial wounds and broken ribs. If you look closely enough," she leaned toward him, while separating strands of blonde hair just above her left ear, "you can see a scar. I keep telling myself, he didn't mean to do it. But he did it anyway."

"You have children. I believe two or three?"

"Two little girls. They were present. They ran and hid in their room. The older girl, eight, was the one who called 9–1–1. They're in a foster home now."

With his fork in one hand and upraised knife in the other, Jonas leaned across the table on his elbows. "Lady, my father beat the hell out of my mother every day. Would slap her across the face with the back of his hand. She had it coming! She was one lazy bitch. When she left me and my brothers for another man, Dad beat the crap out of him. He'd shake his fist at us. 'See this. It's the best problem solver you'll ever have.' He made us box each other. If we didn't hit hard enough, he'd hit us with his bare fist. It only took one blow to make you hit back. Yes, sir! You don't ever let nobody insult you."

"Is that what happened? Did you hit someone?" asked Darby. "We know you've been put on leave. We try to be helpful."

"Now aren't you being noble! Who told you that? It's no one's damn business what I do or did!"

"Yes, but I get the feeling you threatened someone. Otherwise, they wouldn't have put you in jail. It's important to be honest here."

"Now aren't you one, smart professor! Mrs. Wagner did say you taught school! Listen! You don't know what happened, or how long I had to put up with that son-of-a-bitch. Day after day he was in my face. I thought he was my friend, somethin' of a mentor, but he changed. We joked around and got a lot of work done, but then he became 'wary,' he said, 'concerned' that we were cutting corners at the expense of the company. He was an embarrassment to work with. The men under us slacked off. They were afraid we would get them in trouble."

"What was your position, if I may ask?"

"It's still my job. When did you hear it wasn't?"

"I was just asking?"

"Well, don't irritate me! You're supposed to help me, not judge me. I don't like being backed into a corner."

"I apologize if you see it that way."

Edna set her fork down and picked up her water glass. Her hands trembled so that droplets sloshed over the lip. "Please, don't argue! That's all I've ever heard. Argue, argue, argue! After my husband left, I couldn't find a job. I couldn't afford sitters for my children. We lost our house, our clothes, most everything we valued. I had so little money, save what my father-in-law gave us. We slept in our car until he put us up in a motel. He did all he could for us, but his pension couldn't handle our bills. Finally, my youngest daughter's teacher found out and reported us to the DSS. It broke my heart when they came for the girls. At least they're in homes now. Vocational Rehab's supposed to help me when I get back, but who knows what good it will do."

"You weren't tough enough!" Jonas said, in between slicing edges of meat off a skewer. "You should of taken your fist to her, to the teacher, or the principal. They think they know so damn much; that they can do whatever they please. The state needs to fire most of them, especially those county boards of education. Public schools aren't worth a crap, and private schools aren't nothin' but cash-cows. Most are more expensive than colleges."

"Where did you attend school, if I may ask?" Darby inquired.

"Public schools! Then to private and back to public before college. In case you're wondering. I'm a civil engineer and work for a private construction company. That bastard I hit was an older man. He was determined to go by the books. Everything had to be documented. Just right! Hell, he was slowing us down on every project. Losin' money. But I showed him!" Jonas raised his still bruised right fist. "I broke his jaw. I would have pissed on him if I could have. He's still in the hospital, faking a coma."

"It's a wonder you weren't fired."

"Nah! The owner knows I'm too damn good to lose. He'll want me back. It's the old bastard who'll get the boot," he smirked. "You don't like that, do you? Well, with me there's no middle ground. It's either black or white. Period!"

Edna's body shook with tremors. Her lips quivered. "You're like my husband," Edna stated with struggle. "Everything had to be his way. He was never wrong. The children and I were never right. We were always in his way, 'whining, demanding, complaining,' he said. He slapped the girls, too. Just abusive, like you, Mr. Sumter! Abusive!" the word slipped off her lips in a visible tremor.

"Well, judge, jury, and verdict! Guilty because I have principles I refuse to compromise. If someone annoys you, strike back! That's my credo!"

"And if you annoy them?" Darby smiled.

"This!" Jonas raised his fist. "This right here, Mr. Professor!" he shook it with an execrable grin. "It'll settle differences immediately!" he glared with menace.

"Jonas, if I may call you by your first name. No one here desires to judge you, nor do we wish to escalate anyone's penchant for vengeance. Edna's simply picking up on your aggressive nature. Call it feedback, if you like, even if you didn't expect it. Plus, civility at the table benefits everyone."

"My God! So I'm to be damned for expressing my views. Yours count, but mine don't. If you don't approve of me, say it."

"No one benefits from another person's impulsive aggressiveness. Not even you, sir. It only escalates into more rancor and pernicious exchanges. Mr. Sumter, this is a good place to be, to spend a few days of looking into the self through the mirror of others."

"Well, Dr. Know-it-all! In my view, you're one sorry-ass of a mirror. There'll be no backing down on my part. My stay here's only purpose is to satisfy the judge's high-mindedness and the opinion of the hospital's psychiatrist. 'He needs a neuroleptic!'" Sumter squealed in a high-pitched mocking voice. "What a wimp that kook was!"

"Maybe, but it got you a lesser sentence, if any. And Haldol, I'm told, can and will work in time."

"Yeah! But who wants to be emasculated? Not me? If that's your best advice, you've got a lot to learn. What did you teach, anyway? Psychology? Sociology? They're all a bunch of screwed-up misfits."

"Neither!" Darby replied. "You really do go for jugulars, don't you?"

"It's the only way! Now that you know that, maybe we can get along!" he smiled. "Edna, if you're not going to eat your other skewer, I want it?" he reached across the table with his fork, awaiting her reply.

The woman let out a sigh, but looked across the table at him with strength in her eyes. "Take it! That's the only way you know, isn't it? Taking what you want?"

His fork paused in mid-air. He withdrew it and wiped the corners of his mouth with his napkin. "If that's how you feel, fine!" he said, strangely without malice.

Darby remained silent. Perhaps the mirror of Edna's eyes had opened Jonas's to something he'd never acknowledged before.

After dinner, Darby stopped by Garnett's office—*his now* he had to remind himself—to peruse its shelves and files for whatever he could find on *anger*. To his discouragement, he found nothing. He sat at Garnett's desk, turned on his computer, and searched under a number of key terms. Finally, under "anger management" several entries popped up. In turn, they direct-ed him to "Borderline Personality Disorders." He had never thought of that connection, but, again, he wasn't a psychologist or physician. He was a philosopher, for whom anger was a personal vice, the child of an undisciplined mind. It had to do with exercising self-control, with the Apollonian seizing the reins from the Dionysian. Aristotle, Plato, and the Stoics had gotten it right. Especially, Aristotle, with his concept of the "mean"—that middle virtue between excess on the one hand and defect on the other. Anger was both an excess and defect. It all depended on how long it was exercised, against whom, and for what reason.

The articles Darby discovered under Borderline Personality Disorders, like so many other disorders, traced the origin to an absence of chemical balance in the brain, requiring such potent neuroleptics as Thorazine, Mellaril, and Haldol. One psychiatrist admitted, however, that he didn't know its true origin, but suspected its psychological catalyst was a person's feelings of abandonment. If a child had been abandoned by a parent, or grandparent, or later on by a spouse, then a pervasive pattern of instability would set in. The latter would affect his or her self-image, emotional stability, and intensify a longing for other people to be around. Self-mutilation was not uncommon, or a desire to become an avenger of past mistreatment—whether real or imagined. Tattoos were also a sign of disgust with oneself. Such a life would be continually a yo-yo between bouts of episodic irritability and self-devaluation, impulsivity and a frantic search for stability. Darby reckoned that fairly well captured Jonas's attitude and threatening behavior. "Months of psychotherapy may be required," the article stressed.[1]

Darby sank into a commiserate depression. Tomorrow he'd try to be more sensitive to Jonas, as well as Edna. The human spirit is so susceptible to being crushed. He thought of Pascal's lines:

> Man is nothing but a reed, the most frail of nature; but a thinking reed. It doesn't take an entire universe to arm itself to crush him: a vapor, a drop of water is sufficient to kill him. But, though the universe should crush him, he is more noble than all that can kill him, because man knows he must die, and the advantage that the universe holds over him; whereas the universe knows nothing of this.[2]

1. See Etkin, *Professional*, 485–487; also Staff, "Borderline Personality Disorder," mayoclinic.org.

2. Pascal, *Pensées*, par. 347.

Chapter 19

Sitting alone at the breakfast table provided the perfect therapy Darby needed that morning, or so he told himself. Perhaps later he'd find time to walk to the overlook and back, or wander peacefully through the orchard. The guests would go home all too soon. He sipped on his coffee and glanced past the dining room's drapes toward the Villa's gates. The first light of morning was just then emblazoning itself on the Inn's stucco piers, casting obelisks of long shadows down the Villa's pebbled drive. It should be a good day.

Only one thing nagged at his thoughts. His night's dream, or nightmare! Why did he have them? What did they signify? He knew they disclosed the truth, at least, in some form. But which truth? The truth of his past, that of the present, or of a time to come? The context remained blurry, but not the details. The four-story hotel appeared under construction, yet its first two floors had been booked. He had climbed the stairs to the fourth floor. Other occupants were doing the same. But, both on his way up and back down, he was startled to confront silent cats—one a crouching lion, the other a dark tawny cougar. The one on his ascent lurked behind the door of an unfinished room. The lion on his descent crouched directly overhead. He hurried to his room, picked up his .30–30, checked its cartridge chamber, and returned to the hall. Scores of people clogged the stairs. Their stares unnerved him. They began backing away. Someone laughed. It was an older man with white hair visible under his cap. Darby turned, gun in hand, as something moved to his left. He raised the rifle and held his breath. It was a fawn, with the longest neck he had ever seen. He relaxed his grip. When he looked again, the fawn had slipped away. What a dream! Some archetype, no doubt! Some deep fear, some unresolved dread, or perhaps dream he had yet to pursue. He smiled as the sun's rays kissed the pebbles white. Ideally, the fawn represented a new birth, a new life, a new being. But why the long neck? After breakfast, he would take a walk.

He was about to ask Linda for breakfast when he heard footsteps in the hall. He rose from his chair as Edna entered. Dressed in a gray sweater, black slacks, and casual pumps, she smiled as she took the seat to his right. She had parted her blonde hair so as to cover the scar above her left ear. Her gray eyes matched the pallor of her lips, to which she had applied only minimal lipstick. An unobtrusive natural beauty defined her somewhat symmetrically shaped face. Perhaps some eye shadow might have enhanced her looks, but she placed her napkin in her lap and sat motionless, as if waiting for Darby to speak.

Picking up on the cue, Darby, reached for the coffee carafe. "May I pour you a cup? It's still very hot."

"Yes, but just a little. Caffeine makes me jittery till I wake up. I appreciate your trying to soften Mr. Sumter's wrath last night. Perhaps I should have been more aggressive, or demanded that my husband see a counselor before it was too late. It didn't happen that way." She stirred in a tiny packet of sweetener before adding a little cream.

"There's no need to blame yourself," Darby offered, as he reseated himself. "Controlling anger is hard to do, even for the best of us. You did what you had to do to protect your children. Was your husband always abusive, or was it something he acquired as time passed?"

"It was there from the first. An outburst here, an angry word there, but nothing unusual till he lost his first job. His boss chewed him out over something—he never said what—then, the next week, he was fired. He came home. We got into an argument. I was frightened. I was trying to help him. Trying to encourage him. He sneered at me. Then slapped me. I felt it was my fault, that I had hurt his feelings, that I was to blame. He found work again, things weren't too bad, but he began finding fault with my cooking, the house, the way I dressed the girls. It went on and on. The same thing every day. I had a job at the bank. I was a teller. We don't make that much, you know. We're at the bottom of the pay scale. We have to look nice, handle money, complaints, deposits and withdrawals. I miscounted a whole stack of bills, $500 worth. Fortunately, the customer brought them back. Our assistant manager, a woman I might add, called me in her office and berated me to no end. I cried. She gave me two days notice and two weeks severance. That's when my husband really got violent—and I mean violent! He left, and after that our lives fell apart." She inhaled a long breath. "Some way to start a breakfast," she smiled. "I just want a new job and my children back. That's all! The Vocational Rehab people have promised that will happen. Oh, I hope they're not lying!"

"They're a state agency, if I'm right. You'll be assigned a counselor, who will help you find training and employment. Your father-in-law must be one fine gentleman."

"He is! He's sacrificed time and again. He loves the girls more than anything in the world. As for his son, his heart's as broken as ours."

Just then Linda came in with a platter of scrambled eggs, sausage links, hash browns, and rye toast. "Come on now, cheer up!" she said. "It's supposed to warm up today. If you want some exercise, Curly'll be here and you can help him dig around the azaleas, or hose off the patio, or rake the drive. Or, do nothing!" she smiled at Edna. "There's plenty to read and cards in the parlor for bridge and solitaire."

"A walk and a read sounds perfect," said Edna. "Do you have a phone? May I call my girls?"

"Certainly! Just let me know when you're ready."

"Well, well!" hummed Jonas, who had slipped in unnoticed, without a sound. "Caught you, didn't I? Who's this Curly? Why should we have to help him? Don't you pay him? Make him do his own job. That's not our task!" he sat down with a heavy thump. "I'll start with juice, if you have any," he said with a stern voice.

"Well, you'll take what we have. Grapefruit or orange! That's it!" Linda glared at him. "Where are your meds? Have you taken your Haldol?"

The big man stared back, incredulous at being challenged. "No! Not yet!" he replied. "I'll take them after breakfast."

"No you won't. There'll be no breakfast until you do. Be a nice boy and go take them!" she grinned sardonically. "Shoo! Go on now, Go!"

"Jonas, she means what she says," stated Darby.

"I believe it," he grumbled. "A big glass! I want all that's comin' to me." He scooted his chair back and returned upstairs.

Linda's face beamed. She placed her fingertips across her lips. "Hopefully, we're off to a better start," she whispered. "Stand your ground, but be nice to him. He'll come around if we try. Maybe! And that's a big one, isn't it?"

When Jonas returned he sat down and drank the large glass of orange juice that Linda had set by his plate in two long gurgling swills. "Ahhh!" he moaned audibly. He swept his arms forward, and, rather than asking for the platter to be passed, laid his plate along the edge of the platter's lip and scooped off all the remaining eggs, hash browns, sausage and toast. "You don't have to look at me that way," he grumbled. "If you don't like it, that's your problem. I'm paying full price. That should be enough. Who is this Curly anyway? Your yardman? Does he know what he's doin'? You don't need to dig around azaleas. Their roots are shallow. What else does he do?" he reached for the carafe. "Empty! Why don't you refill it, Mr. Host?" he stared smugly.

"You're the only one who needs it," Darby rejoined. "Jon Paul will be glad to fill it for you. Have you met him?"

"Who's he?"

"Linda's husband, our chef, and co-partner of Montesereno."

Just then Jon Paul pushed his way past the swiveled door into the dining room. His large chest and groomed beard, big hands and fists would have caught the eye of the most burly of men. "Mr. Sumter! Do you need something? Linda's taking a break. How may I help you?"

Jonas's eyes opened wide. Flecks of grease about his lips sparkled in his moustache. "Some more coffee, please!" he mumbled in a meeker voice.

"Bring the carafe to the kitchen, and I'll refill it for you." Jon Paul returned to his kitchen, leaving the door still swinging.

Neither Darby nor Edna said a word. "I'll have some when you get back," Darby added.

Anger flashed in Jonas's eyes. His arms trembled, along with his hands. He jerked up the carafe and sauntered with ursine movement to the kitchen. Darby listened and motioned for Edna to remain still.

"Listen, Mr. Sumter!" Jon Paul said. "You act rude like that again, and I'll knock your teeth out! Do you understand? You will go back in there and apologize, or your ass will be out of here by noon."

A long silence followed. Darby could hear the carafe being filled. Jonas returned, as angry as ever and set the carafe down next to Edna. With swelling cheeks he said: "I apologize if I've been rude." Still standing, he turned and simply glared at Darby.

"Thank you," said Darby, as he poured Edna a full cup. "Jonas! You might enjoy meeting Curly and walking about the estate."

Jonas struggled to regain his dignity and, with simmering silence, plopped into his seat. He rubbed his eyes with his fists. His whole body quivered. "I'm sorry I've acted like an ass. I've been so angry for so long I don't know what not being angry feels like. Thanks for putting up with me," he managed to mutter. "I'll try harder. Goddamn but it hurts. Maybe some outside work would help."

* * *

With Curly and Hettie's arrival, Darby noted a friendlier attitude on Jonas's part. The man obviously liked Curly, as Curly was everybody's likeable man. They were standing on the patio in the morning's cold shadows.

"Well, it ain't fittin' you should do nothin' you don't want to," Curly studied Jonas's face. "But any help would be graciously aplenty around here," he winked at Darby. "Doc here's our *in-tee-lectual*! He does all his work in his head. But you'ens look fit to do whatever's tolerable."

"Name it!" Jonas said.

"How about helpin' with them huge urns," he pointed to the large planters, home to the Villa's tall lacy ornamental firs. "They need movin', cleaning about their pedestals, and pluckin' dead needles out of the tags. You up for that?"

"That and more!"

"There's gloves in the shed and whatever else you need. Thank you, sir! As for you, Doc, why don't you'ens clean around the driveway and rake them pebbles some."

"Consider it done! I'll help till noon. After that, I've got to get back to my study. I want to submit an article on Montesereno. The paper ignored Garnett's death. Somebody needs to correct it."

"I ain't disagreein'. That was kind of him to leave me and Hettie what he done. Two thousand each."

"I didn't realize that."

"Yep! The lawyer's office notified us this past week. We was surprised but shore grateful. That's $4,000 all together. We'll get the checks next month. We hope to put 'em down on a new trailer: a doublewide. Hettie's *ekk-static*, if that's the right word?" he smiled at Jonas. "I love shockin' Doc with words he don't think I know."

All three smiled.

"Well, let's get to work, 'fore this here weather changes and cold sets in." Curly pointed to the sky. "They're callin' for ice and snow next week. Ain't gonna be nice after that. And your road up here's gonna be closed. If you need anything in town, you'd best get it soon."

"Thanks for the warning." Darby walked toward the shed to find a rake. He would love to see Dianne. Or at least call her before Curly's forecast set in. He didn't even have her number, but hopefully Linda did. After lunch, he'd attempt to call.

Midway through his project Darby looked up to observe a sheriff's patrol car pull past the gates. Its side panels read: "Deputy Sheriff, Haywood County." Slowly it crept to a halt, crunching the driveway's pebbles under the weight of its tires. Two deputies emerged. Both unfastened their pistol's holster flap as they approached. The older of the two glanced about. He was tall, fit, with a pleasant smile. "This is Montesereno? Yes?"

"Indeed!" replied Darby. He relaxed his grip on the rake's handle to study the two figures. The taller older man pushed his hat back, revealing a head of perfectly combed gray hair; the younger, slightly shorter and equally trim, glanced uneasily about. The older man spoke:

"We're looking for a Mr. Jonas Sumter. We've been advised that he's here somewhere. We've got a warrant for his arrest. We ask you to remain calm and let us do what we must."

"Is he inside or out?" the younger deputy partly smirked, adjusting his holster about his waist. "We ain't here for a party."

"Enough!" reprimanded the older man. "I apologize. Can you tell us, sir, where is he?"

"Out! In back," Darby nodded in the direction of the Garden. "He's helping our maintenance man."

"Is he armed?"

"I don't know. I don't think so."

"Well just remain calm and stay here."

The two fanned out—the elder toward the Garden end of the Villa; the other its northern side. Moments passed as Darby watched with anxiety. Suddenly, Jonas began running up through the orchard. Both deputies followed in hot pursuit. The younger caught up with the big man first, tackled him, while the older deputy applied handcuffs. Jonas fought to free himself, but the younger deputy struck him with a rubber club. Curly had run up behind them, but, seeing the two attackers were deputies, retreated toward the work-shed. By the time the deputies dragged Jonas to the car, his face and beard were wet with blood. His mouth—a seething orifice of anger—opened pink in the midst of his black beard. While still lunging and twisting, he knocked the deputies about the side of the car until they secured him in its backseat and locked the door. "Damn!" the younger man said with relief. "That'll hold you!" he glared at Jonas.

Just then, Curly came around the corner of the house. "What goin' on?" he mumbled with a tremor in his voice. "We ain't done nothin' wrong!"

"Maybe not you, but that man has," the older officer pointed to Jonas.

The latter sat staring at them, dazed, if not shocked, in the right corner of the backseat.

"What's this about?" asked Darby.

"You don't know?" quipped the younger officer.

"No. But I can guess."

"Well, guess! And if you guess he's killed someone, you've guessed right. He's wanted for homicide. We just make arrests."

"We apologize for the commotion," the older deputy stated. "Ours isn't an easy business, but," as he glanced about the estate, "you've got one beautiful place here. I'd love coming back at a more peaceful time. Good day, sir!" he tipped his hat.

* * *

As the afternoon sun reached its apogee, Darby pulled on his warmest coat and took a seat in the Garden near the ginkgo. The air had turned cold. A brisk breeze, drifting up from the bottom, whispered past the dark limbs of the oaks and stung Darby's cheeks. He crammed his hands deeper into his pockets and, tilting his head back, turned his face toward the sun.

He wondered what mitigating circumstances, if any, Jonas's case might involve. If the hospital's psychiatrist, whom Jonas had mocked, came to his defense, some sort of "disorder" might apply. Still, whatever one's condition, the consequences were difficult to dispel. An angry man, with a history of violence, had killed an older man, simply because he resented his opinion and feared his own slack actions would be exposed. Darby mulled his own *existence*, recalling the moments when he and Julia had exchanged their bitterest barbs, words he regretted ever having said. One never forgets some things, however noble one feels. How he wished such memories never resurfaced.

Enduring the Garden's cold temperatures anesthetized his cheeks, while the laurel leaves whispered their solace of absolution. *Abba, Father, may this cup pass from me!*

While still in a contemplative mood, he looked up to find Edna walking his way. She had clad herself in a hip-length green woolen coat, tan cap, and brown jeans. White acrylic socks peeked over the tops of her ankle-high shoes. She seemed preoccupied, as if unaware of his presence. Upon discovering him, she jumped with alarm. "Oh! Dr. Peterson!" she placed her hand across her chest. "You scared me! I didn't see you there. Jumpy, I guess!"

Darby stood up. "Sorry to frighten you. I feel dazed myself."

"I feel so sorry for Mr. Sumter. As crude and arrogant as he was, you can't help but feel sorry for him. What do you think will happen?"

"I don't know. Arraignment, jail, bond, trial! Hard to say! I feel sorry for his jury. Please sit down, if you will. The sun's warmer here. Temperatures plunge at night, you know. We're long overdue another snow."

"Thank you," she said, taking a seat next to his, facing the sun. "I'm sad. So deep down inside sad! I called the girls, but of course they're still in school. The foster mother said that after school, her husband plans to take them skating. Then they're going for pizza. My own girls! And I can't be part of them anymore." She placed her cold hands to her face and shook her head with grief. "I would cry, but I'm all cried out," she turned toward Darby. She placed her hands in her lap and struggled to smile.

"Edna, it's all right to be sad."

"Please hold my hands," she said.

He leaned to his side and clasped her hands in his.

"Thank you," she said. "I'll be OK in a while."

Just then, Hettie came to the backdoor. Looking first to her right and then to her left, the spirited woman called out in as loud a voice as she was capable: "There ya are! We got jobs for you, Doc! You, too, Mrs. Miller! Linda says to get in here. You ain't got no idea what's to be done."

Once inside, Linda explained. "Darby, with all that's happened, I haven't done the first thing to prepare for Christmas. Edna, would you like to help? Hettie's dragged out all the decorations and tree ornaments."

"I'd love to," said Edna. "I need the distraction. Thanks for asking."

"There's only one problem, Darby. No trees!" said Linda. "That's your job. Curly can help you haul them in, but you'll need to select at least two. Curly can show you where to find them." Her eyes conveyed her message with determined sassiness.

"The honor is mine," he smiled, "even if I don't have a choice."

* * *

By dark, two splendid firs stood fresh and tall in their stands in the hallway; by midnight, both glowed decorated in tinsel, ornaments, and colored lights. The bulbs' soft radiance of blue and green, red and gold filled the house with wonder and joy. The taller of the trees Darby left in the hallway, the shorter he set up in the living room. Soon the downstairs was redolent of crisp resin fragrance. A clean, airy scent permeated the dining room, as well as the upstairs hallway.

All six—Jon Paul, Linda, Hettie, Curly, Edna, and Darby celebrated by downing Dominetti's last two bottles of white wine, then went to their respective places to bed.

Chapter 20

Five days before Christmas, Jon Paul asked Darby if he'd join him in the study. "Our CPA wants to see us and go over our accounts. I've asked him to drive up, but he prefers to meet us in his office. I need to bake hams and prepare dishes for the holidays. He said it'd be all right if just you and Linda go."

"I accept that," Darby replied. "I don't want to be a burden. Surely there are obligations I can assume."

"There are, though Linda and I can handle them," he said in a brusque tone.

Darby stared at the robust figure, at his thick blond hair but graying goatee. An ominous pallor had ensconced itself in his face. How should he respond? "I'm not prepared for this either, Jon Paul. I can bow out if I need to. That you and Linda are used to running the business, I understand. It's a great place to live, as well as a gracious place to work. I can surrender my part in the estate."

"You're in it with us now," he snapped. "Whatever we do, we do together, at least until we work out the kinks. There's a lot of marketing you can do, some writing and lecturing. Plus, Linda and I haven't had a vacation in years. I mean, *years!* I want the two of us to take off and let you manage the place for a while. There are chefs we can hire from schools in Charleston or Atlanta, kids who'd give their eyeteeth to intern here. We get requests every year."

"Fine, then! I'll go down with Linda to see him."

Jon Paul turned away, while fidgeting with a corkscrew he produced from his pocket. "One thing," he leaned in toward Darby, "watch yourself with Linda. I don't like the casual way she butters up to you, or you look at her! You understand? I'm not accusing you of anything inappropriate. But watch it." He twisted the wine opener in his hands. "You get the point?"

"You don't have to be nasty about it," Darby replied. "Linda's your wife. I'm no fool. I have no intention of coming between the two of you. I know from past experience how much betrayal hurts. But," he stared hard into Jon

Paul's eyes, "don't misjudge my character or read into my thoughts your own jealousy. Are we together or not?" he offered Jon Paul his hand.

The chef measured Darby with mixed emotion. He shook his hand in silence. "Let Linda drive," was all he said.

* * *

Mid-way down the mountain, Linda suspended her busy chatter and, slowing the car before each curve, turned ever so slightly toward Darby: "Darby, I was in the hallway and heard JP. I'm sorry! I hate it when he acts that way. He'll get over it. I'll see to that. But he's hurt. Neither of us ever thought about a third party. Even I'm a little rebuffed, but you don't have to worry about me."

"I'm not, Linda. I'm prepared to bow out if I need to. I love Montesereno, but I can find another life, or return to teaching. The Dean at Oglesbee would gladly take me back. I can rent somewhere in Atlanta until my apartment is free again."

"Darby, that's not the point."

He could hear the lump in her throat constricting her words. Tears moistened her eyelids. What tiny amount of blue eye shadow she had applied to her lids only heightened her desirable features. Her petite frame and delicate bearing seemed to transcend her anguish, transforming her into that quintessential wholesome woman Darby had always admired. The tightness in her voice eased up as she swallowed.

"Darby, you're still missing the point. Don't you realize, I *love* you?" she touched his hand quickly before grasping the steering wheel again. "I *do!* Don't you realize how jealous I've been? You're all I've ever wanted in a man—as far back as the first time you and Julia came. I never trusted or liked her." Her voice regained control. "That's impossible to hide or deny. Jon Paul didn't want Garnett to call you. He suspected as much. We didn't know what to do. Too late now," she smiled. "You're awfully quiet. Am I barking up the wrong tree?"

"No!" He leaned toward her and patted her right hand. "You know I've always had an eye for you. But I promised Jon Paul. I know you heard that, too. As for Dianne, she's found someone else. She told me so the day I drove down for Garnett's ashes. She's like me, Linda. She's just lonely and searching. I don't know what else to say."

"Don't say anything. But that night she joined you in the cottage, I thought I'd die. I cried myself to sleep while JP snored. Darby! I'd leave Monteserono for you, but I love it, too. Just hang on with me for a while. You never know how things might turn out."

Darby fought to contain his wits. Here was the *real woman* to love, seated beside him right now. Who would have predicted it? No amount of Aristotle, Seneca, Heidegger, or Camus had prepared him for the angst he felt or the passion her words aroused. "Linda!"

She slowed the car and pulled over to the side. Momentarily they embraced. She looked into his eyes and kissed his lips. "Darby, there is something you need to know, that I've kept from you for a long time. Promise me you will keep it a secret and never let it change your opinion of Jon Paul or me."

"Do I really need to hear it? If it's about Julia Laine, I doubt if you've forgotten any more than I that thump we heard in the kitchen, while in the cellar that day. Remember?"

"Yes. But now that Jon Paul's said what he has, it's time to speak. The last time you and Julia Laine visited the Villa, Julia coaxed JP to slip upstairs with her, to one of the guest rooms, 'to ask about a painting,' as she put it. He was eager to go. He always harbored a fascination for her. I watched them tiptoe upstairs. After a while, I followed behind them, fearing the worst but hoping it wouldn't be so. I heard a commotion in the room, coming from one of the beds—you know the kind of noise lovers make. I hurried downstairs, but returned after they left to discover a pair of panties hooked around one of the bedposts where it had slid down by the bedspread. My respect for Jon Paul plummeted after that, and I still bear the hurt. You don't have to feel a loss of any integrity if you don't want to." She kissed him again before driving on.

Upon their return from the CPA, Linda said to JP: "Everything's fine. We'll not quite break even, but we'll not take a hit either. You and I will have to pay taxes on our salaries, but only the minimum. Egghead here," she winked at Jon Paul while nodding toward Darby, "will get it next year." She hugged the burly chef and nudged him in the ribs. "Come on, Hun, we've got a host of chores before the next guests arrive."

Jon Paul beamed with vindication. Any self-reassurance he had lost earlier rebounded with Linda's display of affection. After she departed, Jon Paul extended Darby his hand. "Sorry I overreacted. Damn, but I need a break!" The big man let out a long and tortured sigh. "Still, I worry," he said with a suspicious eye. "You might want to brush up on your religion. A jejune minister's coming sometime after Christmas. Says he's lost his faith. Maybe you can help him find it, or whatever. He'll arrive mid-January or so."

Lost his faith? Darby pondered. What was that in comparison to how he felt just now? He knew JP was angry, jealous; yet, strangely, Darby felt no animosity toward him. Julia Laine's behavior no longer numbed him. Now things had metamorphosed into a future neither he nor Linda had scripted.

Lost his faith! The thought repeated itself in his mind. Would he be meeting himself in this man?

"What does he know about me?" Darby asked. "I hope Linda hasn't told him that I was a priest. That can get in the way, you know."

"I suspect she has. She's rather proud of it," Jon Paul half smirked. "Says it helps for guests to know."

* * *

"We're in for a lucky break," Linda announced as Darby stepped from the office. "Our Christmas guests appear to be a handful of normal people—thank God, *normal*! A Dr. and his wife, a South Carolina poet, Horne and his wife, yes—Jeff Horne of Body Parts Inc.—and your lady friend, Dianne!" she puckered her lips with a knowing frown. "She's bringing a guest. His name's Reeves St. Matthew. She's only booked one room. What do you make of that?" a huge grin spread across her mouth. "Darby, take it as good news! She's moving on. I'm sorry for you, but," she lowered her voice, "happy for *me*. Let her go! Shhhhh! Let's leave it at that."

He had to smile. He half wanted to scold her about the minister and whatever she might have told him, but, more pressingly, he perceived that she wanted to kiss him, to reach out and touch his arm, his wrist, or hand, more to comfort herself than anything else. "That's just as well," he shelved his numb emotions. "I need to return to my own work and create some ads for the Villa. Thanks for the warning," he stated. "Oh, by the way," he finally couldn't repress it any longer, "Is it true that a minister might be coming here soon, someone whose lost his faith? JP mentioned it."

"O Darby, forget it. You'll be able to handle him. Right now, it's you I'm worried about." Suddenly she kissed him; then turned away.

* * *

Jeff and his wife were the first guests to arrive. They drove up a in a spiffy, gray, new Land Rover, crammed with boots, warm jackets, Christmas gifts, and guns. One would have thought they had packed for a safari.

"I wanna hunt those hogs!" Horne smiled as Darby greeted him in the drive. "Dr. Peterson, my wife, Emma Mae."

Mrs. Horne stepped out, bundled in a flannel-lined denim jacket, blue jeans, and hiking boots. "It's a pleasure to meet you," the plump, middle-aged, gray-haired lady smiled. "Jeffrey told me all about you and this beautiful place. It's lovely, isn't it?" she gawked up at the Villa's Italian architecture and iron grillwork. "I just had to see it. Along with you! He's very grateful for all you did."

Darby smiled. "I know you'll enjoy your stay, and Jeff his hike to the bottom. Hopefully, he'll kill a hog, if not several."

"We plan to bring them home, if he does," she beamed. "So long as they're pigs and not boars! I love to cook game. I suppose he's told you about his duck hunts on the rivers near Raleigh?"

"Yes. He's a great outdoorsman, no?"

"That's right."

The next guests were the Dr. and his wife—Brandon and Susan James—followed by the poet, and, lastly, Dianne and her friend, Reeves St. Matthew.

As evening descended, Darby sat in his usual place and listened to the banter about the table. The young doctor and his wife seemed fascinated with Reeves and Dianne. Reeves, a man in his late-forties of medium build, black hair, handsome eyes, face, and chin, with a slight offset cant to his nose, sat clad in a red turtleneck sweater and faux faded jeans. He appeared relaxed and at home. The youthful doctor was extremely tall, with wavy reddish hair, a cleft chin, chiseled face, noticeable cheekbones, with large ears and a broad smile. The latter displayed a perfectly straight set of gleaming teeth that glowed white in the chandelier's light. His slender blonde wife sat beside him, ebullient and eager to know about Dianne and Mr. St. Matthews. Her long eyelashes all but shadowed her face. The poet sat to Darby's right. Somewhat shy to reticent, she listened intently to the others. She had drawn her long brown hair into a single glossy ponytail, which dangled down the back of her neck. She wore a blue Christmas sweater, decorated with snowflakes and reindeer. Dark brown eyebrows framed her slender face. In spite of her shyness, she evinced a wholesome vibrancy.

"And how long have you been a pilot?" the doctor's wife asked St. Matthews.

"Since the First Gulf War. Our duty was to protect the armored divisions as they moved out of Kuwait. Our squadron flew over eighty missions. We did a lot of damage to Saddam's army. It was exciting at the time, but we killed a lot of people. It was like shooting rats in a crowded maze. In retrospect, not so fun, but at the time I was flying on adrenalin."

"And now?" she asked.

"I fly out of Charlotte for Comair and Delta. That's where I met Dianne," his face lit up.

"Where do you practice?" Dianne asked the doctor, as she glanced toward Darby. A slight flush of embarrassment reddened her cheeks.

"In Cincinnati. I read about Montesereno in one of our medical magazines. The ad appealed to me instantly: '*A place to rest, recuperate, and find yourself again.'* A picture of the Villa accompanied the ad. One of my colleagues from Birmingham encouraged us to come. How pleased we are! Incidentally," he turned toward Darby, "Mrs. Riley tells me you're a retired professor and, at one time, a cleric. True?"

"I'm afraid so, but no longer a practicing priest. I taught philosophy and other subjects. I chose an early retirement to be of assistance here, as needed."

"How fortunate for us!" smiled the physician. "My favorite philosopher is Bentham. I love his commonsense outlook. His principle of utility: *if something augments happiness, that's good; if it diminishes happiness, then reconsider.* That's direct and useful. The same is true in medicine. If what we do improves life, then society's better served." He sat forward slightly. "For that reason I favor whatever medical advances help rather than hurt people. If I were a surgeon, I'd be into transplants and maybe cloning," he offered with a deft smile.

"I've no complaint with that," said Darby."

"Goodness!" the poet spoke up. "I'm just a daydreamer. Lost in a world of rhyme and meter, of the inner life. The Taoist in me pulls me away from the 'madding crowd.' I would have made Henry David Thoreau a jealous companion."

"Well, can you recite one of your poems for us?" Emma Mae asked. "I'd love to hear one. Nature boy, here, might too," she elbowed her silent husband.

"Don't mind me!" Horne chuckled. "I'm here for the food, hike, and view. And, of course, the guests!" he raised his water glass. "As for this fellow Bentham, what the doc said makes sense to me. Thanks, Doc," he nodded toward the physician.

"Please, Miss . . ." Emma addressed the poet. "I've forgotten your name already. I'm so embarrassed. Please tell me again."

"Jennie Leigh Boykin," she answered. "It's not a name many know. But, honestly, I'll recite a poem, but promise you won't laugh." She sat erect:

> *To begin the day in a negative way*
> *Will break your heart in two.*
> *Better by far to look up at a star*
> *And let it inspire you.*

"I know that's simple, but I do write more subtle verse."

"No doubt!" rejoined the doctor. "Maybe you'll treat us to more. Yes?"

"Please! I'm working on a chapbook. Perhaps tomorrow evening. You're very kind."

Chapter 21

Early the next morning, Darby watched from the edge of the Garden as Jeff descended the logging road, rifle in hand. "Come join me!" Horne called. Darby waved a thank you and continued his walk through the orchard. The bundled figure of Horne disappeared down the lane and out of sight.

Darby walked to the edge of the overlook and scanned the cold sky. Dark banks of sullen clouds had formed all across the west and southwest, hanging low and dark mauve over the mountains. The vista toward Waynesville lay cloaked in massive bands of fog. Dampness floated in the air; nothing stirred. Vapor from his breath lingered before dissipating into a frosty blur. It was certainly too cold to hunt. Let alone wander down to the bottom. He guessed Horne knew what he was doing. Darby flailed his arms, pumped them beside his chest, and returned through the orchard. Near the *Ginkgo Garden*, as he preferred to dub it, he surprised Dianne and Reeves, holding hands. They were seated on a bench. She blushed as he passed her. "Certainly, cold enough!" he commented to Reeves. "Think I'll head for the cottage."

"So that's where you stay?" Reeves intimated. "It must be quaint?"

"Yes. You might say so," Darby smiled. "Keep warm!" he advised the pair. "It'll probably snow soon. It's certainly bitter enough." He glanced up at the sky; then entered the cottage.

He built up his fire in the hearth and settled down on the couch with Goethe's *Autobiography* in hand. He turned to its Chapter VI, with its descriptions of Romer Hall and the seats of the Kings and Electors. With Gretchen in arm, the poet described visits to the home of his tutor along with debates with his teacher. The latter insisted that philosophy preceded poetry, nor could be composed if not founded on philosophical presumptions. Not so for Goethe! For him, philosophy was already contained both in poetry and religion. Poetry was "a certain belief in the impossible"; religion "a belief in the undemonstrable."[1] In spite of his preference for philosophy, Darby tended toward Goethe. After all, the poets preceded Socrates and Plato; so also the hymns of the Vedas before the sages of the Upanishads. For the former, there was no "ontological gap" between being and knowing. The latter only made manifest what the former struggled to observe, narrate, and proclaim. One can refute and disagree with philosophical principles, but not with a poet's insight into the human soul.

Darby read late into the morning, almost oblivious to time, until he heard a lone, distant, rifle report. "Horne!" he mumbled. He must have shot a hog in the bottom. Should he pull on his boots and go down? A second report rumbled, slightly muffled; then a third. Quickly he leapt up, pulled on his hiking boots, coat and heavy gloves, and opened the door. Driving flakes of snow stung him in the face. He realized the snow had been falling for at least an hour. Three inches or more covered the ground. An unforgiving wind groaned eerily in the trees, hurling its puffy flakes before its wrath.

Pressing forward into the wind, Darby headed toward the logging road scarcely able to see more than ten yards ahead. An hour passed as he slogged through the descending snow. He listened for any sounds of Jeff's voice, struggle, or commotion in the bottom. Only the wind howled back in his ears. He passed under an overhanging ledge, paused, listened. All was silent. Quickly, he moved on. Finally, toward the bottom, he spotted Horne, hunched against the stump the two had sat on in November. He was cleaning a hog, while nursing his leg. His rifle lay across his lap.

"I hoped you'd hear and come. I've been hit, but I'm all right," Horne all but shouted into the wind. "The bastard came out of nowhere. Clipped my leg! I was bending over, bleeding this one," he pointed to the pig he was cleaning, "when the son-of-a-bitch hit me. This one's just right," he smiled. "Not too small; not too big! Perfect for a backyard barbecue!"

"Better let me see that wound," Darby removed his gloves, flexing his numb fingers. "How bad is it bleeding?"

"Stopped long ago. Just sore. Here, pull me to my feet," he held up his right hand. "I can carry the hog if you'll carry the gun."

Darkness had fallen by the time the two struggled exhausted into the Villa's backyard. More than a foot of snow lay everywhere. Drier, finer flakes drifted in the wind. Jon Paul had turned on the Inn's outside lights. The tractor's motor rumbled—its headlight beams covered with snow. Someone sat hunched in its iron seat. Clad in her denim coat, jeans, and boots, Emma Mae wagged her head as they came into view. "Well, well! They were about to give up, but I told them to wait till dark. Then I'd search for you. If you

---

1. *Goethe, Autobiography,* 188.

two aren't a mess!" She watched as they approached. "You're limping!" she scolded Jeff. "You never learn, do you?"

"Just get off your ass an help us," he snorted. "Don't be so fractious. At least I'm sober. And it is Christmas Eve!"

She turned off the tractor, slid off its seat, and gave him a huge hug. There were icy tears in her eyes. "Don't scare me like that again," she kissed him. She noticed the hog, blanketed in snow, draped across his shoulders. "I knew you'd get one," she smiled. She turned toward Darby. "Thanks, Dr. Peterson for going after him. That lovely couple told us they'd seen you going down after the last rifle shot. You're a dear, sir!"

Darby licked his numb fingers and attempted a smile. "We might want Dr. James to examine Jeff's leg, or at least have Linda clean it. You never know about infections from hogs."

"Oh, heavens!" she glared at the pig about Horne's neck. "Pack that thing in the snow and get inside."

* * *

That night as the guests gathered about the fireplace, James complimented Horne on his hardiness. "As strong as a boar," he stated.

Darby, upon entering the room, nodded with approval; then walked back to the kitchen to present Jon Paul and Linda with the gifts he had purchased in Waynesville.

"You shouldn't have," Jon Paul reflected, a bit miffed, as he opened the box and slipped out the bone-handle knife. "I know these are expensive." He opened the blade, ran his thumb along its edge; then closed it. "Well, it's back to work," he turned toward the oven.

Slowly Linda unwrapped her gift. A pleasant shock filled her eyes. "O my gosh!" she whispered discreetly, with a nervous glance toward JP's back. Quickly she rewrapped the sweater. "You'd better get back to the guests. They were pretty somber at dinner. I guess you didn't feel like coming in?"

"No. I needed a break."

As Darby returned to the living room, he could hear the doctor requesting Miss Boykin to recite another poem. "Perhaps you've something for the season," he suggested, "or even for Christmas Eve. I'd love to hear one."

The woman had changed from her sweater of yesterday into an ankle-length, brick-red corduroy dress with a silver necklace about her throat. She had untied her brown hair to let it fall in limp strands about her shoulders and down her back. Her eyes sparkled in the firelight. She blushed but sat forward. "This is for Mary," she began. I wrote it years ago:

Hail, Mary, full of grace,
Had I been in your awkward place
I'm not sure what I might have done,
O Sacred Holy Mother!

To think I might have climbed a stile
Down some rat-infested aisle
And, glancing back, dislodged the child
Fills my heart with horror.

You bore it all, the angry gall
Of those who judged and dismissed you
Yet something higher gave you the power
To endure with grace and love.

And so I kneel before his cross
Your rosary in my hand
That you instead lay on that bed
Though but a manager stall.

And in your pain preferred the gain
Of birthing that sweet child
And held him to your lips to kiss
His tiny hands and smile.

James stared into the fire, as if mesmerized by her poem. Horne rubbed his leg and adjusted the bandage on his shin. Finally, Darby, who had seated himself beside Miss Boykin, leaned in and whispered, "St. Luke couldn't have said it better," he smiled.

After a long while, James turned toward Darby. "Darby, if I may call you that," he paused, "Ms. Boykin's poem makes me wonder." He glanced about, then back to Darby. "What in your mind is the truth about the Virgin Birth? I hate to ask the question, but there it is."

Darby absorbed the awkward thought, with something of a shock. He hated to add anything to her poem. It said what needed to be said, beautifully! For all his modernity, he respected the sentiment the Church had invested in Mary. Not that he believed it, literally. Yet, Mary was too embedded in his heart to deny the story's simple appeal. He knew he owed it to James to say something, but what? "It's a good question," he began. "Both honest and blunt? But on reflection, it's an incarnation story; an inquiry of how the divine can possibly enter our world. It's a facet of all the great religions, at least in some form," he smiled. "That we can transcend the bonds of our darker natures, or that God can be born in us, is the heart of the story. It doesn't matter how we define God, or even think of Mary. In the end, the story's about something far greater; it's about something we can become."

No one replied. Moments later the group fell into chatter and light banter. Linda and Jon Paul entered with a tray of champagne glasses and Italian Asti. JP poured each a flute of the bubbly effervescence, with cider for Jeffrey.

"How pleasant a Christmas Eve," Susan thanked JP. "Hopefully tomorrow the snow will stop and we can drive home."

"That might not be possible," Jon Paul said. "I checked with the county's highway department. Toward late tomorrow, they'll start scraping the road, but who knows when they'll get here. Conditions will be hazardous at best. You're welcome to stay an extra night, free of charge."

"Well, by dang! We might just take you up on that!" chortled Horne. "I'd love to scrape and pepper that hog and cook him proper for you."

"That I'd like!" smiled St. Matthews. "I'll even help," he kissed Dianne's ear.

Darby finished his champagne. "I need to retire," he said. "A Merry Christmas to all."

"And to you!" the others enjoined.

As he left the room, he observed the group over his shoulder: some gravitated toward the fire to warm their hands, others toward more comfortable chairs, while Dianne and Reeves walked into the hallway. Linda's eyes followed Darby's. Their message was crystal clear. He smiled, slipped on his coat, and opened the door.

"Good night!" St. Matthews gestured toward Darby. With a blush, he followed Dianne up the stairs. "Until tomorrow!" he bade politely.

"Thank, you! And Good Night!"

* * *

When Darby awoke on Christmas Morning, the fragrance of pork simmering over hot coals permeated the cottage. Once dressed and outside, he discovered Horne, cloaked in a camouflage coat, slowly basting the butchered hog over a trench of coals. Iron rods supported the huge grill on which the twin-halves of the pig were spread.

"Been up since four," the haggard, unshaven man drawled. "You heard what happened in the night?" he glanced over his shoulder toward the house.

"No!"

"I guess that's why the rest aren't up, but it was something, let me tell you." He continued brushing the pink flesh of the big pig amid the fire's pleasant aroma. He stopped—brush in hand—and stared at Darby. "Ms. Riley's boyfriend, it was. I guess she didn't know. He began screaming in the night. Oh, not so loud, maybe, but moaning and crying. He was reliving a bombing run, he said. They were strafing Saddam's Republican Guard. Half of 'em didn't have shoes. Only a few carried weapons. They were fleeing in broken down trucks. He fired rockets into the mob—those phosphorus kind that burn flesh. As he pulled up, he could see the bastards writhing in orange flames. They were falling off trucks like charred maggots. When he woke, he had bloody saliva on his sleeves. Emma Mae helped Dianne clean him up. If Delta knew that, they'd probably fire him. I suppose that's what you call 'post-traumatic stress.'"

"It's a wonder James didn't help."

"Oh, he did. He gave him a syringe of something. One of my mechanics has that syndrome. His nightmares recur about every three weeks. Sometimes he just lays under the cars, totally helpless and scared as hell. If he sees a military truck, he gets the shakes. I can't bring myself to fire him. Like that other guy I help, I pay for his therapy and drugs. It's part of our health plan. He's on Paxil, for whatever good it does." Horne paused and studied Darby's emotionless eyes, mouth, and face. "Hell, Doc! Some life, ain't it? Were you ever in the army?"

"No."

"Nor I. I missed Korea by five years. I think I could have killed men. It's just as well I'll never know."

Chapter 22

With the passing of Christmas Day and the departure of the last guests—Horne and Emma Mae—Darby longed for a break. Only New Year's Eve to go, he thought as he sat by Garnett's computer. It was eleven-thirty a.m.

"You don't have to worry about that," Linda nodded toward the computer. She had come into the office, where Darby was perusing medical journals and travel magazines online.

"Trying to post a few ads," he said. "I've already placed a dozen."

She put her hand on his shoulder, smiled, and leaned toward him. "We must have at least twenty to thirty out there ourselves. In any event, we cancelled the Gibson's reservations. They and two other couples were the only registered parties we had for New Years anyway."

"How bad is that for the Villa, business wise?"

"Enough. But from mid-January on, we have a catalog of guests to balance out the ledger. Nobody's scheduled, however, for the rest of the week."

"Jon Paul said a clergyman's due. Is that the one I asked about?"

"Yes. He'll be here Wednesday week, and a quartet after that. As you know, JP's made plans for a couple from Charleston's Salley Wailes School to chef until we return. He's hell bent on our leaving for a vacation, as soon as we can. He never cleared it with me. I don't want to go, Darby. I just want to stay here. With you," she bent forward and kissed his lips.

Darby reached up with his hands and pulled her down closer. He placed his arm about her waist, shoulders, and neck. "Ah, Linda!" he mumbled, as he returned her kiss, smoothing out her lipstick with his right hand.

She kissed his hand, before releasing it. "They'll arrive around the 7th or 8th," she said with dejection. "Just put them in one of the guest rooms. Jon Paul's made a list of dos and don'ts, where to find things, etc., so you don't have to worry about that. Your only concern will be the minister and quartet, and possibly one other guest—a writer, but she hasn't confirmed. She'll either email or call," she touched his hand, running her fingertips lightly across his knuckles. She sighed and stood erect. "You'll enjoy them—the quartet," her eyes glistened in the room's dim light. "They're here mainly to practice." Linda pressed her fingertips against the desk, bent forward, stared searchingly into his eyes, hesitated; then said: "If only we could have met earlier."

"Be careful! Let me know before you leave."

"There's not much time for that. We should be gone by mid-afternoon," she replied. She cocked her head sadly and hurried from the room.

* * *

"Well, we're off!" Jon Paul stated, as he glanced at his watch. "Four o'clock now! We fly out at seven. Should be in Phoenix by eight—their time. I know you can handle it. We've needed this vacation for years! Truly, we have!" he announced in a self-reassuring voice, making no attempt to conceal the passive-aggressive undertone he evinced. "Linda needs to get away! So do I!" he smiled grumpily.

Darby walked to their car with Linda. She stopped and gave him a hug. "Water the violets in the kitchen, if you remember." She climbed in while Darby held her door. Before he could completely close it, Jon Paul clicked the lock button. He had to click it a second time. As JP backed out, Linda stared straight ahead. Slowly, the car drove off.

After their departure, Darby felt miserable. What to do? He had never thought of Linda not being there. What am I supposed to do? He could drive to Waynesville, or down to Asheville to kill time, but darkness was already creeping in. He could listen to music? Take a long walk? Or bury himself in books and writing? All seemed worth doing—either tomorrow or later in the week. But not now. Then a thought occurred to him. Yes. Why not? He would carry his personal items into Garnett's room and make it his own. It was time he bedded down in the house. That seemed the wiser course and wisest use of the Inn's resources. Its fireplace was larger, its couches more comfortable, and if he fell asleep, who would care? Hettie and Curly could always wake him, he mused—whenever they were next due. He had forgotten to ask. That Jon Paul was so eager to exit and Linda so quiet and demure deepened his loneliness and dispelled any reservations of civility he harbored toward Jon Paul. "Bastard!" He whispered. He exhaled a deep breath.

Eating alone that evening depressed him all the more. His mind succumbed to dredging up a host of disparaging thoughts. Nietzsche's phrase "the loneliest loneliness" came to mind, symbolizing a reality Darby could not evade. According to Nietzsche, once stripped of life's crutches, a "loneliest loneliness" becomes the inexorable condition under which all humankind exists. In Nietzsche's mind, that "loneliest loneliness" is always present.

Becoming conscious of it only adds to human pain. To fill that *loneliness* with anything other than *loneliness* is to betray the self. Why? Because it is only in the depths of that *loneliness* that existence springs to life again. As Darby mulled the thought, he knew how true it was. That's what made Weimar, or Nietzsche's home during his last years of dementia, the terminus ad quem of his new project, and Wittenberg its terminus ad quo. Therein lay the theme for that new book he wanted to write: *From Wittenberg to Weimar.* In the rag shop of his own loneliness, Luther had turned to faith in God to rescue himself from his loneliness. It was only in Goethe and Nietzsche that Luther's *credo Deum* was reversed and belief in the self as one's incorrigible true redeemer reinstated. It was the Occident's Gateless Gate through which once passed, the universe may be wandered in freedom. Darby wanted to attempt that in a scholarly work, provided he still had the mental patience to do it.

Early the following morning, Darby showered, shaved, dressed and drove down to Waynesville. He grabbed breakfast at Whitmore's sandwich shop and purchased a pair of flannel-lined jeans from Mast; afterwards, he drove out by Lake Junaluska. While standing beside the lake, he fed a lone duck a handful of breadcrumbs he had pocketed at the restaurant. Finally, he returned to his car and began the long climb home—to Montesereno.

Up past the leafless oaks, maples, gums, and poplars he drove. A gray fox darted out from a wooded cove, then sauntered sardonically along the roadside, its eyes cut back toward Darby. "Don't worry! I'm not going to hit you." Slowly the fox picked up its pace and raced on a few yards before leaping off into a patch of flaxen grass. Its reddish-brown tail flopped up before it disappeared. As the road climbed higher and the shadows darker, Darby swerved to avoid icy patches, while dropping the transmission into a lower gear. On he climbed, taking the curves in methodical fashion, observing the changing landscape, as laurel and rhododendron bushes increasingly dominated the alpine scene. Pines, firs, and steep icicled-covered rocks swung more and more into view. At one bend, a flock of tiny juncos fed along the snow-packed edge. Cardinals and chickadees hopped among them. He spotted an energetic nuthatch clinging upside down on the trunk of a yellow birch. The bird's activity renewed Darby's spirit. On the road climbed, past another meadow, its field of purple grasses bending in the cold wind. Finally, the Villa's gates came within sight. Darby drove between them, down the pebbled drive, and back behind the house. To his surprise, a vehicle was parked there. A thin thread of smoke rose from the cottage's chimney. Had he forgotten to lock the door? He must have. As he slowed his car he realized the parked vehicle was a Lexus—the Martin's car! Had Linda forgotten to tell him that they were coming?

As Darby parked his car, the cottage door opened slightly, but no one stepped out. He closed his own and eyed the *petit maison* cautiously. He took a deep breath and approached the cottage. What sort of surprise was this? What if it were Celeste, all alone? He'd never forgotten her words about returning, or her kiss in the night, or her long fur coat, swept back about her hips and breasts. From deep inside his heart, his manhood ached; his chest trembled. The door opened fully. It was she. Her eyes met his as she smiled. Slowly, he stepped inside. He looked past her and about the room. She was alone. Clothed only in a loosely tied white bathrobe, she placed her arms about his neck, stared up into his face, and drew him down to her lips. "I told you I'd come back." She let the robe slide off her shoulders. In spite of himself, his groin grew tight, his manhood hard. He lifted her in his arms and carried her into the bedroom. She had already turned the sheets down. Heat radiated from the floor wallboards. She had fluffed the pillows—all two. A bottle of champagne and two flutes awaited christening. His heart raced, his loins ached. *Get behind me, conscience*, his manhood whispered. He knelt quietly by the bed, kissed her tiny breasts, and laid her gently on the warm sheets. His thoughts soared, racing high beyond his reach. He felt like Ikarios mounting the sky; Phaeton clasping the handrails of Apollo's chariot. *Darby! Darby!* His Muse cried. He fell on her with trembling passion. She kissed his lips, his neck, his chest. Their breasts rose and fell in syncopated harmony, a dance of carnal *love*, he told himself, *not lust, not lust, but love*! But he knew it was lust. When later they lay back to pause, he held her hand to his heart to feel the thumping. They rolled together and kissed again.

As night approached, they dressed, secured the screen in front of the fireplace, and relocated to the house. For dinner, they raided the refrigerator, heated up a dish of leftover shrimp-Creole, and opened a bottle of Bordeaux white wine. They carried their plates into the living room, built a fire, and ate their supper quietly together. Darby returned to the cellar for a second bottle, this time selecting a fine Spumante. He picked up a box of French butter cookies along the way.

"You know how to live!" Celeste kissed him as he refilled her glass. "Just one of those wafers, please! You need an exercise bike here, you know."

"I've thought of that on cold mornings, but we've plenty of paths to the overlook, and there's always the logging road for the courageous few."

"Perhaps you'll take me there tomorrow," she cuddled up against his right shoulder. "I brought boots, cap, and gloves. Here," she placed his hand in her lap and pressed down on it. "I want to feel you there as long as I can." She ran her hand along the inside of his right thigh.

Darby yielded, kissing her mouth as he did. Her brown eyes and glossy hair heightened her desirability more than he had ever imagined. Had she always been this way, in need of intense sex, beyond what Parker could provide? Or he for Julia Laine for that matter! He stared into her eyes. How could anyone not want such a passionate woman? Or was her deportment a cruel veneer, one she had perfected in her acquisition of her nymphomaniac lifestyle? Whatever, Darby felt like a cheap accomplice, culpable in every way. "Have you always been this deprived? Gnawing for something constant and different?" he asked above a whisper.

She clutched his hand, set aside her glass, and leaned back in the chair. "Please! Just hold me! Just do what you're doing. It feels so good!" she sat up and ran her own hands between his thighs. She slipped onto the floor and unzipped his trousers. He slid out of the chair and lay down beside her on the carpet. Their mouths fumbled and lips searched for each other's erotic core. "O God!" she moaned. "Don't stop! Don't stop!"

Afterwards she lay panting beside him. "Can you pour me one more drink? I just want to lie here and stare at the ceiling, the fire's glow, and your face. Just one more, that's all."

Darby rolled to his side, pushed up, and poured her the last few sips from the wine bottle. He lay again beside her and stared up at the ceiling. "Celeste, whatever really happened between you and Parker? If my wife had come on to me the way you do, our marriage might have survived. She wanted me, but I was too involved in my own career to meet her needs. I guess I'll never know."

Celeste turned her face toward his, kissed his lips, and laid her right leg over his hips and thighs. "We had great sex at first, but it exhausted him. I've read where hot sex exhausts some men; they can't sustain it and lose interest. That's when I asked for an open relationship. I wanted more. I wanted to experiment, to experience other men, to take it to the limit and beyond. And that's when I crossed the line, some invisible line I hadn't counted on. The bondage and cuffs were daring, different, arousing." She raised herself on an elbow. "But that wasn't enough," she lay back down. "I moved into masochism—light and playful at first—then into heavier and painful stuff. I wanted to be choked, raped, abused, slapped, my hair pulled, just plain *fucked* harder and harder. Parker wanted to come along. That's about the time he became re-interested. Brought in his friends. They all wanted in on it, on me. I gave them everything they wanted; everything they imagined. That's when Parker went ballistic, into a rage. He slapped and hit me. His friends had to claw him off. I felt like a whore in a cage. I felt angry, yet ashamed. I engaged in a number of nights like that, with strangers and many of his friends; all behind his back. That's when I came home that night, frightened and hurt, trembling and silent, because I had crossed the line. I bit a guy's cock hard. Really hard! He slapped me so hard I cried." She stopped and ran her fingertips down Darby's chest, around his navel, and groin. "I went to see a psychiatrist. I told him what I've told you. He just sat there, maybe in disbelief. He'd never heard of such a 'tale' he told me. He wanted to know if I had been abused as a child, molested by my father or uncles. Had I grow up on a farm? Had I seen livestock cohabitating in a field? Did their genitals fascinate me? Was I aroused by the beastly way they mounted their own? I laughed at him. He wrote all my answers down. Of course, they were 'No.' He prescribed Lexapro; twenty milligrams a day. Told me to exercise, to stay off the Internet, to seek reconciliation with Parker. Plus, go see a sex therapist in an office next to his. He said I needed hormone therapy. Except for that, he was a thorough waste of time. I'm just who I am. That's all. Just who I am! I should have been a whore. At least they know who they are and don't have to apologize."

"I'm no saint," Darby swallowed. "If Garnett knew I was having sex with Montesereno's guests, he'd be shocked, if not horrified. That's not why he chose me. But, from what I've read, a person's neurotransmitters have to be redirected for therapy to be successful. That takes time and effort. But who am I to counsel anyone?" he rolled her back and kissed her neck and breasts.

Suddenly, she sat up. "Darby, what I need is someone like you. That's the sum of it," she smiled. "I'm not abnormal or any different from any other woman. We've been liberated, Darby," she leaned forward to kiss him. "We've been taught to think and 'hunt' and go all the way. It's a marvelous feeling, a feeling our mothers never had. I just wish you were younger," she stared into his eyes from the depths of her own. "After ten years or more, I'd be after someone again. I'd never work, would it?" She brushed his hair back with her hands. "Let's have one more bottle, then fall to sleep, right here on the carpet."

"Ok!" he whispered. "Can you stay one more night?"

"Sure! I want to hike tomorrow, get a little air; maybe dance once more, like we did that time before. I want you to hold me as we dance to 'Soul Sister' and do anything else we like."

He pulled her down and into his arms. "Let's just go to bed. I don't think I'm good for another glass or even a sip."

"Sounds like a plan," she kissed him. "I'm close to drunk anyway."

In the morning they rose early, made love, and hiked to the mine and back. That evening, they ate leftovers; then returned to the living room to dance.

"Here's one I love," said Celeste, holding the disc in the air.

"What is it?"

"Just come here and listen. Put your arms around me. That's right, like that. Now kiss me," she slipped her sweater off, then dropped her panties. With silence he slipped out of his own clothes and embraced her. She smiled and pressed down on the player's key. Slowly their feet and bodies moved to the soul-breaking lyrics of "The Tennessee Waltz." A tear formed and trickled down Darby's right cheek. He held her ever tighter as he realized just how lonely he had been, and how much life had slipped by. She began humming the words, but he smothered her lips with his own in order to silence her, as the lyrics were too eviscerating to bear.

Early the next morning, they embraced one last time. "Farewell," Darby kissed her neck and lips. He helped her in her car and watched her drive away. As her Lexus passed through the gates, he wandered into the Garden, sat facing the sun, and let his heart sink into the numbest recesses of his sub-consciousness.

O God, what have I done? O Mary, Mother of God! I so miss being loved and having someone to love in turn!

PART THREE

Spoleto

Chapter 23

T he white Chevrolet van that chugged down the Villa's drive all but died at the back entrance. Its motor coughed and engine stalled in a cloud of oily exhaust and blue fumes. Darby rose from where he was seated in the Garden to greet the interim chefs: a young couple dressed in jeans, sweaters, long scarves, and orthopedic shoes. "I'm Darby Peterson, part owner and host," he smiled. "Welcome to Montesereno!" he extended his hand, first to the tall bearded man and next to his distaff companion. She had gathered her long black hair into a tight bun, pinned just above the back of her slender neck. Pink freckles dotted her face just beneath a radiant pair of cheerful green eyes. Her cheeks burned red from the cold.

"Greetings to you!" the girl spoke first. "I didn't think we'd ever find this place, but, oh, it's so beautiful!" she stared at the patio and then the house. "How exciting to be here."

"Our pleasure!" the young man replied, adjusting his scarf as he slid back the van's left door to drag out two duffle bags. "How long's this place been here?"

"Since the forties, at least," Darby answered, "but in truth I don't know. Your room's in the wing just off the kitchen. It comes with a large double bed, along with a twin bed and sagging sofa, private bath, etc. It's past the freezer and refrigerators. You know we've got guests coming in tonight, probably around five o'clock."

"Hey, man, we're good to go. Here, man, carry this for me," he handed Darby a bag of fresh collards. "Just lead the way. Incidentally, I'm Joshua Long and this is Brandy Sisk. Just call me 'Josh.' We're both from the Low Country, near Wadmalaw Island. Your guests are in for a treat."

"Gullah cuisine, no doubt?"

"We hope so. Your chef said the freezer was stocked with everything imaginable, from seafood to poultry to steaks. I brought the collards for at least one meal of fresh greens. Just leave it to us, sir. All we need to know is how many palates to please."

"A minister's, if he comes, plus four more, the two of you, plus myself. Eight maximum!"

"Hey, we got it!" Josh grinned. He bent forward and snatched up his duffle bag, leaving Brandy to fend for herself.

"This way," said Darby as he led off. He glanced back over his shoulder. They made a cute pair: cocky, eager, ready to work. It'd be interesting to see what they'd come up with. "Well, here's the kitchen; your room's just beyond the passageway," he pointed. He set the collards down near the sink. "If you'd prefer separate rooms, there's plenty of space upstairs. The Villa can sleep up to thirty, when it has to."

"Oh, we'll be fine!" Brandy smiled, cutting her eyes first toward Darby and then Josh. "We've been buddies a long time. Besides, we're roommates. It's the only way you can make it through school these day," her eyes studied Darby's, uncertain as to what his take might be.

"That's fine. I'll check with you later, once the guests come in." Darby nodded as if tipping a cap. "Till then."

Just after four-thirty, the members of the string quartet arrived. They drove up in a Ford Explorer, packed with valises and instrument cases. Darby stepped out on the porch to greet them. The first to get out was the male driver and a passenger behind him in the backseat, then two other women from the opposite side. The man's diminutive stature caught Darby's eye first. Five feet tall at the most, his baldhead and pudgy figure reminded him of Tunstan, but his eyes radiated with a merriment ready to be unleashed if given an inkling of permission. Darby smiled and shook his hand. "Good afternoon! A gracious welcome to all of you! Gather your things and come on in. The office is just past the stairwell. I've got your room assignments and keys ready. Just let me know how best to help. Dinner's at seven-thirty. Please, this way! Do come in."

After they registered, Darby suggested: "Why not leave your instruments in the hallway? You can practice in the living room? We've one other guest coming—a minister. He can relax in my office, or in the cottage out back, or enjoy your music. It's up to him."

"That's a splendid idea!" the director's wife replied. She had registered their names as Merle and Aileen Velesky. She was taller than her husband, slender, with short dyed red hair and large brown eyes. "We want to practice before dinner; then an hour or so into the night. Hopefully we won't be a boor. Is the minister Episcopalian or Presbyterian by chance? I ask because they tend to be more liturgical. They often engage us to play during Advent and Easter. But, then Baptists do, too."

"Don't worry about him. He'll probably enjoy every note, along with every squeak and grind."

"There'll be plenty of those," the youngest member of the group laughed. "We're hoping to perform at this year's Spoleto," she held Darby in her gaze. "In case you've forgotten, my name's Tracy," she smiled. "This one," she leaned toward a quieter older girl, "is my sister, Melanie. We're from Asheville, but Sis and I grew up in Charleston. Can you imagine performing at Spoleto! We want it to be perfect."

Darby eyed both girls—women, he should say, as they were easily in their late twenties or thirties. Neither wore wedding rings. If the minister weren't married, maybe he'd find his match here. He smiled and thought of Linda. If it weren't for Jon Paul, would she be his match? They'd been gone a week and not a peep from either. "Tracy, Melanie, I'll try not to forget your names. I'm looking forward to your presence. Maybe you'll favor us with several pieces. Our interim chefs are from Charleston."

"We promise you that!" Merle assured. "Now to our rooms, maybe some tea?" he hinted, "and down to practice."

Darby notified Brandy. "Hot tea for the foursome!" he called. "I'll be outside for a while." With that he pulled on his coat and cap and wandered into the orchard.

In less than an hour the winter's orb would dip below the dark horizon. He thought of Julia Laine, Dianne, Celeste, and Linda. How could a man in his late-fifties, and a philosopher at that, have arrived at this point in life and still not know the ebb and tide of lasting love? Where had it all gone wrong? He tightened his coat about his shoulders and chest and walked to the edge of the overlook. In something of a wistful mood, he stared out across the shadows that blanketed the cold mountains. Soon the deep ravines of fir and leafless oaks would plunge into darkness again. Chuang-tzu in his *Inner Chapters* had urged ancient China to return to Nature to rediscover its roots. Rousseau had advised the same for his generation. But Nature was only nature. Darby rubbed his hands together and watched as the oblique rays of the sun's soft bulge sank dark orange into the earth. He let his mind slip into neutral as he walked back to the house.

Sounds of Sibelius drifted from the living room. With passion, the quartet's strings sang to the chords of the Finn's melody. Darby recognized the piece as *Finlandia*. He sought out a chair in the hallway, sat down quietly, and listened. The violins' strings, cello and viola's deep tones filled the two spaces with the composer's majestic anthem. He didn't want the music to end. Darby glanced up at the hall clock. Seven p.m. and still no minister. Darby slipped silently out of his chair and entered the office. He pulled out the man's folder and read again what Linda had entered:

Charles Wythe Sanders, AB, BD, ThM. Methodist. Wofford Col-
lege, Duke Divinity School. Pastorates: Bethel United, Shiloh
United, Marion Central, Weaverville Chapel, Chaplain Effert
College. Age 48. Caucasian male. January 8th–12th, put in room
35 at end of hall at guest's request. Not taking antidepressants.
Conference recommends solitude, reflection, conversation,
hikes, rest. Room and board paid in full by The Bishop's Pastoral
Counseling Fund. Notify latter if cancellation.

Darby replaced the folder and returned to the hallway. He peeked in the
dining room. Brandy had set the table with the Villa's finest china, sterling
ware, silver goblets—all spread on white linen with purple-and-green-
striped napkins in silver rings above each plate. Linda must have left her
detailed suggestions. All was perfectly arranged.

The clock in the hall chimed seven-fifteen. Brandy hurried to Darby's
side. "Shall I announce dinner on time?" she queried. "Who's not here yet?"

"The clergyman. Maybe he got lost. Let's delay an extra five minutes.
Can our chefs handle that?"

"Of course!" she smiled. "But the shrimp and grits don't need to steep
too long. Nor, the collards!" Her hands seemed a little nervous and sweat
beads had formed on her brow.

"Right! At seven thirty-five sharp we start. If the parson's late, we'll seat
him whenever he comes in. I'll worry about his room later."

"Thanks, Doc," she nudged him with her elbow. "Jon Paul did say you
were a professor."

"True! But Darby's good enough. Thanks, just the same."

* * *

They were at table, well into the evening's second course and a third bottle of
wine, when bright headlight beams, accompanied by the crunch of pebbles,
announced a vehicle's arrival. A vehicle door opened and closed. "Excuse
me," said Darby as he scooted his chair back and walked to the door. Without hesitating, he opened it. "You must be Sanders?" he said to the lean,
middle-aged man who stood on the steps opposite him, suitcase in hand.

"Yes," answered the blond-headed figure, dressed in dark brown cords,
a green sweater, and Docker moccasins. His hair lay parted in the middle,
his ears loomed large and eyebrows a little too long and bushy, arched awkwardly above deep-set blue eyes. "This is Montesereno? Yes?"

"Of course! Come in! Sit down and eat. We'll do the rest later," he shook
his hand. "Ladies and gentleman, Mr. Sanders. Charles Wythe by name."

"Thank you," he nodded toward the guests. "I'm sorry to be late. I missed the turn at the forks and didn't realize it for several miles." He set his valise just inside the hallway. "The drive up must be beautiful by day. I couldn't see much in the dark." He located his place at the table and took a seat.

"Welcome, sir!" Merle greeted him. "We hope our music doesn't drive you to distraction. We're here to practice. We hear you're a minister. True?"

"Yes, a Methodist; I love good music," he smiled.

"We'll be gone by the weekend," Tracy said. "We're part of a string quartet. This is my sister, Melanie."

"And I'm Aileen!" the director's wife smiled. "I go with Merle. We're the Veleskys. You must tell us about yourself."

The man's eyes lost their sparkle; a restive uneasiness filled them. He looked up uncomfortably. "There's not much to tell," he replied in a quiet voice. "I'll take some wine," he nodded toward Merle, before whom the third half-filled bottle's contents glistened in the chandelier's light.

"So glad you drink!" Velesky said. "That makes the four of us very comfortable."

"Thank you!" Sanders nodded.

The door to the kitchen swung open and out popped Brandy. "Oh great, you're here! I've been saving your plate. Everything's still hot and tasty. You're not allergic to shellfish, I hope. Are you?"

"No. Not at all!" Sanders drank in her spunky manner with an uplifted change of face.

"Well, it's shrimp and grits, Gullah style! A tad spicy—just a little pepper that is—with greens and black-eye peas! Can you handle that? Plus corncakes?"

Sanders smiled, nodding acceptance. "Yes. Many thanks, yes!"

"How do you prefer to be addressed?" Mrs. Velesky asked, with a polite flash of her brown eyes. "I . . . I don't mean to sound impertinent. Please, I don't mean it that way."

"Just Charles or Wythe. I go by both. I've never been one for titles. My denomination has enough."

"Well! Charles, Charles it shall be!" she offered in a friendly spirit. "I think you'll like our music."

"Dr. Peterson," Merle leaned forward, "How did you ever come by way of your career? I've only met one other professor of philosophy, and his specialty was epistemology, he claimed. But after he explained it, it made no sense at all," the man smiled. "You wouldn't mind trying, would you?"

"Please!" Darby choked. "I wish you hadn't raised the question. But, let me try. And I will be brief," he smiled at the guests about the table. "Here goes. Epistemology itself is a rather modern field, made possible by the works of Descartes, Kant, and many others. But its roots go back to Plato, if not the Sophists. It asks the question: 'How can I justify what I believe I know?' Or, 'what is my justification for anything I believe?' That's sort of it in a nutshell. I could give you the history of it, but it would bore you to tears. Seriously," he smiled. "The field has now moved into language analysis and post-modernism. My own training preceded much of that. I'm more old-school, still lost in the likes of Plato and Aristotle, or folk like Hegel, Nietzsche, Heidegger, and Sartre—a kind of smattering of philosophical fig- ures most college profs teach. I taught it all, but most of us have our favorites and limitations."

"If I asked you to single out a favorite, who would it be?"

"I couldn't answer. I've beholden to everyone, to all of them. They've all energized my mind in one form or other."

"Still! You must have a favorite."

"I suppose Plato and Nietzsche vie in there somewhere, along with Heidegger and Camus' *absurd man*."

"And what's the *absurd man*? You might be describing me," Merle smiled.

Darby stared at Merle and the others about the table. He hadn't meant for the conversation to stall in his hands, or end in his lap. Like Kierkeg- aard's "Knight of Faith," a man's deepest beliefs are private and incommu- nicable, hidden in a place even he guards against entry. He wet his lips and moved uneasily in his seat. "It's a long story with many antecedents. But, in brief, it's one of Camus' ideas. For Camus, we'd give our lives to know if life has a purpose, but it doesn't. We long for meaning. But it's not there. There isn't any purpose or meaning to life—though we *crave* one. And that's what makes it *absurd*. Life ought to have a meaning, we think, but it doesn't. The only meaning it has is what we give it. And we have to accept that, period."

"Absolutely horrible! Unthinkable!" Aileen objected, as she coughed on a sip of wine.

Velesky's lips parted in silence. He stared at his glass and turned its stem slowly in his hand. "Another bottle would help, wouldn't it?" he laughed.

"I'll get one," said Darby. "Something light to go with dessert."

* * *

Later that evening, after registering Sanders and showing him to his room, Darby bundled up in a long black coat from Garnett's closet, pressed his cap down about his ears, and wandered outside. The stars seemed especially bright, Jupiter in particular. He walked past the large urns and down the flagstone steps to the Garden. The cottage loomed lonely and empty, indeed, surreal in the soft light of the milky stars. He wished Celeste or Dianne were back, awkward as that made him feel. He wondered how Linda was holding up under Jon Paul's surveillance. Taking a deep breath, he glanced up into the night sky. As his eyes adjusted, he walked past the cottage and took a seat near the ginkgo tree. He thought of Goethe's statement: "Only one thing is indispensable, love!"

He let his mind sink into itself: his thoughts bubble up, as Hindu meditation guidelines encourage. "Just let your errant thoughts bubble up," his Hindu friend Ramasitachara had coached him. "Don't try to stop them, or cling to them, or even try to manage them. Just let them go. And out they'll slip, one by one. And you'll find peace, experience calm. It's better than prayer, for it lets God into that space your mind vacates." Chara believed that, Darby knew. Maybe that's why the Hindu always seemed at peace. "Then people won't see you, but God!" the man would smile triumphantly.

Darby wondered if Camus had ever tried that but wound up with the *absurd* rather than with God. Now that would be something? God descending in the form of the *absurd*! That was for theologians to argue, not philosophers. The problem of being was problematic enough. Better to concentrate on the problem of consciousness, the problem of reason, and the problem of personhood, as Rorty insisted, and leave mysticism to the mystics. His conscience remembered what he had said to Garnett: that philosophy is more like poetry than science, a lifting of the human spirit beyond its boundaries of fear and exuberance.

Suddenly aware of how cold it was, Darby stood up, flailed his arms back and forth, and returned inside. The quartet's strings were midway into the theme of Ken Burn's documentary on the Civil War—Jay Ungar's *Ashokan Farewell*. The music emptied him of any pretentions he had entertained and humbled him with its mournful notes of national regret. What a mixed bag! He was eager for whatever tomorrow might bring. But just now the music of the violins' strings, to the accompanying sweep of Merle's viola and Aileen's cello, bore his heart to the home place of his childhood and the hearths of a memory that still empowered him everyday.

Chapter 24

While alone the next morning at his desk, Darby looked up to discover Melanie peeping in. He hadn't really given her much thought at yesterday's table but now found himself quite taken by her serene and inquisitive manner. Tall, nicely shaped (certainly enough to catch a man's eye), of handsome cheekbones, a thin nose, soft-rounded lips, and fine facial lines, she actually appeared striking. She approached quietly, with a wide smile, tossing her long black hair back across her neck. She had clad herself in a mid-length, red-black-and-gray plaid skirt, white blouse, and black slippers. On closer examination, he placed her age somewhere between middle-to-late-thirties. He stood and returned her smile.

"Good morning!" she greeted him. "With whom of your absurd philosophers are you identifying today?"

"You got me!" he stammered, somewhat surprised. "I'm just sipping coffee. Would you care for some? There's plenty on the table. Or tea?"

"Tea! But, please, don't let me disturb you," she glanced about the room. "Some office! And quiet comfortable. Are you the decorator?"

"Not hardly! That's Linda's domain. She's the real energy bunny behind the throne. You probably know that."

"I do. We've been here before. She's a bundle all right!"

"Let's get your coffee, or tea."

"Can we bring it back in here?"

"Of course!"

"I like this quiet, relaxed atmosphere," she turned her face about, still admiring the room.

Darby followed her into the dining room, refilling his cup while she prepared a cup of tea.

Back in the office, he sat in the sofa. She smiled and sat at his desk. "You don't mind, do you?"

"And if I did?" he queried with bemused interest. "What could I do?"

She inhaled a slow, deep breath, while toying with her cup. "You saw how cute my sister can be! Precious little Tracy, with her big smiling eyes!

From the moment she came into our parents' lives, I dropped from first to second *fiddle*," she frowned. "Literally! O to be sure, I love her, and wouldn't know how to act without her. But here I am an old maid, and all she could talk about last night before bedtime was 'that handsome poor lonely minister, Charles. Isn't he a dear?'" she cut her eyes comically at Darby. "So I go along with it," she exhaled. "I'm taller than she, which doesn't help either. And I'm really not all that talented. Did you notice how Merle kept nudging me during practice and drowning me out with his viola? Watch him this morning, or afternoon, if you're about. You'll see what I mean. But, look! I'm doing all the talking. I wanted you to do some," she looked across the desk and into his eyes. "So who's the mentor today? Or is it just yourself? I haven't had this kind of fun in years."

"Melanie, you are quite refreshing!" he smiled. "As for today, I'm just myself with a ton of things to do. I need to drive into Asheville, fetch the mail, and clean out the fireplaces when I get back. Maybe our housekeeper and handyman will show up. We certainly need them."

"I love them," Melanie said. "They're so down-to-earth! I was hoping they'd be here. I haven't seen Hettie or Curly in two years."

"Hopefully, they'll come. I forgot to ask Linda their schedule. There's ample work to be done."

Melanie sat up, clacked her cup in its saucer and quickly stood up. "I hear Tracy coming. I'd know her footsteps anywhere. It's been so nice, just sitting here."

"The honor's been mine," Darby replied. "Let's see what's for breakfast. I'll tell Brandy we're ready."

"Well! Good morning!" Tracy uttered, as the two stepped out of the office. "I see you have an *understudy*," she arched her eyebrows at Darby.

"You are impossible!" Melanie retorted. "Honestly!" she sighed, struggling to let the innuendo slough off.

The two women took seats at the table as Darby notified Brandy of their presence. "Whenever you're ready!" he called back into the kitchen. He smiled and sat in his customary place.

"I do hope the minister's coming down," Tracy opined, glancing over her shoulder into the hallway. "He seems so lost, so lonely. I wonder why he chose this place?"

"Maybe he favors the view," Melanie replied. "Or heard you were coming."

"Well *do* be jealous! And right in front of our host! She isn't always this sarcastic," Tracy frowned at Darby. "You're not having your *monthly visitor*, are you?"

"You are disgusting!" Melanie blushed. "Honestly!" she shook her head. "And we have to play together!" she smiled at Darby. "*Monthly visitor?*"

"Well, I could have said *menstrual cycle*, you know. Or your *red-haired cousin.*"

"Good heavens!" Darby sputtered. "Are you always this pleasant to each other? Who's first violin anyway?"

"I am!" Tracy announced. "Though we do complement each other," the girl finally smiled. "I just love to tease Sis, especially in front of handsome men."

"You are awful, Tracy. You are behaving like an idiot! Seriously!" Melanie smiled toward Darby.

His face couldn't help but beam. He loved Melanie's poise and deep green eyes. So this is how sisters treat each other! "What's in store today, anyway?" he asked.

"Beethoven and Haydn!" Tracy answered. "Mozart tomorrow! We'll be performing twice at the Festival. Once as a chamber group and, toward the end, with an ensemble of others, playing medleys of folk tunes in celebration of the past Sesquicentennial."

"I must come!" Darby stated. "If it isn't too late to buy tickets."

"You'll be fine," Melanie promised. "The sponsors have guaranteed us tickets for family and friends. I will send you one."

Just then the Veleskys and Sanders entered. With good-natured smiles, they took seats. The banter moved in a score of friendly directions. Hot cakes were served, along with fried potatoes, sausage, and syrup. After downing his last bite, Darby rose quietly. "I'll be off this morning for a while, but should be back by noon. Please enjoy yourselves and don't hesitate to ask our chefs for whatever you need."

"Fine!" said Merle. "We've got our work, too. If you're going by the post office, I've a letter I wish you'd mail."

"Will be glad to. Just leave it on the hall table and I'll pick it up on my way out."

"Dr. Peterson, when you return, let's talk some," Sanders looked up. "How muddy is the logging road behind here?"

"Wet and slick. Please, just call me 'Darby.' If you go, keep an eye out for pigs. There're a few wild ones in the area. If you'd care to wait till tomorrow, I'll go with you."

"Thanks! I'll keep that in mind."

Tracy exchanged glances with Melanie, but neither said a word.

* * *

While backing out of the drive, Josh hailed Darby from the kitchen's back door. "Here!" he called, as he hurried toward the car. He handed Darby a grocery list. "Mainly greens. Anything fresh and green! We've got everything else we need."

"OK!" Darby ran his eye down the list. "Should be back around noon or slightly later. See you then."

As he drove along, he wondered how the Wagners had managed to run the Villa, keep its books straight and storehouse stocked without a vacation before now. He knew the Inn was low on wine and possibly household supplies. Any uncertainties he pondered, however, evaporated when, midway down the road, he spotted a food distribution truck whining up the mountain. He slowed his car and lowered his window. As he approached the truck, he leaned out and waved to the driver. The man rolled his window down while shifting into a lower gear. "Check for bathroom supplies!" Darby called.

"Will do!" the driver smiled. "Gottcha!"

When four hours later Darby returned, he was relieved to find the delivery truck gone and Curly and Hettie's pickup parked behind the Villa. The noise from Curly's chainsaw was deafening. Goggled with his cap on backwards, the wiry man was sawing a log into manageable firewood sections. Near the cottage, Sanders was swinging an ax, splitting the circular pieces into kindling and smaller units. A wheelbarrow full of ashes remained to be dumped. Sanders looked up, smiled and mopped a line of sweat from his brow. "You said, 'Noon,'" Sanders relaxed with the ax by his side.

"I know. Sorry."

Curly cut off the chainsaw's motor and eyed Darby in his customary way. "Anythin' to get out of work! Ain't that right, Doc? What's it feel like bein' the chief now? I bet you miss Jon Paul a'ready."

"Linda more! Glad you're here, though. Sure Hettie's busy, too?"

"Yep! We'll be headin' down soon. The weatherman's callin' for another round of ice and snow. Ain't sure which!"

Sanders laid his ax beside a pile of firewood and hunched his shoulders and neck back and forth. "Mr. Curly, I believe I'll empty these ashes, then crash for the day. Where should I take them?"

"That's my secret," Curly smiled. "Actually, I dump 'em outback over a compost pit where asparagus comes up in the spring. Come May, they'll poke their heads up. I appreciate y'ur help."

Sanders removed his work gloves and laid them on the ax handle. He ran his right hand over his forehead and back across his thick patch of blond hair. "My privilege, sir!" He placed both hands on his hips while stretching backwards. "I need to shower," he said to Darby. "Then I need to bend your ear, if you don't mind."

"Once I deliver these groceries," he nodded toward the car, "I'll be out here. By the laurel and azaleas. Come May, they'll be beautiful."

Charles was not long in returning to the Garden. He had dressed in a casual but warm pair of jeans, tan cardigan sweater, light jacket, and hiking shoes. Darby watched as the clergyman approached.

"Beautiful here, isn't it?" Wythe stated as he took a seat beside Darby. "Do you mind if we walk around? I feel peripatetic."

"Not at all! There's a nice path through the orchard to an overlook beyond it. It's one of my favorite walks."

As the two walked toward the orchard, Sanders began: "My bishop sent me up here. At least suggested I come! I'm actually married, with two small boys, but my wife and I separated last year. We agreed I needed space, some time to myself, to rethink my life and ministry. I miss her and the boys, but, Darby—if I may call you that—I was on edge every day, more and more. Becoming more aggressive, easily hurt, and discouraged. To tell you the truth, I wish I were dead, could just die; they'd be better off if I were. Nora—my wife—would receive full survivor's benefits, and she and the boys would make it on their own." He stopped and looked out through the apple limbs toward the distant ridges, gray and white in the sun. "It is beautiful, isn't it? I'm repeating myself, I know."

"Perhaps it's just burnout. I'm sure that's not uncommon."

"Maybe it is burnout. I don't know. But with me it's deeper than that. It's something else. It's like I don't care anymore, because I don't believe it anymore. You know, we're big on *telling the story*. That's the catch phrase now. If you just tell the Story, that's supposed to change things. But if you don't believe the Story to start with, it doesn't matter. Does it?"

Darby listened with hidden remorse. Had he not morphed from a similar background, only Catholic?

"All my ministry I've followed the lectionary every Sunday," Sanders continued. "Whatever the texts are, I've based my homilies on them. We're big on social issues, you know, political flashpoints, inclusiveness, political correctness. But that kind of preaching dulls one's soul after a while. I spend hours crafting my sermons, but to what avail? I hate what I'm doing. Besides, who really needs clergymen anymore, or the Church? We're big on the Trinity! Imagine, believing in a God of three persons, each co-eternal, with Christ fully human and fully divine? I'd rather be doing what Curly's doing."

Darby listened, awash in his own remembrances.

"Darby, the church is all I know. I don't know what else to do. I've become sour. I just want to go away. But where? I want Nora and my children back. But what good would I be to them? Still, here's the odd part," he paused and stopped walking momentarily. "There're times when I'm in my robe, with my stole about my neck, and I glance down and see it bouncing about, just above my shoe tops, and look out into the faces of the members kneeling to receive communion, and I think of Christ's words: '*This is my body, broken for you.*' And I wish I could believe. But what I believe, I'm not sure. I wish I could tell them the truth. That none of us knows what to believe. That we're all in it together! All of us! And the dogma of the church is nothing in comparison with our wounds and doubts. That *that's* who we are! And to hell with the rest!" He expelled a long sigh. They walked a little farther and finally arrived at the overlook. Sunlight dazzled on its rock wall, illuminating the fine granules of quartz and mica that streaked the weathered stone.

"Quite a view! Isn't it?" stated Darby.

"If I may ask," said Sanders, turning toward him, "how did you handle your misgivings when you demitted from the Church? Or so Mrs. Wagner hinted when I called. I don't mean to be nosy or personally improper."

Darby stared out across the mountains and down into its dark coves. The stark scene, with its far-off ridgelines glowing in the cold sunlight, broke across his thoughts with both radiance and sadness. His religious views had gone South long ago, his priesthood ending with them. How could he explain that to Wythe? "It's a long story," he began, "I'm not sure it's worth telling. You really don't demit the priesthood, you just walk away from it once you disavow celibacy, and, of course, sign out so to speak."

"Try me, seriously."

"Well, it goes something like this. I grew up in the mountains in East Tennessee and southwest Virginia. As a child, the 'Nobs—as we called them—terrified me. They symbolized the frightful world of catamounts and bears. Then as I matured, I came to respect them—their shadows, game trails, trickling springs, their summer shade and fall colors. Wherever I wandered, I felt at home. Their spirits spoke to me; comforted me. I camped by their streams, fished in their brooks, and hunted in their woods."

Darby paused as he looked toward the mountains in the distance.

"Go on."

"Well, one day while reading a book on natural theology, I realized that ancient man must have felt similarly; then as he matured, he advanced beyond animism to forms of polytheism and, eventually, to monotheism. That's when he learned to identify the sun, the mother earth, and the sky as One Immortal Mystery: Creator, Protector, and Savior of all. I don't know! Maybe I'm just a mystic, a Vitalist at heart. In any event, as cultures emerged, the religions of the world took shape, especially in India and Buddhist Nepal. But what advanced Christianity in the West were Plato's ideas, those eternal forms, distinct from the world, accessible only to the soul—those perfect patterns that Philo and Augustine placed in the mind of God."

"As a Methodist, I believe that too."

"In any case, after college, I entered a Catholic seminary and for several years served as a priest. Then, I became disillusioned. After that I pursued an academic degree. Now, I look upon religion as a friend, a comforter of hearts and not as a judge. As for the Church, at best, it represents longings for a definitive answer that can never be had. There are no definitive answers, for there's no definitive ground from which to launch them. In truth, Wythe, it's all right to have doubts about the Church and still love it. If a priest or minister came at his task as he should, and sought only to comfort and enlighten people, then religion might be worth practicing. I chose teaching instead. I was lucky, that's all."

"Yours is more than luck." Charles replied. "I'd like to believe that the world is good, but that's a tall order. If I decide while here that I've had enough of it, then I want out. I'd rather be an atheist or a wanderer in your Knobs, or find something better to do."

Darby glanced toward Charles, but remained silent. The afternoon sun had reached its zenith. All around, the woods mirrored its winter glory. A biting wind blew raw across Darby's face and neck. He bit his lower lip and stared across the bare woods and the cliffs below. Quietly, he listened to the soughing of the wind as it passed through the firs and gnarled rhododendron. "Perhaps you might care to pursue this tomorrow?"

"Perhaps. Right now I'm on the ropes and want out of the ring. I'm tired of it, Darby. Just tired and want the emptiness to go away."

* * *

For dinner that evening, the Charleston duo outdid themselves: salmon loaf, bristling with toasted breadcrumbs, steaming under a sauce of whipped cream, diced cucumbers, and lemons, served with tomatoes in wine and wild rice. And for dessert, an egg custard, topped with brown sugar and more cream!

"My goodness!" Aileen groaned when she tasted the dessert. "Absolutely divine! The Wagners would be envious, I assure you," she smiled at Brandy.

"Thank you so much! We love it here."

"And how long do you stay?" asked Merle. "When will Jon Paul and Linda be back?"

"In two weeks, they told us. Around the nineteenth. We're here only for eight-to-nine days. We're just pleased that you like our fare!"

"Like it? Love it, is more like it!" Melanie smiled. "I'm sure I've gained at least three pounds since yesterday."

"If not more!" Tracy interjected.

"You girls are horrible!" Aileen chuckled. "Seriously! Once in Charleston, you have to behave yourselves! You simply must, or we'll never get invited back."

"Provided we do well to start with!" Merle corrected. "We'd best rehearse at least one more selection before retiring."

"May I sit and listen?" asked Wythe, as he glanced at Tracy.

"We would love that!" Melanie answered for her. "Won't you join us, too?" she asked Darby.

"I'd love, too, but I've a pile of mail to sort through and some bills I need to review. And even answer a letter from some folk who want to come next week."

"Sounds like you've already become the new manager," Merle quipped.

"I'm afraid so. More on-the-job training than I bargained for."

"You can handle it," Aileen smiled. "I did want to ask you a few questions, but they can wait. Before she left, Hettie said it's supposed to snow tonight or in the morning. Wouldn't that be beautiful!"

"Please!" moaned her husband. "We've got to get home after tomorrow. One more day and night and that's it. Reverend," he addressed Sanders, "maybe you'd better say a special prayer."

Wythe looked up from his plate, shocked! Darby could feel the man's traumatized reaction. Sanders forced a smile about the edges of his mouth.

"We can all do that!" said Darby. "Besides, it's too cold to snow without sufficient moisture. We'll just have to see what Old Man Winter's got in store. Maybe you should play something from Mussorgsky's *Night on Bald Mountain*. Maybe that might keep the witches engaged."

"I'd love that!" beamed Tracy. "I wouldn't mind getting snowbound with the right people around," she glanced across the table at Charles.

Melanie caught her sister's eyes in the process. "Tracy!" she shook her head. "You're as bad as Mussorgsky's hags." Suddenly, she glanced in turn toward Darby, blushed; then looked away."

"My perfect sister!" Tracy smirked.

Aileen rapped on her water glass with a spoon. "Enough! Come, now! To the living room."

"That's right! Back to the pit, the chamber pit," said Merle.

"Ah, yes! The *chamber*!" Tracy laughed. "If we make it to Spoleto, it'll be a miracle."

"Up, up!" Aileen ordered. "Beethoven's waiting, and it's going to be good."

And good it was! Darby stood by the office door and listened. Their passion brought out every nuance of the composer's suite. With the door open, he walked toward the desk and stared down at the mound of mail he had retrieved at the post office. He sat in Garnett's chair—his chair now— and began sorting through the bills and letters, prioritizing what he'd need to do first. He'd wait another week for Linda's return. If the couple hadn't returned by then, he'd have to contact the CPA, determine what bills needed immediate attention, and request to have himself put on the Villa's checking account. *Garnett, you should have warned me! Prepared me.* He slumped slightly forward in his chair, fighting the temptation to sink into self-pity. No, no! He chided himself. But how he wanted to listen just then to the sisters' violins, Merle's viola, and Aileen's cello! They were playing his favorite suite of Borodin's *Nocturne*. It swept into his soul with intensity, infatuation, and sorrow. How could the composer have captured life, its heart and depth, so powerfully? Spread out like Eliot's patient, numb upon a table.

Chapter 25

M id-way in the night, the sound of ice pelting against the Villa's windows awakened Darby. He rose and pulled back the curtain in Garnett's bedroom. The glistening precipitation created a crackling drone against the panes. He could see the sleet in the lamplight by the outbuildings. An inch or more already covered the patio, its driveway, the cottage roof, and the Garden area.

He glanced at his watch. Three-thirty a.m. He was about to return to bed when he noticed the office phone's red message light blinking. He hadn't remembered hearing it ring, nor had he noticed it before retiring to bed. He pulled on a night robe and made his way to the phone. Darby picked up the receiver and pressed the "message" button. It was Linda's voice:

"*Darby*," her voice muffled in a whisper. "*Delete this message once you've heard it. I can't speak any louder. I'm on my cell in a restaurant in Phoenix in the bathroom. Call our attorney and bank and have your name added to the Villa's checkbook. You'll find it in the bottom of the file cabinet near the window. At the rate JPs going, he'll max our credit card soon. Knowing him, he'll start on the Villa's next. He's spending way too much. He won't say it, but I know he wants you out of the will and out of the Villa. He's going to have it contested. He's been passive-aggressive all day, ever since we got here. I'm so sorry all this is happening. Give us another week or ten days. I'll take care of any management problems when I get home. Guard your back. JP's up to something, but I don't know what. I love you, Gotta go!*" her voice ended abruptly.

Darby pressed "one" to repeat the message. He sat at the desk, opened the drawer and slipped out the credit card. He'd have to call Sheratt's office. He'd know what to do. In the meanwhile, he turned the card over and wondered if he should call the twenty-four-hour eight-hundred number. An English-speaking Asian came online, a young woman. "Yes, I need the balance on our business card. Can you do that? Yes, I'm the manager and co-owner of the business. Yes. The Villa Montesereno! Visa! The number is . . . ; the code on the back is . . ." Slowly Darby read the numbers, plus the

expiration date. "Good! Excellent! Thank you! Yes! A good-day to you, too."
He should have asked her location. Probably Bangladesh! The Philippines!
Or Mumbai! Who knew? At least he felt better. The balance owed was neg-
ligible and the credit line close to $10,000.

He sat back and rubbed his face with his hands. The sleet made a
pleasant sound, tugging and lulling him back to bed, whispering its lullaby
of sleep. But how could he? He had come to serve as a host to befriend
and stimulate Garnett's guests—the healthy as well as depressed. But what
now! Co-owner and manager, with no background to pull it off! And an . . .
adulterer . . . to boot! He held his hands out in the dim light; they were trembling slightly. His dream was to write books, especially *From Wittenberg to
Weimar*, a true exploration of that unique timeframe—*from the rebirth of
Luther's God to the death of God in Nietzsche.* Or something even better! Had
not Garnett chosen him to entertain the Villa's guests with his philosophical
banter and upbeat anecdotes? To listen to their fears and infirmities without
passing judgment? To be a facet of their therapy; not a hindrance? He felt
sick on his stomach, if not ashamed. Linda would be back; so also Jon Paul.
He would have to regroup and do what he could. Montesereno was too valuable an asset to allow personal vicissitudes to destroy its place in the sun. He
dropped the card back in the drawer and returned to bed.

At six a.m., he aroused again. He peered out the window to discover
that only a light fluffy glaze of snow encrusted the night's finer layer of sleet.
Too dark to see the dawn, stars twinkled in the winter's cold black sky. At
least, it would not snow again. That should please the Veleskys and facilitate
their departure. He thought of Melanie and smiled. She seemed so pluperfect in every pluperfect way! He expelled his usual sigh. He had enough pluperfect worries of his own to worry about anyone else's pluperfect problems.

At breakfast, everyone save Merle expressed delight over the snowfall.

"It's so clean and crisp. Look, not a footprint to mar its beauty!" Tracy
observed from the dining room window.

"Like white frosting on a vanilla cake!" Brandy cooed. "We rarely, if
ever, have snow in Charleston. And when we do, it never sticks."

Josh had come into the dining room, too. Dressed in blue jeans and
frayed sneakers, a tall white chef's hat and a white starched double-breasted
chef's jacket, he smiled and uttered the momentous word: "Cool!" He gave
Tracy a peck on the cheek. "How would everyone like a Charleston spice
cake with sea-foam icing on it? I feel inspired! Man, I do. I can have it ready
by dinner. This is awesome. Really!" he reiterated, as he glanced out the
window. "Absolutely!"

"Will that give you enough time for the icing to stiffen?" Aileen
questioned.

"Not a problem!" Josh fired back. "It'll be moist, warm, and delicious. Just leave it to me."

"Well! It's to the living room by nine!" Merle stated, glancing at his wristwatch. "We'll break after lunch and tromp around outside, if it's not too icy. Are the roads ever cleared up here after a storm?"

"Yes, and no!" replied Darby. "It takes a day or two for the road crews to get up here, and we're not always their first priority. But they came on Christmas Day. Chances are, you'll make it home tomorrow. I'll take a walk in a while and see how extensive the storm was. Sometimes, we only get grazed by the ice, and the rest of the mountain receives but a dusting."

"Save some walk time for me," Tracy requested, with a restive glance toward Wythe. "Sitting erect with a violin under your chin all day's no joy. I'd covet such a break."

Melanie winced slightly but looked straight into Darby's eyes. "I'd love to walk down that logging road and admire the snow, too. It looked so beautiful, so restful, from my upstairs window."

"It's a great walk. If you'd like company, I'll wait and go with you," Darby offered. "I've got plenty to keep me busy until then."

"All right!" Merle announced. "The living room by nine! I'll see you there," he addressed his wife and the two sisters. "Nine, promptly!"

* * *

By mid-morning, Darby had attended to the Villa's most pressing problems and had received assurances from Sheratt and the bank that he was fully authorized to sign checks. There remained one other item on his desk—a letter from a woman in Knoxville, eager to bring her daughter to the Inn for a three-day rest. Darby read the letter in silence:

Dear Management:

My daughter, Harriett, is twenty-two and recovering from her eleventh cleft-palate surgery. She is so depressed, more so than ever. Since birth we have all had to suffer with her. Her disfigurement has not abated significantly since childhood, and each successive operation has only exacerbated her self-consciousness. It has truly added to her sense of public embarrassment. Her doctors have suggested she get away for a while, free of family, friends, and others, who, in spite of themselves, are often repulsed by her looks, though as family we don't mean to. It is just so hard to hide. She feels so rejected. Please register us for two rooms, the nights of the 11th and 12th of this month. She likes to have her own. Please advise any staff to treat her like anyone else. We have learned the hard way not to overindulge her. That has only deepened her feelings of rejection. Below you will find my phone number. I apologize for such a short notice. We look forward to spending these days with you at Montesereno. Sincerely, Evelyn Corsey Mays

Darby picked up the receiver, called Mrs. Mays, waited for the dial tone but ended up having to leave his message on voice mail. "This is the Villa Montesereno. We shall look forward to your arrival on the 11th and are confirming your request for two rooms. Thank you for choosing Montesereno." Darby hung up, pulled on his coat and cap and wandered outside. A bitter breeze slapped him in the face. The wind blowing off the icy surface of the snow-covered glistening sleet made any outdoor hike unlikely. The sunlight flooded the frozen surface with a brilliant glare, turning the icy ground into a gleaming lake of sparkling wonder. Crunching through the snow would be exhilarating, but was it too cold? The challenge beckoned his sense of manhood. Still, was it advisable? He could see sharp prints in the ice where deer had fed earlier on the sedges and lower branches in the orchard. Hopefully they wouldn't start on the azaleas! He inhaled a breath of stinging air and let it out slip out warm through his lips. He would have to let the "girls" decide if they were up for such a jaunt. He was about to reenter when he noticed someone sliding along on the road past the orchard. The figure seemed to be skating on the ice, holding his arms out for balance. It was Charles Wythe, bundled in a mound of padded coats with a toboggan cap pulled over his ears. The clergyman saw Darby and waved his arms. With his head tucked low into the wind, he began trudging toward the gate. Darby kicked the ice off his shoes and stepped back into the house. The string quartet was still at it, but Darby didn't recognize the suite they were practicing. He hung up his coat and wandered into the office. The front door opened and footsteps resounded along the hall. Moments later Charles appeared at the door. He removed his cap, unbuttoned his coat, and sank into the sofa by the desk.

"Oh, that was great! Cold. I mean cold! But it's what I needed." He removed his coat and ran his hands through his tussled hair. "You seem very sedate," he stated. "I guess running this place isn't all that fun."

"I've been occupied," Darby replied.

"I've been thinking about our conversation yesterday. I keep vacillating between euphoria and depression. Euphoria at the thought of leaving the ministry; depression at the thought of what happens afterwards. I've crossed the threshold where you can't go back. You just go on. Is that how you felt when you left the priesthood?"

Darby sat forward and picked up a paperclip to turn in his fingers. "Sort of like a worry bead!" he held it up and smiled. "You know the Greeks are big on these things." He dropped it back on the desk. "Students would sometimes ask me why I wasn't an atheist. They couldn't imagine how I could teach philosophy—above all lecture on Nietzsche and Hume—and still take religion seriously." He expelled a quiet sigh. "I look at it this way. If God exists, God exceeds anything our minds are capable of seizing. And that's true of every religion. They're all tainted with cultural and linguistic limitations. And just enough contentment to leave it at that!"

"No wonder you left the priesthood. I would have, too, if I felt that way. I never studied philosophy in depth. What philosophy I gleaned, I picked up as it pertained to theology."

"If you can forbear for a while, let me try something. Are you familiar with Tillich, or his Augustinian interpretation of the philosophy of religion?"

"Actually, no."

Darby stood up momentarily and walked toward the window. He glanced out, then returned and sat down. "According to Tillich, who was a Protestant theologian, there are only two ways of coming at God. One, he calls the Aristotelian, or Thomist—named for Aristotle and Thomas Aquinas; the other, Augustinian—named for Augustine and his Neo-Platonic leanings. In the first, God is a phenomenon *outside* ourselves and the universe. That means his existence has to be proven. The second, posits God as *something within ourselves*, whose presence we already sense. The first method has to demonstrate that God exists and possesses the attributes we assign God, you know—all-knowing, all-good, all-wise, all-loving. The second is already aware of these attributes, so that whenever we experience any gradations of truth and goodness, we're already experiencing the mystery of God. Good Catholic theologians acknowledge the same. I know that doesn't quite answer the question the way you want it. Nor was it enough to keep me in the priesthood, but atheism is another thing."

Sanders moved uneasily on the sofa. He sat a little more erect and stared out the window. A pair of cardinals was just then flitting from bush to bush about the urns. The birds' bright red feathers compelled Darby to glance past the cardinals and the urns' shadows that crisscrossed the snow. It was a moment of single clarity.

"You're about as helpful as Satan on a godless day!" Charles muttered. "It is beautiful, isn't it?" he smiled, as he stared out the window with Darby. "There aren't any easy answers, are there?"

"Unfortunately, not!"

* * *

Soon after the noonday buffet, Tracy and Melanie knocked on Darby's door.

"Aren't you forgetting something?" Tracy queried. "Like, our hike!" she smiled. "We're game and ready," Melanie added.

Both women had donned coats, scarves, gloves, and knee-high boots. Darby rose and returned their smile.

"Well? Are we or aren't we?" Tracy repeated. She looked over her shoulder into the hallway. "Is Charles coming?" she feigned a pout.

"We'll have to find out. But I warn you; it's cold. Are you sure you want to brave it?"

"Yes!" Tracy carped. "Why not?"

Just then Sanders came to the door. "I haven't forgotten our promise," he eyed Tracy. "But it's *bitter*. And I mean, bitter!" He too was dressed for the hike. "What do you say, Darby? We could all use the exercise."

"Please, Darby! Come with us!" Melanie pleaded. "If only for half an hour!"

Darby studied her face, eyes, and smile. "OK! But don't say I didn't warn you. Incidentally, there are skis and sleds in the shed out back, if you're interested. I'll bundle up and join you."

"We'll see you outside, then," Charles replied.

Twenty minutes later, the four stood huddled and laughing at the top of the logging road. Charles and Tracy had selected a sled, Melanie and Darby ski poles.

"Come on, Granny, we'll race you downhill!" Tracy called back as she and Charles shoved off and scooted down the frozen path.

"How she galls me!" Melanie bristled. "She knows my trigger points like the back of her hand! My sister! I hope she crashes into a tree!"

"Don't say that! They'd freeze to death before we could drag them out."

"You know I don't mean it," she turned and smiled at Darby. She put her left arm in the crook of his right. "You don't mind, do you? I can't afford to break my bow arm," she locked herself in place with a gentle squeeze. "I haven't walked in snow for years. The woods are so bright and beautiful! You must love it up here?"

"I do. But it does grow lonely from time to time. The truth is, I stay so busy I can't get any of the writing projects going I want to. Not that it would make a difference if I don't."

"Now don't talk like that! You're sounding like me. I noticed two of your books in the living room—the novel set at sea and the one in Paris. I read the first eight chapters of the Paris story last night." She stopped and leaned into his body. "Is any of that true? I mean, the love scenes and all the visits to the Louvre, cafes, and gardens? I couldn't put it down. I hope to finish it tonight," she resumed trudging beside Darby. "Is it? I mean, how could anyone make that up? It's all so real. I won't tell anybody if it is."

"Some is and some isn't. My wife and I studied in Paris for two years. Afterwards, we rented a car and drove about France and down into Spain. The gossip in the *pension* is pretty much as it was. The sex scenes," Darby looked down at her as he clutched her arm, "are maybe a little exaggerated. After all, it is a novel."

"I wish I could experience what your Christine enjoyed. They came so close to falling in love. Their intimacy together, I mean their sex! Single women long for that. At least once! Was that part real? I'd love to know," she slipped, falling against his arm while struggling with her ski pole to stay aright. "Darby, can we stop here?" she looked into his eyes. "I won't tell anybody, I promise." She steadied herself against his shoulder and reached up and touched his cheek. Her lips were full, purple, and waiting.

Darby thought of Dianne! Celeste! Of Linda! Linda would be back soon. Maybe there was a future with her. He didn't know. He hadn't planned on this, especially not sex with the Villa's clients. Holy Mother of God! What kind of host was he? He felt guilty, cheap. He looked down into Melanie's eyes and full lips. She was ripe for love! Even if younger than he! How could she have gone this long without some male wanting her? He leaned down. Just as he did, she pressed her lips to his, then placed her arm about his waist and smiled.

"Holy Mother of God!" he whispered. Their lips touched again.

"Oh, God! I've wet my pants!" she laughed. "I just felt a warm gush between my legs. Let's do that again."

They turned toward each other.

"Shall we walk on or walk back?" he whispered. He could feel her heart beating through her coat.

Melanie looked around, to her right, past Darby, and over her shoulder. "Nobody's following us," she said uneasily.

He could feel her body trembling next to his.

"What do you think," she smiled awkwardly, unable to take her eyes off his.

For the next ten or fifteen minutes they struggled on, holding hands and leaning into the ski poles for support. They could see the sled's tracks in front of them, where its riders had fallen off but gotten back on. "They must be having fun," Melanie observed in a quiet voice. Suddenly she stopped and looked up at Darby. "Where? Where would we go? I may never have this opportunity again," she spoke softly. "Everything inside me's tingling. Have you ever felt that way?"

"Yes."

"Could we go back to the cottage? We'd be alone." She looked up again, her cheeks and lips burning red. "I've never done it before," her voice quivered with excitement. "Christine seemed to know what to do."

"Well, that was in a novel. We can just walk on. I am supposed to be the host."

"You're not helping, you know," she muttered in a trance-like moan. She swallowed the lump in her throat and began trembling again. "Please! Please take me, Darby. Let's go back. Please!"

When forty-minutes later they slipped into the cottage, Darby could feel Melanie's heart thump across her entire upper chest as he slipped off her brassiere and pulled it over her head. Her D-cup breasts spilled into his hands. He kissed each in turn, as she watched, uncertain what to do. With an excited blush, she pulled down her panties and lay back on the bed. Her eyes followed his every move as he undressed in turn.

"I'm not sure what to do," she whispered. "What do I do?"

"Just lie back and let me kiss your legs and breasts. You'll know what to do."

Soon, she spread her legs, and, with fumbling fingers, guided his hard manhood into her soft, wet chamber. "O, Oh, O!" she clung to him. "O, Oh!"

Twenty minutes later, relaxed, dressed, yet still excited, Melanie turned and peered out the window. All was quiet about the back shed. Tiny snowflakes were falling again. Then, figures appeared on the logging road. "O Lord! They're coming back! They look exhausted. Can we slip out of here, unseen?"

"There's a rear door. It exits by the orchard. Come, we'll go that way."

Melanie pulled on her coat and wraps. "Thank you!" she kissed him. "I'm still trembling. O God!" she hugged him.

"You're blushing," he said.

"So are you! I hope Tracy sees me and eats her heart out! The imp! At last, I'm one up on her!" She kissed Darby as they went out the door. As they ran toward the orchard she clasped Darby's gloved hand. "Wait! Wait up!" she stopped to catch her breath. "What if I don't want this to end? What if I want to come back?"

He caught her hand and held it. His heart raced in his chest; he felt as exhilarated as she. "Girl! You're too young. How old are you?"

"Thirty-five! I've always looked younger than I am. Darby, please! I feel so happy. So absolutely happy!" She all but threw herself in his arms. "Darby, you make me so happy, I'm going to cry."

"God woman! You're just supposed to be here as part of a chamber quartet. Come! Hurry!"

They ran up into the orchard before pausing and turning back. "Happy?" Thought Darby. "You're happy! And I? I guess I'm happy too," though he kept the thought to himself. He smiled at her, as he inhaled a deep breath. "Smell that?"

"Smell what?"

"That wonderful aroma! It's Josh's cake! We'll have it with champagne tonight. It'll be our secret. Just for us, unless your sister finds out."

"Let her! I've longed for this day all my life. Just to hold hands and be happy! Not even she can take that from me." She kissed Darby as they stumbled through the snow toward the Garden.

Chapter 26

The Swiss steak Brandy and Josh served that evening dissolved at the touch of a fork. Josh had obviously pounded the ground steak into tender filets before rolling them in peppered flour and stewing them with green peppers and onions. His side dish consisted of buttered carrots and a lime Jell-O salad. The savory meat fell apart in creamy bite-size morsels. It exceeded anything Darby had expected of the young couple.

"O my stars, Brandy, what I would give to cook like this!" Aileen exclaimed. "I must have you cater a dinner for us when we come for Spoleto."

"We can do that!" Brandy flashed her eyes with a smile. "There's a restaurant off Bay Street that hires us on the weekends and lets us do parties in their private dining room. We'd love to."

"Just leave us your card!" said Merle. "I certainly echo Aileen's thought."

"Speaking of echoes, Charles and I never heard a peep from you guys," Tracy addressed her sister. "But I did see where two sets of footprints entered the cottage with none coming out!"

"Oh! Did you? Isn't that something?" Melanie smiled with a triumphant gleam in her eyes. "Maybe you missed your calling! No?"

"Please!" Aileen objected. "You're worse than our own daughters. Thank heavens they're married and on their own!"

Tracy was about to respond when she caught Charles' eye. She blushed and dabbed her napkin to her lips. "Well, maybe as sisters we have similar *callings*," she pronounced with a guarded smile.

Charles glanced toward Darby, then down at his plate. "Are you performing for us?" he asked Merle. "A sort of dress rehearsal?"

"We are! Provided we stop eating soon. I won't be able to get my chin across my viola rest. Maybe we can save dessert for later."

"Can do!" Brandy replied, as she scurried about, refilling water glasses. "Wait till you see Josh's cake! I applied the icing, in case you fall into it."

"Well, I've been smelling it all afternoon," Merle confessed. "Incidentally, have any of you been up on the road? Guess what? Our storm stopped right past the gates. Yes! All this side of the mountain is covered. But the ice

176

never made it across the top. Just a little smattering of snow here and there. It's almost clear. We'll have no trouble departing in the morning. Isn't that great?" he expostulated with joy.

The two sisters looked horrified. Disappointment slipped indelibly into each woman's face. Tracy looked across the table at Charles, then toward Darby. Melanie moved uneasily in her chair and sank back in reflection.

"We can pack as soon as our rehearsal's over!" Aileen suggested. "That should save a lot of time tomorrow."

"Not until we have our cake!" Merle objected. "Just the instruments. We're not in that huge a hurry to vacate this charming Inn. No?"

"Agreed!" Tracy said sadly. "What a wonderful respite this has been!"

"For me, too." Charles added softly. "I'll be staying another day. I'll surely miss your company. All of you!" he turned toward each member of the quartet. "I needed this time to myself; you've made it all the more reassuring. I'll not forget this, nor you," his gaze returned to Tracy.

Everyone sat quietly.

"OK! Time to move!" Merle broke the silence. "Let's take a quick break, then reassemble in the living room to show our hosts how grateful we are."

* * *

Once Charles, Josh, Brandy, and Darby had taken seats in the living room, Merle raised his bow, and, nodding to his quartet partners, led the players with intensity into Debussy's "Scherzo" from the composer's Opus 10. Darby recognized the piece's modernistic tempo and dissonant notes, hardly his favorite. He fell into a stupor until the suite ended. The four listeners responded with polite applause. The quartet noisily turned pages to their next piece. What followed more than compensated for their technically perfect opening. With exuberance and expressiveness, they played selections from Haydn, Mozart, and Beethoven. At Darby's request, they performed Borodin's *Nocturne*; then concluded with a medley of their forthcoming selections for Spoleto. All four dropped their bows to their laps and bowed their heads with pleasing smiles. Darby and the others rose quickly to their feet to provide a loud ovation of eight, clapping hands.

Melanie sat drained, momentarily emotionless, still cradling her violin in the crook of her left arm. Darby placed his hand over hers and kissed her cheek. He also kissed Aileen's and Tracy's. "I'll never forget this," he smiled. "Whenever I hear Haydn or Mozart again, I'll think of you; all four of you."

"The pleasure was ours," Merle said. He stood up, replaced his viola in its case, and mopped his forehead with the handkerchief he had used to protect his chin.

"To the table, Messieurs Dames!" Josh announced from the hallway. "*Notre fete de bon appetit commence!*"

With an outburst of "Oooohs!" and "Ahhhs!" the guests moved noisily into the dining room.

"Would you look at that!" muttered Merle.

There in the center of the table, on an elegant Bavarian dish, set Josh's spice cake, topped with layers of Brandy's sea-foam icing, with bottles and flutes of champagne beside it. Matching dessert plates and silverware accompanied the cake.

"Come!" Brandy beamed, as she sliced each a wedge of light brown cake and laid it gently on their plate.

Darby popped the corks on the two bottles of champagne and poured each a flute full. "By the way," Darby asked Merle, "what were those Mozart pieces you were playing, after the Debussy one? I loved them all."

"Haydn's No. 67 in F major, Mozart's No. 14 in G, and Beethoven's No. 7 in F major. They thrill even us time after time."

"I should say so!"

The party moved back into the living room to enjoy dessert. After downing her cake as politely as she could, Melanie caught Darby's eye and returned to the dining room for him to fill her glass a second time. As he did, she caressed his fingers with the tips of her own. "Can we slip into your office after this?" she gazed into his eyes.

"That's kind of risky, isn't it?"

Melanie glanced over her shoulder, past his, and sipped from her drink. "I'll just mosey that way after thanking Brandy," she took a second sip.

"OK! I may need to go down to the cellar for a few more bottles. Why not come with me?"

"I'll wait in the office," she studied his eyes. "I'll get another drink and just look around at the books."

Minutes later Darby found her relaxed, cuddled up on his office's sofa, barely griping her champagne flute by its stem. "One more of these and I'd be wasted," she looked up as he walked in. An air of melancholy played about the corners of her mouth.

Darby stepped over to the sofa, bent forward and kissed her. "It's been a tiring three days, hasn't it?"

"Emotional, is more like it! Mercurial! Do you still want me," she explored his eyes. "I want you. I guess that's obvious?"

"It's mutual!" he ran his right hand across her breasts. "I'm not getting any younger, you know."

"Darby, I want to get pregnant," she looked up at him, as she propped herself on her elbows. "I'd love another glass of champagne; then I want you to get me pregnant." Suddenly, she sat up. "You think I'm drunk, don't you? I'm not!" she lay back, handing him her glass.

"Melanie! Goodness! Wait till the others have gone to bed. But, pregnancy?" he shook his head. "We can't risk that."

"How do you know? I'm thirty-five, remember? I don't want a deformed child. Do you?"

He stared at her, bemused and shocked. "Listen," he took her hand as he sat beside her. "Love is a serious thing! You know, it's not something you just fall into, like into a river, and never surface again. A lot goes on once you come up for air. You'd be wonderful, but, at least, give it another week!" he kissed her with a smile from ear to ear. "I might get fired if I rush into this too soon." He could tell she was drained, emotionally and physically, and if not tipsy, close to it. "We'll be OK! What do you say?"

"Help me sit up!" she stated with slurred speech. "I'm sober, I tell you. If you don't get me pregnant, who will?"

"Give me a little time. Rest this off and we'll talk in the morning."

"I don't want morning to come," she replied with deadpan effect. "Seriously!" she put her arms around his neck. "Just a little bit right here," she spread her legs.

Darby couldn't help but laugh. "Melanie, there's no such thing as 'a little bit.' It's all or nothing. That's how a guy functions. He can't help it. We've got a lot to learn, you and me. You'll love it. I promise."

She tucked her chin and burped quietly. "Ugghhh! I could taste that," she gulped. "God, but I'm dizzy. That champagne went right to my ass. Shhhh! Just let me sleep here. OK?"

Darby wrapped both arms about her waist and let her collapse back gently onto the sofa. He placed a pillow under her head, picked up her legs, scooted them onto the sofa, and wedged them with another pillow. He covered her with a quilt on the back of the couch, tucked it about her shoulders and breasts, and kissed her. He stared at her sleeping form, her eyes, lips, and brow. He knelt beside her, put her left hand in his, and kissed it. What if he were *to let her* into his life the way Adam let Eve in? She'd make one hell of a precious stand-in, wouldn't she? He leaned in closer and gripped her hand. *Abba, Father, if only it were possible* . . . He paused and stared down at her again. He sat back, exhaled a long breath, and lay on the floor beside her.

Chapter 27

With the departure of Melanie and the members of the quartet, Darby's thoughts turned to the upcoming visit of Mrs. Mays and her daughter, Harriett.

"Brandy," he called to the young girl, "There'll be two guests arriving here this afternoon. Hettie and Curly should arrive, too. They'll be a huge help with all the laundry, dust, and ashes we've got to cart out."

"Thank heavens you remembered! Josh says we're out of fresh salad again. How in the world do you guys manage up here? No grocery store, no Wal-Mart, no mail delivery? Primitive! This is the twenty-first century. Hasn't the news gotten here yet?" she smirked with pretend insolence and the flick of her long black hair.

"Look, I know. Why don't you and Josh take off for the rest of the morning and shop for us? I'll give you the Villa's credit card, and you can stop by the post office on the way back and pick up the mail. They'll let you have it if you show them the card. Even Curly picks it up sometimes. Wythe and I can take care of ourselves. Just be back in time for the dinner guests. OK?"

"Sure! We can do that! As long as the road's not slick. We're not used to driving on snow."

"If the Veleskys made it out of here, so can you. Go on, now! We'll be fine."

"All right! But I'll make you and Charles sandwiches before we leave. There's plenty of cold beer and cokes in the refrigerator."

"Thanks. That would be perfect."

"Yes! It's really wonderful here. Snow, ice, sun, and all! We'll be back by three."

As the morning wore by, Darby welcomed Hettie and Curly's return. As for himself, he slipped into the office. Wythe would have to take care of himself. Darby rummaged about searching for the reservation log in the event future guests should arrive before Linda and Jon Paul returned. He found the log and made a mental note of pre-registered guests. Linda had not attached any addenda beside their names. Hopefully that signified "nor-mal" clients simply seeking a mountain getaway.

While still perusing the log, the office phone rang. Not expecting the call, Darby halfway jumped as he dropped the reservations book to the floor. He bent over, picked it up, and hurried to the phone. "Yes? Hello! The Montesereno Villa speaking."

"No, Darby! Not the Montesereno Villa, but you!" Linda's voice caught him off-guard. "It's so good to hear you."

"How are you? Where are you? You didn't train me enough. I'm having to do it all!"

"Please! Listen! We'll be leaving here Thursday. We should be home by eleven. Late, but home! I'm so tired, Darby. I just want to crash and give you a huge hug."

Darby could sense the fatigue in her voice along with the excitement in the word *hug*. How could he tell her about Melanie? What would her reaction be? "I'll wait up for you if you'd like. I'll have a glass of wine ready, or whatever you and Jon Paul want. Incidentally, the chef kids have been superb. You couldn't have chosen a finer couple."

A silence met his last words. Darby waited for Linda's reply. "Are you there? Are you Ok? Linda, tell me the truth. What's going on?"

"I'm worn out. I've picked up a rash. It itches all the time. As for JP, his mood swings come and go. I don't think he wants to come home. I don't think he knows what he wants. He's been sweeter the last few days, but he's still cross. Maybe we'll keep the 'kids,' as you call them, a week or so longer, until we can settle back in. I'm just sad, Darby. We need a long ride together. I miss you. Two weeks away have been two weeks too long."

"I know. We're having some guests from Tennessee who called unex-pectedly. They'll arrive later today. But we're ready for them."

"Well, don't fall in love with anyone. I know how women love to chat with you. Like Dianne and Celeste! You will be a good boy, promise? Yes? You will?"

"Yes! I'll try."

"Darby! You've lost it, haven't you? Which one was it? Aileen? Tracy? Her sister? I can hear it in your voice!" Her anxiety was unmistakable. It sank heavily into Darby's chest, burning its way painfully into his esophagus.

"Please; don't worry!" he mumbled.

"O Darby! I wish I had never left!"

A long silence ensued on his part.

"Can we talk about it, at least?" she whispered.

"Of course! You're still number one."

"Darby!" she blurted. "'Number One! Darby, I want to be the *only one*! That's what I'm trying to say."

"Linda! You know I love you. Hurry home."

"Darby! I'm going to cry now. Good-bye! Thursday night." The phone clicked. She had hung up.

Darby expelled a loud sigh and slumped in the sofa. He ran his hands along the couch where Melanie had lain on her side. One of the pillows still retained the faint impression of her face. He stretched out on the pillow and let his mind drift.

At lunchtime, he bundled up and walked outside, munching on a ham sandwich Brandy had prepared. A beer poked out of his left coat pocket. Spotting Sanders in the Garden, he wandered toward him and sat down.

"Damn good sandwich, isn't it?" Sanders said. "Where'd you get the beer?"

"In the refrigerator. You can have this one. I'll get another later." Darby twisted off the cap and handed it to Charles. "You know the one thing that epitomizes you clerics is your eternal sense of entitlement. You know that? I'm serious," he smiled.

Wythe looked at him, stunned. "Well, you did offer! You did, didn't you?"

"Of course, enjoy it!"

As the two crunched through the lettuce, ham, and bread, Wythe took a long draught of beer, wiped his mouth with his coat sleeve, and paused. "You know, Darby, my father was a cabinet maker, and so also my uncle. Dad's dead, but not my uncle. I used to work in his shop when I was a kid. I saved a lot of money for college that way." He took another drink and a bite out of his sandwich. "He's still alive, still making furniture. And you know what? Before I came up here, he asked me to join him." Charles held his sandwich in the fingers of his left hand and turned the beer about in the other to take one last swallow. "He makes customized pieces: china cabinets, dressers, tables, chairs, you name it. Got lots of clients, too." He turned and stared at Darby. "I guess you know where this conversation's leading?"

"I think I do." A draft of cold air ruffled Darby's collar, as the bright sunlight transfigured the snowy woods into a blinding glare.

"Shall I say it or you?"

Darby smiled and nodded his head for Wythe to continue.

"I'm going back. I'm going to take him up on his offer. Hammers and wood you can see. Finished products as well! Lots of satisfaction in running your hands over polished tabletops, corner cabinets, and lathe-turned lamps. The only thing you have to do is wait for the stain or varnish to dry."

He finished his sandwich. "Let me bring you a beer and let's sit here a while longer."

"OK! The sun's quite warm now. A beer'll taste good," Darby stared up through the bare tree limbs and out toward the orchard.

While Darby waited for Charles to return, he stood up and walked toward the clearing at the head of the logging road. Yesterday's footprints were still visible, though their soft edges had melted and settled into a gray mush. The prints had turned purple, thanks to the forest's long shadows and the sun's slanting rays. What if Plato had not *let* Socrates *into* his life, or Marcus Aurelius, the Stoic ideal; or Saint Francis the eyes and sores of the poor? What if Kant had never allowed Hume's essays to arouse him from his dogmatic slumbers, or Hegel had discarded the notion of *Zeitgeist*, or Nietzsche had laughed at the nihilistic ramblings of *Zarathustra*? What if none had ever let their ideas in? Darby stared down the road. He thought of Melanie; then of Charles. It was Sanders' life. Not his! It was Wythe's choice. Hadn't he made his own when he chose philosophy over the priesthood, and, later, over Julia? What sort of a bigot was he?

Darby walked back to the Garden, sat down, and waited for Wythe to return. For whatever reason, however, Charles failed to show. After enduring a prolonged wait in the now stinging cold, Darby rose and returned to the house and his study.

*   *   *

When the Mays arrived, Brandy must have noticed them, Darby concluded, through one of the dining room windows, as she shouted: "They're here! A rather attractive lady and, well, a somewhat despondent passenger! You'd better go out and help them," she muttered as he came out into the hall where she was standing. "Here are the receipts. I'll see you at dinner." She patted her hand across her mouth before returning to the kitchen.

Darby opened the front door and stepped out onto the Villa's narrow porch. Mrs. Mays had parked her car behind Sanders'. Snow and ice still covered his, its windshield, hood and trunk. The Mays' car, however, bore the messy streaks of salt and highway spray. Mrs. Mays struggled toward him, the weight of her large brown vinyl suitcase more than she could bear. Harriett followed, face down, slipping along the icy path that Curly had cleaned. The mother glanced up and smiled. Gray hair poked out from under a tight pink scarf. Her eyes and cheeks, lips and chin, glowed with freshness, in spite of the vertical grooves that witnessed to a life of stress. Harriett looked up just then, her thin face titled sideways to reveal her right cheek, lower lip and small chin, concealing her cleft lip and left side. She wore a long tan coat and burgundy beret. Her eyes burned into Darby's as if pleading: *Please, please like me! Please don't find me ugly!*

Darby smiled and stepped down to help. He gave each a hug. "Welcome to Montesereno. We've been looking forward to your visit. We'll register; then I'll show you to your rooms. You did want two? Yes?"

"Yes!" the young woman stated, turning her face fully for Darby to see. She set her suitcase down as they entered the hall. She slipped off her beret and shook out a long full head of shiny red hair. It fell in glossy strands past her shoulder blades, indeed, past her breasts. A cruel red scar with ugly white tissue marred her smile. It cut across her mouth from below her nose to just under her upper lip. "I'm still undergoing surgery," she mumbled with a nasal tone. "It's not pretty, is it? Nor my speech?"

"On the contrary, it's coming along! Both of them!" Darby answered. "There's an old Gullah saying: 'A boy's just a boy and that's that!' Or 'a lips just a lip, and that's all. Just a lip,'" he picked up her bag, along with her mother's. "This way!" he smiled. "You'll enjoy the view."

About that time, Sanders entered the hallway from the back. His mouth fell somewhat open upon seeing the guests. He slid off his cap and took the girl's suitcase from Darby's left hand. "Allow me," he said, as he eyed the girl. "My name's Charles. Charles Wythe Sanders! The food's unbelievable and the vistas equally great. I can vouch for both."

"Thank you," the girl replied. "I'm Harriett Mays and this is my mother. Thanks for making us feel welcome."

After showing the women their rooms, Darby returned downstairs to find Wythe in the Villa's office, seated in the sofa, with his feet propped up on the desk.

"That was gracious of you to greet the daughter that way. You were decent to do so."

"Don't thank me!" he said, removing his feet. "Something inside insisted I do it. It just came natural to do."

That evening Josh and Brandy served a pork loin, rubbed with mild herbs, baked to a delectable tenderness, preceded by a cold salad of sliced cucumbers in vinegar, with a platter of mixed vegetables to accompany the entrée. A white wine from the Saumur region of France supplemented the meal with its own *gout de la résistance parfaite!*

"I see what you mean about the cuisine!" Evelyn complimented Brandy.

The two chefs had come in and, at Darby's insistence, were seated with them.

"We try our best!" the girl replied with a proud jerk of her head and wink toward Joshua. "We're going to miss here, too."

"Oh! You're not staying? How sad! You must be bound for some five star resort!"

"No! School! We're just temporary," Josh stated, "till the real chef and hostess return."

Mrs. Mays turned toward Darby. "You mean it gets better?"

"Not really! Josh and Brandy have been perfect. But the Wagners—our chef and his wife—are on vacation and won't return till the end of the week. Or perhaps even later! You'll have to come back when they're here."

"I can't imagine they'd upstage you two," Mrs. Mays smiled at the couple.

"Nor I," mumbled Harriett in her distinct nasal voice. "Maybe the Wagners will get lost!"

"Don't count on that. They're part owners and managers of the Villa. We couldn't survive without them," stated Darby.

"Well! Back to the kitchen!" announced Joshua. "I hope you don't mind some leftover cake. It's still fresh, but the icing's a bit crusty."

"Not at all!" added Charles. "Mrs. Mays, he's referring to his Charleston spice cake, buried under folds of rich sea foam frosting, created by none other than Brandy," he deferred to her.

Harriett studied Brandy's pretty face, bright eyes, black hair, and sassy looks.

Darby noted the girl's envious countenance. With just a little work, surely surgeons could eliminate the remaining scar tissue and eradicate her disfigurement forever.

Harriett caught Darby's eyes exploring hers. A look of fear filled her face. She blushed and turned slightly away.

Darby smiled and raised his glass. "To our guests and to Brandy and Josh!" he hailed, as the couple slipped out to serve dessert.

Later that evening, Mrs. Mays knocked on the office door, opened it, and entered. "Dr. Peterson, won't you join Harriett and me in the living room. We've a host of questions we'd love to ask. Mr. Sanders tells us you're a retired professor, and of philosophy at that. I studied early child development, taught for a while, but have stayed home with Harriett most of my adult life. Please do join us! Please, sir!"

Darby laid aside the accounts he'd been reviewing and scooted his chair back. He felt awkward, uneasy, yet flattered. "I wouldn't trust everything Mr. Sanders says. But, you've put me on the spot. How can I refuse?" he smiled. "You must tell me about yourself." He gestured with his hand for her to lead the way into the living room. He followed at a respectful distance.

Harriett had seated herself near the fireplace while her mother sat in a sofa facing the oriental chair. Darby settled into the richly upholstered armchair and waited for either woman to begin.

"I do know some philosophy," Mrs. Mays opened, "mainly Dewey, Piaget, and Adler's childbirth order. Dealing with school kids required patience, which I lost over time. Public school isn't what it used to be. And I say that with sadness, for I've always been an advocate of public schools. But each year, discipline got harder and harder." She glanced toward Harriett. "God knows it was hard on her."

Darby stared down, momentarily, then back at Mrs. Mays. "I was fortunate. Philosophy was and remains a popular subject. However, in the mid-seventies and early eighties, I had kids falling asleep in the classroom from smoking pot. But by the mid-80s, things calmed down."

"You were lucky," she said. "The hardest moments for me were when children would sass back, or their parents lash out at PTO gatherings. I've been kicked, clawed, and spat on. Our principal did his best to support us, but after fifteen years, I had enough. We had to take Harriett out of school and place her in a private academy, but that was bad for academic reasons," she offered as she glanced toward Harriett.

"Mama! Please! Dr. Peterson," she turned to address him, "everyone thinks you're a freak if you're disfigured. I used to sit under the bleachers during recess and cry. My therapist said I had to stop it. But I still feel like a misfit, like a circus spectacle when people stare at me."

Mrs. Mays leaned toward Harriett and touched her hand. "Sweetie, tell the good professor what you asked your therapist. He'll understand. Please! Go ahead! Maybe he'll have an answer that the therapist didn't have. The therapist couldn't come up with one," Evelyn stated.

Harriett cleared her throat and placed her left hand to her lips. Tears seeped into her eyelashes before trickling down her left cheek. She wiped them back and smiled. "It doesn't hurt as much now as it did. I was fourteen at the time. I asked him if any boy would ever want to kiss my lips as marred as they were. He sort of crumpled, not knowing what to say. I guess there's no answer for it," she brushed back the remaining tears with the sleeve of her silky shirt. "Kind of silly, wasn't it?" she tried putting the pain behind her.

Darby rose and leaned toward her. He hesitated momentarily, but his heart felt it was the right thing to do. Quietly, he covered her hands with his and kissed the corner of her lips, gently—cleft scar and all. Then he brushed a strand of her glossy red hair out of her face with his right hand. The strand had stuck to her cheek and was still moist with tears. He resumed his seat in the massive oriental chair and smiled.

Harriett appeared somewhat startled, then smiled in turn, as she ran her fingers across her lips, stood, and kissed his cheek, beside his lips.

Suddenly, Mrs. Mays put her hands to her mouth and emitted a low-pitched sob. She sucked back her tears, strangling and coughing in the process. She began to moan and press Harriett's hands in her own. "O God, Honey! O God! O my God!" Her tears had now turned into a glistening flood of release, if not shock. She looked up at Darby and wept even more. She shook her head from side to side, rose and kissed her daughter. "O darling. Darling! If only you could see your smile! If only I had done the same long ago!"

As she sat back down, Darby pressed his hands over hers and continued to hold them as she sobbed. While searching for the right words, any words to comfort her, the phone rang in the office. "Excuse me," Darby nodded, as he released her hands, rose and left the living room for the office.

"Hello! The Villa Montesereno here!"

"Darby! Don't sound so serious!" It was Linda's voice. "We're stuck here. Our flight's been cancelled. We've had to return to the resort."

"What's happened?"

"Massive snowstorm! Blizzard conditions all the way from New Mexico, up across the country. No way of getting out before Monday or Tuesday. So we've registered to stay another week. O Darby! How I want to come home! O no! Here comes Jon Paul! Mad as hell! He's up to something, I tell you. Good-bye," she whispered in a choking voice.

"Ummmmph!" Darby muttered aloud. As if he didn't have his hands full enough! Poor Linda! What in the hell was going on? He'd love to know. He hung up the receiver and stepped out to gaze at the stars. How lambent the sheds, the icy patches, and dark woods appeared in the night's translucent glow! From the quiet in the living room, he could still hear mother and daughter crying.

* * *

With the weekend over and the Mays' and Sander's departure, Darby was stunned by Josh's unanticipated announcement. "Sir, Brandy and I have to go now. We can't miss any more classes. Can you pay us, like the Wagners promised?"

"Of course! But we'll be short two chefs if anyone shows up."

"I'm sorry, sir, but Jon Paul said eight days and we've already stayed nine. There's a big storm coming, too. We heard it on the news. It'll hit Atlanta this weekend and Asheville by Saturday. We gotta get back. Plus, is anybody coming? You haven't said, if they are."

"No. They're not in the registry, at least!"

"No offense, Doc, but you've got tons of food in the freezer and ample stores in the pantry. All sorts of seafood, steaks, chicken, pork, even duck! Plus, the pantry's overflowing with everything anyone could need."

"If you say so. How much did Jon Paul promise you?"

"Nine hundred each. Separate checks. We may live together, but Brandy's as tight-fisted as they come. She'll want her own moo-lah."

Darby rose and walked back into the office. "OK!" he grumbled as he removed the business checkbook from the desk drawer. "Nine hundred each!" He reiterated. "Bring Brandy in for hers," he looked up at Joshua as he sat down. Opening the checkbook, he wrote each a check. He could hear Brandy's slippers sliding along the hall floor as she hurried in. "Nine hundred for you, Ms. Sisk," he handed her the check. "And nine hundred for you, Mr. Long," he handed Josh his. "You've been fabulous. I wish you the very best," he smiled as he stood and shook Joshua's hand, then Brandy's.

"I'm sorry, we're leaving you like this," Brandy replied with embarrassment. "The time flew! I want to come back, if you ever need us. I'll even come alone, if Josh can't."

"Whoa, woman! We're a team!" Josh blurted. "Who'd help share the rent and cook for me?" he winked at Darby.

Brandy ignored his slam and, standing on her tiptoes, kissed Darby's neck. "Just let me know!" she stated with a perky flop of her long hair. "Really!"

"I'll not forget." Darby hugged her about her slender waist. "Besides, we're family now," he winked at Josh. "As a retired Prof, I collect kids like you. I never let go. You'll always be part of me. Like it or not! It comes with the territory."

"It's mutual," Joshua replied. He stared down at his check and kissed it. "Much obliged. We'll be splitting within the hour."

Brandy grimaced and stared at her own. She snapped it and slipped it in her bosom. "Bye, Darby!" she shook his hand, quickly following Joshua into the hallway.

Chapter 28

T hursday came and passed, the original day of JP and Linda's return. If a blizzard were coming, Darby knew he needed to drive into Asheville, check the mail, go by the bank, and pick up any personal items his toiletry required. He wanted to locate Melanie's phone number, but his Socratic *daemon*[1] whispered "No! Leave well enough alone. Head on to Asheville and get back."

Darby reserved the mail pickup to last item on his list. Linda, he noted, had sent a postcard from Sedona. The area's red cliffs and dusty mesas formed a mirage on the face of the card. In small print on the back the town boasted its identify as the *film site of John Wayne and Jimmy Stewart movies.* Linda's message contained cryptic bites at best:

> *Hot! Stunning! Tiring! No time to think or write. You know my wishes. Must run. Eyes everywhere. Leg itching like hell! Our secret's safe! Mailing now. Linda.*

The remainder of the mail consisted of credit card statement, ads, catalogs for bed-and-breakfast inns, plus a passel of junk mail. One letter, postmarked "Raleigh," did appear to be a request for lodging; best of all, however, was a pink envelope whose return address read: *Stephanie Gay. 10 East Oyster Bay, Charleston, SC.* Tearing it open, Darby scanned it quickly:

> *We hope to be there soon . . . Joel and I want you to marry us . . .
> he's been assigned as marshal in the Charleston area . . . I'm back
> in school. Love, Stephie.*

The envelope was postmarked the 11th. Stephanie had not indicated when they might come. Probably too excited. Darby laid the note aside, turned on the ignition switch, and drove back toward the Villa. Marry them? What were they thinking? Didn't Stephanie have the slightest clue? It wasn't possible. True, he hadn't renounced his defection per se. But he could

---

1. The voice of conscience that Socrates extolled and relied on. Interestingly enough, it only warned him what not to do.

still hear his bishop's shocked reprimand! "What! Not in my lifetime! You will always be a priest. You can't undo the Sacrament of Ordination!" "But I may want to marry!" Darby objected. "Well, that'll just be too damn bad!" the old bishop retorted. Then he embraced Darby with a sad kiss.

Ah, Jesus! He wouldn't be able to officiate, but he'd come up with something.

While driving back, black clouds had formed into roiling swells behind the mountains to the south. As far as the eye could see, their barrier brooded opaque above the treeline. Leafless poplars, maples, gums and oaks bristled in an endless web of scaly branches. Darby broke his speed to allow a small herd of deer to leap across the road. He watched as they bounded down slope to graze in a pine-protected meadow. Others followed in the underbrush, creating a graceful illusion of cinnamon silhouettes amid flaming white tails. By the time he reached the four-thousand-foot elevation, snowflakes began intermittently to dart past the windshield. He turned the car's heater up to keep warm. Increasingly, icy flakes swirled past the windows and lodged in the wiper blades. At the five-thousand-foot elevation, all became dark. He turned on his headlights and sped as fast as the car would safely climb. As he pulled into the drive, huge tumbling snowflakes descended in cascading wonder. He had to roll his windshield down just to see. It was all he could do to grope his way around to the back of the Villa and park near the cottage. He glanced at his watch! It was two p.m. Better get inside for one history-making snowfall.

Whatever reprieve Darby had anticipated came to an abrupt end. While closing the car's door, the humming, tire-spinning sound of a vehicle caught his attention. He walked toward the Garden to gain a more advantageous view. A handsome canary yellow Hummer, towing a small car behind it, had stalled at the gates' entrance. Its bright yellow top lay flecked with dirty slush. Its headlights canted crazily into the snowy gloom. The driver spotted Darby, waved and started the Hummer again. Slowly it descended the drive, the smaller vehicle still in tow. The two cars came to rest in front of the Villa. By then, Darby had trudged across the estate's icy lawn to greet them. The passengers in the small vehicle—a white Honda—emerged first. Darby recognized Joel and Stephanie instantly, neither quite clad for the impending conditions. Stephanie wore only black jeans, a black sweater, tan suede jacket, and pink scarf fluffed about her head. Joel stood tall as ever in his western boots, wool-lined denim vest, and khaki trousers. A cowboy hat concealed his lean face and professional demeanor. He favored his right leg as he limped toward Darby. A black sling held his left arm in place against his chest. The handgrip of a .45 caliber pistol protruded from a brown holster strapped to his waist. The young marshal smiled, then paused and looked over his shoulder for Stephanie.

Darby's attention focused next on the three occupants climbing out of the Hummer. One walked to the rear of the vehicle and unfastened the chain between it and the Honda. He wore a bearskin coat, Russian pull-down cap, and black duck-hunter's boots. The other two passengers were dressed similarly: in warm coats, hunting boots, gloves, and felt hats. When Darby peered into their vehicle, a heap of camping, hunting, and fishing gear filled the rear compartment.

Darby shook Joel's hand, hugged Stephanie, and waited for the Hummer's occupants to speak.

"I guess you didn't get our letter," the driver spoke first, "seeing you appear a bit shocked." He was slightly taller than Joel, clearly muscular, with deep brown eyes, chiseled facial features and broad shoulders. "We mailed it off two days ago. Maybe three! If you've not read it yet, Jeff Horne recommended we come. He said you'd probably have room for us."

"Yes! Plenty of rooms! But no cooks! They left yesterday. Our real chef and hostess are stranded in Arizona, waiting for this storm to clear," Darby glanced up. "You're welcome to stay, but you'll have to cook for yourself."

Darby turned to Joel and Stephanie. "You can have the cottage if you wish, or first pick of any rooms you want. Stephanie, can you cook?"

"Not to worry! You're in luck," the driver said. "Ed here," he nodded to the man in the bearskin coat, "is a chef. That is, of our hunt club," he grinned. "Actually, he's a prosthesis rep. Reed and I," he deferred to the third man, "are buddies from way back. We've been hunting, fishing, and camping for years. Horne's our club's president. We have our own plantation, bird fields, kennels, and lodge just east of Raleigh. By the way, I'm Rice Abel, retired Army and this is Reed Haney, an attorney. We take jaunts like this every year. We hope to shoot a hog or two, and maybe bag that beast Jeff missed."

"Well! Pull around to the back, if you don't mind. I'm just returning from town. There's a lot of work to be done. Fireplace needs to be cleaned out and logs brought in, along with clean sheets and towels for the rooms upstairs. I haven't been that diligent. Still interested? I'll show you to your rooms and knock off thirty-percent of the usual rate. Does that sound reasonable?"

"Sir, we're not beggars. We're all gainfully employed. But ten percent would be nice, provided that includes night caps and beverages," he grinned. "Fortunately, unlike Jeff, we're not alcoholics. You do serve beer and liquor, and a little wine?"

"We have a full *cave* of connoisseur wines, French and Italian. Plus ample reserves of bourbon, scotch, malts, and whiskeys! You'll survive! Please follow me. Let's get you registered and settled in." Darby looked up at the sky. "At the rate this snow's falling, we'll see at least eight to ten inches before it stops."

"The deeper the better!" the man in the bearskin coat boasted. He had black shining eyes, a thick beard, and long black hair tied in a knot. "I'll scout the kitchen out if someone else will take care of the ashes. Name's Ed Horton," he shook Darby's hand.

"Fair enough!" said the attorney, "I'll do the ashes."

Darby stared at the gentleman, judging him to be in his mid-sixties. The man's face glowed pink in the cold. Bushy eyebrows, sloping shoulders, and a prickly moustache gave him the appearance of a leprous sea lion.

"We can tend to the rest!" Rice added. "Just don't tell Doris! She's my wife," he smiled at Darby. "OK! Let's head 'round back," he ordered. He stopped and stared into Darby's eyes. "Sorry about that. I was a colonel in the Army. No offense!"

"I'll be up for the story," Darby replied. "See you in the office. Just come in the back hall."

After the three had registered and selected their rooms, Darby walked to the cottage with Stephanie and Joel. "This will be on us," he said. "Don't worry about the rate." He opened the door for Stephanie to enter first.

"Uhhh! It's cold," moaned Stephanie.

"It'll warm up," Darby assured her. "The fireplace is already clean. Plenty of firewood piled in the back. When is your event, anyway?"

"Not until after May exams!" Stephanie replied. "If that's OK with you?"

"I've nothing scheduled to my knowledge. We can check the registry to see who Linda's booked."

"Her exams should be through by the middle of May!" said Joel. "I've already checked with central office. They've cleared the week for me." He placed his right arm about Stephanie's waist and hugged her against his shoulder.

She kissed his cheek, careful not to bump his sling.

"Dominetti?" Darby inquired.

"Yeah! Took two in the chest, one in the upper arm, and one in the left thigh. I'm lucky to be alive. Dominetti didn't have a chance. They gunned him down as I stepped around to assist him. They didn't get away though. We had agents at the end of the block. They were disguised as garbage collectors. They got the garbage all right!" He looked down at Stephanie. "As

I went down, you're all I could think of. And this place! I wanted to come back. That's all I could think of. To marry you and come back."

"I've told him about Daddy's grave. How we crawled inside and barely escaped. We're gonna go down tomorrow to see it, no matter how much it snows. I want be near Daddy again. I want tell him about Joel. That I'm all right now! That whatever happened is OK! I have to do that Dr. D. I have to. Will you join us?"

Darby smiled. "Let me think about it."

They entered the cottage and turned on the lights. A cold musty redolence stung Darby's nostrils. The dampness had settled in the walls. "You can stay inside, if you want," Darby said.

"No! This is fine!" Stephanie chirped up. "Will you go down with us? Please!"

Darby drew in a deep breath. Linda might call. If Horne's three friends joined them in the bottom, anything might happen. His *daemon* knew what to do, what to say. "I'd love to, but I'd better stay here. You and Joel can take your time, savor the moment, or whole day. You need to be together."

* * *

As darkness fell, Horton's kitchen skills produced a fine cuisine. Everyone but Darby had pitched in. His sole task was to set the table and open bottles of wine. He worried briefly about the latter, so fond had he become of the grape, but he knew when to stop, or so he told himself.

Horton's "group specialty," as he duped it, consisted of marinated pork chops, baked in garlic butter, served with mashed potatoes, parsley flakes, asparagus, green peppers, and cherry pie for dessert.

"Breakfasts, I do even better!" the man bragged. "I mean pancakes, sausage links, fried potatoes, and scrambled eggs! Any objections?"

"None here!"

"Nor here!"

"Nor me," Stephanie exhaled a deep breath. Without thinking, she pressed her hands on her stomach; then all of a sudden looked up at Darby. "Don't think it!" she blushed. "I'm not. Really, I'm not."

The five men eyed each other, Joel receiving the clumsy stares of the four.

Joel held up his hands in innocent protest. "I'm just a guest!" he winked at Darby, before kissing Stephanie on the cheek. Everyone laughed.

"Enjoy it!" Reed stated. "We've all been there. I've no regrets."

"Nor I!" said Horton.

Haney glanced about the table. "I can talk here, can't I?" he paused. "I've got one, condescending son-in-law. Truly I do. He's tall, surly, hairy—like Ed here, but arrogant and rude. On his wedding day he had the gall to inform me that he could hardly wait to get my daughter as far away from us as possible. Imagine that? To his father-in-law, of all people! As for his mother, he pushed her down a flight of steps when he was fourteen, he confessed, because she nagged him about his room. None of this came out until after the wedding. I wondered why his parents sat alone. His own father hated him as a child, he claims, because he was awkward and clumsy as a boy. His father was an ace football star in high school and college. When he got tall and old enough, he claims, he shouted at his father, 'Why don't you like me?' then he hit him. His own father! I want to believe in the man, but he's so abusive, so incommunicable."

"Wait a minute! Maybe you'd want to hit back too, if you had a father like that?" Rice said. "Maybe the guy needs a break. What son-in-law doesn't want to get his bride as far away from her parents as possible? There's really no harm in that. Without a decent father, what boy can grow up normal?"

"I know. I really want to believe in him, but you can't imagine how hard he is to love. He's threatening to leave Allison if I don't help them with their mortgage."

"What does he do?" asked Joel. "Has he ever been jailed?"

"Maybe he's suffering some kind of disorder?" Rice queried. "We had our share of angry men in the Army. Nam attracted an over-supply. They'd scream at their men; shout in their faces; order them around like pigs. They were afraid to lead. They had to have someone to blame. One of our units fragged an officer like that. Placed a grenade in his poncho one night in the rain. A master sergeant confessed. I told him to report it as a friendly, gone down. It was the wisest thing I ever did, cause after that he protected my ass every time we came under fire."

"I'm afraid my son-in-law wouldn't qualify for 4-F, if it still exists. He's a draftsman. It's just that he's so obnoxious. He worked for an architectural firm out of Georgia, but got laid off. Fortunately, he's been recruited to work for the Boeing plant in Charleston. Right now he's unemployed, ungrateful, and searching for someone to blame. Maybe I shouldn't be so hard on him."

Darby thought for a moment, not wanting to interject his views, but with reluctance offered: "There are drugs he can take, you know. That might calm him enough to take cognizance of his behavior. But I'm not convinced that drugs work in the long run. They just postpone recovery."

"I'd love to give him the benefit of the doubt, but I think he's just genetically programmed to be disrespectful; plus being abused by his father didn't help." Reed smiled with pain in his eyes.

"I guess you've had cases like his before?" Rice deferred to Darby.

"We have, but I'm not qualified to make the call. I've sometimes thought that what we really need here is a psychologist. But, then, I don't think any of us wants to see Montesereno become a sanatorium, although, in the beginning, that's what it was. We advertise as a haven of respite, relaxation, and rest, a place to repose and regain peace. I've placed several ads using those very words: *'respite, relaxation, rest; a place to repose and regain peace!'* A sort of high-end bed-and-breakfast, but much, much more."

"That's how Jeff described you," Haney replied. "I like it here! You're much more than a lodge. Plus, Horne boasts that you're a retired professor."

Darby smiled. "Yes. I guess so, though I try not to bore guests. Some of my views are pretty antiquated."

"Listen, if yours are antiquated, then mine would qualify as Neanderthal!" Rice struggled to grin.

"Why not gravitate toward the fireplace," Ed suggested. "After we, and I mean *we*, clean off the table and wash the dishes. I didn't volunteer for that!"

* * *

Everyone's pitching in to clean up proved to be a godsend for Darby. Stephanie could see he needed to be alone for a while. "Go on; get out of the kitchen," she scolded him. She and Joel had elected to dry while Horne's friends began scrubbing the pots and pans.

While the guests were engaged in their KP duties, Darby slipped into the office to search the files for Melanie's phone number. Surely, it had to be in the registration folder somewhere? Finally, after emptying several cabinet drawers, he located the Velesky's card. Yes! All four of the group's phone numbers were listed. He replaced the folder, sat somewhat uneasily at the desk, and punched in Melanie's number. Should he be doing this? His Socratic conscience remained suspiciously uncommitted. A tightness swelled in his groin. He thought of Linda as he listened to the dial tone. Someone picked up. "Melanie! Is that you?"

"Darby! O God! I'm so embarrassed! I can't believe what we did! I mean, what I did! Tracy says I really acted out. I'm sorry. I've been afraid you'd call."

"Don't worry, Melanie. I'm the one who needs to apologize."

"No, no! That's quite all right. My monthly visitor shocked me back into reality. I began my period yesterday," she muttered. "You know I live with my sister? Tracy's on a date right now. With Charles! He's decided to leave his wife. He told her as much the morning we left."

Darby could hear her restricted breathing, its silent frightful tenor. His old companion "ambivalence" hunkered within his chest. "I hate to hear that about Charles, but I know the feeling!" he mumbled. "You were so perfect."

"Thanks," she whispered melancholically. "It's not fun, is it? Wanting what you know won't work?"

"Please don't say that. You were wonderful. Special!"

"You're sweet to say that, but, thank God, I'm not pregnant. I loved every moment of it. Thanks for calling," she whispered. "I'll never forget you. I'm so sorry."

She mumbled something else, but Darby couldn't decipher it. He held his breath to listen as quietly as he could. Perhaps Tracy had come into the room. He counted the seconds slowly up to ten before hanging up. He thought of Heraclitus's famous statement:

> In the same river, we both step and do not step, we are and we are not.[2]

"Come join us in the living room!" Rice called. He had peered into the office from the hallway. "Quite nice!" he glanced about. "Join us and let's chat."

Reed and Ed had chosen the largest and most comfortable chairs. Rice walked to the fireplace, removed the screen, and poked the glowing logs. A shower of red sparks popped and crackled before disintegrating in the hearth. Rice replaced the screen and sat with the others. Stephanie and Joel wandered in from the dining room and sat quietly in a loveseat near the CD player. They looked toward Darby, then at each other, and blushed.

"How did you get into the teaching business, anyway, Peterson?" Rice asked. "I majored in military history at the Citadel, though philosophy was my favorite subject. I took two electives—the Intro course and one on European Philosophers. It went from Descartes to Heidegger. The latter enthralled me, but I hated all the gobbledygook devoted to epistemology. What's your take?"

"Don't get me started. Yes. Epistemology is the bane of modern philosophy. Let's just say that only its devotees know what to espouse."

"Can't you give us a hint; at least a one-sentence definition? Jeff said it was your field, isn't it? Or was?"

Darby did not want to explain it; not in the least. It was enough that he had defined it for Merle; nonetheless, he suspired as he cleared his mind. "Epistemology has to do with justifying what we think we know, as well as

---

2. Heraclitus, *Philosophy*, 12–13.

justifying the grounds on which we base that justification. It is the most important field of all."

"Why?"

"Because it underlies all else?"

"Well! Go on." stated Rice.

"I'd rather talk about Heidegger," Darby smiled.

"Well, tell us about Heidegger, then. I'm game."

Darby stared at the man before glancing around the room. "Don't say I didn't warn you. It goes something like this. Heidegger was more of a priest, a metaphysics man in search of a new belief system, than hung up on epistemology. He liked to talk about the default of the gods, figures like Jesus and Dionysus, whose believers believed they'd return one day, but neither has nor ever will. That era is over. Gone. Past. Now we're stuck with having to come up with a new reason for being, one that will do justice to our time." Darby stopped, uncertain that what he was saying was worth it, or as sound as it should be.

"Please! Go on," Rice insisted. "The legal field is quite similar."

"Well, Heidegger didn't exactly abandon the spiritual mythology of the ancient world. In the poet, Hölderlin, he found a clue to his search. Hölderlin argued that the great gods like Jesus and Dionysus had left traces of themselves in bread and wine, which the great poets still explore. By living on the earth, or *dwelling* on it, as Heidegger preferred, we still live under the stars, on the earth, acknowledging the passing of the gods, yet as mortals who must die, and precisely to that extent find meaning in accepting our being as such. By so living, we display a merit worthy of our being mortal, while our eyes remain fixed on the heavens, in quest of new 'gods,' or a more contemporary belief system."

"Well, you got us all listening now," Ed blurted. "Might as well finish us off," he laughed.

"Don't say I didn't warn you. The best place to read all this is in Heidegger's *Poetry, Language, Thought*. Once I discovered it, I fell in love with it, as it is so much like Sartre's view—that we are responsible for our own lives, what we believe, what we do, and how we live them. We alone write the history of our lives, for good or evil; and we alone are responsible for that." Darby paused. "Is that enough?" he smiled. "It just gets more boring."

"How about a conclusion, then? I want to be able to explain it myself," Rice averred.

"You would," groaned Ed.

"Ok, but this will be it. To sum it up, we each enjoy a limited time of life, of *Sein und Zeit*, as Heidegger spelled it out. In essence, our lives are sort of thrown into a great Void, a Nothingness, not knowing how it will turn out. But only the extent to which we enter that nothingness, that *das Nicht*, without overlaying it with our present presuppositions, can we hope to find meaning and value, our own beingness, or *Dasein*, as he called it. Fail to do that, and you'll end up with a remorseful inauthentic life, in which you let other people determine how and what you'll do, believe, and become. That's it!" Darby stopped.

"And where do you stand?" asked Joel.

"I'm just a generalist," Darby stared toward the fireplace. "I favor a commonsense approach. We simply have to do the best we can with what we have, and understand that we're accountable for our beliefs and actions. And, yes, sadly, sometimes we do things we can't justify, or don't even want to justify. Which is what makes us remarkable as either pernicious or angelic. That's a woeful over-simplification, I know! It's just that it's so hard to generalize without twisting the truth."

"I can accept that!" said Rice.

"I'm just a cook and prosthesis fitter!" Horton threw up his hands in mock horror. "I don't have a leg to stand on."

"Oh! That's awful!" blurted Stephanie.

"I couldn't help it," Horton smirked. "In any event, let's break out the *real stuff*. Scotch and Bourbon! What do you say?"

"Enjoy it, gentleman! But it's off to bed for me!" bade Darby.

Before retiring he stepped out on the patio for a breath of cold air. Snow was still falling, light and fluffy. It had to be at least ten inches deep. What were Horne's companions thinking? To hunt and hike in this? Tomorrow, he guessed, he'd know.

Chapter 29

The morning roll call came with a startle. The sounds of a camp dinner bell ringing with vigorous clanging filled the air with loud vibrations. Darby, who had been up for about an hour, peered out the office's rear window. Horton was standing in knee-deep snow beside the Hummer, banging away on an iron triangle with an iron rod, apparently part of their camping gear. A window from upstairs opened, and Rice's voice rose above the clangor. "That's enough!" He must have glanced at his watch. "OK! I'll get Reed up and we'll be down as soon as possible." The panes in the French window rattled with a slam. Darby glanced toward the cottage. Light puffs of gray smoke rose from its chimney. It hovered cold over the cottage and the barren orchard beyond. Everything huddled near the freezing mark. Horton replaced the iron in the Hummer and waded toward the kitchen in the snow. He saw Darby's image in the window and waved. "Cold as hell!" he shouted. A good-natured smile emanated from the man's bearded face.

Once breakfast was downed, the Villa's guests lined up by the Hummer, eager to descend the snowy face of the logging road. The sun had crept out of its own hiding, causing the snow's icy crystals to sparkle like diamonds. Horne's companions urged Darby to join them.

"You know it'll be fun. Lots of adventure!" Stephanie assured him. "Please! Please come!" she held Joel's left hand while tugging at her gloves. The two were bundled in warm coats and caps they had found in the cottage. Joel's pistol and holster bulged noticeably beneath his coat.

"Thanks! But I've plenty to do here. Plus, I want to be available in case the Wagners call. I wouldn't take your Hummer, though," he addressed Rice, "unless it can pull through deep drifts. There'll be plenty to encounter."

"Stephie, you're the only one who knows the way down and back. Rice, take her advice and be cautious. It's pretty boggy near the bottom and we've no way to haul you uphill."

"Listen!" Rice replied. "This Hummer can go anywhere through anything that nature can throw at it. Sure you don't want to come along?"

"Thanks. Just be careful. Fire three times if you get in trouble. Maybe our old tractor can pull you out if it has to. Good luck!" he waved from the patio. With several kicks against the steps, he knocked off the cakes of snow that had clumped up under his boots. Glancing over his shoulder, he watched as the group climbed into the yellow vehicle. As the Hummer's engine purred softly, he waved again and re-entered the house. From the office window, he observed Rice back up the big vehicle; then listened as its tires crunched forward over the heavy snowpack and down the logging road. Stephanie waved from the back seat.

They would be gone for at least four hours, he reasoned. Time to read, to trudge out to the overlook, as well as reflect on encroachments that pre-occupied his thoughts: mainly Linda, Jon Paul, the Villa, and its needs. And then there were his dreams, which seemed less definable with each passing day. Did he really think he could pull it off? An actual history of ideas from Wittenberg to Weimar, from Luther to Nietzsche, and down that long road of hypostatizing the universals to reifying the particular within one's self? Why not just publish three statements, period? *You are here! One day you must die! Can you handle that and not despair?* Ex-priest or not, wasn't that the truth?

Midway into studying facets of Goethe's prose, Darby broke his con-centration long enough to prepare a sandwich and heat water for a pot of English tea. He let the bags seep until the steam whistled from the kettle. Carrying his lunch into the office, he reopened Goethe's *Italian Journey* to compare the poet's German text with its English translation. If anyone knew how to weather the vicissitudes of life, it was Goethe. Born of a princely family, he had witnessed his share of Teutonic political turbulence and fi-nancial straits. Gifted with enviable artistic powers and reared amidst the privileged classes of Frankfurt and Weimar, his career had drawn him into the forefront of the German States' fascination with *Freiheit und Frieden*, which in turn had inspired his inquiry into the German Romantic Move-ment, with all its *Sturm und Drang*. O to be the Goethe of one's time!

As he listed the characteristics of Goethe's period, he noted the passing of a shadow outside his window and looked up to see Reed struggling by. The attorney's thin moustache and heavy eyebrows glistened with ice. His pink complexion had turned red. He panted heavily as he reached the door. Darby quickly pushed his chair back and strode toward the hallway.

"God, but I'm exhausted!" Reed expelled as he bumbled into the hall. "I left my gun in the Hummer. The others are still down there. Is that tea I smell? Please fix me a cup."

"By all means! Rest in the office. I'll be right back."

Upon his return, Darby found Reed perusing a hardcover volume from one of Garnett's shelves. He had carried the book to the leather sofa and was marking pages with light pencil checks. Darby set down the tray. "Your cup, sir!" he intoned gravely. "Would you care for anything more?"

"Forgive me," the lawyer glanced up. "Here it is! This book perfectly describes my son-in-law. He's suffering from a narcissistic disorder. It's all right here!" he lifted the book for Darby to see. *Advances in Psychotherapy of the Borderline Patient*, by LeBoit and Capponi. "Listen to this:

> The grandiose self screens a hungry, infantile character with exaggerated dependency needs, considerably oral rage and envy. [It is characterized] by a manic pursuit of gratification, an intense ambition and a craving for recognition and applause . . . With an ability to contrive a surface social adjustment, the narcissistic individual can achieve in fields such as theatre, politics, or business, where an inflated self-concept and charismatic veneer are not detriments.[1]

He let the book flop closed. "That's my daughter's husband, Darby! Capponi has described him to a T! He can't get enough adulation or applause. Capponi claims when such people suppress their omnipotent feelings and find themselves confronted by a superior person, their 'destructive facets explode with anger and aggression.' If only I could get him to seek help!"

"Try drinking your tea. It's a great English blend," Darby consoled him. He sat beside him, rather than at his desk. "Some people we just have to tolerate, even when they lash back. And sometimes, we just have to forgive people. I know he's hurt you, hurt you deeply. But at some point we just have to forgive some people, especially those who hurt us most."

Suddenly, a quiet moan rose from Reed's throat and, burying his face in his sleeve, he let out a wrenching sob. "Ah, God, Darby! If only you knew! I've carried this hurt so long. I just want it to go away!"

"Then let it go. Why don't we just walk out there in the snow and let it go. Do you really need his respect to validate your self-worth? Think of all you've accomplished? All the cases you've won, all the people you've helped. Reed, all that stands regardless of his opinion of you. Isn't that true?"

Reed sucked in his tears and wiped his face with a tissue he had found nearby. He sat there for a long while, wiping his tears away. "You're right!" he finally said. "Let's go outside. I need a slap of clean cold air," he smiled.

"Aside from meds, I don't know what else to say. I hate to think that we're just victims of mindless neural processes, compounded by chemical imbalances. I hate to see disorders prevail over an examined life. I fear it's

1. LeBoit, *Advances*, 32–33.

happening more and more in our culture. We've all become unrestrained narcissists."

"Darby! I didn't mean to drown you in my own depression. Sounds like you need help yourself."

Darby thought for a moment. "The one thing Hegel was right about is that every era gives rise to one that finds its predecessor quaint, cruel, and outmoded. Thus the pendulum of revulsion swings full arc, ushering in a new era. Sometimes the changes are good; sometimes nihilistic and blind. But it makes for an interesting mix. That's the optimist speaking in me, Reed," his mouth widened into a grin. "A pessimist would drive off a cliff and be done with it."

"Well, I'm no pessimist. I love life too much to want to miss even the worst of it, including my son-in-law."

"We'd better get outside before we become maudlin." Darby smiled.

"Did you hear that?" Reed suddenly noted, his neck erect and senses startled.

"Sounds like a shotgun. Perhaps they jumped a grouse or rabbit. At least, it means they're still alive."

The two pulled on their coats and went outside by means of the office's back door.

"Here," said Darby, as he rolled a clump of snow into a tight ball and handed it to Reed. "Stephanie and I once hurled apples off the overlook instead of jumping off ourselves. Lets see how many snowballs we can roll and pepper the shed with, just for the hell of it."

"You're on!" laughed Reed, as he threw the one Darby had handed him and quickly rolled up another.

When three hours later the Hummer expedition returned to the Villa, its driver and passengers crawled out with cheerless expressions. Mud and snow splattered their trousers, faces, and gloves. Weary and exhausted, they lined up to retrieve personal items from the vehicle. Suddenly, Rice broke the silence with a mammoth grin. Turning about to face Darby and Reed, he held up a ruffled turkey, head down, with its spurred claws clutched in his left glove. Blood dripped from its gray and black feathers and red comb. Its beard had been blown off. "I know it's not in season," Rice smiled, "but it'll make a great dinner, provided you've got a deep-fat fryer."

"You do," answered Ed. "Give me four hours, and we'll dine with the best."

Darby glanced at his watch. It was 3:30. "That'll do!" His eyes met Joel's and Stephanie's. Tears had frozen on her cheeks. "You didn't try to go in, did you? She didn't, did she?" he stared at Joel.

"No, sir! We sat down by the entrance and stared inside. I saw bear tracks, but they were obliterated by churned up snow. No hogs, though. I figure they heard us coming and retreated. Have you ever been down the mountain past the mine or the creek beside it? The trail has to empty some-where, where they either trucked out the mica or dragged out logs."

"No, I haven't. The bottom's as far down as I've ventured."

Joel glanced about, as if waiting for privacy. "Listen! I found the place where you hid the car. It's in remarkable condition. If you ever need to start it up or drive it out, I'll be glad to help. It all depends on the battery and how stiff the oil is. It'd make a great roust-about sedan! I can get tags for it anytime you'd need."

"I don't know. But thanks for the offer. Incidentally, you and Stepha-nie will need to acquire your license in Hayward or Buncombe County. I can't officially marry you. You'll need to find a magistrate to conduct how-ever brief a ceremony you want, and then have him or her sign the license. According to what I know, there will be a fee. Then when you're ready to come to the Villa, I'll come up with the best possible ceremony I can create. Stephanie's too sweet to let down."

"I never thought about that! We'll come prepared."

*　*　*

By noon Sunday, the state highway department's scrapers had cleared a path from the forks below to the Villa's gates. Darby walked out and waved to the operators as they descended the mountain. Two hours later, Horne's com-panions, along with Stephanie and Joel boarded their cars and slipped out of sight. The wind bit into Darby's face, stung his ears and lips, as he watched the Hummer and Honda steal from view. Shuddering from the cold, he bur-ied his face inside his coat's collar and returned to the house.

More than ever, he felt lonely. More than ever, he wanted Linda. He wanted Melanie, too. Melanie was sweet and loving. Ripe and ready for mar-riage! But she was gone. At least he and Linda shared a bond together, a history and chemistry. Except for one factor: Jon Paul! What was he up to? Should he offer to buy him out? Where would he secure such funds?

Darby stirred the logs in the fireplace, added a new one to the blaze, and sank back in the great Oriental chair. He had arrived at the hall to lec-ture. But where was his folder? In the car! Yes, in the car. But where was the car? It was not in the parking lot. Yes, the car in the bottom! Perhaps the folder was there. Down the road he ran. In the snow, in the slush, in the mud! Where was he? Where was the car? He couldn't find the car. Damm! He had just seen it. Ah, there! In the tangles! He couldn't break through the tangles. The vines had enlaced the car in a cage of frozen tendrils. *Alors*! Someone was in the car! The man had his folder! He tugged at the handle. He had to have that folder! It was lecture time. He looked down. His hands were bleeding. Blood was everywhere. The car's occupant was smiling at him. Son-of-a-bitch! It was Jon Paul! He banged on the window. "You son-of-a-bitch!" he shouted. "It's mine. The folder's mine!" The door opened. It wasn't Jon Paul. Who was it? "The folder! The folder!" It was Dominetti! No! Hughes! No, someone else! The man was big. He could smell his body odor; he was ugly! The man laughed and threw the folder in Darby' face.

"Darby! Darby! For God's sake! Wake up!"

Darby opened his eyes. He'd been dreaming. His mouth felt dry, his mind paralyzed, his lips too numb to move. It was Linda! The room swam dizzily about him. His shirt clung damp against his body; his face trickled wet with perspiration.

"Darby, you're feverish! We're home, Darby! It's me, Linda. We got home earlier than we thought. Are you all right?" She pressed her hand to his forehead. "Better get a cold wash cloth, JP. He's burning with fever. We should never have left you!"

"Linda, for heaven's sake! He'll be fine!" Jon Paul's voice rose with agitation.

His image wavered in the gloaming darkness as Darby struggled to rise but fell back.

"What do you expect from an academic, anyway?" JP uttered with impatience. "Most couldn't hold a job if they had to."

"JP! That's despicable! You promised there'd be no more of that! No more! I want no more it! And that's final."

"Have it your way! But you'll regret it! You'll see."

Darby wanted to rise, to engage JP with his fists. He tried lifting his head, but Linda's face began to spin. The fireplace had turned upside down. He felt drunk or drugged, part of a Chagall painting, revolving around delusional images and gross faces. "Linda!" he whispered, raising his hand, only to be pulled up and hoisted over Jon Paul's shoulder. With audible grunts, the unhappy chef carted him through the office and dumped him on the bed.

"Careful!" said Linda. She removed Darby's shoes and covered him with a bathrobe. "I'll wipe his face with something cool."

"Suit yourself! You'll see. Hopefully, we still have some beer."

Chapter 30

When Darby rolled over to discover himself in his flannel pajamas and a glass of tepid water beside his bed, he blinked twice, sat up, and rubbed his head. The sour olid odor of his own body made him wince. He looked up to see Linda seated by the door, half in the office; half in his bedroom.

"Welcome back to sanity!" she smiled. "You've been out for two days. I tried sponging you down, but JP got too jealous. I did put you into your pajamas," she smiled. "Nice package, but a little droopy."

"You are the best!" moaned Darby. "I feel like a freight train hit me."

"It did!"

"I ache all over!"

"You should. Probably some forty-eight hour flu." She leaned forward and suddenly began scratching her right leg with methodic vigor. "Oh, but I itch!" she clawed her leg before sitting back.

"What's wrong?"

"I don't know. I've had it since we visited Arizona. Just some allergy or bug bite. Possibly poison ivy. Ah!" she sighed with relief.

Darby pressed his hands to his face. "What's going to happen here? JP wants me out, doesn't he? As if I cared."

"Not sure what he's up to, but flying back he kept smiling to himself. Kind of cocky! We had drinks in Atlanta. He got mushy, sentimental. He's pissed, but he might come around."

"Sure! With an ax handle! I feel weak!"

"Where'd you get your muscles? You've been doing more than sitting at a desk all these years, or leaning over a podium."

"I ran cross-country in college. Used to jog until it bothered my knees," he swung his legs out of bed. "Aaah, Linda, but my ass aches! I'd be nice to have a few weights or spinning bikes here, just for us to exercise, if no one else."

"We've thought of that. But, listen, you've got to buck up. We've got a list of guests coming in over the next few weeks, indeed, months. One woman wants to stay a month. She's a writer."

"Ohh!"

"Yes, oooh!" Linda raised her voice in a mock, seductive tone. "Darby, for goodness sake! Besides, she's ugly. I've seen her photos on the back of her dust jackets. Ugggly!" she emphasized, with a flirtatious wink of her eyes. "You'd better shower and get dressed. We've a doctor and his wife coming in tonight. He was drawn, he said, by one of your ads in a physician's bulletin. He called last night. So," she sighed, as she got up and approached his bed, "time to resume your duties, sweet man. And brush your teeth!" she bent down and half-kissed his lips. "What I don't do for you! Darby, at some point we've got to . . . you know?" she nudged his shoulder with her fingertips. Her eyes stared intently into his. Her dark irises sparkled in spite of the room's dim light.

He stared back, with a tired smile. "You know the answer to that," he whispered.

She slipped away from his side and left the room.

* * *

Toward mid-afternoon, Darby decided it was time to confront Jon Paul. He felt alert and keen enough to do it. He found the chef in the kitchen, slicing plump purple medallions of filet mignon. The burly man glanced over his shoulder as Darby entered.

"You want something?" he quipped with an edge of annoyance in his tone.

"It's time we had a talk. Don't you think so?"

"I'm busy, can't you see?" he turned, gripping the butcher knife loosely in his right hand. "Don't get me upset."

"I believe there's a good reason to be upset. It's obvious you want me out of here. That you're angry over Garnett's will! Look, neither of us planned on this, or foresaw it. You're on the payroll. I'm not. My income's based on my retirement: TIAA and CREF. The Foundation pays yours. We're just the Villa's caretakers. And that's an honor in itself."

"I don't need your lecturing me, or need you in here." He turned again with a menacing glare. "Take it to your clandestine sweetheart. *My wife!*" he hissed. He raised the knife and waved it in Darby's face. "I don't give a damn about you! Why don't you take a vacation? Go to France or wherever. And don't come back!"

Darby shook his head from side to side. He knew he couldn't let the moment pass. He stepped inside Jon Paul's comfort zone—his male territorial realm—placed his right foot suddenly behind JP's right leg, and, striking him in the face with the palm of his right hand, knocked the stunned chef to the floor. JP's head struck the corner of the kitchen's chopping block as he went down, opening an ugly gash behind his left ear. The knife skidded across the floor as the big man landed on his back. Shocked at the unceremonious manner in which he was toppled, he rolled to one side, nursing his bloodied ear with his left hand. In something of a stupor, he looked up, dazed.

"You will not talk to me that way! Ever again!" said Darby. "Do you understand?"

"Help me up!" the bruised man wheezed. He lifted his left hand toward Darby.

Darby bent forward and pulled him up. In the process, he handed Jon Paul a wet dishcloth from the sink. "You'll need this."

"I'm sorry I lost it!" Jon Paul heaved, catching his breath. "O God!" he sighed, as he pressed the cloth to his ear. "I worked for this all my life!" he glanced about the kitchen and out its side-back window toward the woods. "Shit!" he pressed his lips together. "Here!" he extended his right hand to Darby's and shook it. "Give me a little time. I'll get used to it. But keep away from Linda!" His eyes all but narrowed into slits.

"That I can't promise, anymore than you kept away from Julia Laine!"

"Then, go to Hell!" the big man huffed, as he continued to nurse his ear. "Get out of my kitchen! Get out!" He bent down to retrieve his butcher knife. He wiped it against his apron, paused; then walked to the sink to wash it. "Let's just call a truce," he mumbled. "What the Hell! Linda's going to be Linda and there's not a damn thing I can do about it."

"Whatever. I plan to move back into the cottage, at least for the nights."

The husky chef shifted his weight as he returned to the chopping block, its surface shimmering with its pile of gourmet cuts. "That's damn noble!" he exhaled with a groan. "Time will tell!" he muttered, keeping his eyes on the block while averting Darby's.

Was there something wrong about this? Darby wondered. Angry one minute, remorseful the next! At least, they had stared at the elephant. Darby inhaled a deep breath and returned to his office. He pulled on his coat, tightened his hiking boots' shoestrings, and strolled out toward the Garden. The sun burned especially bright; many patches of snow glistened in its melting warmth. He thought of Aristotle's line:

> For one swallow does not make a spring, nor does one sunny
> day . . . make a man blessed and happy.[1]

Well did the Greeks fathom that mortal man can never cease to contemplate his *glassy essence*, as Shakespeare put it! Darby walked up through the orchard, stopped at the overlook, took in its mountainous vista; then returned by way of the cottage. Its fireplace had been cleaned and logs arranged to be lit. Curly must have attended to the details while he was knocked out with the flu. He turned on the floorboard's heating elements, slipped Longfellow's *Evangeline* off its shelf, and, with the poem in his lap, turned the pages gently as he relished each verse. In the quiet recesses of his soul, he could hear the poet's Acadian pines soughing their plaintiff lament. The Buddha had it right: suffering is universal.

With the advent of evening, Darby changed shirts, trousers, and jacket and walked back to *le grand maison*. Hettie must have polished the dining room's chandelier, for its glass pendants cast elongated ovals of rotating light into the hallway and across its waxed floor. The couple seated at the table rose when he entered.

"We are so pleased to meet you!" said the man. "My wife, Pamela! I'm Hampton Cochrane, director and staff coordinator of my new clinic. We are pleased to be here."

Darby bowed toward Mrs. Cochrane, who offered him her hand. Her shiny auburn hair, sparkling eyes, and tapered nose caught his attention at once. "My honor!" he shook her hand. "Please, be seated. Both of you."

The doctor leaned across the table and shook Darby's hand. "A genuine pleasure!" He smiled and took his seat as Peterson assisted his wife into hers again. Darby watched her as she unfolded her napkin, her eyes fixed admiringly on her husband's.

"This is almost like our honeymoon!" Cochrane's face lit up with a blush. "This is our eighth anniversary."

"Congratulations! Please, help yourself to more wine. A toast to both of you!" Darby raised his glass.

"Thank you!" the three touched glasses.

"I can hardly wait to tell you what I'm up to in Beaufort! I've been wanting to do it for years. Have you ever been there?"

"Yes. I love its quaint dreamscape, its old-timey downtown, and the smell of its tidal marshes."

"We, too!" his wife replied cheerily. "You'll love what we've done there."

---

1. Aristotle, *Nicomachean Ethics*, 17–18.

"Yes, not to brag, but I've built a wellness clinic that integrates all the forms of what's now being called 'complementary medicine,' or CAM. Are you familiar with it?"

"Only vaguely. I assume you mean alternative medicine?"

"Yes! But *complementary* expresses it better. You know, close to forty percent of all adults now favor CAM, as it's called. That's not to disparage allopatheic medicine at all. I'm a family doctor, myself. But prescriptive drugs and traditional practices don't offer the holistic therapies many patients need. And that's where you come in, or Montesereno. I liked your ad's description as a place of 'rest, relaxation, and recuperation,' or however you put it. That's what most people need. Just someone to listen to them, to touch their shoulder or arm, to provide a relaxing massage or a calming arena for catharsis, then provide prescriptive medication or talk therapy, as needed. That's what I'm trying to do."

"Oh, goodness! But these medallions are scrumptious!" his wife interjected. "I must know how to prepare them," she smiled.

"Our chef *is* good!" Darby allowed. He turned toward the swinging door where Linda was reentering. "Save room for dessert," she winked at Darby. With her eye still on him, she refilled their water glasses. How wholesome, perky, and elegant she looked in her white pearl necklace, svelte green dress, and tiny diamond earrings. Her short black hair and fiery eyes captured his heart *de nouveau* in spite of his lost soul.

"It sounds like we might want to recommend some of our guests to you," Darby continued.

"By all means, vice-versa! We'd love to send our more contemplative types to you. Your location is excellent. And this house, your estate! It's unequalled! I assure you."

"I love it, myself. I must confess."

"Well, let me tell you more. I might want to borrow you from time to time. We do a lot of integrative medicine. I've not eliminated anything. For example, we offer herbal botanicals, dietary supplements, mind-body therapy, acupuncture, yoga, meditation, spinal manipulation, even exercise, pilates, and psychotherapy. We do it all. Even Reike, as well as light and magnet therapy! I assure you, none of it's quackery," he paused, glancing down at his plate before looking again at Darby, "though some of my older colleagues shun our clinic and ignore us at the Country Club."

Mrs. Cochrane lowered her eyes and sipped on her water.

Darby helped himself to a second glass of wine—a dark mild *vin rouge de Le Midi*. "I'm not surprised," Darby swallowed. Just then he raised his glass. "To the delicious mauve nectar of Bacchus," he smiled, lowering his glass. "You know, philosophy gets a bad rap, too. I'm glad you're here and we can talk like this, openly and freely."

"It's amazing, isn't it, what silence and stillness can do? A touch of the hand! A glance of the eye! A relaxing massage, a patient listener, and the right setting! Naturopathy! The Chinese were big on it. And the Romans and Greeks as well, with their baths and gardens." He paused and smiled at his wife. "Pamela's our receptionist. I have to detoxify the over-stimulated males who fall in love with her."

"I can see why," Darby tipped his glass toward the man's wife.

"I'm eager to walk about tomorrow," Cochrane continued. "We offer calmness, but we can't compete with your setting here. Perhaps, this summer, or earlier, we could experiment by recommending some of our clients to spend a weekend, if not a whole week with you. If I prescribe it, insurance companies will cover it; Medicare will even pay for it, if you accept their minimal reimbursement."

"That's the rub, I know. We can't afford to settle for less than half our registration fee."

"That I can well accept. I had to visit this place for myself. If you give lectures, I'd love to listen in, whatever topics you cover."

Darby's face felt flushed. Lectures? "You are quite complimentary, sir, but I fear my lecturing days are over. I left those behind in the classroom, or in recurring nightmares. Plus, I'd hate to impugn this wonderful Villa's reputation."

"Now, now! I doubt that would happen. Would it?" Cochrane asked Linda, as she carried in a tray, arranged with three, glazed, royal blue petit pots de crème, filled with tiramisu.

Linda glanced at Darby with embarrassment as she served each guest a cup. "I don't know," she smiled. "Everyone loves Darby. Now, be good and eat your dessert. I made it myself, fresh, this afternoon, with a hint of kirsch in the bottom of each cup." Her face lit up with its typical magical fire and inimitable mystique.

Darby winked at the silent doctor as Linda slipped away. "*C'est bon, non*? She hasn't served this in some time."

"I was thinking perhaps the *bon* referred to her!" he smiled. "Or should I say, *la belle*? Isn't that right, darling?" he deferred to his wife.

"Whatever you say!" she stared in return before glancing at Darby.

* * *

Preparing to move back into the cottage proved more difficult than Darby had anticipated. For a long while, he sat at his desk—the Villa's desk—he reminded himself, and stared at its faded green blotter, penholder, stapler, telephone and small dish of varied colored plastic-coated paperclips. He would miss the room, as well as its adjoining sleeping quarters. But, perhaps it was for the best.

While feeling sorry for himself, he glanced up to discover Linda standing in the doorway. "You're an interesting study, you know?" she said with wistful candor. "JP told me what you said, about moving out. 'No, siree!' I replied. 'He's staying here! This is his office and quarters as much as ours.' So I told him." She stepped closer, glancing over her shoulder as she approached his desk. "Darby! I want you in here, near me! Not out there! I don't trust JP anymore." She raised herself to the corner of the desk and sat facing him. Her petite hands, body, short hair, left thigh, and dark eyes converged in a collusion of visible tender desire. He could hear her silky dress squeak. She bent forward and placed his left hand on her thigh. She pressed it gently into her firm and sensuous quad and covered his hand with her own. Leaning closer and closer, she smiled, as her lips touched his. "I want you right here. Where I can keep an eye on you." She glanced about the office, its books, furniture, and file cabinets. "JP's asleep! Snoring, in fact." She eased off the desk with her hand still on his; then entwined her fingers about his. Her eyes wandered toward the bedroom. "We can at least cuddle and lie in each other's arms."

Darby rose, his hand tightly gripping hers. He bent down and kissed her and followed her into the bedroom. When two hours later she slid out of bed, he walked with her through the office toward the door. He kissed her again, opened it, and watched as she slipped quietly down the hall. The fire was still glowing in the living room. He peeked in. Hampton and his wife had their shoes off and were listening to music on the CD player. Chopin! He returned to his room, undressed, climbed in bed, and stared at the ceiling. Bright moonlight filled the office with a silent silvery glow. Wide awake, he lay there long into the night before drifting off to sleep.

* * *

"A remarkable night!" Hampton greeted Darby as he stepped into the dining room for breakfast. "About midnight I awakened. The moonlight was so bright I could count the limbs on the ginkgo tree. I love those trees. Summer or winter! To think, they carry us back to the carboniferous era. Or is it the Pleistocene, when dinosaurs roamed the earth? Plus, they have medicinal value. Anyway, I need an adventure today. Your chef tells me there's a wonderful path down to a bottom and back. Will you go with me? I would love to pursue our conversation of last night. Pamela wishes to stay here and read."

Darby felt only half awake, but his instincts welcomed the invitation. It seemed like weeks since his last outing of any significance. "Yes! I could use a long walk. As soon as the sun dries the trail a bit, let's go."

"Perfect!"

"Just be prepared for mud! That's all!"

* * *

Mud, indeed! Darby mused as they sank past their bootlaces near the bottom. The road down had been soft, but firm enough. Snowmelt and runoff, however, had turned the base of the trail into a bog. Carefully, they negotiated the soggiest areas and came to the entrance of the mica mine.

"This must have been some operation in its day?" Hampton queried. He leaned back and stared up at the brown web of vines that dangled rope-like from the granite crags above. "A daredevil might try that!" he observed.

"He just might!" Darby's mind exploded with curiosity. He wondered if that's what happened to Stephanie's father? Had he wandered too close to the overlook's edge and fallen off?

"Can we sit here?" Cochrane motioned toward one of the larger rocks. "This would make a great place for a bench, or a small gazebo, or perhaps to be left just as it is."

"I think so. It's hard to improve on Nature, though clearing back brush might heighten its effect. One can create the gift of rustic wholeness, as Japanese landscapers do, if not disturbing an area's natural beauty and rugged aura. The designer of our ginkgo garden achieved that somewhat. I love sitting amid its azaleas, its laurel and rhododendron, and yielding to its arcane and unadorned spell. I can see a thatched hut here, but I think it'd be better to leave it natural, as it is. Maybe a wooden bench might do."

Hampton stood up and turned toward the creek. Around and about him towered the forest's stark and leafless oaks, laced with graceful hemlocks and lone pines, all indigenous to the mountains' soil. A hawk cried overhead. Darby could see its massive broad wings and reddish-brown tail feathers. It circled high above, cried a second time, then, in a long silent graceful dive, glided swiftly into the woods.

"I must come back," said Hampton. "You are fortunate! Indeed! What I would give to have my clinic here!"

PART FOUR

Misty

Chapter 31

January's frigid weather ushered in a still snowier February. For two weeks, guests cancelled reservations at the Villa. They would try again in March or April, they wrote. Drifts, seven-to-eight feet deep, prevented the Haywood County's Maintenance Department's ablest crews from clearing little past the forks below.

Darby spent the snowy reprieve holed up in the office in the mornings, moving out to the cottage in the afternoons. He scoured both libraries—Garnett and the cottage's—for any resources on seventeenth, eighteenth, and nineteenth century German literature and philosophy he could find. Insufficient data made research difficult, but Internet access to Princeton's library provided the basic resources he required. Perusing Kant, Leibnitz, Hegel and others bolstered his descent (or was it ascent he wondered?) into his project: *From Wittenberg to Weimar*. The question, when and if completed: would any scholars take him seriously? In particular, Friedrich Schleiermacher's thesis that the "feeling of absolute dependence upon the Infinite is inseparable from one's own self-consciousness" summed up the German's belief that the Eternal is known primarily *in one's self-consciousness* and cannot be isolated from one's deepest sense of self.[1] One simply cannot be a person without being in relation to God. Then Feuerbach and Nietzsche came along and dismantled Schleiermacher's conviction, underscoring his own thesis all the more: that the human condition must find *within* itself the grace and courage that it had formerly hypothesized lay *outside and beyond the self*. If anything, the story of humankind meant that God had moved from outside man's consciousness to inside man's essential mystery. And to be that man was to be free. It made such perfect sense to Darby. But would anyone else see it? Nietzsche was wrong to conclude that God was dead, but he was right to insist on the need of the *Übermensch* to become one's own center of value. Can I pull that off, Darby wondered.

1. Schleiermacher, 1768–1834. *Faith*, Vol. 1, 17.

* * *

The writer of whom Linda had spoken arrived the first weekend in March. Snow still lingered in the shadows about the Garden. Icy clumps covered the ground around the gateposts, and in the orchard melting patches glittered in the sunlight.

Darby had just returned from the bottom. While there, he had assembled a log bench, fastened with wooden pegs. He had arranged it near the site where he and Hampton had rested beside the brook. Tired and muddy, he was in the process of scraping mud off the insteps of his boots when Linda appeared at the backdoor.

"Ah-hum! Dr. Peterson!" she cleared her throat. "Allow me to introduce Trudy Belle Hartley. Miss Hartley, Dr. Peterson!"

Darby looked up at a rather full-bodied woman. Homely, yes! But ugly? No! A half-smirk drifted across Darby's mouth as he studied Linda's. Women, he knew, always loved to disparage a man's interest in another woman. "My honor!" Darby extended the woman his hand as he ascended the steps to greet her. She clasped it with some hesitation, but with a friendly smile. Dressed in a tight short black skirt, knee-high chestnut leather boots, black jacket and green blouse, she hardly disseminated the looks of a romance writer or historical novelist, whichever she was. Nor did her plumb cheeks, square face, plucked eye brows, thin eye lashes, and plum lipstick enhance the woman's beauty either. Perhaps she knew that, but just didn't care. He guessed her to be in her late fifties. Silver earrings dangled almost to the top of her shoulders. Long auburn strands of hair descended straight down the back of her neck. If she had combed it recently, or in the past month, no one but a hairdresser would know. "I shall look forward to your stay and any conversation you might choose to share."

"I too!" she replied with cordiality. "Don't be offended if I remain aloof. I'm really a recluse. I prefer it that way. I love to write and that's about all. But I will be civil." She turned toward Linda. "I'm tired now and wish to see my room."

Linda's eyes betrayed her own estimate of the woman's geniality. "This way!" she replied politely. "Darby, we will see you at dinner."

"Yes, ma'am!" he responded. "I know my place!"

Both women looked at him as only women are capable of glaring. Whether they were disguising humor or disgust, he couldn't tell.

"I'll be there!" he emphasized, with a squeeze of Linda's hand.

* * *

With Miss Hartley's being the only guest, Linda set the table with the writer to Darby's right. Close enough for conviviality, but no closer! Darby noticed the unusual arrangement, but kept his thoughts to himself. Having changed clothes and put on a fresh shirt, tie, and navy blue double-breasted jacket, he was somewhat surprised when Miss Hartley entered in the same outfit in which she had arrived. She had rolled her long hair into a bun and had affixed it with a sharp silver needle the size of a large straight pin. The point reminded him of a trash-man's pick-up stick.

"Do you always stare at guests like that?" she said as he rose to pull back her chair. "I can take care of myself."

Darby assisted her, nonetheless, and reseated himself. "It's an old habit, I suppose. My mother insisted on such manners."

"Actually, I like it!" she shook the strands of a few hairs that were tickling her neck. "I write historical romances, set in palaces and bedrooms," she rolled her eyes, "in castles in the mist, and on lonely battlefields amid carnage." She smiled briefly, as if to test his interest.

Darby noticed, but responded with only a feigned nod of his head.

"My critics deplore the latter and consider the former shameless. Frankly, sir, I don't care. It's a good living. Not art, poesy or literature, but a living. What about you? Mrs. Wagner tells me you're a scholar. My, but I'm talking more than I have in weeks!" she placed her hands on her bosom, with an affected release of excited breath. "It's a lonely life, writing, you know? I expect you agree."

"I haven't written that much fiction, but scholarship exacts its pound of flesh. I know what it is to be abased and criticized for the slightest discrepancies. A professor's rise to fame can be dashed by a single review. It happened with my *History of Western Philosophy*. 'Too much on the classics!' 'Not enough in-depth attention to current literature.' Critics can be mean. But tell me, please, what all you've done."

"Not in the mood tonight! I did find my first novel—*Canals in the Moonlight*—in your living room, though. The story of Byron's last days! It took additional novels before I ever became noticed. Now, I'm struggling to hang in. I'm in the twilight, if not moonlight of my years. I'm hoping this retreat will help me complete a biography on Catherine the Great. Now, there's a woman for you! But that's for another time. No offense, sir! I'm just tired."

"I, too! Would you care for some wine? I know Linda will be out with our salads soon."

"Thank you, but no! It dulls my senses," she sipped on her glass of water. "You must tell me sometime all that you've done. Ah!" she turned, as Linda placed a crisp endive salad before her, and one before Darby.

Darby winked at Linda and, for the remainder of the dinner, ate for the most part in silence observing and listening to what minimal muttering Miss Hartley deigned to share.

The next two weeks found Miss Hartley equally reticent. She descended for breakfast only after Darby left, and slipped down for lunch only before Linda gathered up the modest spread. Occasionally, Darby caught glimpses of her wandering about the yard, sitting in the Garden, or walking along the road parallel with the orchard. Yet, as the evenings progressed, she relaxed and become more voluble.

"What can you tell me about Catherine the Great that's caught your interest so?" Darby asked. "Just curious. All I remember his her sordid affairs with younger men and her fascination for horses."

"That's rubbish! The horses, I mean! There's no proof of it at all. Her detractors hated her and concocted that nonsense only to hurt her."

"What nonsense is that?" Linda asked, as she served the main entrée. "I've never cared for biographies, unless they're exceptionally well-written. Or loaded with gossip!"

"Unfortunately, there are plenty of those. Maybe Dr. Peterson is more qualified to answer your question," the woman stared up at Linda.

"Well?" Linda arched her eyebrows, as she set Darby's plate in front of him. "What about the horses?"

"You don't want to know. Seriously, Linda! I misspoke," he averted the writer's gaze.

A thin smirk formed on Hartley's lips. "Shall I tell her? I think I should!" she relished the sudden attention. "Rumors have it that Catherine craved well-endowed men. She could never get enough. She went through numerous lovers, or paramours, we should say. Night after night!"

"And?" Linda pressed the woman, winking at Darby as she did. "Where do the horses fit in?"

"Well, your words *fit in* pretty much answer that. Do I have to spell it out for you?" Hartley emphasized the word *spell*.

"I got ya!" Linda laughed. "Fit! I wonder if she was fit to be tied?"

Hartley stared at her plate, clenched her teeth and set her jaw. She would not be humiliated by such a pun or deign to respond.

"I'm sorry, Miss Hartley! It was just too good to turn down."

"Oh, forget it!" she waved her away. "I had it coming," the writer finally smiled. Suddenly she bent forward, almost touching her plate with her forehead. "*Fit!*" she laughed. Her sides heaved with convulsions. "Oh, God! I needed that! I've been so pent up for days! You can't believe how worried I've been! *Fit*," she chuckled one more time. "Fit!" she repeated. "Oh, God! Maybe I should include that!" she continued laughing.

Toward the end of March, a warm mass of air blew in from the south-west. Below the three-thousand-foot level, buds on the hardwoods' branch-es turned mauve to deep purple. Twig ends bulged with pollen, and breezes blew unending clouds of green mists across the yard and into the woods. Ornamental pear trees bloomed along the highway into Waynesville. Stalks of bright jonquils filled the ditches and shoulders of the town's streets and roads, lining the way with graceful custard-colored blossoms.

A number of guests kept the Villa solvent. Among Darby's favorite re-turnees were the Hutchinsons, Brandon and Susan James, and the Gibsons. Midway through the month, two sisters showed up, chatty and affable at the table, but each sibling harboring resentment for the other. Their hurt surfaced in between meals or while Darby was in his study or in the Garden.

The older of the two, a very polite, thin-faced brunette, with a kindly smile motioned to him one afternoon just as he was returning from the overlook. The cerulean sky glowed especially blue and filled the Garden with a fresh, subtle scent of earth and air.

"May I bend your ear?" she asked, as she glanced toward one of the metal chairs.

"Of course. Let's sit here," Darby suggested, as he gestured toward a bench near the ginkgo tree. "This is one of those rare beautiful days we've not had in a long time."

He waited for her to take a seat; then sat beside her.

"You've met my sister. We're both so pleasant at the table. But reality is quite different," she raised her eyes to look into his. "Our mother was bipolar. Had us within five years of one another. Then she fell ill, actually went into a postpartum depression from which she never recovered. That dumped everything on Dad. As Mom grew worse, more and more respon-sibilities fell on him, but since he had to be out of the house so early for work, I became my sister's nanny. Dad's last words every morning were: 'Be sure to see that Carol gets up, has breakfast, and gets to school on time.' He never asked about me. Mom just lay in bed or stared at the wall. Eventually, she had to be committed. She died from a heart attack. At that point, Dad began seeing another woman and rarely cared for us at all. Oh, he was there at night, but Carol and I fell through the cracks. Whenever she'd cry, Dad always took her part and scolded me as if I were to blame. I don't know how we made it through high school, let alone college, or got married and moved out on our own, but after Dad's death, Carol never wanted anything to do with me. That was true even before I left home. She still hates me for 'bully-ing her as a child,' she claims. But, God, it was all I could do to care for her and myself—let alone our father when he came in. We came up here to try to mend things, but the hurt I harbor still burns in my heart." She looked up sadly toward Darby. "If you wonder why, it's because Carol's never expressed anything but antipathy for me. That's a sad story, but true," she glanced again toward Darby. "You're one of the few who really knows how I feel. Thank you for listening."

The evening before the two sisters left, Carol, Mary Allen's sister, knocked rather loudly on the office door before entering. "May I come in?" she asked. She was taller than her sister, with high shiny red cheekbones and a dark complexion. Her gray eyes never once blinked as she sat in the closest chair near Darby's desk.

Darby rose; then sat down again.

"I saw my sister out there in the garden yesterday with you. I don't know what she told you, but I wouldn't believe a word of it. All my childhood she bossed and yanked me around, like I was some kind of dummy: 'Get up. Get dressed! Brush your teeth. Hurry, hurry! We haven't all day.' And on and on! I tried to be nice and still try. I've tried to forgive her, but she's always been that way. It began when I was just a little girl. She's hated me all her life. I really don't like her at all and wish she would die. The only one who ever loved me was my daddy. But once Mama got sick, poor Daddy just faded away. It's been hard, Dr. Peterson, It really has. How about that for enmity? Ha! As if I should care! Maybe some day we'll see things differently, but if she were to die tonight, I'd not shed a single tear."

Darby sat forward at his desk. "The loss of a mother at an early age wounds everyone, doesn't it? Your father, you especially, even your sister? That you wanted to come and rediscover your lives speaks volumes about each of you." He looked thoughtfully into her eyes. "Maybe you might tell your sister sometime how much your parents' death hurt you and changed your feelings for her, how you always felt abandoned and unloved, except by your father. Mary Allen may well feel the same way and just doesn't know how to tell you. You only have each other now, other than your husbands and children. You're each other's only link to your parents, their living dream beyond themselves. I have the feeling you care for each other more than you realize, or you'd never have wandered up to Montesereno."

Carol stared at him uncomfortably. In silence! Tears welled up in her eyes. She placed her hands to her face, snuffled back her tears, and got up. She hurried toward the door, paused as she looked back; then ran quickly down the hall. Later that night, he saw her in the Garden. She and her sister were sitting together, hugging each other and crying. When they left the next morning, they each gave Darby a hug and kissed his neck. Together, they walked toward their car, laughing, hand in hand.

Chapter 32

With the advent of April, the bikers returned, and many sections of the Blue Ridge Parkway reopened. Curly came up with several helpers and pruned the orchard. Slowly, the Villa's grounds awakened to the changing mountain climes. Dogwoods bloomed; so also the estate's daffodils, along with the Garden's azaleas and the first white clusters of rhododendron. Spectacular tendrils of wisteria blossomed along the lower road, inching ever-closer up the mountain as temperatures rose. Hiking to the bottom provided an equally inspiring treat, since the walk brought the Inn's guests into the heart of the mountains' swaths of trillium, may apples, Galax, and jacks-in-the pulpit. Above all, the forest's songbirds filled the air with melodious warbles and tinkling calls. Once more deer appeared in the orchard to nibble on the pruned buds. In the moonlight, their coats glowed greenish-white with pollen.

None of this beauty or wonder, however, could forestall Darby's concern for Linda. The scaly itchy patch on her right leg had become swollen. A purple crust had formed about its edges.

"You've got to see about that!" Darby stated. "Looks imflamed. Pus filled! Are you sure you're OK?"

"Just tired! I've been bathing it with Epsom salt and spraying an antibacterial on it at night. The mist's very soothing. I'll do something if it gets worse."

During the last week of April, two guests arrived, their stay coinciding with the writer's final evening. Miss Hartley was shocked to learn of their identity.

"I was a brothel girl," laughed the female, "just outside Vegas. My name's Glenda Collins." She rolled her eyes at Darby, Miss Hartley, and the male guest.

"I'm a priest, turned Buddhist, then back to Catholicism," smiled the man. His tan baldhead glistened under the chandelier's light. "Now I'm a member of a new religious order—Our Lady's Brothers of Anselm. We're located in Abbeville, a little town near Augusta but in South Carolina." He wore a long blue smock, which hung loosely over his blue jeans, with open-toed sandals on his feet. Not quite as tall as Darby, the gaunt man exhibited an air of refinement and dignity. Darby surmised the monk to be at least seventy-seven, if not older.

"I'm in transition!" Ms. Collins offered. "I'm not sure what I'm going to do."

Darby could not take his eyes off her. To describe her as beautiful would be an understatement. Long blonde hair plunged down her back to the top of her buttocks. It shimmered flaxen in the evening light. Her light-tan silky knee-length dress, slightly exposed breasts, slender body, hazel eyes, long eyelashes and long fingers exacerbated his fascination, all of which was heightened by her smooth and delicate white skin.

She stared back at Darby with a twinkle in her eyes. If she had applied any makeup at all, he certainly couldn't vouch for it. She was just naturally gorgeous. He guessed her to be in her late-thirties, maybe even forty.

"Forgive me for staring," he said. "You must have been very successful?"

"Well, of all the things to ask!" Miss Hartley blurted. "Aren't you over-stepping yourself, sir?"

"Not at all!" Ms. Collins chuckled. "I'd be disappointed if he hadn't. Yes, I was! And banked every penny. And enjoyed it, too. I was young and wouldn't exchange the experience for anything."

Miss Hartley raised her eyebrows, casting a desperate glance across the table toward the priest. He smiled but remained silent. "Well, I . . . would . . . never . . . have thought of *that* as a calling," she muttered. "Seriously! I've written about anything and everything, but not *that*! Goodness!"

"I hope to put it in a book some day," the girl replied. "Incidentally, please just call me Misty! That was my brothel name. Misty Daze!" she threw her head back and laughed. "What a time I had with that label!"

"I bet!" the monk joined her in laughter. "I've seen it all myself! As a Buddhist, I wandered all over France. As for my name, I go by Brother Aurelius—St. Augustine's first name. My birth name remains Antonio D'Maricio."

"How kind of you to say that!" Misty patted his arm. "I learned long ago not to judge people, either. But, of course, I had some losers! I mean, ugh! As in, 'God, help me! Please, God!' Somehow I'd manage to survive."

"Now that you have my curiosity up, what in the world motivated you to go there and do *that*? Weren't you afraid?" asked Hartley.

"Afraid? No! But curious? Yes! I began at an early age, right out of high school. I first went to New Orleans, got involved in a bad way—you know, drugs and things, then read where Vegas needed cocktail girls to work in their lounges. So off I went," she smiled. "And that's where it really began. I mean men all but dragged me to their rooms and threw me on the bed. One was a manager of a ranch outside town. That's what they call the brothels—*ranches*. You know, like for horses, stallions, studs, like 'The Cock Farm!' He liked me. Gave me a thousand dollars to think about it. I mean, a thousand dollars! I'd never even seen a hundred dollar bill except in New Orleans. He gave me his room number. Wrote it down on one of the bills. So, the next morning, I got up early, showered, brushed my teeth, flounced my hair, and put on the sexiest outfit I had—this little skimpy pink cocktail dress I'd been saving back. I mean, I knocked on his door. I didn't hesitate. 'Get your things, Honey,' he said. 'We'll be out there in an hour.'"

"I can't believe you did that!" Miss Hartley stared wide-eyed at Misty. "I'd have been terrified! I get goose bumps just describing erotica, let alone doing it with strangers. Weren't you afraid of disease? Of being hurt? Beaten up by some drunk? Forced to do . . . just, well, I mean, whatever? Think of that! How did you manage that? My goodness!"

"There were moments. But the ranch didn't attract the clientele you're describing. We were upscale, only for gentlemen with money. You know, guys with good salaries, meeting for conferences in Vegas, eager to have a good time, to romp just once with a beautiful girl. That's what we did. I rarely saw the same man twice. Unless he'd come back before flying east."

"Did you ever fall in love?" asked Darby. "I can't imagine that men didn't fall in love with you."

"Some did! One guy wanted me to return to New York with him. Said he'd put me up in a townhouse and fete me with anything I'd ever need. But he was married. So were most of them. They weren't about to compromise their careers for a . . . a *prostitute*. That's all I was. Sadly, there were girls who didn't understand. They'd fall for some dude. Maybe he'd seen them twice. They'd pack their suitcase, hide it in the closet, and wait for the guy to return. Of course, they never did."

"Didn't you get depressed, living amid all that?" Hartley crooned. "That would break anyone's heart. Truly!"

"A little, if I let it. But by then I was in my late twenties! I was earning up to a thousand dollars a night. Plus, I loved sex, and was horny! Most of the girls were like me. Just there for adventure and money! I did it for sixteen years. Yes, I grew tired occasionally. In fact, a lot! It had its boring side. Its down time, with limousines full of losers. But it was my job. Deep down, I enjoy pleasing men. I wanted to be the best experience they'd ever had."

Darby looked at her longingly, embarrassed to do so. Hopefully, no one was staring at him. "Misty! I can't image anyone not wanting you, or a guy returning in his limousine, knowing that he'd never be able to forget you. That he'd carry you in his soul for the rest of his life."

Misty studied Darby's face with something of an attentive smile. "If I had thought like that, I couldn't have survived. The clientele began to change, anyway. Lots of Orientals, Russians, and Arabs! It wasn't the same. Plus one night two Russians got in a fight. One knifed the other. Blood ran everywhere. I put my hands to my face and screamed. Violence is one thing I can't take. I left the ranch after that. I went independent for a while. But that got depressing and lonely. I missed the girls, the excitement, our jokes and laughter, even our tears."

"What are your plans, now?" Hartley asked. "Heavens, it's not my business, but still! You didn't make that much money, did you?"

"Enough! I'll not starve. I can make it," she laid her hand once again on the monk's forearm. "Besides, remember, I'm in *transition*. Maybe some 'Hail Marys' would help?" she teased. "I wouldn't object."

"That would be an honor," Aurelius smiled. "I was arrogant enough as a priest, and lost and empty as a Buddhist novice. It took me twenty years to come around and reclaim my heritage as a Catholic. I'll be seventy-eight my birthday. I just want to die in a monastery, or curled up in the corner of a vineyard somewhere, or quiet chapel; be buried in an unmarked grave, one that simply reads: 'Brother Aurelius.' That's all God needs to remember me by."

* * *

On the morning after Miss Hartley's departure, Darby spotted Misty taking a walk through the orchard. With binoculars in one hand and a backpack slung over her right shoulder, she appeared to be scribbling notes. "I'm a bird watcher!" she intoned as he approached her. "Love it! Look at the list of birds I've spotted already." She showed him her note pad, handing it to Darby while securing the binoculars against her jacket. "See!" A camera dangled about her neck.

Darby ran his eyes down the list of birds she had sighted: Nuthatches, Indigo Buntings, Juncos, Toe-hees, Blue birds, White-throated sparrows, Purple Finches, four different kinds of warblers, Titmice, Chickadees, a hawk!

"Hardly an ornithologist's list," she admitted. "But it's a start. I take their pictures, select the best, and transfer them to my laptop. I'm hoping to turn them into gift cards, you know, like the kind you'd buy in a stationery shop or at a bookstore. Maybe a hobby that could become a career! Or part of my *transition*," she smiled with a drop in her voice. "Who knows?"

"You and your *transition*!" Darby grinned. "Sounds like a long road to me." He re-handed her the list. "Impressive, I will say." He glanced up through the trees, their swollen buds and white blossoms. "Have you ever thought of going back and trying college? Or matriculating somewhere, or enrolling in a *nursing program*? Old professors are prone to think like that, you know."

"I have! But not ready yet. I want to try Charlotte, or Raleigh, or Savannah for that matter. Or better still, Charleston. Somewhere a little artsy. But, the thought of waiting tables again or becoming a real *whore*—I mean a *lifetime whore*—that really scares me. I don't want that! Not any more!" her eyes met his.

Darby's lips parted, not quite knowing what to say. "There's a shop in Waynesville, in fact, many, where they'd take those cards. But you'd starve waiting to be discovered." He glanced at her neck, her lips, her shoulders, her eyes. "I don't envy your transition. My own aches my heart enough."

"Would that you had been one of my clients! But!" she raised her voice with spirit. "I did what I did. I loved it! And I made money. Enough to go back to college, or that nursing program you've mentioned." She flounced her long hair from shoulder to shoulder. "If worse comes to worse, I know what to do."

The gleam in her eye would have seduced Jesus, he thought. Maybe she was Mary Magdalene, reincarnate! Or the woman dragged in front of Jesus and flung at his feet. What in the hell were those Pharisees thinking? How spiteful the human heart can be! He thought about what Jesus had said to the woman, before glancing back at Misty. Did you just stop stone cold? he wanted to ask her. He couldn't help but stare at Misty, his thoughts captive to his libido in the worst sort of way. "You are beautiful, Misty. Forgive me, but you are."

"Thanks," she gave him a little kiss on his cheek. "Be careful, Doctor D. Remember, I'm still in transition."

* * *

While reviewing notes on the German poet, Hölderlin, Linda knocked on the office door; then entered. "Hey! You goober! Your Ms. Collins is something! A refreshing gem, isn't she? Darby, you aren't going to bolt on me, are you?" She sat beside him at the desk. "I need you. You know that. We need each other," she ran her fingers across his right hand. "She keeps using the word *transition*. Every time I come into a room, she mentions it. Darby, that's our word—*transition*. We can do it. I'm confident. JP and I don't even sleep together any more. We sleep in different beds. It's no good, Darby. He wants both of us *out*! It's as plain as day." She released his hand and sank back in the chair, her shoulders forward.

Darby leaned sideways and kissed her. "I'm yours, sweetheart. I liked what Brother Aurelius said about being lost and empty. Twenty years it took him. I love you and want to stay here."

"That's all I ask," she whispered, as she sat forward to scratch her leg.

"You've got to see about that. If JP won't take you in, I'll drive you to a doctor myself. You've had that long enough."

"I know. The swelling's gone down some. Give me another week. I'll make the appointment. I promise." She pressed her lips to his; then left the room.

* * *

As the afternoon wore by, Darby chanced upon Brother Aurelius in the Garden.

"Splendid place!" the monk stated. "What a location for a retreat! Our little cottage and cloister in Abbeville scarcely measures up to yours, but it's been all I need the past few years. Thank God I'm in my late-seventies now. It's been a long life."

"I take it you were elsewhere, no?"

"Your 'no' reminds me of my days in France. '*Non!*' '*Oui?*' Every sentence seemed to end with a '*Non*' or a '*Oui*.' Not that I'm complaining. Please join me," the good brother stood. "Such a beautiful place and beautiful view."

"Thank you," Darby sat with his back to the orchard. "I studied in France years ago, back in the mid-80s. I loved Paris. Could have stayed there the rest of my life."

"I passed through it in 1970, on my way to southern France," Aurelius stated. "That was right after my defection from the priesthood in favor of becoming an eclectic mystic—part Buddhist, part Taoist, part Zen. I wanted to experience it all."

"I'm sure it was quite valuable."

"It was. Incidentally, the Villa's website lists you as a retired philosophy professor. True?"

"Yes. My preference was the Classics and German Idealism, with a bit of Existentialism thrown in, plus Nietzsche. A kind of a Renaissance Prof. Nothing special."

"Have you ever read anything by the philosopher Clayton Rogers Clarke? I ran into him while in Paris. He was on sabbatical. We had quite a tiff one afternoon in the Garden of Luxembourg. He was keen on epistemology. Didn't care for my eclectic views or intention to 'run off to a monastery,' as he put it. I later read the man's work: *An Epistemology of Doubt: From Descartes to Rousseau*. Very interesting."

Darby smiled with bemused surprise. "Indeed! I read that book in grad school. My professors took a dim view of it. Said he was more into mythology than epistemology. Still, we were required to read it. Frankly, I liked it."

"I too," replied Brother Aurelius. "His emphasis on the inescapability of the self brought me back to the Church. Deep down in my heart, I couldn't deny the presence of a mystery that pointed me in the direction of transcendence. Plus his love for the Greek myths, which he took from Carl Sullivan, he claimed. In them he found the secret to his own life, he said, and the need to balance inspiration with reason. They say his death at thirty-five came as a blow to philosophy. It was a shame for such a pen to be silenced."

"His work partly inspired my own," said Darby. "Particularly his interest in Greek Mythology and the mystery of the self. It took Nietzsche to resolve the problem for me, though I've moved on since."

"People wonder why I want to be a monk. 'A wasted life,' some have charged, right to my face. But when I think of all the striving for ends that perish, versus the spiritual gains that endure, the Buddha was right. So also the Christ! There's nothing wrong with a monk's life or his love of peace and harmony, or search for solitude and silence. God has blessed you, Professor Darby, to place you in this Villa, whatever you might think. Thanks for letting me share my thoughts with you."

* * *

Darkness had long stolen over the Villa when someone's hands began pulling on Darby's shoulder. "Darby. Dr. Peterson! Wake up! Please!" The hands shook him again. "Sir! Please! Wake up!" It was a woman's voice, low, almost in a whisper. Soft, dream-like, yet urgent. "Darby! It's me, Misty. Glenda! Listen, Linda's sick. Jon Paul needs your help. Come quickly!" her hands continued to shake him.

Darby sat up in the darkened room. He could scarcely make out the woman's frame, silhouetted against the glow of the office. "Misty? What's happened?" He struggled to lift the bedcovers. "What is it?"

"Mr. Wagner's trying to sponge her down. I've been helping. She's sick. Running a fever—102. He's asked for help. I'm going with him to the hospital. Better get dressed." She squeezed his hand. "I'll tell him you're getting dressed."

Darby slid out of bed, flipped on the ceiling light, and, grabbing his bathrobe, hurried to JP and Linda's room.

Linda appeared half-dressed, limp, unconscious. "She's delirious!" moaned JP. "Can't get her temperature down. I'm taking her in. Ms. Collins's going with me. Can you two carry Linda to the car? I've already pulled it around. Keep near the phone. I'll call when I can." He turned toward Misty. She gathered up her purse, jacket, and a pillow and followed the two to the door.

Darby carried Linda in his arms. Her petite body felt as airy as an angel's wings. The threesome wrestled their way through the kitchen and out the side door. Misty opened the car's back door and arranged the pillow. Darby eased Linda into a fetal position; then closed the door while Misty slipped into the front seat. A grim look tormented JP's face. Whatever the man was thinking, Darby realized he hadn't expected this. Darby looked into the back seat. Linda seemed so small, rag like. He watched helplessly as the car pulled away. He returned inside and fell on his bed. His mind raced from thought to thought. He made himself sit up for a phone call. At three a.m., he finally fell asleep.

Chapter 33

When Darby awoke the next morning, the house seemed strangely silent. Still in his bathrobe, he stumbled out into the hallway. Someone was in the dining room. Its dim light cast a yellow glow into the hall. He could smell coffee. As he turned the corner, there sat Aurelius by himself.

"And a good morning to you!" the monk smiled. "What's happened? Are we the only people here?"

"Right now, yes! Linda became ill in the night. Jon Paul and Misty took her to the hospital. Now that I think of it, they didn't say which one."

"In Asheville, I would imagine. Or is Waynesville closer?"

"The former, I'm sure. They didn't call, did they?"

"If they did, I never heard the phone. How serious is she? Do they know the problem?"

"Serious, I know. As for the problem, I don't. When she returned from Arizona about two months ago, she had this scratch on her leg. It must have become infected. When they left last night, her temperature had climbed into the 100s. Hopefully, Misty will call soon. JP's out of his senses right now. It's a long story. Would you care for breakfast?"

"No thanks! I found a frozen baguette and sliced off a piece. For years in France, that's all I had for breakfast: a morsel of bread, spread with butter and a smidgen of *confiture*. I'd feel guilty if I ate more."

"I feel the same. I will have some coffee."

* * *

For two hours, Darby paced the office, staring at the desk and sometimes sitting by the phone. When it finally rang at 9:30, his arm jerked, his hand lunging straight for the receiver. "Hello! Yes! Montesereno here!"

"Darby!" It was Misty's voice. "We're driving back soon. Linda's fever hasn't broken. It's climbed even higher. She's hot as fire. Her face and cheeks, arms and hands are burning to the touch. I just felt them moments ago."

"Where are you? Which hospital? Are they keeping her, or what?"

"In Asheville, at the Central Hospital. They plan to keep her. She's in ICU, packed in ice. JP's been belligerent since we got here. He keeps saying it's his fault, but is taking it out on the staff. I'm dead for sleep. Linda looks bad. There are welts all over her body, big sores and bumps. I think she's suffering from a snake or spider bite, but nobody here will listen."

Darby didn't know how to respond. "As soon as you return, I'll drive down and sit with her. You'll have to be the hostess. You can do that. Several families are coming in over the next day or two."

"I guess my *transition's* coming to an end. My wardrobe's so limited. Just skimpy things you know, or casuals for hiking."

"Don't worry about that. I know a lady in Asheville whose clothes would fit you. She's very high class and discrete."

"Thanks, but no thanks! Wait till we get there. JP's signaling now!"

The receiver clicked. Belligerent! Would that Garnett had never added him to the will! His fault. Darby rubbed his face and placed it on the desk's blotter. Time to shower, shave, and get dressed. He heard a rapt on the window. It was Aurelius. "Come and join me in the Garden!" the monk summoned in a loud voice. "You need to get out of the house."

"OK!" Darby nodded. "Give me a few minutes, if you will."

* * *

Pacing about with the monk in the Garden brought Darby zero relief. His heart quickened, however, the instant he heard Jon Paul's car pass through the gates. Slowly JP drove the vehicle around to the back. Accompanied by Brother Aurelius, Darby hurried to the car as Misty and JP got out. Jon Paul glanced Darby's way, but said nothing. With head bowed, the chef closed his door and ascended the steps to the kitchen.

Misty approached Darby and touched his forearm. "He's worried. He said nothing all the way up. I told him what you said about my hosting for a while. He half-smiled but kept driving. I wouldn't do this for anyone but you." Her hands were trembling.

Brother Aurelius gave her a hug.

Misty smiled. "She's in room 532. They have her on IVs and monitors. She's a sick girl."

"I'll go soon. A family from Georgetown's supposed to arrive around three o'clock. Put them in any room you want. Just follow me to the office and we'll set up their registration."

"Sure!" she stared into his eyes. "It'll be like old times. Greeting clients you've never met and wondering what to expect."

Darby had to smile. "You never know until they arrive. You've got the skills." Darby stepped back to admire her long hair and slender beauty.

"I can handle myself," she kissed his cheek. "Better go check on Linda."

* * *

The drive to the hospital passed as if in a time warp. Darby took the curves faster than normal, scarcely noticing the changes nature had wrought. Twice he slammed on brakes, first, to avoid a deer; second, a groundhog, whose fur glistened red with mud where it had been feeding on the road's shoulder. He looked up into the rearview mirror to see the poor creature tumbling in the grass. He must have clipped it.

Once on Linda's floor, he made his way quickly to her room. She appeared so small, so punctured with needles, taped to her tiny arms, and all connected to chrome stands by yards of plastic tubing. Overhead a screen tracked her breathing, brain waves, and heartbeat. He leaned forward to touch her, to place his hand on hers. "Linda. It's Darby." But if she were breathing he couldn't tell. He glanced up at the screen. Its data seemed so erratic, dancing with rapid, elongated, and looping lines. Glancing about for a chair, he pulled one up beside her bed. "Linda!" he whispered. "Linda!" For the next hour he sat there, waiting and keeping watch. A nurse entered, checked her readings, then left. A while later a doctor came in, followed by the nurse.

"Who are you?" the doctor asked.

"A business colleague and close friend."

"Do you mind moving?" he stared at Darby, with an annoying edge in his voice.

Darby pushed back the chair and stood.

The doctor bent forward and placed his stethoscope on Linda's chest. "Here!" he said to the nurse. The two lifted Linda up, as the doctor ran his stethoscope across her back and lower ribs. They laid her down gently. "Does she have close family nearby?" he asked.

"Other than her husband and me, no. Not that I know of."

The doctor examined her chart. "Mrs. Wagner's very ill. If her temperature rises another degree, I can't promise she'll make it."

"What's happened? Do you know?"

"Not yet! It's just one of those damn idiopathic occurrences we're seeing too much of. We've taken all sorts of blood samples and fluids. I think it's Lyme disease. Not always fatal. But," he turned and looked down at Linda, "we don't know yet. It's very difficult to diagnose. It might be too late. If she has family, they need to get here immediately. I mean as in *now*! She's at a critical point. I'm sorry, but that's the truth." With that the doctor nodded to the nurse and the two left the room.

Darby sat down by her bedside. Outside, in the hallway, the sky had grown increasingly dark. Black clouds had gathered overhead; a heavy rain began pelting the windows. It drowned out the beeping sounds of the monitor. Sheets of rain slid off the panes in a dreary stream. Mist formed on the windows. For some unknown reason, Darby got up and ran his right hand across the windows. The moisture left his fingers wet and cold. He stared out over the hospital's lower rooftops where the water was gathering in shimmering pools. Quickly, he spun about and returned to Linda's bedside. He pressed her hand in his, bent forward and kissed her cheek.

For the remainder of the afternoon and long into the night, Darby sat beside her, clasping her hand in his, relinquishing it only when hospital staff entered. He broke off long enough to call the Villa. Misty answered the phone.

"Darby, is this you?"

"Yes. It's not looking good. I plan to stay the night, as long as they'll let me. How's everything?"

"Raining, but busy! The Georgetown guests have been cussing out each other over old hurts since their arrival. Brother Aurelius has been marvelous. He's managed to listen to all their grievances and calm them a bit."

"Give him my regards. I'll call again in the morning."

As dawn broke to the somber clatter of rain. Darby stood up, stiff and miserable and looked down at Linda. He put his hand to her feverish cheeks. They burned with heat. Quietly, he left the room to visit the closest restroom and, after splashing water in his face, returned. Outside it was raining even harder. It was impossible to see the rooftops. Darby reseated himself and began stroking Linda's hand. He rose and peered down at her face, her complexion, and closed eyes. Tiny wrinkles had trapped drops of perspiration about her brow, eyelids, and nose. Her tangled short hair struck him as such an anomaly in comparison to her normal, energetic, and healthy state. "Linda!" he whispered, wiping beads of moisture from her cheeks. He sat back to hold her hand again.

Why had he delayed so long before loving her with all his heart! Now he wanted only her. Julia would never come back. Dianne but a flicker in the night; Celeste, hot, erotic, a hungry man's one-time dream; Melanie, but a girl, too young to know her own heart. But Linda! He leaned down, ever so close, and brushed his lips gently against her inflamed cheeks. Darling! Darling. Please don't go away. Please! Please!

Suddenly, a beeping noise sounded and the screen over her bed went flat. A bell rang. Footsteps reverberated in the hall. A nurse pushed Darby aside. "Dammit!" someone cursed. It was a doctor. He slapped Linda's chest and pressed his hands down hard on her torso. "Damn!" the doctor kept muttering. "Sir, you will have to leave the room. She's critical. Please, step out!"

As Darby backed out, the doctor gave Linda a shock to restart her heart. The door closed. Twenty minutes later when it reopened, the nurse stood in the doorway. Hall lights blinked and an aide, pushing a gurney, hurried toward the room. The doctor stepped out and looked up at Darby. "Please, sir, we have procedures to follow. We're taking her to the morgue. I'm sorry. We're all sorry. You can view her there."

Chapter 34

Linda's death occurred so suddenly that neither Jon Paul nor Darby had prepared an obituary. The one that appeared in the papers incensed Darby's conscience. Jon Paul had provided the scantiest of information. Date of birth, date of marriage, date of death, plus length of years at Montesereno. "*Her presence will be missed*," was all Jon Paul was quoted as offering. Aside from the death announcement in the paper, few, if any of the Villa's friends knew of Linda's demise, let alone funeral arrangements.

In a small cemetery just east of Waynesville, Darby stood silently beside Hettie and Curly, Aileen and Merle. Jon Paul stood opposite the casket where it rested atop the open grave. Brother Aurelius and Misty stood at the foot with heads bowed. The minister—a pastor of a nearby rural church—had just uttered a somber "Amen," when suddenly he turned toward Darby. "Mr. Wagner tells me you were once a priest. Would you like to offer a closing prayer?" Numbness fell across Darby. What was he to say? He had no holy water or even a cross to sway across the casket. Would his heart permit him anyway? He wanted only to savor Linda's memory and bury his heart in sorrow. He looked about at the small band of mourners and, searching his mind for what to say, stared with emptiness toward Brother Aurelius.

Instantly, the good monk stepped forward, cross in hand. "May we pray?" he said. "Let us bow our heads." A hush fell upon the tiny band. "Almighty God. Dear Holy Mother. We return Mrs. Wagner into your arms. Her life touched so many and blessed them with charm. She was the rose of the Villa's Garden, the angel of its joy. Hear our prayers and comfort our hearts." Then he began to pray the LORD's Prayer, followed by those haunting words of the Hail Mary. As he prayed, "be with us sinners now and at the hour of our death," Darby's eyes filled with tears! "Holy Mary, enfold her in thy arms," Aurelius concluded.

Darby crossed himself and stared down into the hole. Its slick sides appalled him, as if mocking her mortality. He wanted to kneel, to kiss her one more time, to hold her hands and press his lips against hers. Tears welled in his eyelids; then ran freely down his face. He fought to hold them back;

but they coursed down his cheeks anyway. When he looked up, the funeral director was indicating for him to move aside. Already the casket's flowers had been removed. The cemetery's workmen needed to lower the coffin. So quickly! So soon! He turned, blinded by his tears. Someone slipped an arm about his. He looked to his side. It was Misty. Brother Aurelius placed his arm about his shoulder. Together all eight, including the Veleskys, returned to the funeral home's limousine and the ride back to the mortuary's parlor. Jon Paul drove off by himself, while Misty and Brother Aurelius rode with Darby to Montesereno.

Following a dinner of soup and salad, rolls and wine, Darby turned to Jon Paul. "We have to talk about this, like it or not. We need to meet in the office, and all three of us—You, Misty, and me—decide what's best to do, at least for the next few weeks. Will you stay, Misty, and help us? You'd make a gracious hostess." He waited quietly for her reply.

"Yes!" she answered. "Provided you want me."

Jon Paul stared at her, then Darby. A thin smile crept across JP's mouth. Wine droplets glistened in his goatee. He had not trimmed or groomed it. Small veins crinkled red under his dark eyes, just above his flushed cheeks. He nodded in agreement. "You don't need me. Set it up yourselves. The Foundation's account paid Linda directly. The bank will transfer whatever salary you arrange once you go down and notify them. I haven't been as slack as you think. No offense, Ms. Collins. I'm too tired to pursue this any further. Good night to both of you."

Brother Aurelius began gathering up the dishes. "I'll help in the kitchen," he whispered. "Life has to go on, as well as your Villa!" He glanced up reflectively at the chandelier, then toward the breakfront's shelves of sterling goblets, fine china, and silver bowls. "Go on!" he smiled at Darby. "We'll be fine in the kitchen."

Chapter 35

As April drew to a close, Misty appeared at the office entrance one morning and stared at Darby. He was clacking away on his laptop, but he could feel her presence.

"Come on in," he smiled. "This can wait!" He saved the entry, looked up, and closed the lid. Her shimmering hair all but pulsated in the morning light. She stood clad in a long-sleeve yellow blouse and long black skirt. She had applied only a hint of rose eye shadow about her eyes and only a thin line of soft red lipstick to her lips. He rose quietly and reached for her hand. "I'm sorry I've been so preoccupied. I didn't mean to make you feel . . . neglected."

"More like a servant," she added. She curled her long fingers about his right hand and reached tenderly for his left. "Remember, I'm still in transition," she whispered in a gentle hush. "I have to have a little attention, too." She placed her arms about his neck and kissed him. "That's all!" She placed his fingers tightly about her own. "I know you've needed distance, time by yourself. You must have loved her deeply and could never show it."

He stared into her eyes, into her deep pools of pure hazel. Slowly he brought her fingertips to his lips and kissed them. He wrapped his arms about her shoulders and bosom. Everything about her was firm, strong, and womanly. Quietly he turned, glanced toward the bedroom, and led her into the sanctuary of that loneliest loneliness that begged to be healed.

"I have longed for this moment, as if from eternity," he kissed her shoulders, as he slipped his hands gently under her yellow blouse and slid them up under her brassiere. The latter fell to the floor as she leaned forward and unfastened its back. She turned and helped him slide her blouse up over her shoulders, about her neck, and over her long silky hair, until her lips met his once again. In turn she unfastened his belt and pulled down his trousers; then knelt and cupped her slender fingers about his scrotum and pressed her mouth against his underwear, tugging at his shorts until they fell off. "Misty!" he ran his fingers about her hair and grasped her ears. "Take off your skirt! Come, come to the bed," he half-gasped, falling backwards, lifting her up as he did, the two collapsing in silence on its downy quilt. He all but ripped off her skirt, as she lay on her back and waited while he sank his stiffness slowly and gently into her sacred passage. "Oh, Darby!" she whispered. "You feel so good. Here, let's try it this way," she whispered as she slid out from under him and climbed on top, covering his handsome face with her flossy hair. When an hour later they sponged off, it was as if Hell's chains and leg irons had finally fallen away and he was young and free again.

"Before you go, would you dance with me?" he asked. "For old time's sake, just the two of us. You and me? You're all I have now. I've several discs on my computer, you know, my iTunes."

"Sure," she seated herself, still nude. Then fluffing her hair, she waited on the edge of the bed as he opened his laptop and selected the piece.

He smiled and held his hands out to her. "God, but you're beautiful."

She stood and placed her arms about his neck. "That's the theme from Moulin Rouge," she whispered. "I used to sing it for customers at the Ranch."

"Would you sing it for me?

She ran her tongue about his lips and, leaning back, let her hair bathe both their naked bodies. Then she began to sing in soft whispers the song. He swung her away and out and around, admiring her beauty, then brought her back gently against his chest. Then holding her ever closer, he buried his face in her hair along with his heart.

Chapter 36

May's first weekend brought a full house of guests. Jon Paul persuaded Hettie to remain overnight to help Misty. "I ain't the politest, Honey," she looked up enviously at Glenda, "but I can tote the food in an' the dishes out. It won't be the first time."

Misty hugged her. "Everybody needs a Hettie. Especially you! We'll get it done."

* * *

With two exceptions, the guests that evening were first timers. They filled the chairs at both the main table and two smaller ones by the tall window. In addition to the glow of the crystal chandelier, Misty had lighted candles on the side tables and placed arrangements of azaleas and mountain laurel in the center of each.

The returning couple was Craig and Ada Gibson. They sat at the main table, Ada to Darby's right and Craig to his left. Other guests sat opposite each other the full length of the table, almost into the hallway. An air of gay informality reigned. Darby felt relaxed and at peace.

"By the way," Craig smiled, as he addressed Darby, "have you ever heard of a Jonas Sumter? He was jailed this past year on manslaughter charges, but escaped only to kill again in Georgia. Ada read it to me from the paper on the drive up."

"I have," Darby uttered with a startle. "He was a guest here. We were concerned about him then, as well as after his arrest. I'm not surprised."

"Well, he's in real trouble now. Apparently he's killed some lawyer's son-in-law. From what I could gather both men were hotheads, neither unwilling to give ground."

"How does the attorney fit in? Or his daughter?"

"They're from North Caroline, the Raleigh area. The son-in-law had lost his job but apparently accosted Sumter in a bar. Their words escalated into an argument. Whatever the issue was, nobody knows. But Sumter reacted with anger and bashed the man's face in with a billiard stick. The thing about it that caught my attention was the father-in-law's comment. Quote: 'I regret to report that my daughter and grandchild will be the happier now for this fortuitous, though brutal blessing.' How about that for a father's estimate of his son-in-law?"

"I know this father-in-law. Both he and Sumter were here, though at different times. The latter was a bully and apparently the son-in-law as well. After Sumter left, I perused a passel of articles on impulsive anger just to trace some of its causes. We've a small library on the subject."

"I need to check it out," a middle-age woman spoke up mid-table. Like Misty, she was tall, but with short, graying hair. With something of a drawn face and sunken cheeks, she appeared to be suffering from anemic or chronic digestive disorder. "My older brother and his wife are experiencing an unimaginable hell, thanks to his sister-in-law. The latter has hated my brother's wife since childhood. Mindy, my sister-in-law, says it began when they were children. She, Mindy, was the younger of the two, but their mother favored her older daughter, Nancy. I know it's confusing. All her life Nancy has been jealous of Mindy. Mindy is cuter, sweeter, busier, smarter, and anything else you can image. Nancy was married, divorced; then remarried to the same man. A year later, she shot him in an argument, but walked clean from the trial. Thanks to his wealth, she inherited tons of money. She never wanted children. Had her tubes tied at thirty-one. My brother and his wife have two sons—both married with children of their own. So, what does Nancy do? She invites her sister's grandchildren to her house on their birthdays and lavishes them with expensive gifts, just to thwart her sister's relationship with her own grandkids. It's been a nightmare for everyone."

"I feel very sorry for all of them, and you, too," said Ada. "She must be very jealous. I think every family's cursed with someone like that, who acts out of spite for the enjoyment of the pain they cause. There's a German word for it: *Schadenfreude*. It means *malicious pleasure*. We work with a clinic at home. Craig and I both volunteer as counselors. The flow of hurt people is endless, while those who hurt them rarely show up. Once in a while, we'll get a person who realizes they need help. Usually it's only after they've wrecked their own lives or strained their relationship with their family. Still they come, nervous and upset, paranoid lest anyone should question their actions or goals. They're rarely wrong, or sorry for the pain they cause others. We've discovered that the medications their doctors prescribe help them maintain a margin of civility, but in their hearts their anger never abates. Craig gets discouraged with them, while I keep trying. What if I were like that, I wonder? Manic one minute, depressed the next? Or narcissistic half the time and angry the rest?"

"I can top that," said a red-haired gentleman from the far end of the table, "though I do so without pleasure. This is true. Every word of it. I have an uncle. His name is 'Hoot.' That's right, Uncle Hoot. He has idiosyncrasies within idiosyncrasies. He needed some cash from the bank. So I brought it to him in the bank envelope, which he hid in his bedroom dresser drawer for safekeeping. Then, to remember where he hid it, he wrote a note with a big red arrow pointing to its location. To save money and not have to buy new carpet, he nailed planks down over the worn paths between his bedroom and kitchen. They've gotten slick, and he's fallen twice, but he won't listen to reason. I could go on, but would rather not. After all, he's my uncle." The man shook his head. "I know since he lost Aunt Lillian, he's been depressed. It's just that his world is so small. He keeps pictures of her in every room, but the glass in two frames is cracked, and the frames are gray with dust."

"That's sad!" Craig interjected. "But, what a beautiful hostess we have!" He raised his wine glass and tilted it toward Misty. "You need to join us yourself. Darby, how fortunate the Villa to have this lady as its hostess!"

"Hear, hear!" guests rallied about the room.

"You must hail from Hollywood!" an elderly gentleman toasted from one of the smaller tables.

"Just one state away!" Misty winked at him, as she made her way about the tables. With a sensuous yet gracious smile, she refilled each goblet with glistening ice crystals and spring-cold water. She paused and glanced toward Darby. "Well, maybe not *that* close, but thank you, sir, nonetheless."

* * *

As the weekend's guests cleared, Darby reminded Jon Paul of Stephanie's wish to celebrate her marriage at the Villa. "She wanted me to officiate, but all I can do is bless it."

"When's that?"

"Late May."

"I'm not sure you ever told me." Jon Paul was busy cleaning oven racks. The gooey cleaning paste had stuck to his gloves. "Linda took care of most of the reservations, you know. Better check the reservations and let me know." With the back of his forearm, he wiped a line of sweat from his brow. "Without Linda, I'm not certain how I'll do." He lowered his eyes and returned to his chore. "I'm in a daze, Darby. I don't give a *shit* whether I live or die. Maybe I'll pick up in a month or so."

"I understand."

"Oh, you do, do you?" He looked hard at Darby. "This was our place. Our dream. We worked as a team. She's gone now. Whatever my faults, we were a team. Not sure I want to remain here anymore. Your Misty's no replacement of Linda."

"I never said she was. But we need each other. I know we've used that line before. I'd buy you out if I could. You know that."

"And I you! I'd settle for half the estate's value if you'd leave. At my death, you could have it all! Why not think about it?" he straightened up, as he pulled off his gloves.

"I'll check the register and contact Stephanie."

"Encourage her to limit her number of guests."

"I'm sure she will." As Darby turned to leave the kitchen, he noticed a daytime photograph of three bikers outside a rustic nightclub. The crinkled photo lay propped on the counter under the wall phone. Someone had scrawled a series of numbers across the photo's face. The bikers sat slouched on Harleys; two with their gloved hands on the handlebars, the third with his arms folded. Each wore a leather vest and black leather biker's cap. A sandy airfield was visible in the background. "Friends?" Darby queried.

"And more!" JP muttered. He picked up the photo and stuffed it in his billfold. "There's such a thing as privacy, you know. Curly and Hettie will be arriving soon. Why don't you find something to do for a change!"

"I might just do that." Darby repressed his anger. He wanted to belt him. How much longer was this sort of crap going to go on? "Listen! We both need to ratchet our face-offs down." He stepped in closer and doubled up his right fist. "Just one thing. If you ever hurt Misty, I will knock your teeth out, if not kill you. Don't put me to the test. Are you willing to be civil?" Darby unclenched his fist and offered him his hand.

Jon Paul looked down, hesitated, then opened his hand and shook Darby's. "Look! After this Stephanie thing, I need a long break, a long time off," he waved him away. "*Kill me!*" he repeated. "And you were a *priest once!*" he smiled with wicked triumph.

Darby held his calm. What the hell! Still, he smarted at the insult.

* * *

Once the Bells arrived, Darby sought out Misty, and, half-smiling, half-embarrassed, kissed her cheek: "Misty, can you help Hettie pull the sheets, maybe dust a little, and ready each room for the guests. I'll work with Curly. We've a lot of brush to burn off in the orchard. OK?"

"Of course!" she kissed his lips. "It'll just be like old times, back at the ranch."

* * *

Around lunch, as Darby returned to the Villa, Misty crooked her finger slyly and motioned for him to follow her upstairs. Her smile aroused his curiosity, along, of course, with his infatuation for her every expression, smile, and curve.

Seeing the look in his eye, she shook her head from side to side. "No, no. Not that! Just come and see what I've done."

She opened the door to the first room; then hurried along the hall, opening each of the other doors. "Go on! Take a look! Be a good sport."

He peered into the room, glanced about, ever charmed by the elegance of the Villa's rooms, their drapes and furnishings.

"Well! Go in. You've got to go inside. Take a look! What do you think?"

He stared again, to the left and right, up and down; then stepped inside with a smile. On the window ledge set a beautiful greeting card, with a photo of the hawk Misty had taken earlier, transferred and printed in full red and brownish-gray colors.

"I put a different one in each room," she said, "with a little note on the back with my name. That's not being too presumptuous, is it? Don't tell me if it is."

He turned and stepped back toward the door, reached for her hand, and kissed her. "Misty! It's beautiful. Handsome! If they're all like that, you'll be getting requests for boxfuls."

"Sure!" she returned his kiss. "Thanks. I stayed up all night working on each one. It's a wonder you didn't hear me. I had to sneak into your office for some of the work."

"You must have closed the door."

"I do have some intelligence," she squeezed his hand. "By the way, a couple called while you were out. A Mr. Donaldson and his fiancée. He said you'd agreed to marry them. Is that true? I didn't know you were a priest." she blushed. "We rarely had those at the ranch. Honestly!"

"Well, I'm not anymore, but even priests have therapeutic needs. And you're very, *very therapeutic!*"

"I know what you mean!" she rolled her eyes with a giggle. "I loved it. In any event, they're coming in tomorrow to talk over arrangements. They've asked for the cottage."

"Well, I'm not authorized to marry them, but I can mutter a few words by way of celebration. You'll love Stephanie. She's still a kid but happy now. Let's go out there and take a look."

After opening the door and stepping into the cottage, Misty took Darby's hand and smiled. "Ah! I have the feeling this is a trysting place, no? You don't have to answer. I just have . . . that feeling."

"Ms. Collins, you know too much. Would you like to see the bedroom? We need to change the sheets, you know, and get Hettie out here before she leaves."

"Sounds like a plan," she tilted her head back with a laugh. "Why not. I'm in your hands, as they say."

"Get in here," he tugged on her wrists. "I'll never tell if you won't."

She pressed her mouth to his and smothered his lips with her own. Slowly, they backed toward the bed and enjoyed what lovers have always enjoyed.

Chapter 37

Joel and Stephanie's arrival coincided with a tetchy event occurring down mountain. Misty and Darby could hear it but couldn't localize or see it. As Joel stepped out of his Honda, he pointed up in the sky. Suddenly a small plane passed overhead, just missing the treetops. It banked, climbed, with engine-whining vibrations, and, gaining speed, swooped past again.

"Not good!" muttered Darby. "He's either lost or about to crash."

"Maybe not!" Joel replied. "Look. He's bracing for another run. Could be taking pictures."

"Here he comes again!" shouted Stephanie, as the small plane's propeller and landing gears all but clipped the huge oaks behind the house. "He's waving to someone! See!"

"Not to us!" said Joel. "That's a hand signal of some kind. Who's back there, anyway?"

"No one that I know of, other than Jon Paul," replied Darby. "And he's in the kitchen!"

"Maybe it's a search party, looking for someone in the woods."

"Or someone interested in buying the property!" Misty offered.

"Or your old boyfriend from New Jersey," Darby teased.

"What's this?" Joel asked. "You are the lady I spoke with, aren't you?"

"I am. Misty's my name. Glenda Collins, to be exact! You must be Mr. Donaldson and, you," she turned to embrace Stephanie, "must be the bride-to-be?"

"I am. We're so sorry to hear of Linda's death. I cried when I heard the news. We'd hoped she'd be with us at the wedding."

"In spirit she will be," Darby hugged the girl. "Let's get your things in the cottage. We can talk after dinner. Remember, you have to get a license and have a magistrate sign and date it before you come up for the *wedding*. Plus a notary or magistrate has to officially marry you. I can't celebrate the Sacrament of Marriage anymore. I can only bless you. I'll come up with a good one, I assure you."

"Don't worry, we've already picked up the license," stated Joel.

"Yeah!" replied Stephanie. "But I'm not going to be happy, Doc, until you pronounce us married. A deal's a deal."

"Well, I'll do what I can," he squeezed her hand.

"I knew you'd say that," her large brown eyes emanated with joy.

* * *

As the dinner hour approached, Jon Paul came around the back of the house and rapped on Darby's office window. He signaled for him to come out. The big chef seemed unduly nervous. He motioned a second time for Darby to step out.

Once outside, Darby asked, "What is it?"

"I'm," he hesitated, "I'm . . . really not certain. I think I'm having chest pains. That's all."

"Should I get a doctor? Call 9–1–1? Maybe you'd better sit down and rest."

"No, no! Not that at all! Just a weird feeling! None of the other symptoms. Arms feel fine. Not clammy or sweating. Just a scare!" he smiled with pain. "See you at the table."

Darby watched the big chef lumber preoccupied back toward the kitchen. Maybe he had misjudged the man. Maybe Jon Paul was OK after all. Darby returned to the office. Just then the phone rang.

"Hello!"

"Darby, it's Jeff here. Got a room for me?"

"Of course! Come on! We've plenty of room. Where are you?"

"On the way. Just out of Asheville. Ready to take out that big, hairy hog."

"That'll be fine. You can hunt all you want! Plus gawk at our new hostess."

"New? What happened to Linda?"

"Linda's dead, died. Only a month ago."

"Damn, that can't be! I'm so sorry to hear that. What happened?"

"A fever took her out, some unexpected idiopathic disease. It broke our hearts."

"I loved her presence; her smile. Her just being who she was."

"Thank you. We too . . . We have a new hostess, though. You'll like her; she's beautiful and quite special. You'll see. We'll have a room ready for you when you get here and set an extra plate. A young couple's here as well. They'll be having their wedding celebration soon. You'll like them. He's a US Marshal and she's a young college student, or soon will be."

Darby walked back to the kitchen. "A Mr. Jeff Horne's coming up to go hunting. He just called. He's on his way! He's gruff, but fun," he said to Misty. "He's an alcoholic, so no wine for him. That'll make it cozy, just the three guests and the three of us. We should all sit at the table. Yes?"

"I prefer to stay in here," replied Jon Paul. "The kitchen's my realm. My domain. You and Misty join them. I'm fine."

"It would be nice if you'd join us," said Misty. "It's like you're in a cage back here."

"My choice! Thanks for asking. You *are* a doll."

"Careful! Dolls can break, you know," she kissed his cheek.

* * *

Horne's vehicle pulled into the driveway just as Joel, Stephanie, and Darby were about to take seats in the dining room. Misty had already placed salads at everyone's place, including Horne's. The gruff, gray-haired, disheveled figure wandered in and immediately pulled back his chair. "Ah! I'd better splash some water in my face and wash my hands!" he groaned.

"You can use the downstairs rest room," Darby stated, "right beside the office. We can wait for you or go ahead."

"Please! Go ahead! You must be the new hostess!" he stared benumbed at Misty. "Thanks for including me. And you, young sir, the marshal, and, you, young lady, the bride to be! Please sit down. I'll be right back."

Upon his return, Misty brought out one of Jon Paul's stock recipes: a simmering stew of chuck-roast, carrots, peas, and new potatoes, drowned in brown gravy, and garnished with leaflets of parsley. She set a basket of hard rolls in middle of the table. Jon Paul stuck his head out to greet Horne, waved to him, and returned to the kitchen.

"You must tell me about yourselves!" Horne directed his attention, first to Misty and then to Joel and Stephanie. "I'm just a *parts* man! Been running an automotive and truck repair shop since a kid. What about you?"

"Just in transition between careers," Misty smiled. "Nothing to crow about."

"I doubt that!"

"The marshal part's right!" Joel mused. "Worked in New Jersey for a while. Now I'm assigned to a post in the Charleston area! And you?"

"Raleigh! Love to hunt. Somewhere in the bottom below there's a huge hog I want to bag. Plus, there's a flock of turkeys and a million deer all over this place. Deer are out of season, but not turkeys. I plan to get up early in the morning and be down in that bottom before daybreak. Ever been there?"

"Yes, sir! Both Stephanie and I! Rugged area. Craggy and soggy! We'll probably wander down about noon."

"My Daddy's buried there," said Stephanie. "In that old mica mine."

"I heard about that!" Jeff answered. "I'll keep him in mind as I go by."

"I didn't realize that," added Misty. "You'll have to tell me sometime."

"Yes, ma'am, I will."

"Stephanie! Just call me Misty!" she patted the girl's arm.

* * *

Evening came early with wind and light rain. Darkness silenced the woods about the mansion and fog settled over the Garden and rhododendron. Everyone had gone to bed save Darby. He wanted to steal upstairs and sleep beside Misty, but, more than that, he wanted the invitation to come from her. She had offered it twice and would offer it again, no doubt. He loved her presence, that feminine élan that defined her and followed her into every room. There wasn't a corner of the house her smile hadn't graced.

For a while, he sat in the office's couch and thumbed thoughtfully through the pages of Whitman's *Leaves of Grass*. His favorites were the War poems, when comrades held the dying in their arms and tinctured their lips with water. But the one that caught his eye tonight was different.

> *O you whom I often and silently come where you are that I may be with you,*
>
> *As I walk by your side or sit near, or remain in the same room with you,*
>
> *Little you know the subtle electric fire that for your sake is playing within me.*

He closed the poet's volume and went to bed.

Chapter 38

"Darby! Wake up! Shhhh! Get up! Darby!" the voice rose in pitch, edged with a tremor of exasperation. It was a man's voice. "Wake up!" the voice reiterated. Hands began to shake him, back and forth with violence.

Darby sat up.

"Listen! You've got to get up. You got to get out of here."

"What time is it?"

"Six-thirty. We've all overslept."

Darby opened his eyes. Shaking him with trembling hands, Jon Paul stood half-bent over the bed. "We got to get the others up."

"Why? What's going on? Are you all right?"

"No! I'm sick. Real sick! But that doesn't matter." The man stood erect. Cold sweat trickled off his face and unkempt goatee.

Darby swung about and sat on the edge of the bed. "I'm still groggy!" he stared at JP. "Do I need to take you to the hospital?"

"No, no! Too late for that." JP pulled up a chair and ran his hands about his face. "I got to explain this, I know. You don't have much time. You gotta get Misty and Joel and Stephanie out of here. I mean, fast. Within the next few minutes."

"Are you in your right mind? Where's Horne?"

"Left! I got him up at four for coffee. He's already in the woods some-where. We don't have to worry about him."

By now, Darby realized that JP's entire body was shaking. His arms and hands, legs and lips were shivering with convulsions. "It's about that airplane? Isn't it?"

"Yes! I never meant it to go this far. I meant to call it off." Jon Paul could scarcely utter his words. A tightened larynx had all but silenced his speech.

"I'm listening. I'll get dressed while you talk."

"Better pull on your boots," JP mumbled in between jitters. "Listen! I was so angry at you and Garnett that I contacted a group of ex-bikers I once rode with and hired them to kill you. The plane overhead was the signal. The time, today! Hour, seven a.m. That's when I told them you'd be eating breakfast. They're armed and will kill you—all three of them. And anyone else who gets in their way."

"You can't be serious!" Darby struggled to his feet. "You must be delirious! You are, aren't you?" He glared at JP, stunned and with shock. "We *don't* have much time, do we?"

"No! I'll get the kids up. You'd better rouse Misty. I didn't know it was going to happen like this. I was going to take Linda off. Get her out of here before they came."

"How will they know who I am?"

"I mailed them a picture, a snapshot Linda carried in her purse. She never knew I took it. I copied it and put the original back." Suddenly, he lunged toward the office's outside door. "You don't have any more time!" he shouted. He flung open the door and left.

By now, Darby had dressed and laced up his hiking boots. He checked the desk's drawer for Tunstan's 9 mm pistol, slipped it in his jacket, and raced up the stairs.

Misty had heard the commotion and was already slipping into a dress.

"No, no!" Darby seized her. "We've got to run for our lives. Something's happened! Bad! Wear something warmer! Rougher! Jeans, sweater, boots! We've got to go now. I'll explain later."

He watched as she shimmied into her clothes. "Good!" he muttered. "Take my hand. Run now."

"OK! Give me a minute!" She stared at herself in the mirror; then clasped his hand. Quickly, the two half-stumbled out into the hall, descended the stairs, and ran out the back door.

JP, Joel and Stephanie stood in the cold air, shivering on the patio. A heavy bank of fog encased the orchard, cottage, and outbuildings. "Where to?" asked Joel.

"Anywhere in the bottom! Listen! I hear motorcycles! Hear them?" JP iterated in a trembling voice.

All five stood in the driveway, listening for the slightest cough of a muffler's rumble.

"Yes! There it is!" said Joel. "Darby! Do you still have the keys to the mobsters' car? We can hide in it. Maybe even start it," he adjusted his holster.

"I've never taken them off my key ring," he held it up for Joel to see. "Even if we could start it, we'd never be able to drive it out. That road's been closed for years."

"Maybe, maybe not! At least we can hide in it."

The muffler roars of bikes heralded their approach with muzzled vibrations.

"Hurry!" JP shoved them. "I'm staying here. Remember, I have a rifle."

"Sure! And once they kill you, what good will that do?" Darby gaped.

JP stared at all of them. "They can't collect their money till they've proven you're dead. I sent it in cash to a navy buddy in Valdosta. They have to show him your head!"

"Head?" Stephanie gasped. "O my God, Mr. Wagner!"

"Yes. Now, run. I'll hold them off." He grabbed Darby by the shoulders and kissed his neck. "Go. Go, dammit!"

Grabbing Misty's hand, Darby pulled her along into the fog. It ebbed lightly about his feet, but when he looked down at the road, he could barely see its sunken ruts. "Come!" he hauled her as she tripped along.

Recent ice had felled limbs across the lane; nonetheless, the four raced past the debris as fast as they could run. Patches of fog began to obscure their way. Darby stopped. "Here," he motioned, "we can form a chain with our hands."

Joel clasped both Darby's and Stephanie's, as she grasped Misty's. Together, they skirted the deadfall and crumbling embankments as they stumbled along. Twice Stephanie fell; twice Joel lifted her up and carried her piggyback. Finally, they had to rest. All four panted for breath. "Take it easy!" Joel encouraged. "We can hide in the mine's entrance if we have to, till we catch our breath."

Just then, gunshots could be heard from the Villa—the pop-pop sounds of pistols, interrupted by the muzzled roar of a rifle. The four paused, looked at each other, and listened. "We've got to keep moving," said Joel. "They'll discover we're not there, or force Wagner to talk. They'll want their money. We haven't long."

"They've got their bikes?" queried Misty. "They'll come on those. I used to ride bikes in Nevada."

"This isn't Nevada. They won't risk their bikes. That's their only way out, their ride home."

Another volley of shots sounded through the fog. Pistol shots, punctuated with two rifle reports.

"That's coming from the orchard!" Darby observed. "He's trying to lead them away."

"The poor man!" grieved Stephanie. "Will they kill him?"

Neither Darby nor Joel replied. "Keep moving," was all Joel said.

When they reached the bottom, cool banks of fog hovered over the stream, concealing the mine's entrance, but not the rocks and timbers outside it.

"No good!" said Joel. He stopped, un-holstered his Colt, and checked its cylinder. "Full load! But that's all."

"This way," said Darby. "The car's over there, somewhere in the thickets," he pointed.

"Guide us the best you can," Joel motioned. "The fog will be lifting soon. We don't have much time."

"Shhh!" Misty whispered. "See?" she pointed uphill into the fog.

Dark shadows were moving slowly downhill: two, one behind the other. Their jackets and black caps formed eerie silhouettes in the fog's drifting wisps. The mist thickened, engulfing the silhouettes. All became silent again.

Darby held Misty's hand while Joel clasped Stephanie's. In his right, Joel raised the pistol; in his left he clutched her cold fingers. Slowly, silently, quietly, they crept toward the enwalled car, somewhere in the fog, behind briars and kudzu. The latter's massive tendrils loomed gray and milky in the thick morning mist.

Voices near the mine broke the silence. "I see their prints!" a coarse voice muttered, just above a guttural whisper.

"Shih!" a second reprimanded. "I can't see a damn thing."

Quietly, silently, closer and closer Darby and Misty, Joel and Stephanie approached the vines. Cautiously, carefully, Darby entered the dark wall, lifting a wet mass of tendrils as he pulled Misty behind him. Joel and Stephanie followed. A crunch came up quietly from the ground, from a rotten branch under Darby's foot. All four held their breath. "Keep moving!" Joel motioned. "We can't stop here."

"Listen!" said a coarse voice near the stream. "I think they're over there somewhere, in that thicket!"

From a distance, an owl hooted. It hooted a second time. A chilling silence fell upon the forest.

"What's that?" erupted the startled voice of one of the bikers.

"It's just an owl. Shut up now and keep quiet," replied his partner.

Darby lifted his arms as they came to a second wall of entanglement. Silently all four passed through the web, then slipped through another.

A turkey gobbled. Waited, then gobbled again. Darby paused. The owl's hoot had warned the flock. Perhaps their clatter would mask their escape.

Darby placed his fingers to his lips for all to keep silent. The fog was beginning to thin. He could see Misty, Joel, and Stephanie's faces. He raised his arms again and slipped through a fourth tangle of briars. Hard thorns tore at his hands, his coat, his jeans. He could feel blood oozing down his face and legs. He pointed to the white disc of the sun, rising in the east, visible now through the silver fog.

"What's that odor?" Misty whispered.

"Hogs!" whispered Darby. "They're around here somewhere; be quiet."

"Listen!" ordered the closest pursuer. "Over there! I think they're over there. By the briars!" A pistol fired. Three shots ripped successively through the foliage.

"Hurry!" Darby pulled on Misty's hand. He buried his face in the briars and struggled to break through the barrier. At last! He all but fell against the car! "This way!" he fumbled with the keys, unlocking its rusted door, to tug on its handle. "I can't get it open!" he stated. "Joel? Where are you!"

"Right here!" Joel replied, as he grabbed the handle and yanked on it with all his might. "Help me! Pull on my body!" he motioned to Darby. "Girls, get under the car. For God's sake, crawl under it."

More shots zipped through the vines. One cracked the rear window of the car.

Once again, the two yanked on the handle. The door flew open. "Inside!" coughed Darby as he helped Misty and Stephanie crawl in the car. "Get in, Joel! Here! Take the keys. Try to start it. I'll hold them off," he pulled out Tunstan's pistol.

"No! Get in here yourself!" Joel grabbed him. "Start it!" With that, the marshal slipped back into the briars, his Colt in hand.

As he did, the fog lightened and lifted even more. There, less than twenty yards away, in the midst of the kudzu, loomed one of the bikers. He smiled, leveled his pistol, and aimed at Darby. "You're the only one we want. Fuck these others!" He pointed the gun toward Darby's face. At the same time, he spotted Joel. "One move, sonny, and I'll kill you. Drop your gun!" he ordered as he approached Darby.

Joel looked stunned. He was not prepared for this ending. Darby could see it in his eyes. Suddenly, the second biker reared up out of the vines and grabbed Joel from behind. What happened next sent Darby staggering back. A horrific explosion splattered blood all over Darby's face. He slumped beside the car and rolled to one side. Standing before him reeled the first biker, his face dripping with blood. A black hole appeared in the man's forehead. The stunned, would-be assassin stumbled backwards and collapsed in the vines. Just then, Joel managed to break the second biker's grip. The man looked up. Kneeling in the woods beyond the car was Horne. He had lowered his rifle to cock it again. The man lunged for Joel and, knocking his pistol out of his hand, began dragging him through the thicket. "Fire! And I'll kill him!" the man shouted. "Just one slip, an' I'll kill him!" Suddenly, a rustling erupted from deep in the vines, a scurrying all around. Dark and menacing, it tore at the vines' roots, snorting and tearing, ripping and thrashing through the tangles. "What's that?" the biker shouted. "What's that?"

Slowly, Horne advanced toward the car, rifle in hand. A look of horror creased his mouth. "Joel! Run! My God, run!"

The biker shoved Joel aside and turned to face the briars. Without warning, a terrifying apparition charged the startled man. The boar! It was the boar! Darby stared at its white eyes, black hair, and mud-caked bristles. With huge yellow tusks, it slammed into the biker, shaking his body like a rag toy, scattering his entrails to the squealing of the piglets, rushing through the underbrush behind it. Joel leapt on top of the car. The boar saw Darby, grunted, and raced toward him. The roar of Horne's rifle exploded in Darby's ear, as its barrel hurled its sphere of death into the pig's skull. The monster boar squealed, spun in a thrashing circle, collapsed in a loud grunt, and died beside the car.

Misty slid out of the back seat and smothered Darby with tearful kisses. Then she pulled Jeff into her arms and kissed him, too.

"God, woman. If I had known you was that good a kisser, I'd a killed that son-of-a bitch hog with my first shot and saved the second for that asshole there," he nodded toward the maimed biker. The look of triumph in his eye was nothing less than magnificence in all its glory.

Darby shook his head with wonderment and embraced the rugged man.

"Hey! I was born for this!" laughed Jeff. "As God is my witness, I love it."

* * *

By the time they climbed back to the top, they found JP's body where Darby suspected it would be. Nearby lay the third biker, as each had shot the other in a running duel through the orchard. Jeff checked Jon Paul's body for signs of life. His left eye had been shot out; red fluid oozed from a dark hole in his chest. Joel rolled the biker's body face up. Jon Paul had managed to shoot him in the neck. The man's eyes ran with blood. Dried cakes had formed purplish crusts about his mouth. Joel shook his head and rolled him back over.

While still peering down at JP's corpse, Darby felt a gentle hand on his shoulder. It was Misty's.

"Horrible, horrible!" she whispered. Her whole body trembled with spasms. "Oh, God!" she put her hands to her face. Her upper body continued to convulse with shivers. "I thought I was stronger than this," she mumbled. Desperation had crept into her face. "O Darby!" her voice cracked. "I'm so sorry."

Darby turned to comfort her. That's not what he had expected to hear. Her *words* had the ring of *shock* about them, abandonment. Surely she wasn't going to buckle, not after all they had been through.

She must have read his thoughts. He could see it in her eyes. Shaken, she patted his hands nervously and looked away. Her face was pasty. Tears sparkled in her eyelashes. A sigh slipped past her lips. With silent sadness, she turned and hurried toward the house.

Stephanie picked up on Misty's reaction and clasped Darby's hand. "It's OK! She'll get over it. We're alive, Darby! We're alive! We're standing here, alive!" She placed her hands on his shoulders, stood on her tiptoes, and kissed his chin.

Darby stared down at her—in all her sweet, innocent goodness. Her longing just to be whole! "You are precious. We'll get this cleaned up," he looked toward Joel and Horne. "I'll get Josh and Brandy back, and we'll have that wedding this May, whenever you want it." Then he glanced hard at the Villa. What to do? Should he follow after Misty to comfort her or what? Surely, she didn't mean what she said!

Joel opened his cell phone. "The sheriff's department, please! In Waynesville! That's right. Yes! This is US Marshal Donaldson with the Justice Department. We've had a murder at Montesereno. Four people killed to be exact. Will stand by for instructions. Yes! Thank you. Over!"

"Well, I'm heading back down to the bottom," said Jeff. "You got a gunny sack of any kind around here?"

"Possibly in the shed," Darby offered. "I'm sure Curly's got a few stowed away somewhere." He glanced toward the Villa again. What was Misty thinking? Her reaction had taken him totally by surprise. His own hands began to tremble.

"Hey! The poor girl's just upset," Horne said. "Come on, Darby, help me. I gotta save that boar's head and have it mounted! Ain't nobody in Raleigh'll believe me unless I do. Those tusks have got to be at least ten inches long, if not longer." He glanced toward Stephanie and gave her a hug. "Better go comfort Blondie," he smiled. "You just never can tell about some women. Come on, Doc. Buck up!" He too stared toward the Villa, with a faint hint of doubt in his voice. He patted Darby on the shoulder, with a nudge from his fist. "She'll be fine. Probably never seen that much blood before in her life."

"I guess not," said Darby, as he turned to help Joel. Together the two lifted JP's body and began carrying it toward the house. Halfway, in the thick of the orchard, still white with apple blooms, Darby looked up to catch a glimpse of Misty. She had stumbled out of the Villa and was throwing her suitcase and art books in her car. She glanced back toward Darby, got in, and drove away.

"Well I'll be damned!" Jeff grunted. "Who would of thought such a thing?"

Darby stopped, paused, and, glancing toward Joel, stood erect, dismayed. Someone reached out and clutched his hand. It was Stephanie. Her eyes betrayed a glisten of tears, her mouth partially open. "Ah, Mother of God!" Darby whispered, as he shook his head in disbelief.

Chapter 39

The breeze that ruffled Stephanie's hair tugged at Darby's white carnation, as well as Joel's. Together, the three faced each other, standing midway between the Garden and the orchard. A cluster of guests smiled, holding on to each other's arms. Darby looked out across the pink rhododendron toward Tunstan, stationed just behind Stephanie. He had flown in from New York to give her away. Darby reached forward and clasped Stephie and Joel's hands in his own. "May God bless you and keep you and make his face to shine upon you and be gracious unto you, now and for evermore!" Raising his head, he paused to take in the small knot of friends one more time. "Ladies and gentlemen, it is my proud honor to introduce Mr. and Mrs. Joel and Stephanie Donaldson. May God bless them and all of you who have come to share this moment."

A grateful ovation rose through the tiny throng as Joel gathered Stephanie in his arms and kissed her. Together, they both turned and hugged Darby. "You are the best," Stephanie muttered, choking back her tears with a smile. She stood on her tiptoes to kiss his cheek. Quickly she turned and hugged Tunstan. "You were so good to come! Look at you! Smiling again."

"I wouldn't have missed it for anything," he kissed her cheek, while pressing a roll of bills into Joel's hand. "Take it! Life is too damn short as it is."

The crowd melted away to gather in the mansion's brightly candle-lighted dining room. Josh and Brandy had spread an enviable table of hors d'oeuvres, decorated with yellow and blue mountain flowers, with a tiered wedding cake rising white in the center. Bottles of champagne bubbled uncorked for the guests to imbibe.

"Here's to the bride and to the groom!" Tunstan toasted. "And to all of you with good cheer!" he raised his glass a second time.

"Hear! Hear!"

"Such a darling couple!" Ada smiled beside Craig.

"Indeed!"

After kissing Stephanie's cheek once more, Darby wandered out to the Garden, champagne glass in hand. He set it down on one of the slate-gray walls and walked on through the orchard. Near the overlook, he watched as Curly worked the last few bricks into place, wiping off slices of damp mortar against his right pant-leg.

"Come, see what I done!" the scraggly haired, good-natured workman called. "It ain't the best, but it ain't the worse, none either," he stepped back to admire his own work.

Darby walked toward him, careful not to slip off the narrow path that bordered the orchard above the asparagus patch. To the west, one could gaze clearly over the treetops to behold the mountains in all their spring and rolling verdure. Green and luxuriant, they rose in majestic ranges as far as the eye could see. Darby paused by the site Curly had now completed. "You've done well," he congratulated him. Slowly, he extended his hand to touch the handsome monument, with its brass plates honoring Garnett, Linda, Jon Paul, and Stephanie's father. Each person's name appeared engraved on a separate small plaque. Curly had inserted a metal box, protected with a brass lid, just under Garnett's name. It contained his ashes. "No one could have done better," Darby assured the swarthy man.

"Here they come!" Curly stated, as he pointed toward Stephanie and her guests. "I shore hope she's pleased. That's all that really matters, Doc."

Slowly the wedding party made it up through the orchard and down to the site. Stephanie had removed her wedding slippers. Threading her way barefoot through the young grass, she stepped in front of the brick monument and stared down at her father's plaque. She stooped and ran her fingers gently across his name. Joel squatted beside her and placed his hand tenderly over hers.

"Poor Daddy! Poor Mama! All those years she thought he'd run off with another woman. All that time, he was right here down in the bottom, in the mine!" She exhaled a slow breath and, rising abruptly, hugged Curly. He placed his denim sleeve carefully across her shoulders and hugged her in return. "Thank you, ma-am," he whispered, not wanting to soil her wedding dress, or its dazzling lace. "Them's all the words I need to hear."

"It's beautiful, Curly! Like an angel's face, staring out across the valley! Thank you," she hugged him.

* * *

The warm days of spring awakened each morning, heavy with dew. June arrived amidst a burst of activity for the Villa. Darby couldn't have been more pleased. Josh's cuisine and Brandy's deportment brought new energy to the

Inn. Their presence renewed his own faith in the Villa, if not in himself. In truth, he enjoyed a trove of amenities most men or women would "kill for," as the saying goes.

If only it weren't for the evenings. The long arm of depression descended with them, cloaking him in their shadows of sadness and remorse. He needed Montesereno, if not a chaplain of his own, a Goethe Garden, a Brother Aurelius, a Dominetti to comfort him in his own loneliness.

Whenever possible, he'd steal into the cottage and listen to recordings of his favorite composers and their orchestral arrangements. How they brought solace as well as tears! He loved his role at the Villa, but how his heart ached for Linda and Misty's smile. Among his favorites were Samuel Barber's *Adagio For Strings*, followed by Ralph Vaughn Williams' *Greensleeves* or *Fantasia on a Theme of Thomas Tallis*. Sometimes he would listen to Tchaikovsky's *Andante Cantabile* or Rachmaninov's *Rhapsody on a Theme of Paganini*. Always the music, with its lush strings and fluid chords, lifted him to wholeness again. Then he would open his laptop and play the song Misty had sung.

*   *   *

Toward early July a gray Porsche pulled into the driveway. The noonday sun transformed its windshield into a blinding glare. Coming around from the Garden, Darby couldn't recognize the car's driver, but to his surprise he recognized its passenger. It was Gloria Gandy. The man who accompanied her slipped out of the driver's seat and held his arm out for Gloria to take as she came around the car. Together, the two walked toward Darby. Gloria had allowed her red hair to grow longer, giving her face a more oval and pleasant appearance. Dressed in a white blouse, blue denim skirt, and yellow sandals, even Horne would have found her stunning. She smiled at Darby and stopped with her companion less than ten feet opposite Darby.

"Dr. Peterson, my husband, Ralph Gandy. He wanted to meet you and see the Villa for himself."

"My pleasure!" the medium-sized, casually dressed man said. His hair reminded Darby's of Jeff's, as it was long, gray, and tied behind his neck. He was wearing a gold-colored golf shirt, tan trousers, and elegant shoes. "Whatever happened here," he glanced about, "changed Gloria. After she sobered up, she went to seek help."

"I did. I'm seeing a psychiatrist in Charlotte. I never knew how sick I was. Schizophrenic. I was hearing voices and imagining you present wherever I was. I could see this place, the Gibsons, and Mr. Horne. I felt ashamed. I wanted to change."

"And she has," her husband affirmed. "The weird thing, though, is what the psychiatrist said about her hallucinations. Both the visual and auditory."

"I was having those here," stated Gloria, "but Dr. MacHagan—my psychiatrist—assured me that that was OK."

"That's what surprised me," said her husband. "I always thought hearing voices and seeing people who aren't present meant you were crazy, but that's not the case. MacHagan says the ego has to do that to protect itself. It goes into a protective shell, surrounded by voices and other people, namely, aspects of one's self. It's the self, sorting out itself. She needed that."

"Plus my meds! I can't tell you how great I feel knowing that all that bizarre activity was OK, just myself trying to sort out my personality. I only wish I could have enjoyed this place more," she smiled at Darby.

"Why don't you stay for dinner? We've always room for extras at the table."

"Thanks!" her husband replied. "We're actually headed over to Waynesville to stay at the Balsam Inn, but," he glanced around, "your place is beautiful."

"Please do come back. You're always welcome."

"We certainly will," he nodded pleasantly, taking Gloria's arm to return to their car.

* * *

He had come to the overlook. Tendrils of ivy and mountain vine draped the rock barrier between the turnaround and the steep granite cliff. Yellow honeysuckle blossoms had opened fully, inviting a hum of bees to flit from flower to flower.

Work remained to be done on his project—*From Wittenberg to Weimar*! He had to smile. Was it worth completing? He brushed off a section of vines to sit on the wall. Would that his marriage had never failed. Would that Linda had not died! Would that Misty had remained to love him and he to love her! He leaned forward and placed his face in his hands.

He had much to be thankful for—Garnett! His career. His books, his teaching, the students he'd inspired across the years. Not every dream comes true for most. Certainly he had enjoyed his share, even here: Stephanie. Dominetti. Tunstan. Horne. Hettie. Curly! Dianne. Misty. And, above all, Linda! He inhaled a deep breath and rose to his feet. Brother Aurelius' image came to mind. His was a life worth living, the monk had insisted. A life of solitude was not to be denigrated. No more than a life in the mountains. So what if God is the only one who remembers us in the end? Or we simply vanish into Heidegger's great *das Nicht*? Or come out somewhere on the other side? Or even on this side, whether shattered and beaten down, or humbled and lifted up, yet all the more cognizant of the mystery and wonder of life?

Darby turned to stare out across the mountains. A chickadee lighted in the vines nearby. It cocked its tiny black crown and white cheeks toward him. Its "peep-peep" stirred Darby's awareness of all he truly loved. He looked off toward the Villa. Montesereno. The Goethe Garden with its ginkgo tree, then back across the mountains.

As he stared at their glory, the Muse of all he loved whispered its faint *pensée* for him alone to hear:

> And so I come to marvel once again
> At stands of fir trees trembling in the wind
> Where fickle Mother Nature's seasons change
> From ice and snow to summer's pelting rain
> And back again to autumn's flaming glow.
> I could do worse and in reverse erase
> Life's footprints of my own defaulted course
> By covering each with folds of gleaming moss.
> But having taken refuge in such thought
> Returns again the summons of Plato's call
> Transcending every shadow of lesser Good
> To seek none but the best and highest cause.

Darby laid his thoughts to rest. If only he had achieved the latter with clearer conscience; nonetheless, lifting his face toward the sun, and squinting at it momentarily, he walked back through the shade of the orchard, toward the Villa and its Garden, awash in the estate's summer glory and filtered streams of light.

Epilogue

S lowly, that summer metamorphosed into fall. Winter followed with its icy gales and veils of rime. Guests came and stayed, took walks in the snow, and sat with Darby in the Garden. Temperatures warmed to the sound of melting snow. Jonquils bloomed in the beds about the Villa. March arrived in a stream of constant wind, rustling the oaks and the pines, and, toward mid-May, the rhododendron and laurel filled the Garden with delicate clusters of pink and white blossoms.

Darby stepped out of the house and walked toward the ginkgo tree to sit beside the floral blossoms. For a long while he sat there, lost in a stream of ruminations that took him back forever. Or so it seemed. Just then a car approached the Villa's gates, stopped, then crept down the driveway. To his knowledge, the Villa wasn't expecting anyone. He rose from where he was seated and stared toward the car. The vehicle came to a quiet rest. With something of hesitation, its driver opened the door and stepped out. It was a woman. Whoever she was, she saw him and, lifting a long skirt to trail in the tender grass, came toward Darby. The woman had tucked her bun of flaxen hair under a large floppy green straw hat.

Was this a dream? A cruel hoax? An apparition? He rubbed his eyes. Was it Misty? He hurried across the lawn. "Yes! Yes," his Socratic voice whispered. He reached out to her, seized her hands, and stared into her eyes.

"Can we try again?" she asked, as she placed her arms about his neck. "I went first to Charlotte, then to Savannah, and wound up in New Orleans again! 'You stupid girl,' I thought. 'Haven't you transitioned enough?'" She looked up and smothered his mouth with kisses. "The truth is, Darby, I wanted it to stop. I just wanted it to end. I can't nay-say what I did. I was young. It was a career. I wasn't ready for it to stop, even while here. But there on Bourbon Street, I wanted it to end. As I stood in its darkness, I realized that I had been nothing but a *prostitute* since my late teens! Living in houses of prostitution, until the ranch at Vegas. And here I was! Back on Bourbon Street, just standing there. I began to cry. I wanted to come back. I wanted to come home; to Montesereno; to the only place . . . *of love* . . . I've ever known," she let out a hushed sob. She caught her breath and kissed his face and cheeks.

Darby pulled her against his chest. "Ah, Glenda! You and your *damn transition*! I guess I've been in one all my life."

She smiled, as her hands groped for his and their lips touched again.

THE END

Bibliography

Aristotle, *Nicomachean Ethics*, translated by Martin Ostwald, The Library of Liberal Arts, Macmillan Publishing Company, New York, 1962.

Dante, Alighieri, *Paradiso, Canto 1, The Divine Comedy*, translated by Allen Mandelbaum, Bantam Classic, New York, 1998.

Goethe, Johann Wolfgang von, *Goethe's Autobiography*, translated by R.O. Moon. Public Affairs Press, Washington D.C. 1949.

Heraclitus, "The Supremacy of Reason," in Abernethy, George and Langford, Thomas, *History of Philosophy: Selected Readings*, Dickenson Publishing Company, Inc. Belmont, California, 1967.

Kaufmann, Walter, *From Shakespeare to Existentialism*, Princeton University Press, Princeton NJ, 1959.

LeBoit, Joseph amd Capponi, Attilio. *Advances in Psychotherapy of the Borderline Patient*. New York: Jason Aronson, 1979.

Mayo Clinic Staff. "Compulsive Sexual Behavior." www.mayoclinic.org.

Mayo Clinic Staff. "Narcissistic Personality Disorders." www.mayoclinic.org.

Pascal, *Pensées*, Editions Garnier Frères, 6, Rue des Saints-Pères, Paris. 1964.

Plotinus, *Enneads, I*, translated by A. H. Armstrong, Lobe Classical Library, Harvard University Press, Cambridge, Massachusetts, 1978.

Schleiermacher, Friedrich, *The Christian Faith*, I. translated by Mackintosh, H.R. and Steward, J.S., Harper Torchbooks, Harper & Row, New York, 1963.

Schopenhauer, Arthur, *The World as Will and Idea*, in Beardsley, Monroe, *The European Philosophers from Descartes to Nietzsche*. Modern Library Press, New York. 1960.

Scott, Etkin, Lender, David P., Mills, Elizabeth Jacqueline (Editors). *Professional Guide to Diseases, Eighth Edition*. New York: Lippincott Williams & Wilkins. 2006.

Yutang, Lin, *Importance of Living*, John Day Company, New York, 1940.

www.ingramcontent.com/pod-product-compliance
Lightning Source LLC
Chambersburg PA
CBHW051146030726
47504CB00004B/1063